DANCING IN THE LIGHT

801 879 6214 James

DANCING IN THE LIGHT

SEQUEL TO *A TIME TO DANCE*

a novel

ANITA STANSFIELD

Covenant Communications, Inc.

Cover image photographed by Picture This . . . by Sara Staker

Cover design copyrighted 2006 by Covenant Communications, Inc.

Published by Covenant Communications, Inc.
American Fork, Utah

Printed in Canada
First Printing: August 2006

11 10 09 08 07 06   10 9 8 7 6 5 4 3 2 1

ISBN 978-1-59811-137-8

For Nathan, my big brother,
Who chose door number three.
I love you and miss you.

CHAPTER 1

Salt Lake City, Utah

Wade Morrison pulled his car up in front of the large, beautiful home where he and his wife, Elena, were currently living. They had been married barely a year, and not so many hours ago he had witnessed the birth of their first child—a healthy baby girl with dark hair like her mother, and big eyes that had immediately taken in the world with interest.

Wade and Elena had been living out of state where he was attending medical school, but they'd come back to stay with his brother's family for the summer so they could be close to family and friends for the arrival of the baby. It wasn't normally acceptable to take a semester off in the middle of medical school, but both Wade and Elena had felt strongly that it was important and the right thing to do, even though it would set him back and could possibly create some future complications. In a little more than a month they would be returning to their apartment back east, and he would resume his education.

Putting the car into park, Wade felt suddenly overcome with a combination of relief, awe, and fear. He felt awe in having seen this child come into the world, and relief in knowing that all was well. But the fear was still there, for reasons he didn't even want to think about. And now that the baby was here and Elena was doing well, he had to admit that his fear had been weighing heavily on him, even though he hadn't wanted to admit it—even to himself. He couldn't hold back a rush of tears while his mind darted through various thoughts and memories. Then he forced some composure upon himself and got out of the car.

Looking up at his brother's home that was more than a hundred and fifty years old, he had to admit that he dreaded leaving here. The house was beautiful and had a wonderful spirit about it. Alex and Jane had purchased the house from Alex's cousin, Susan, with the agreement that she and her husband, Donald, would live with them for as long as they needed to. But at the moment, Donald and Susan were away serving their second mission. Wade loved this house, but it wasn't just the house he would miss. He loved being so close to Alex and Jane and their children, although he felt sure separate living quarters would be preferable. At least it probably would be for Alex and Jane. Personally, he loved being in their home, and he knew that Elena did too. On top of that, they had truly missed Utah and the connection with family.

Wade unlocked the front door, then locked it behind him, certain everyone else had already gone to bed. The light in the stairwell had been left on, and he headed in that direction until he heard Alex say, "So how's that new baby?"

Wade turned to see his brother coming out of the study. More specifically, Alexander Keane was his half-brother, and fifteen years his senior. Their relationship was unique for many reasons, not the least of which was the fact that neither one of them had known of the other's existence until just a couple of years ago. But they'd bonded immediately and had been the best of friends ever since.

At six foot two, Alex was the same height as Wade, and their build was similar. Alex's hair was darker than Wade's, which was sandy brown, but they wore it much the same way, combed back off the face. Technically their features differed considerably, since Wade strongly resembled their father, and Alex bore a strong likeness to his mother's side of the family. But people often commented on how they looked like brothers. It had been concluded that the resemblance was more in mannerisms and behavior. They'd been told they walked the same, and talked the same, and people couldn't be with the two of them without commenting on the similarities. And that was more than fine with Wade. In his opinion, Alex was a man worthy of exemplifying, whether he did it consciously or not. Wade felt closer to Alex than any other blood relative; the relationship they shared was profound and irreplaceable—and not something Wade took for granted. Staying here with Alex and his family, along with becoming a new father, had by far made this the best summer of his life.

"She's perfect," Wade said in answer to his brother's question.

"And Elena?" Alex asked.

Wade had to fight the emotion he'd been struggling with in the car. "She's fine," he said, and saw Alex furrow his brow.

"Then what's wrong?" Alex asked, and Wade didn't know if he should bless or curse his brother's perception. He leaned more toward cursing it as tears overtook him so quickly there was no point in trying to hide them.

"Wade?" Alex pressed. "What is it?"

When Wade didn't answer, Alex took his arm and guided him into the study where a lamp was on. They sat together on the old leather couch before Alex demanded gently, "What's happened?"

"Nothing's happened, Alex. The baby's perfect. Elena's fine. I just . . ."

Wade only had to wonder for a moment if he should share what he was feeling with his brother. Perhaps this moment was a blessing. Maybe he'd held it inside long enough.

"What?" Alex urged gently when Wade hesitated.

"Have you ever just . . . had a feeling . . . like a spiritual impression, but . . . subtle? Subtle, maybe, but . . . still undeniable? And it's like . . . you're being prepared for something?"

Alex leaned back and drew a deep breath. "I'm assuming by your countenance that you're not talking about something positive." Wade didn't answer, and Alex added, "Yeah, I've had an experience like that."

Wade felt relieved, freed of the burden of trying to explain it any further. "What were you being prepared for?" Wade asked quietly, almost reverently.

"I didn't know at the time. I just felt . . . uneasy, but then . . . I had a strong impression that God would see my family through any trial that might come up." He paused and sighed. "It was just a couple of days before we discovered Barrett's leukemia."

Wade drew a harsh breath and looked away. His nephew's illness had been a nightmare for the family. But somehow he found the comparison viable. Alex asked gently, "What is it, Wade?"

Wade attempted to gather his words, and Alex allowed him the silence to do so. "Um . . . soon after I asked Elena to marry me, I just . . . had the feeling that it wouldn't last."

"You mean, like . . . the marriage wouldn't work out, or . . ."

"I didn't know at first. I just felt like it wouldn't last. I told myself I was just paranoid, thinking it was all too good to be true. But I knew beyond any doubt—I still do—that marrying her was the right thing to do. Through the engagement I kept struggling with it; every once in a while that feeling would come to me. Subtle, but . . . real. Like . . . I needed to enjoy this while it lasted, and make the most of every moment. I was managing to push the thoughts away, and rationalize that it was just me, until . . ."

"Until?"

Wade sighed loudly and looked at the floor, leaning his forearms on his thighs. "Until Elena sat me down for a little heart-to-heart talk."

"This was before you were married?"

"That's right," Wade said and found the courage to put his thoughts to words. "Apparently her patriarchal blessing has some indication that her mortal life will not be long."

"Good heavens," Alex muttered breathlessly.

"But more than that . . . she just . . . said that she's always felt . . . her life would be brief." He chuckled with no sign of humor. "She told me then that she felt surprised she'd made it that far; she never expected to go to college or be married. Every once in a while she'll comment on it." He was quiet a minute, then sighed again. "Now, I realize that patriarchal blessings can be interpreted in different ways, and maybe its meaning isn't what it seems. But when I consider what that could mean, in addition to her feelings and mine, I cannot ignore my belief that we are . . ." his voice cracked, "being prepared. But we made the decision to be married in the temple, knowing that no matter what happens, we will have forever. We've both taken the attitude of making the most of every minute we have, and at the same time live as if we will have fifty years or better together. And if . . . when . . . she is taken from me, I will be able to find peace in knowing that it was meant to be."

Again there was silence until Alex asked, "So . . . what happened today . . . that's prompted the way you're feeling?"

Wade had to take a minute to get his tears under control. He finally managed to say, "She gave birth with absolutely no complications; everything's fine." He sobbed quietly. "Just last week she told me she'd been having these . . . feelings, more strongly. She was afraid something would go wrong, that she wouldn't make it through. But she did. Everything's fine." He sobbed again. "Still, I had a hard time leaving her there, because . . . because . . . I'm feeling it too, Alex. I've asked myself a hundred times if I'm just being paranoid. A part of me wanted to stay there with her tonight, but I felt so wrung out I thought it would be better to cry privately. And she insisted that I should come home and get some decent sleep. We certainly didn't get much last night, with her labor starting when it did."

Alex attempted to absorb what he'd just been told, but all he could feel was shock. He had a deep regard for such spiritual promptings, especially considering his own personal experiences. While Wade cried quietly, Alex put a hand on his shoulder and wished he had any idea what to say. He couldn't tell his brother that there was nothing to be concerned about, or that he shouldn't worry. He finally managed to ask, "So, what now, Wade? Tell me what I can do."

"There's nothing anyone can do," Wade said and reached for a tissue from a box on the end table. He blew his nose, then took a deep breath. "I really hadn't intended to tell you, but . . . I'm glad I did. I've carried this burden alone since Elena and I first talked about it—before we were married. I can't do it any more, not when we're both feeling this way. I haven't told anyone else, and I'm not going to. I don't want family and friends speculating and reading stuff into this. What we have felt is sacred and private, but . . . I need you to be my rock. You always have been, since the day we met."

"And vice versa," Alex said.

"It's between me and you, Alex. I don't even want Jane to know."

"Okay," Alex said.

Wade shook his head. "I don't know how long it will be, Alex, but I know that it will happen. And when I lose her . . . I pray that you're standing close enough to scrape me up off the floor." He pressed his fingers over his eyes, and his voice quavered. "I love her more than life, Alex."

"I know. And she loves you."

"Yes, she does," Wade said and took a sustaining breath. "For that and many other reasons, I am the happiest man alive." He shook his head, and laughter emerged through his tears. "We have such a beautiful little girl; she is incredible. And she looks like her mother."

"Can't wait to see her," Alex said. "Do you have a name?"

"Rebecca Elena Morrison," Wade said proudly, then he stood up to declare an end to the conversation. "I need some sleep," he said. "Thanks for listening."

"Any time," Alex said and stood beside him, offering a firm, brotherly embrace. "Hey," Alex added, "whatever happens . . . whenever it happens . . . God will be with you, Wade, and so will I."

"I know," Wade said and hugged him again. "I'll see you tomorrow."

Once alone in his room, Wade had a good cry while he prayed to find peace—to be reassured that his uneasy feelings would not interfere with the joy in their lives. Then he slept deeply. He woke up with nothing but a desire to be with his little family, but he couldn't leave the house without first searching out Barrett to see what he was up to. Barrett was Alex and Jane's oldest child, and at the age of eight he had already experienced more of life than some adults. He'd been diagnosed with leukemia at the age of four, and had literally hovered at death's door a number of times. There was no sign of cancer in the child now, but he was small for his age and needing to catch up the growth he'd lost. Still, he was alive and getting more healthy every day. And Wade felt a compelling bond with Barrett. Logically, it could have something to do with the fact that Wade had donated the bone marrow that had saved Barrett's life, which meant they literally had the same blood. But their bond went much deeper than that. Alex had told Wade that Barrett had been wise for his age even before the cancer; he was always a smart kid with a sharp wit and a strong spirit. But hovering near death, along with the suffering he'd endured, had added a refinement to little Barrett's character that continually fascinated Wade. He felt as if Barrett were somehow older in spirit, and just being with him fed something in Wade's own spirit.

"Hey there, buddy," Wade said when he found Barrett in his room, concentrating on something at his little desk. "What are you up to?"

"I'm drawing Batman," he said pensively without looking up.

Wade looked over Barrett's shoulder to see a library book open on the desk that, sure enough, showed how to draw Batman. And Barrett was doing a relatively decent job of it. "Batman is *awesome,*" Wade commented, noting there were three other Batman books on the desk. Barrett had shown the same interest in Batman that any little boy might, and he had a few Batman toys. But Wade had heard nothing about it recently. He felt sure that finding a book at the library had stirred a new interest, and finding one book would have sent him searching for more. That's how Barrett was.

"You got that right," Barrett said as if he were ten years older, making Wade chuckle. It was a phrase Wade often used himself, and he knew the child had picked it up from him. "You know what's so awesome about Batman?" he asked without disturbing his concentration.

"I do," he said, "but I want you to tell me what *you* think."

"He's not like Superman or Spiderman; they have super powers. Batman is just like a real guy who fights criminals and helps people."

"So like . . . *you* could be Batman when you grow up, right?"

Barrett looked up at him with mild disgust. "He's like . . . filthy rich. How do you think he can afford that Batmobile and all that other stuff?"

"Okay, well . . . but if you were filthy rich, you could be Batman, right?"

Barrett let out a sigh that implied Wade was immature and required great patience. Wade chuckled and added, "Well, that's some very good artwork. Do you think you could draw a picture of Batman for me? I'd really like one."

"Sure," Barrett said. "Did you like Batman when you were a kid?"

"Still do," Wade said, as if it should have been obvious. He tousled Barrett's dark hair, still not quite used to it, since he'd met Barrett during chemotherapy when he'd had no hair at all. "Hey, guess what?"

Barrett looked up with animated eyes as if he'd remembered the news and knew what Wade was going to say. "You're a daddy now, huh?"

"I sure am," he said with pride. "So that means you have a new cousin."

"Was it a girl like you thought it was going to be?"

"Yes, and her name is Rebecca, after your Aunt Rebecca."

"But we call her Becca," Barrett said. "Are you going to call the baby Becca?"

"No, we'll call her Rebecca. I think she's coming home tomorrow, and you can meet her. I've got to go, but you have a good day, okay?"

"You too," Barrett said, and Wade moved toward the door. "Uncle Wade?" he added, and Wade turned back. "How long before you guys have to move out?"

"About a month," Wade said.

"I don't want you to go," Barrett said, and Wade felt touched.

"I don't want to go either." Wade moved back into the room and squatted to face Barrett. "But when I'm done with medical school, we're going to move back here and buy a house really close so we can see each other all the time, okay?"

"Okay," Barrett said and threw his arms around Wade. They shared a tight hug before Wade went down to the kitchen where Alex was refereeing the other children at the breakfast table, while Jane held their youngest, Ruth, against her shoulder. Katharine was six, and Preston three. They were adorable kids, and Wade loved them, but there was no comparing his relationship with them to the one he had with Barrett.

After grabbing a piece of toast and some juice, Wade hurried to the hospital where he found Elena looking cheerful and rested, and little Rebecca looking even more adorable than he'd remembered. He stayed with his wife and daughter throughout the remainder of the day, enjoying the visits of family and friends who came to see the new baby. He spent the night there as well and stayed until it was time for Elena and Rebecca to be released from the hospital.

Wade felt nothing but perfect joy as he and Elena settled into a routine, adjusting to parenthood with the help of more experienced loved ones around them. Alex and Jane were helpful and supportive without being intrusive, and they both clearly found great joy in Rebecca's presence in their home. Ironically, their youngest daughter, Ruth, was only a couple of weeks older than Rebecca, and they all had a great time taking pictures of the babies together, and making comparisons between the two little cousins.

When Rebecca was two weeks old, Wade realized one morning that he hadn't given a second thought to his concerns about losing Elena since the night he'd talked to Alex about it. He felt certain that he and Elena had naturally been drawn to thinking about it more as they faced the birth of a child. But now that it was behind them, and all was well, he had no reason to believe that they didn't have a great deal of time left together on this earth. He put the matter into God's hands and once again forgot all about it, enjoying every moment of life with his new little family.

* * *

Wade was thrilled when a friend from high school called. Kirk had heard from Wade's mother that he was in town, and he wanted to meet him for lunch. Elena strongly encouraged him to go, even though it was at the same time as Rebecca's two-week checkup with the pediatrician. Elena assured him that she could handle it, and convinced him that he should meet with his friend and have a marvelous time.

When Wade saw Kirk at the restaurant, they laughed and shared a firm embrace. They'd not seen each other much since high-school graduation, but they'd kept in touch here and there, and through their teen years they'd been the best of friends.

"Hey, it's good to see you," Kirk said.

"And you," Wade replied.

After they were shown to a table and had ordered their meal, Wade asked Kirk to catch him up on everything he was doing. He was married and had two children, and he was working for a software company. After Kirk had talked about his life well into the meal, he said, "Now it's your turn. Your mother told me you're going to medical school. That's great. And you have a new baby."

Wade chuckled. "That about covers it." He talked more specifically about where they were living back east, and went on at some length about his wife and new daughter and how thoroughly happy he was.

"So, where are you staying while you're in town?" Kirk asked.

"With my brother, actually. His home is huge, so it works out nicely."

"Would that be Lance or David?" Kirk asked, and Wade felt caught off guard. He'd not seen Kirk since great changes had occurred in his life. Now he had no choice but to explain. He'd gotten over feeling ashamed or embarrassed by the circumstances, but it was still a sensitive issue.

"Brian's still living at home, isn't he?" Kirk asked.

"Uh . . . yeah . . . Brian's getting ready to submit mission papers."

While he was wondering how to open this up, Kirk asked, "Is something wrong? Something hasn't happened to one of your brothers, I hope."

"No, no. They're fine. Nothing's wrong. It's just that . . . I made a rather startling discovery a couple of years ago, and sometimes I forget about the changes because I've gotten used to them. But I haven't seen you for . . . what? Three years or so."

"Probably." Kirk was clearly concerned. "I was living out of state when you got married; I was sorry to miss it."

"It would have been good to have you there, but I understand."

"So, are you going to tell me?" Kirk pressed.

"Well, I'm not staying with Lance or David. I'm staying with my brother Alex. And before you point out that you weren't aware I had a brother named Alex—and you, of all people, should know all of my brothers—let me say that I didn't know either."

Kirk's expression was stunned. "Okay," he drawled. "So . . . what? You were adopted?"

"Uh . . . no."

"Your mother gave a child up for adoption."

"No to that too."

"Maybe you'd better just start at the beginning."

"I would if you'd let me," Wade said facetiously. "Still impatient, I see."

"Always," Kirk chuckled. "Okay, I'll shut up and listen."

Wade took a deep breath. "You know, of course, that I was raised in a good home; couldn't be better, really. The gospel was strong in my home. My parents are good people."

"Yes."

"Well, apparently before I was born it wasn't that way. Apparently my father—he readily admits this—was a pretty lousy husband. My mother's efforts to get him to treat her better went unheeded, so she left him; lived with a guy for a couple of years."

Kirk's eyes widened. "Are you *serious?*"

"Do I look like I'm joking? Obviously my father took her back, but she came back pregnant—with me. She was excommunicated, and my father took a great deal of accountability for driving her away. From that point on they both worked very hard to do everything right. They went through a lot of counseling, had two more kids after me. My parents are wonderful people, but you know that."

"Yeah," Kirk said, visibly shaken. In a solemn voice, he asked, "How did you find out?"

Wade drew a deep sigh. "I was taking a genetics class; volunteered to do DNA testing in my family for a project. I thought I'd screwed it up somehow, then I had to go home and ask my parents why I didn't have any of my father's DNA."

"You must have been pretty upset."

"Upset?" He chuckled with no humor. "Initially I blew up; the family fell apart. I could barely breathe for weeks. I even tried to kill myself." Kirk gasped. "Of course, I'm glad I failed at that. For being a pre-med student I did a lousy job of it."

"And now?"

"Now, I am the happiest man alive." Wade marveled at his own serenity over the issue. "Everyone has come to terms with it—especially me. Back to your original question: I am staying with my brother Alex who is the son of my biological father. He's an amazing man, and my closest friend. I would be utterly lost without him. Now that I've adjusted, I can honestly say that I'm glad I found out, and I'm glad it came out in the open. I am fortunate enough to have two families—and they're both wonderful. They all came to the wedding."

"You're kidding." Kirk chuckled. "In the temple?"

"That's right. My parents—all three of them—are all wonderful examples of repentance and forgiveness."

"So . . . the father who raised you . . . and your mother . . . are on friendly terms with the man she had an affair with?"

"My biological father; that's right."

"That's incredible."

"It's the miracle of forgiveness," Wade said with a smile.

"I still find it difficult to believe," Kirk said. "I mean . . . you grew up in the ideal family. I always loved being in your home. Your parents are incredible people."

"Yes, they are. But you have to understand that they became that way because they went through some pretty horrible stuff. It's like I told my mom once. She made some really bad choices, but she followed them up with some really good ones. Once I realized that, I was able to find peace with it."

"How? How do you find peace with suddenly learning that everything you had believed was true suddenly wasn't?"

"Well, that was the question that made me cut my wrist, Kirk. But I found the answer. You grew up in the Church, served a mission. You know the answer."

"The Atonement."

"That's right. I learned that what Christ did performs its greatest miracle in circumstances that will never make sense logically. I am the consequence of a grievous sin, but it's okay because God loves me, and so do my parents. I've been very blessed."

"Wow," Kirk said. "So, if you're living with this new brother you found, obviously it's no secret that this happened."

"We don't go shouting it in the streets, but no, it's not a secret."

"Isn't that hard on your parents?"

"Sometimes. It brings up awkward moments occasionally, but my mother has said many times that she would endure any amount of ridicule in exchange for my having peace with the issue. I knew in my heart it was good and right to be actively involved with both families. I can't do that and keep it a secret, but Mom has become pretty tough through having her past sins discussed openly. She's an incredible woman."

"And you're a pretty incredible guy," Kirk said, but Wade made a scoffing noise. "No, seriously. To come through something like that with such a good attitude . . . I'm inspired."

"All I did was give it to God. Like I said, I'm the happiest man alive."

They talked long after they'd finished eating, and Kirk said that he'd like to invite Wade and Elena over to have dinner at his home, and to meet his wife. He promised to call in a few days to set a time.

Wade returned home feeling grateful for the opportunity to renew his friendship with Kirk, and to catch up on all that had happened in their lives. He sat close to Elena while she fed the baby, and he told her all about his lunchtime conversation, and he shared some tender and funny memories related to Kirk from his youth.

"How did the checkup go?" he asked her.

"It was great," she said. "They told me that Rebecca is perfect in every way. The nurse—I think her name is Laura—she was so cute with Rebecca. She coddled her like she was the most beautiful baby in the world."

"Well, she is, of course," Wade said.

"We actually talked for a while. She's very sweet."

"It's too bad we're moving. You could take her out to lunch or something."

"Yeah, too bad," she said, and a cloud came over her countenance. He knew she didn't want to go back to their apartment, a thousand miles away from loved ones, any more than he did. But they'd talked about it a dozen times. They knew it was the right course, and it was only temporary. Still, settling in there with a new baby would bring on new challenges—especially for Elena.

"Hey, it'll be okay," he said, lifting her chin so that he could look into her eyes. "It may just be the three of us, but together we can get through anything."

She smiled, and her face brightened. "I love you, Wade," she said and kissed him.

"I love you too," he replied and kissed her again.

The following day Wade's mother called to ask if he would help her with a project. Apparently a family reunion was being thrown together for her father's descendants, and his mother was taking the bulk of the responsibility. The family wanted to do it before summer's end, which was fast approaching. She also wanted to do it before he and Elena left the state to go back to medical school. And since Wade was the only one of her children who wasn't presently busy with work or school, he was the obvious candidate to give her some assistance. He told her he'd be more than happy to help, especially since he and his mother were friends as well, and he always enjoyed spending time with her.

The following evening Wade went to his parents' home to go over the plans in detail, but they also ended up visiting a great deal, and he returned home late. Elena had stayed at home with the baby, since evenings were Rebecca's fussy time, and she hadn't wanted the baby to be a distraction to their business.

Wade pulled up in front of the house and hurried inside. The light on the stairs had been left on, and he headed in that direction.

In the hall Wade heard an infant crying, but quickly realized it wasn't Rebecca. Jane and Elena had unanimously decided that Ruth and Rebecca were destined to be great friends, since they were both competing so well at waking the entire household every night.

Wade quietly entered the bedroom he shared with his little family. Guided by the light from the hall he crept to Rebecca's bassinet and found her sleeping soundly. *She is so beautiful,* he thought and touched her wispy, dark hair. He then moved to where Elena was sleeping and thought the same thing. She was an amazing woman and he loved her dearly. Struck by her beauty and serenity as she slept, he couldn't resist just watching her for what seemed endless minutes. He brushed a stray lock of dark hair back off her face, grateful that he hadn't disturbed her. Seemingly out of nowhere he felt deeply touched by gratitude for knowing their marriage was eternal, and their love was beyond any earthly description. The enormity of the forever relationship he shared with her felt suddenly so intense that tears burned into his eyes. He loved her so much!

Feeling exhausted, he forced himself to change into pajama pants and a T-shirt. After a couple of minutes in the bathroom he crawled into bed and quickly slept. He woke to Rebecca's cries, followed by the familiar sounds of Elena speaking in a tender voice to their daughter as she changed her diaper, then settled into the rocker to nurse her. He knew better than to offer to help; she always insisted that she had to get up to feed the baby anyway, and it wasn't so hard to change a diaper while she was at it. But Wade rolled over and fought the sleep in his eyes to just watch her on the other side of the room, illuminated by the glow of a lamp, singing softly to the baby. With the flowing white robe she wore, and with the baby wrapped in a white blanket, they almost looked angelic together that way.

After putting Rebecca back into her bassinet, Elena turned off the lamp and climbed back into bed. "Hello, my love," he murmured, easing closer to her.

"Hi," she said and turned toward him, touching his face in the darkness.

He touched hers in return and gave her a savoring kiss. "I love you, Elena," he said. "Do you have any idea how happy you have made me?"

She laughed softly. "It's the other way around," she said. "I could never ask for anything more than what I have right here in this room. My life is complete." She settled her head on his shoulder and relaxed while he silently agreed with her.

Wade came awake, aware that Rebecca was crying. When the normal sounds didn't follow, he became more alert. Certain that Elena was simply exhausted from all the nighttime feedings, he got up and turned on the lamp. Rebecca continued to fuss while he changed her diaper. He wasn't nearly as proficient at the task as her mother, but he managed well enough and wrapped her up tightly again before he carried her to Elena's side of the bed to be nursed. Rebecca quieted down as if she knew she would soon get what she needed. Wade's heart began to thud before he consciously took in the fact that something wasn't right. He laid the baby back in the bassinet before he went to his knees beside his wife, nudging her gently, whispering her name. He let out a gaspy scream and retracted so quickly that he fell backward. The baby started to cry again as he scrambled to his feet, struggling to breathe, feeling as if he were somehow in the middle of a horror movie, and if he didn't get out of the room something terrible would overtake him.

In the hall Wade leaned his face to the wall, muttering over and over, "God, please help me. Please, God, help me." He was shaking, and his stomach hurt. His chest burned painfully, and his legs threatened to forsake him. He couldn't move, couldn't think, couldn't breathe, couldn't go back in there. It was a nightmare. It had to be a nightmare. *Had to be!* The baby was screaming, but he could only grasp what that meant through some kind of mental fog. Only one thought came together in his brain enough to prompt him to any action at all. His brother was in the house, and he needed him. And when Alex's name charged out of his throat, it threatened to bring the house down.

CHAPTER 2

Alex awoke to the sound of a baby's cries, but it was muffled and distant, and he knew it wasn't Ruth. When the crying persisted an unusually long time, he heard Jane express his own thoughts. "Maybe Rebecca's getting some colic or something."

"Maybe," Alex said and rolled over. A moment later he heard Wade scream his name as if he were sinking into fire and brimstone.

"What on earth?" Jane gasped as Alex flew toward the door and into the hall, heart pounding. With Jane right behind him he flipped on the hall light and ran around the corner to see Wade's face and hands pressed to the wall as if it were barely keeping him from total collapse. He was heaving for breath and visibly shaking.

"Wade," he muttered, putting a hand on his arm. Their eyes met, and everything inside of Alex that hadn't already been terrified turned to painful knots. Wade's entire countenance betrayed that he had encountered some unspeakable horror. "What is it?" Alex asked, aware of the baby screaming. He sensed Jane wanting to rush in there and rescue Rebecca, but she seemed hesitant, and he wondered if her instincts were bristling as his were.

"Tell me," Wade sputtered. "Tell me . . . I'm hallucinating. Tell me . . . I'm having a nightmare. Tell me anything, but . . .

don't tell me that . . . that . . ." He groaned. "Oh, Heavenly Father, please help me."

"Tell you what, Wade?" Alex asked, while he could only think of one possibility that fit the circumstances—from a conversation not so long ago.

Wade fought to catch his breath, looking at Alex as if he might save him. "You go in there, Alex, and . . . tell me . . . there's a reason that she's . . . she's . . ."

Alex didn't wait another second. He took a deep breath and went into the room, telling himself he was an ER physician, and he could handle whatever he might find. As if his entering the room had given Jane a burst of courage, she rushed for the baby and picked her up. He was vaguely aware of Jane's soothing noises as she attempted to calm the baby down, while he stepped slowly toward the bed. He didn't even have to touch Elena to know, but he did anyway, and a heartsickness beyond description consumed him. The baby quieted from screaming to whimpering while he attempted to accept the reality.

"Should we be calling 911?" Jane asked as Alex knelt beside the bed.

"There's no need," he said with reverence. "She's been dead at least a couple of hours."

He heard Jane gasping, protesting, crying, and he quickly took her in his arms, whispering hotly close to her ear, "We've got to stay calm, Jane. We can scream and cry later. Do you understand?"

She nodded firmly, but he could hear her struggling to catch her breath. "Take the baby to our room and feed her. I need to tell Wade."

She nodded again and rushed from the room so quickly that he knew she wanted to get out of Wade's hearing in order to respond to what he'd just told her. He wished he could follow her. But his brother needed him. *Scream and cry later,* he reminded himself. Right now Wade needed him to be strong.

Alex uttered a silent prayer and stepped into the hall to find Wade sitting on the floor, leaning back against the wall. He looked up, his eyes registering both expectation and resignation. He seemed more calm, more lucid, probably in shock. Alex knew exactly what Wade was thinking even before he said, "I won't believe it until you tell me."

Alex sat on the floor, facing Wade. He cleared his throat and forced himself to say it. "She's gone, Wade."

Wade felt the words and their implication pierce his heart, validating what he'd seen and felt for himself. Still, he couldn't bring himself to accept it. He wondered why he wasn't crying, screaming, sobbing. Instead he looked hard at Alex and had to ask, "She's really . . . dead, then?"

Alex swallowed hard. "She is."

Wade groaned and hung his head, wrapping his arms around it. He groaned again and asked, "Do you know . . . how?"

"No. It could have been . . . a number of . . . possibilities."

Wade felt the shock wearing off, and he gasped for breath, suddenly finding it difficult to breathe. He hung his head further and a series of heated sobs rushed out of him. Alex's arms came around him, and he lost all sense of time as the grief rushed out of him and then back in, over and over, until the pain threatened to eat him alive. He felt like a lost child, wrapped in his brother's embrace, feeling as if he had to be dreaming, because it just couldn't be real.

When the torrents of grief receded into a numb sense of shock, Wade pondered the feelings he'd had since he'd first fallen in love with Elena, and the conversations they'd shared. As much as he'd tried to be prepared for this moment, he didn't feel at all prepared. He couldn't believe it! She was gone. His sweet Elena was beyond his reach. In his heart he knew he would be with her again, but a lifetime was a long time to be separated from the person who had become a part of his life more than any other. He couldn't believe it. It couldn't be real.

Suddenly needing some kind of irrefutable proof, he looked hard at Alex and heard himself say in a raspy voice, "I need to see her. Will you come with me?"

"Of course," Alex said and came to his feet, helping Wade stand beside him.

They moved stealthily toward the door, then Wade stopped and had to reach deep inside himself for courage before he moved on, aware of Alex's hand over his arm. He gasped as he approached the bed. She looked so beautiful, but she also looked dead. He swallowed hard and went to his knees beside her, hesitating only a moment before he touched her face, startled by its coldness. In the flash of an instant, volumes of doctrine regarding life and death, the spirit world, the resurrection, and eternal marriage all rushed into his mind, leaving him profoundly grateful for the gospel in his life and the understanding it gave him. Peace tempered his aching for this loss. But still, the ache was there.

For several minutes he just looked at her, grateful for the numb sensation guarding the pain that he knew was present. He was aware of Alex beside him, keeping a hand on his shoulder, offering silent support. After his thoughts had tumbled for immeasurable minutes, he kept his eyes on Elena while he said to Alex, "Tell me what to do now. Is the baby—"

"Jane's got her. She'll take care of Rebecca for as long as you need. We should call Elena's parents . . . and yours. They might want to see her before . . . she's moved."

Wade turned to Alex while it took a moment to perceive what he meant. He nodded and said, "Would you call them for me?"

"Of course."

"And call Dad; I need Dad."

"Of course," Alex said again.

"It's the middle of the night," Wade said, as if Alex might not have noticed.

"It doesn't matter. They need to know."

Wade briefly pondered how those phone conversations might go and said, "I should do it; I shouldn't leave you to have to do something so—"

"If you want to do it, that's fine. But I'm okay with it if you can't. I mean it, Wade. I'll do whatever you want . . . whatever you need. Just say the word."

Wade nodded and felt a hard knot gather in his throat. "I can't call them," he admitted. "I'd be very grateful if . . ." He couldn't finish.

"It's okay. Do you want to stay here or—"

"Yes," he said, "I need some time. Thank you."

"I'll be in the study if you need me," Alex said and hurried from the room. He first went to check on Jane. He found her sobbing quietly while she nursed Rebecca.

"How is she?" Alex asked, alerting her to his presence. Jane looked down as if she'd forgotten about the baby.

"She's asleep," Jane said, her voice trembling. "I . . . I . . . know we've got some formula samples the hospital sent home . . . somewhere around here, but . . . I couldn't find them, and . . ."

"It's okay," he said, gently taking Rebecca from her. He placed her carefully into Ruth's little baby-carry seat that was sitting on the floor near the crib where Ruth was sleeping. "We'll deal with that tomorrow." He tucked a little blanket around her.

"Alex," Jane said as he turned back to face her, "tell me it's not true." He knelt in front of her and took her hands. "How can . . . how can a woman just . . . go to sleep and not . . . not wake up?"

"I don't know, Jane," he said carefully. "The medical examiner will have to determine that."

She looked horrified, then her crying increased as she took hold of him. "I can't believe it," she muttered. "I can't believe it."

"I can't believe it either," Alex said and took her shoulders. "Listen, I've got to make some calls. I don't want to leave you alone, but . . . there are people who need to know. Will you be alright?"

She nodded firmly, and he hurried downstairs to the study, quietly peeking into Wade's bedroom to make sure he was still sitting there quietly beside the bed. In the study, Alex dug out the phone book and quickly found the number for Elena's parents. He had to say a prayer before he dialed the phone, but his heart was still pounding. How could he possibly say what they needed to hear and keep himself together? He'd had moments like this as an ER physician when he'd had to deliver bad news to the patient's loved ones, but this was personal. He felt himself shaking as the phone began to ring. Alex was grateful that he'd gotten to know these people rather well during the weeks that Wade and Elena had been living with them.

"Hello," a sleepy but alarmed male voice answered.

"Is this Harry?" Alex asked.

"It is," he said firmly.

"This is Alex Keane, Wade's brother."

"Yes," Harry said with an impatience that implied he should get to the point.

"I'm afraid I have some very difficult news." Alex swallowed carefully and put a hand over the pounding in his chest. "Elena has passed away."

He wasn't surprised by the disbelief and emotion he heard from the other end of the phone. He just listened and cried silent tears while his own shaking continued. Harry finally asked, "What happened, Alex?"

"Please tell us," Melba said tearfully, and he realized she was on another extension.

"She just . . . went to sleep and didn't wake up," Alex said. "That's all I know. Wade found her gone when the baby woke up to be fed. We thought you might want to see her before we . . ."

"Of course," Harry said, saving Alex from having to say that he needed to call the medical examiner. "We'll be there as soon as we can get dressed."

Once the call ended Alex heaved with emotion for several minutes before he could compose himself enough to call Brad and Marilyn. Marilyn was Wade's mother, and Brad was the father who had raised Wade. Through the trauma of coming to terms with the unique circumstances surrounding Wade's existence, Alex had come to know Wade's parents well.

Marilyn answered the phone without a hello; she simply said, "What's happened?" Of course a phone call at four in the morning would indicate a problem.

"It's Alex," he said. "Wade asked me to call you."

"What is it, Alex? What's wrong?"

"Elena has passed away," he said, and Marilyn responded much as Harry had done. He gave her the same explanation and asked that they come over as quickly as possible.

Again Alex had to take a few minutes to calm down and catch his breath before he called his father. His stepmother, Roxanne, answered the phone.

"It's Alex," he said. "I need to talk to Dad."

"He's right here," she said, sounding panicked.

"Dad," Alex said, hearing more emotion in his own voice this time. Perhaps it was because Neil Keane was someone he knew would sustain him. They had a great deal of practical experience with that.

"What is it, son?" Neil asked.

"Elena has passed away," Alex said, his voice breaking. "She just . . . didn't wake up."

Again he listened to the shock and horror in response to the news, then Neil said firmly, "We're on our way. Don't do anything until we get there."

"Thanks, Dad," Alex said and hung up the phone.

He cried just long enough to vent the pain smoldering in his head and chest, then he hurried upstairs where he found Wade crying silent tears, holding Elena's hand in his. He peeked in but didn't disturb him before he found Jane pacing the bedroom, trembling and crying, while both babies continued to sleep. He took her in his arms and let her cry for a few minutes before he said, "I need to be with Wade. All of the parents are on their way over. If you can just . . . watch out for the babies, I'll—"

"Of course," she said. "And I'll listen for the door. You stay with Wade."

"Thank you," he said and kissed her brow. He turned to leave the room, then turned back, feeling compelled to share something with her that he knew would help give her perspective. "Jane," he said, taking both her hands into his, "a couple of weeks ago . . . right after Rebecca was born, Wade told me that . . . he and Elena had both . . . felt . . . believed . . . for a long time that . . . she wouldn't . . . live long."

Her eyes widened and filled with fresh tears, but he caught a hint of serenity there before he kissed her brow and muttered, "We'll talk more later." She nodded, and he left the room.

Alex sat near Wade in silence until Elena's parents arrived. Their shock and grief were difficult to witness, but their love and compassion for Wade were readily evident, and Alex was pleased to be able to stand back and allow them to share their love for Elena. Brad and Marilyn arrived a few minutes later, and Wade clung to each of them for long minutes, crying like a child while they gave him perfect understanding. The love between them and the strength of their relationships were readily evident. When Neil and Roxanne arrived, Wade took hold of his father and broke down again. Neil just held Wade and cried with him.

Wade couldn't possibly find words to express his gratitude for the love and support of the people surrounding him. When the initial reactions had settled somewhat, Neil and Roxanne left the room to go help Jane with the babies, who were both awake. Neil and Wade were close, but Neil always made a conscious effort to appropriately remain in the background and allow Wade's parents to be more actively involved when situations arose where they would all be present. Brad and Marilyn and Elena's parents stayed near Wade, sitting around Elena's bed, talking and crying softly. Wade shared with them his feelings that went back prior to their marriage, as well as Elena's feelings and their related conversations. Elena's parents were not surprised; they had been aware of their daughter's premonition, and had even had some related impressions of their own. Wade's parents were somewhat stunned, but it seemed they found some comfort in the evidence that those who loved Elena most had been prepared.

The conversation went on for quite some time until Wade reached a point where he said, "I can't stay in here any longer. Alex, will you please . . . call . . ." He couldn't finish.

"We'll take care of everything," Alex said. "Why don't you go find another bed and get some sleep."

With Wade in the care of Brad and Marilyn, Neil went with Alex to make the necessary calls. Roxanne continued to help Jane with both babies. Jane was having trouble getting Ruthie to go back to sleep, even though she'd been fed and changed, and Rebecca was fussing excessively as if she sensed the change in her habits and security. Elena's parents wanted a few minutes alone with their daughter.

Once the calls were completed, Alex checked on the situation with the babies, glad to know that Jane had found the formula samples, and that Rebecca had reluctantly accepted the bottle after fussing for a long while. Roxanne fed Rebecca while Jane was again nursing little Ruth, and both women wept silently as their maternal instincts were clearly anguished on Rebecca's behalf.

Soon after Elena's body had been taken away, the sun came up and the day began. Wade was sleeping with the help of an over-the-counter sleeping pill that Alex had given him, and Harry and Melba went home to inform the rest of the family and get some rest—once they were assured that Jane and Alex could manage taking care of the baby for the time being. Brad and Marilyn also returned home once Wade was asleep, so that they could call family members and make plans. Alex was grateful to have his father and stepmother insist that they were staying. Neil helped Alex tell the children that their Aunt Elena had gone to live with Heavenly Father, and both Neil and Roxanne helped console the children's grief. Roxanne fixed breakfast for everyone, then, while both of the babies were sleeping, she went to the grocery store with Jane in order to buy bottles and formula so that Rebecca could make the adjustment to not having her mother to feed her.

Grateful for competent and loving family to help cover all the bases, Alex went to the room where Wade was sleeping. He dozed off and on in an overstuffed chair, wanting to be sure his brother wasn't alone when he woke up.

* * *

Wade came awake feeling groggy and disoriented. He forced his eyes open and realized he wasn't in the room where he'd become accustomed to sleeping. Then the reasons rushed into his conscious mind, and he squeezed his eyes tightly closed, as if he could block out the reality. The memories of the previous night all catapulted into his mind, leaving him weak with a combination of gratitude and horror. He thought of Alex at his side, and Jane caring for the baby. He thought of his parents—all of them—rushing here in the middle of the night, crying with him, mutually sustaining him. He marveled that the strange circumstances of his birth had merged into the healing and peace that allowed his parents to work together to help him through a crisis without any ill feelings or discomfort.

Wade thought of Elena's parents, and his heartache deepened. She was his wife, but she was also their daughter. Their love for her and their relationships with her had been different. But the loss was surely as deep for them as it was for him. And yet they had offered such perfect compassion and concern for him. He wondered for a moment what it might have been like if this had occurred while they'd been living back east, more than a thousand miles from family. He couldn't even fathom it! His gratitude for the Lord's tender mercy deepened. Still, his thankfulness was counterpointed by the horror that his sweet wife, his dear Elena, was dead. He groaned at the stark truth, and a harsh sob rushed out of him. Then another.

"Wade," Alex said gently, putting his hand on his brother's shoulder, "it's okay."

Wade focused on Alex's face and asked, "How long have you been here?"

"Long enough to make sure you didn't wake up alone."

"She's really gone, isn't she," he said, taking his brother's hand. "She's really dead?"

He knew it was a rhetorical question, but perhaps believed that if he heard the answer enough he might come to believe it.

"She really is," Alex said, and Wade could only cry like a child while Alex stayed close to him, clearly exhibiting his ability to mourn with those that mourn.

When Wade had once again receded into a numb, foggy sensation, Alex said gently, "We have the option of making funeral arrangements this afternoon, or waiting until tomorrow morning. Which would you prefer?"

Wade put a hand over his pounding, aching heart as it grasped the implication. "Um . . . I think I'd like to get it over with."

"Okay, I'll call them back. You need to get something to eat. Even if you don't feel like it, you need to eat."

"And a shower wouldn't hurt." Wade then looked hard at Alex and asked, "Do we know yet what happened?"

Alex shook his head. "We'll know tomorrow morning."

Wade nodded and tried to discern his reasons for feeling uneasy. When it finally occurred to him, he felt sick. He had a daughter; a *motherless* daughter. "Rebecca," he said, hearing panic in his own voice, as if she might have been thoroughly neglected through the hours since her mother had died. "Is she—"

"She's fine. Jane and Roxanne are taking very good care of her. She was a little reluctant over the formula at first, but she's taken to it fine now."

Wade sighed deeply and looked down. "I wish I could help her understand what's happened."

Alex put a hand on Wade's shoulder. "Or maybe she understands better than the rest of us." Wade looked into his brother's eyes. "It's not so long since she left the place where her mother is now. I'm certain Elena will keep very close track of her daughter—and you."

Tears overtook Wade anew, but Alex put an arm around him, guiding Wade's head to his shoulder. "We're going to get through this," Alex said in a voice that made it evident he was crying too. "I don't know how, but we are—together. Understand?"

Wade could only nod, and a few minutes later the tears once again receded into shock. It was as if his mind had been created with some kind of internal coping mechanism that kept him from feeling too much of the pain before it was dulled enough for him to stand back and take a breath.

At Wade's insistence, Alex left him to get cleaned up. He had no choice but to go to the room where Elena had died in order to find clean clothes. The bed had been stripped down to a bare mattress, and all the linens were absent. He hurried to get what he needed and got in the shower where he once again had a bout of volatile crying.

Feeling calm and somewhat dazed, Wade went down to the kitchen where he found his father and stepmother, along with Alex and Jane. Neil was holding little Ruth, who was quietly looking around. Roxanne held Rebecca, who was asleep.

"How are you?" his father asked.

"I think it would be better if I didn't try to answer that," Wade said, taking the baby from Roxanne. He pressed the side of his face against the baby's little head, breathing in her infant aroma, her new little life, while he barely managed to keep the tears back.

Jane put some soup and a sandwich in front of him, and Alex held the baby while he ate, even though he had no appetite. Rebecca was still asleep and in Jane's care when he left with Alex and their father to go to the mortuary to make arrangements for the funeral. They met Elena's parents there, and he was glad to have their support as well as their opinions. It all felt distant and surreal to Wade, and he was immeasurably grateful for his brother and father and their clear thinking as decisions needed to be made. On the drive from the mortuary to the cemetery to purchase a burial plot, Neil said from the backseat, "I don't want you to worry about the cost of any of this, Wade. I'm more than happy to pay for whatever needs to be done."

"It's not a problem, Dad," Wade said, looking out the window, aware of Alex glancing at him from where he was driving. "But thank you anyway."

"What do you mean it's not a problem?" Neil asked.

Wade could hear the toneless shock in his own voice. "I mean that the life insurance will be more than adequate."

"You had life insurance?" Neil asked, and Wade tossed him a questioning glance. "I mean . . . it's obviously very wise and mature to have it at any age, but most people don't think of it at your stage of life. Or if they do, it's only the bare minimum. You've got child care to consider, and your education, and—"

"I appreciate your concern, Dad, but we had a very good life insurance policy." He realized now that Neil and Roxanne had been absent when he'd told the others about the premonitions related to Elena's death. He didn't want to talk about it, but he took a deep breath and forced himself to explain. "Elena took care of it herself, a long time ago. And she made certain it was excellent coverage. The premiums have been paid diligently. It was just below tithing on the budget priority list."

Alex stopped the car and put it in park since they'd arrived at their destination, but nobody moved. Neil asked quietly, "What are you saying, Wade?"

Wade sighed loudly and shared a poignant glance with Alex before he turned to face his father. "She knew she was going to die, Dad," he said, and Neil took a sharp breath. "She's felt for years that her life would be brief. I had similar feelings before we were married. We talked about it then and decided to just make the most of every day. There were times when I was afraid it would happen any minute, and other times when I believed we would have years together."

"That's incredible," Neil said breathlessly, reverently. "Then . . . you were . . . prepared for this."

Wade gave a humorless chuckle. "I don't feel prepared. I feel shocked and horrified and scared out of my mind. Maybe eventually I'll feel that being . . . prepared . . . actually means something. But at the moment it's just . . . I can't even think of a word to describe it." He put a hand over his eyes. "I mean . . . what are we doing here? We're buying a burial plot for my *wife!*" He groaned. "Yesterday at this time we were . . ." his voice broke, "playing with the baby, and . . . comparing . . . Pampers to Huggies."

Neil put a firm hand on Wade's shoulder. Alex said in a hushed voice, "I don't know what to say, Wade. I sit and try to think of something—anything—I can say to give some perspective, some peace, some hope. But there's nothing I can tell you that you don't already know. And as wonderful as the gospel is, there's no getting around the fact that . . . she's gone from this world . . . and we're going to have to live without her for a long time." He made a noise of frustration. "I just . . . don't know what to say."

"You don't have to say anything," Wade insisted. "I'd prefer silence over patronizing words that will never make any difference. Just your being with me means more than I could ever tell you, both of you." He sighed deeply. "I thank God that it happened here, and not next month after we'd moved." He shook his head. "I don't even know what I'm going to do. How can I go back there and go to school and take care of an infant?"

"You can't," Alex said. "You need to be with family. Maybe it's too soon to be thinking of such things, but—"

"Or maybe I need to figure such things out so I don't lose my mind," Wade said. "Help me here. Everything that's been so carefully planned has just been blown to pieces. I don't even know which way is up. But I know I have to keep going. I have a daughter to take care of." He heard himself talking and wondered how he could be so calm and rational when something inside of him felt as if it would implode. He could only give credit to the Comforter for giving him the strength to have this conversation.

"Well, obviously it's going to take time to iron everything out," Alex said, "but there are some things that simply can't be altered. You need to go to school here where you have family to help with Rebecca. It's the only way."

"I agree," Neil said.

"My tuition is already paid elsewhere," Wade argued. "How can I—"

"You can apply for an emergency refund," Neil said. "I'll help you; I know it can be done. If you have proof of extenuating circumstances, and you certainly do, then you can usually get a refund of the tuition."

"Okay," Wade said, glad to hear that one problem could be solved. "But how do I get registered at such a late date somewhere else? Somewhere local?"

"I'll work on that too," Neil said. "I might have a few connections, and we'll just pray for a miracle."

"And if you actually miss a term in order to get all this straightened out," Alex said, "the world won't end."

"I don't know," Wade said. "I think the world *did* end. It sure feels like it at the moment."

"Come on," Neil said, opening the car door, "let's get this over with."

Again Wade was grateful to have his father and brother beside him as seemingly gruesome decisions needed to be made. He was surprised when Neil suggested that three plots should be purchased in the same place. Wade turned to him, whispering in astonishment, "Why three?"

Neil looked at him firmly with a gaze that seemed to preamble words that Wade wouldn't appreciate. "You'll want to be buried beside Elena, and your second wife will want to be buried beside you."

An indescribable anger slapped Wade hard, and he stood abruptly, saying, "Fine. Whatever. You take care of it. I'll be outside."

Alex watched Wade leave the sexton's office. He met his father's eyes and said quietly, "Just get three in the place we talked about. He'll thank you for it later."

Neil signed the papers and wrote out a check for three burial plots, an amount that Alex knew Wade would insist on paying back once the life insurance came through.

"How are *you?*" Neil asked as they stepped outside.

"I feel sick to my stomach," Alex admitted. "I want to just put my arms around him and take the hurt away, but I can't."

"Yeah, I know what you mean," Neil said and patted Alex on the back as they walked toward the car where Wade was leaning against it, his arms folded over his chest, gazing out across the vast sea of graves.

"It's a beautiful cemetery," Neil said, putting a hand on Wade's shoulder.

Wade didn't comment, but Alex said, "Yes, it is. My mother is buried here."

Wade looked toward Alex in surprise, wondering why he'd never known that. Alex added, "I bring her flowers for Mother's Day and her birthday, every year."

"I bring her flowers too," Neil said, his eyes distant, and Alex felt surprised. He knew that his parents had become friends following their divorce, but flowers?

"Her birthday?" Alex asked, although he'd never noticed any other flowers left at the times when he'd left them.

"No, actually. There are two dates I always think of her most. Our wedding anniversary, and the day I left her for another woman."

Wade looked sharply at his father, then at Alex; they all knew the other woman was Wade's mother. Neil added serenely, "I just want her to never forget how grateful I am that she forgave me." Neil looked at one son, then the other, adding gently, "And I'm grateful the two of you forgave me as well. I'm glad I don't have to take *that* with me when I go."

Alex put an arm around his father's shoulders. "We've come a long way, Dad."

"Yes, we have," he said and put an arm around each of his sons. "All of us." He looked at Wade directly and added, "We'll get through this, son, whatever it takes. Together. Do you understand?"

Wade nodded but couldn't speak. He just got into the car and was grateful to be going home. They decided to save choosing a headstone for another day.

CHAPTER 3

Back at the house, Wade admired his daughter where she slept. The baby's bassinet and all of her things, as well as his own, had been moved to a different room in the house. He couldn't deny being grateful that he didn't have to sleep tonight in the bed where Elena had died.

Rebecca was still sleeping when the bishop and one of his counselors came to visit. Apparently the Relief Society presidency had come while the men had been gone, insisting that meals would be brought in for the family for the next three days, and they would be taking care of a family luncheon following the funeral. The bishop was compassionate and kind, and he eagerly agreed to oversee the funeral. Wade appreciated the time and concern of these good men, but it all felt distant and hazy and too horrible to be real.

Soon after they left, Rebecca woke up, but Jane got to her before he did. However, he took the baby from Jane and proceeded to change her diaper.

"Do you want me to feed her?" Jane asked.

"No," he said. "I want you to show me how to fix the bottle and what to do." They both knew Elena had always nursed Rebecca, so Wade had never actually fed her.

"I really don't mind taking care of her for the time being, Wade," Jane said. "You must be in shock right now and—"

"I *am* in shock," he said evenly, wrapping a little blanket tightly around his freshly diapered little girl. "We're all in shock. I feel sick and I can't stop shaking, but I need to take care of my daughter." He picked Rebecca up and looked directly at his sister-in-law, who had tears in her eyes. "I appreciate your help, Jane, and if I need you I won't be afraid to ask; I promise. Please, just show me how to fix the formula. I already know how to get a burp out of her. Okay?"

"Okay," Jane said, and he followed her to the bathroom off Wade's room where everything that was needed had been spread out on the spacious counter. She only got partway through the explanation of mixing formula before she collapsed in tears, and Wade put one arm around her while he held the baby with the other. Wade cried with her, barely able to understand her as she muttered through her tears, "I miss her so much. She was as much a sister to me as the sisters I grew up with."

"I know," Wade said. "She loved you dearly; I'm sure she still does. She never wanted to leave here."

Jane wiped at her tears and sniffled loudly. "Now she'll never have to."

Wade just nodded and took the tissue she handed him. They both struggled for composure when Rebecca made it clear she was hungry. Jane showed him the simple procedure of mixing the formula and making certain the temperature was right, then she left him to feed the baby. He sat in the rocking chair where Elena had sat the night before to nurse Rebecca. Now it all felt like a dream.

The following morning after breakfast, Wade left Rebecca sleeping and carried the baby monitor with him to the study where he found Alex sitting in the chair by the desk, just staring at the wall.

"Why aren't you working?" Wade asked, leaning his shoulder against the doorjamb.

"I've traded some shifts, so I have the next few days off. I thought you could probably use a brother."

Wade sighed and sat on the couch. "And my best friend," he added, indescribably relieved. Alex had stood by him through some of the worst moments of his life. He couldn't even fathom how he would ever get through this without him.

"How are you?" Alex asked.

"How should I be?" Wade countered. "I know all those stages of grief, and I'm becoming friendly with every one of them. Sometimes I feel shocked, numb, horrified. Sometimes I feel angry enough to break something. Sometimes I cry so hard I think I'm going to puke. But then . . . you've pretty much seen me in all of those stages—years ago."

"Yes, that's true," Alex said.

"And you still love me."

"Yes, I do," Alex said firmly.

Wade's voice cracked. "For which I am eternally grateful."

"You've stood by me, too," Alex said. "You saved my son's life, for starters."

Their eyes met for a long moment as the memories filled the air around them. The hospital vigils had been long and difficult, but the bonds they had created ran deep.

"It was nothing," Wade said, referring to his offering of bone marrow. But because of the bond he'd found with Barrett, he couldn't deny that the experience had left a deep impression on him.

Little Preston ran into the room with a picture he'd drawn in orange crayon that only vaguely resembled an elephant if viewed with a great deal of imagination. Alex fussed over the picture and hung it on the wall by the computer before he hugged Preston tightly, and the child ran off to play just before the phone rang. Wade watched Alex glance at the caller ID, then he scowled.

"Who is it?" Wade asked.

Alex said cautiously, "The medical examiner." He stood up as he answered, as if being on his feet might make him better able to take the news.

Wade's heart beat painfully hard as Alex held the phone and mostly listened. He couldn't tell anything at all from this side of the conversation. Pondering the meaning of such a phone call, Wade knew that his own lack of emotion pointed more to the fact that he was in shock rather than indicating that he was handling this well.

"Okay, give it to me, Doctor," he said after Alex hung up the phone. When Alex hesitated he asked, "Did it have anything to do with the baby?"

"No," Alex said firmly.

Wade heaved a sigh. "Good. I don't ever want to have to tell Rebecca that her mother's death had anything to do with her." He looked up at Alex, who was still standing. "Just tell me."

Alex sat down on the couch close to Wade and turned to face him. "It was a cerebral hemorrhage. She died instantly, Wade. Painlessly, no warning. Even if you had been sitting in front of her, wide awake, there would have been nothing that you—or anyone else—could have done."

Wade drew a deep breath and squeezed his eyes shut. "At least it wasn't cancer," he muttered quietly. "I cannot begin to tell you how many times I prayed that whatever might take her, it wouldn't be cancer."

"It's getting more and more common. There's hardly a family that hasn't been touched by it. Cancer is like an epidemic these days."

"I know. That's why I was so afraid it would be that, or some other horrible, debilitating disease." He looked at Alex while moisture burned into in his eyes. "At least she didn't suffer. I'm grateful for that, Alex."

"So am I," he said.

"And I'm so grateful for Rebecca." He hung his head, and his voice quavered. "I don't know how I'm going to do it alone, Alex, but I thank God she left me a daughter."

"You don't have to do it alone, Wade."

Wade gave a humorless chuckle. "You know . . . taking a semester off to stay here for the summer wasn't an easy thing to do, and I've been worried about how that would affect my education. But we both felt so strongly that we needed to do it. We didn't question the reasons; we just went with it." His voice broke. "What would I have done if it hadn't happened here, Alex; what if I'd been in the middle of a term? It would have all fallen to pieces, and it would have been worse than not being in school at all. I just . . . can't believe . . . how we've been guided . . . and blessed. And I would be so lost without you."

"We're here for you, whatever it takes."

Wade groaned and tugged at his hair. "I don't even know what to think, what to do. Help me, Alex."

"Well, first of all we're going to get through the funeral. And then . . . well, you want my opinion?"

"I just asked for it, didn't I? Someone's got to have some brain capacity around here, and it's not me."

"Well I agree with what Dad said yesterday. I think you need to file for an emergency refund on your tuition and see if there's any possible way to get on here at the U. You can't take care of Rebecca and get through medical school alone. You need your family. And I've already talked to Jane; we want you to stay here. There's plenty of room, and we can help with the baby. Before you even consider protesting, I want you to know that we would consider it a *privilege* to help you get through this. We've been blessed with this huge home, and we are more than happy to share that blessing, especially under such circumstances. We love you, Wade, and we want you to be here as long as you need to be. We love Rebecca, and we love Elena; we always will. And Barrett's been saying every day that he doesn't want you to leave." Alex put his hands on Wade's shoulders. "We'll get through this together, little brother; whatever it takes."

Wade felt so overcome with gratitude that he could only say, "I just . . . need to think about it."

"Of course. As I said, let's get through the funeral first." He urged Wade to his feet. "Come along; you need to eat something—even if you still don't feel like it."

Wade went with Alex to the kitchen, wondering what he would have ever done if he'd not discovered that Alex Keane was his brother.

That evening Wade was sitting alone in the family room, feeding Rebecca, while the rest of the family was in the kitchen. The room was dimly lit from a lamp on the end table and the light emitting from the hallway. The baby drifted to sleep in his arms, and he set the bottle aside, then he found himself just staring at nothing, while the memory of finding Elena cold in their bed rolled over and over in his mind. A subtle noise pulled him from his morbid thoughts, and he glanced up to see Barrett standing in the doorway, his hands behind his back, his expression timid. Wade realized then that he hadn't even seen the child since Elena had died. Barrett's eyes were puffy, and there were red splotches around them that always appeared when he'd been crying. Wade wondered for just a moment how all of this had affected Barrett, then he pushed the thought away, knowing he couldn't handle any more heartbreak.

Forcing a steady voice, he said, "Hey there, buddy. What are you up to?"

Barrett moved tentatively closer, then pulled a piece of paper from behind his back. He held it toward Wade, saying quietly, "Here's the picture of Batman you asked me to draw for you."

Wade took it from him, recalling their conversation the day after Rebecca had been born. How different life had been then! He couldn't help smiling to see what a fine job Barrett had done; he'd clearly put a great deal of time into the drawing.

"Wow," Wade said. "That's amazing. Thank you. I'm going to hang it on my wall."

Barrett's expression didn't change; he said nothing. Wade felt certain that bringing him the picture now had just been an excuse to open a conversation. There was an expectancy in the child that was impossible to miss.

"I'm glad you like it," Barrett said, his eyes wide and cautious.

"I really do," he said, then added, "What's up, buddy?"

Tears immediately fell over Barrett's little cheeks. "I'm so sorry Elena died."

Wade shifted the baby to one arm and set the picture aside so that he could pull Barrett close. He couldn't hold back his own tears as the child clutched onto him and cried harder. "I miss her so much," he said.

"I know. So do I."

Barrett eased back a little, looking alarmed. "I didn't want to make you cry more."

"It's okay," Wade said, wondering if that's why he hadn't seen Barrett. Had he been trying to keep his own grief away from Wade's view? As always, Wade marveled at the insight and sensitivity of this child, as well as his emotional maturity, which was often beyond description.

"Maybe we needed to cry together," Wade added. "Did you know in the Book of Mormon it says that when we're baptized, we make a promise to mourn with those that mourn?"

"It does?" Barrett asked, as if the idea made complete sense to him. And perhaps it helped him feel validated somehow.

"And since you were baptized not so long ago, and since you're one of my very best friends, I think it's probably a good thing that we can cry together. What do you think?"

Barrett nodded, and his tears increased. Wade held him close until they both quieted down. Neither of them had anything to say for several minutes, but Wade could unmistakably feel the love and compassion of his sweet little nephew.

"The place she went to is much better than this one," Barrett said out of the silence, as if he were much older than his years.

"I'm certain it is," Wade said.

"It's very bright there," Barrett added as if he knew, and Wade's heart quickened. Everyone who knew Barrett was well aware that he'd gone to the edge of death multiple times through the course of his war with leukemia. But Wade had never heard him say any such thing before. He turned to look at the child and found him staring into space, his eyes intense but distant. "And it's very beautiful."

Not wanting to break the spell surrounding them, he asked in little more than a whisper, "What does it look like?"

Barrett turned to gaze at him, his eyes glowing with the wisdom of an old man, while his countenance shone with the innocence of a child. "I don't remember," he said matter-of-factly. "Only that it was bright. But I remember how it felt. It was like . . . more happy there than it is here. I don't know any words to explain how happy it feels."

"You were there?" Wade asked, wondering if he was jumping to conclusions or misconstruing a child's attempt to offer comfort.

"Only for a minute; it felt like a minute. But maybe it was just a dream." *Or maybe it wasn't,* Wade thought. "I had lots of dreams when I was sick." That wasn't a surprise, Wade concluded, considering the time he'd spent comatose, or drugged with pain meds, or just so ill that he'd seemed emotionally vacant for weeks.

Barrett went on. "There were people there, lots of them. My grandma who died before I was born." Wade knew he meant Alex's mother. "And my grandpa who died when I was sick." That would be Jane's father. "And I thought my dad was there; it looked like my dad, but it wasn't him. And other people too that I didn't know. They were all grownups, but not old." Barrett sighed loudly. "I wanted to stay, but they told me I had to come back. Now Aunt Elena is there. It's a happy place. I think the Holy Ghost wanted me to tell you that."

A different kind of tears overtook Wade as he felt a burning witness of the truth of what Barrett had just said. They gazed into each other's eyes while Wade felt the unspoken bond between them deepen. He felt as if they were equals in spirit somehow; no—Barrett was more likely much further progressed in that regard than Wade, even if he didn't have the actual knowledge and experience of an adult.

Barrett touched the tears on Wade's face and wiped them away with his little fingers. "It's going to be okay, Uncle Wade."

Wade could only nod, but he felt certain Barrett was right. Oh, the faith of a child!

While Wade was struck anew with the deep closeness he felt with Barrett, he concluded their thoughts were in the same vein when the boy said, "We have the same blood."

"Yes, we do," Wade said firmly.

"If you had died, I would have died too," he added, and once again Wade's heart quickened. How could he not recall that the week prior to his donating the bone marrow that had saved Barrett, he had attempted to end his own life? But Barrett didn't know that. Or did he? He wondered if Alex had told him, although he couldn't imagine why.

"What do you mean, Barrett?" Wade asked gently.

"I had a dream about you," he said.

"When did you have this dream?"

"After I saw you at the hospital."

"The first time we met?" Wade asked, and Barrett nodded. "I only saw you for a minute before you fell asleep. And then you were so sick that it was weeks before we saw each other again."

"In between then," Barrett said. "I had a dream . . . that you died, and then you came to get me when I died, and we walked down a long tunnel together, toward the light. But then it was like . . . I was in the light, and you were in the tunnel, and you grabbed me out of the light and pulled me back. You put me in the bed in the hospital, then you were sitting by the bed, reading the Bible."

Wade swallowed hard, but still couldn't speak. How could he ever tell Barrett what the symbolism he'd just heard meant to him? He'd pondered many times the horrific irony of what would have happened if he'd succeeded in that suicide attempt, especially in regard to Barrett's life. But he *had* sat at Barrett's bedside, reading from the Bible, waiting to see if the bone marrow would take hold, while Barrett had seemed mentally absent, what little time he'd been awake at all. The enormity of this conversation and its implications left Wade feeling awed and deeply comforted for reasons he could never put into words. It didn't matter whether or not Barrett's experiences had been real or whether they had been dreams. They were a clear reminder that the life they were living was more spiritual than temporal, even if it was difficult to see or understand that in the midst of earthly struggles.

Barrett apparently had nothing more to say. He snuggled up close to Wade and relaxed, and a few minutes later Wade realized he was asleep. Wade savored the serenity of the moment while he held the sleeping Rebecca in one arm, and kept the other around his nephew. He silently thanked God for the message of peace and perspective he'd just been given through the tender insight of this incredible child. He couldn't even imagine what great things Barrett might accomplish throughout the remainder of his life.

"Oh, there he is," Alex said, entering the room. "I've been looking all over for him. It's past his bedtime."

"We were just having a little chat," Wade said and watched Alex pick up the sleeping child, who hardly seemed to notice as he settled his head against his father's shoulder. Alex chuckled and hugged the boy tightly as he left the room. Wade turned his attention to his little daughter, wondering what *her* life might be like. What challenges might she face as a result of losing her mother in infancy? He prayed they would not be too great. Rebecca deserved a good life; he could only hope he had what it took to give it to her.

"You okay?" he heard Alex say and looked up to see him standing nearby.

"Is Barrett all tucked in?"

"He is," Alex said and sat down.

Wade noticed the picture Barrett had drawn and held it up for Alex to see. "I bet you don't have one of these."

"No, I don't," Alex said. "But I do know he's been working very hard on it; he was hoping it might cheer you up."

"Well, it certainly did," Wade said as contradictory tears rolled down his face, and he set the picture down.

"So, may I ask what you were chatting about? Batman?"

"Not even close." Wade said and turned to look more directly at Alex. "Did you ever tell Barrett that I tried to take my own life?"

"No," Alex said firmly. "There's no reason he should have to know that."

"It's not likely anyone else would have told him," Wade said.

"Of course not." Alex sounded alarmed and puzzled. "Why?"

"Do you know what he said to me?"

"What?"

"He said that if I had died he would have died too." Wade saw Alex abruptly put a hand over his mouth. He knew that was Alex's way of attempting to hold back unforeseen emotion. Wade went on. "He said he had a dream about me, that I had died, and then I came to get him when he died, and we walked together down a tunnel—toward the light, he said. Then he said it was like he was in the light, and I was in the tunnel, and I pulled him back and put him in the bed in the hospital, and then I was sitting by the bed, reading the Bible."

Wade realized Alex was crying when he closed his eyes and looked the other way. He sniffled and said, "That's a pretty incredible dream. Or maybe he was more aware of what was going on around him than we thought he was."

"Or both," Wade said. They sat in silent contemplation until Wade added, "Did Barrett . . . ever . . . share with you . . . anything that might remotely sound like . . ."

"Like what?" Alex pressed while Wade tried to consider how to say it without sounding hokey.

The only words he could come up with *did* sound a bit that way. "A . . . near-death experience."

Alex's eyes went wide. "He said that his grandma and grandpa had told him he needed to stay here so that he could be baptized, and grow up, and go on a mission. He made it clear he was talking about the grandparents who were dead." He almost looked wary as he asked, "Why?"

Wade sighed. "I think I just got a little more detail on that. He . . . uh . . . he told me that Elena was . . ." Tears overtook him, and he paused for a minute to gain some measure of composure. "That the place . . . she'd gone to was . . . bright . . . and beautiful . . . and more happy than he could find words to explain."

Wade saw Alex put a hand over the center of his chest; his expression looked dazed, stunned.

"He told me that maybe it was a dream, that it felt like he was only there for a minute. There were many people there—who were grownups but not old. His grandparents were there, and someone that he thought was you at first, but it wasn't."

Wade heard Alex take a sharp breath. They both knew he bore an uncanny resemblance to his great-great-grandfather, whose portrait was in the attic.

"That's incredible," Alex said breathlessly.

"Why do you suppose he's never brought it up before?"

"Maybe he didn't feel the need to," Alex suggested.

"He said he felt like the Holy Ghost wanted him to tell me."

Alex shook his head in disbelief. "Did he say anything else about it?"

"Only that he'd wanted to stay there, but he was told he needed to come back." Wade let out an ironic chuckle and wiped away a fresh stream of tears. "We were sure praying hard that he wouldn't leave us."

"Yes, we were," Alex agreed, equally emotional.

"He's the most amazing child I have ever known, Alex."

"Yes, he is." Alex sniffled and wiped his face with his shirt-sleeve. "And you saved his life."

Wade sighed. "You really don't need to keep bringing that up. I didn't do anything that magnanimous, Alex. God put the right kind of marrow in my bones. All I did was share it."

"For which I am eternally grateful."

Far into the night Wade pondered his conversation with Barrett. It didn't take away the harsh reality that he had to live without Elena for a very long time, and that he missed her beyond description. But he couldn't deny the added peace he felt from the perspective Barrett had given him.

The following morning Wade sought Barrett out and found him putting a puzzle together. Wade helped him put in a few pieces before he said casually, "I wanted to thank you for the things you told me last night. I'm glad to know that Elena is in a better place. She will never have to be sick or grow old, and even though I'm sad for myself because I have to be without her, I'm very happy that she's in a place that's so bright and beautiful."

Barrett gave him a big smile and a tight hug, muttering close to Wade's ear, "I love you, Uncle Wade."

"I love you too, Barrett," he said. "I'm so glad we're friends." He added in a whisper, "You're my favorite nephew, you know. But don't tell anybody. We wouldn't want my other nephews to get their feelings hurt."

"It'll be our secret," Barrett said and hugged him again.

A short while later, Alex sat in the kitchen with Wade while he ate a late breakfast and Rebecca slept. Wade was nearly finished eating when Alex said, "I have one of those questions to ask you that's not easy."

"Okay," Wade drawled.

"The mortuary called. They want to know if you would like to keep Elena's wedding rings, or if they should be left on her hand."

Wade felt utterly stunned. But he had to admit that he didn't know the answer. As if Alex could read his mind he added, "I asked what they usually do; they said people do either. You might want to give them to Rebecca someday, or you might prefer that they remain with her. It's up to you."

"Okay," Wade said again, and tears came from a source that should have surely gone dry. "I want them to stay with Elena. We're married forever, right?"

"Right. I'll call and tell them."

"Thank you."

The phone rang, and Alex reached for a cordless handset that was sitting on the table. Wade wiped his tears and took the last bite of his breakfast. After Alex said hello, he glanced warily at Wade while he said, "Um . . . I'm not sure if he's available at the moment. May I ask who's calling? Okay, hold on a minute and I'll see if he can come to the phone." He pushed the mute button and said, "Says he's a friend of yours—Kirk."

Wade felt a little sick to his stomach. How many days had it been since he'd had lunch with Kirk? And he'd declared himself to be the happiest man alive. Now Kirk was calling to set a time to have dinner together—with their wives.

Wade shook his head. "I can't talk to him. He needs to know what happened, but I can't tell him. And you're getting so good at it with all the practice you've had."

"Yeah," Alex said with chagrin, then turned off the mute before he spoke into the phone. "Kirk," he said, "Wade really isn't up to talking right now. I'm afraid he's having a fairly rough time at the moment. His wife passed away."

Wade knew from Alex's expression that Kirk was expressing his shock and horror. Alex tossed Wade a cautious glance before he said, "Uh . . . it was a cerebral hemorrhage. She died in her sleep. Wade found her."

Wade listened to the words as if he'd never heard them before, feeling almost as if Alex had to be lying. "Yeah, it's pretty rough," Alex went on to say. He stated the time and place of the funeral, and added, "I'll tell him you called. I will, thank you."

Alex hung up the phone and said, "He sends his love. He was crying."

"I had lunch with him a few days ago. Everything was perfect then."

"Yeah, life can change in a heartbeat," Alex said and stood up, taking the phone with him. "I'll call the mortuary."

Wade sat at the table and cried, feeling downright angry at the fact that life could change in a heartbeat.

* * *

Throughout the hours and days leading up to the funeral, Wade was inexpressibly grateful for the people who surrounded him with love and support, making certain everything was taken care of, and every need was met. All of his family members, and Elena's as well, were so good to him that he hardly knew how to respond. But he was especially grateful for his little daughter. Her presence gave him something to live for, someone to take care of, and a reason to feel needed. He looked forward to the times when she was awake and needed to be changed, and fed, and burped, even when it was the middle of the night. And sometimes he just held her while she slept, feeling deeply comforted by her very existence. She was a part of Elena and bore a strong resemblance to her mother that he prayed she would never grow out of. He gave thanks hourly that his sweet wife had lived long enough to bring this beautiful child into the world and into his life to help fill the void left by her absence. And while the loss of Elena felt horrific and completely unfair, he had to admit that he wouldn't go back and change a thing. The pain he felt over losing her had been more than fairly balanced by the joy she'd brought into his life while she had lived. His grief felt harsh and inescapable, but as he prayed for strength, and peace, and comfort, he felt those prayers answered. He knew beyond any doubt that it had been her time to go, and that his own mission on this earth was to remain and move forward. While that seemed impossible at the moment, he told himself that he only had to move forward one hour at a time, and those hours became measured by Rebecca's feedings.

Seeing Elena in the casket was initially difficult, but the peace in her countenance soothed something in him, and he tried to find comfort in thinking of all the struggles of life and old age that she would never have to endure. Through the viewing he kept his sleeping daughter in the crook of his arm while he hovered beside the casket with Elena's parents and siblings nearby. He found it odd that he felt composed and calm, while most people who came to offer their condolences were consumed with varying degrees of grief. Tears were being shed all around him while he saved his own tears for another time. People who loved and cared for Elena were more often than not drawn to Rebecca, as if the infant's presence somehow assuaged the pain of losing Elena, but at the same time, a young mother leaving behind a newborn child added another element of tragedy to this untimely death.

Kirk was one of many friends who came to the viewing. He hugged Wade and expressed his sorrow tearfully. He commented on how beautiful Elena was, and then he introduced Wade to his own wife. Wade smiled and shook her hand while he thanked them for coming, but inside he wanted to scream. It was as if some inner maniacal side of him felt hard pressed to keep from shouting, *You get to keep your wife and I don't! It's not fair and I hate you for it!*

Later at home, Alex sat with Wade while he fed Rebecca. Wade confessed his horrible thoughts to his brother, who readily admitted, "Oh, yeah. I felt that way often when Barrett was sick. My son was in isolation, puking all the time, and I would look at people with healthy children, clearly taking them for granted, and sometimes I'd feel so angry that I questioned my sanity. It's all a part of grief, little brother. Just make sure you vent your anger to me and not to the poor innocent bystanders who did nothing to deserve it."

"I'll do that," Wade said, glad to know that at least his thoughts weren't borderline insane.

The funeral was beautiful, and Wade couldn't deny that he felt a great deal of inner peace. He even felt Elena's presence close to him more than once, as if she wanted him to know of her love for him, and that she would always be mindful of him in spite of the many years ahead that they would be separated.

The day after the funeral, Wade had to wonder where the peace had gone. He felt so utterly consumed with grief that he could barely function. He hated leaving Rebecca's care to others, but he couldn't deny his gratitude for having Jane and Alex around to help with her when he couldn't seem to stop crying and preferred to do it alone in his room. Brad and Marilyn spent a good part of the day there, helping with the baby and sharing Wade's grief. He was grateful for their presence and their ability to offer perfect compassion and simply allow him to vent his emotions. Elena's parents stopped by, but he only visited with them for a few minutes before he admitted that he needed to be alone. They hugged him and expressed their love and said they would stay for a while and visit with the baby. A couple of hours after everyone else left, Neil and Roxanne stopped by, and again Wade was too upset to even want to come out of his room longer than to say hello. He was curled up on the bed, staring at the wall, when Alex knocked lightly before he came in and sat close by.

"How about if Dad and I give you a blessing? I think you could use one."

"I won't argue with that," Wade said and sat up. A moment later, Neil came into the room and closed the door.

Wade was even more grateful for the blessing than he'd anticipated. Afterward he took something to help him sleep, but when he woke up in the night to care for Rebecca, he felt a discernable peace surrounding him that had softened his grief immensely. He prayed that he could hold onto that peace and the source of strength that came with it. He was going to need it.

CHAPTER 4

The following morning Wade was surprised when Brad, the father who had raised him, stopped by unexpectedly. Wade knew he was supposed to be working, and he wondered what might warrant taking the time for such a visit, especially when he'd been here a long while the previous day.

After giving Wade a tight hug, he simply said, "Could we talk for a few minutes?"

"Sure," Wade said and led him to the study. He closed the door, and they were both seated.

"How are you, son?" Brad asked.

"It comes and goes," Wade said. "Sometimes it doesn't feel real, and I almost think I can get through it. At other times . . ." his voice cracked, "I can barely breathe."

"Yes, I know what you mean," Brad said gently, seeming slightly nervous.

Wade wondered what loved one his father might have lost tragically that Wade didn't know about. Had he lost a friend, a sibling? Was there a story Wade hadn't heard or had brushed off in his youth?

"I guess that's what I wanted to say, really," Brad went on. "I just want you to know that I *do* know how you feel. Of course, the circumstances are different, and emotions can vary, but . . . I know what it's like to have the woman you love suddenly snatched from the center of your life, and you've got a crying baby to remind you of her absence."

Wade's heart began to pound as he saw Brad's empathy in his eyes, heard it in his voice. But knowing what he did of his father's history, he couldn't figure how such an experience would have fit into his life. He was waiting for a clarification when Brad said, "That's how it was when your mother left me."

Wade took a ragged breath as it all came together. Brad's empathy hadn't come from the death of a loved one, but from betrayal.

Brad went on in a hushed voice, "I'm ashamed to admit that I wished a thousand times that she had died as opposed to leaving me, especially when I came to accept that I had some responsibility in driving her away. But when she left, your oldest brother wasn't quite four. Your other brother was barely two, and the baby was not quite crawling. I had spent years depending on her to do *everything* beyond my actually making a living. And then she was gone, and I had no choice but to do it all. I'll never forget those nights of being up with the baby, and I was as terrified as I was lonely."

Brad snapped himself out of a daze and turned to look at Wade. "I just wanted you to know that I understand how you feel, and I'm there for you, anytime, day or night. If you need to talk, or scream, or cry, or if you just need some company. I'll always be there for you, Wade."

Wade felt too touched to speak. He knew his chin was quivering as he nodded in response. His father smiled as if he understood, then he hugged him tightly, and Wade held to him, feeling like a child again, reminded of the countless times this man had ushered him through the pains and joys of life, knowing what Wade hadn't known until his adulthood—that Wade wasn't actually his blood son. But Brad had never treated him any differently than the other children. He'd always been there for him, and he could never express what that meant to him now.

"Thank you," was all he could manage to say.

Brad nodded and eased back, setting his hands on Wade's shoulders. "There are a couple of big differences in my situation and yours. I made some bad choices that contributed to her leaving. You didn't do anything to warrant this; it's just life. At least you can have peace in knowing that." Brad gave a wan smile and added, "The other difference is that you have the opportunity to live with your brother's family and have their help and support. I'm very grateful that you were able to come to know this part of your family, Wade. I thank Heavenly Father every day that you have such blessings in your life to compensate for some of the difficulties."

Wade nodded and struggled to say, "I think Him for that too. I am very blessed."

"Yes, and somehow you'll get through this. I know it doesn't feel like it now, but you will. And one day, you will know such joy in your life that you will not be able to comprehend the pain and suffering of this time."

"I'll have to take your word on that," Wade said, unable to even imagine such a thing.

They visited a while longer while Brad encouraged Wade to talk about what he was feeling, and even to shed more tears. When Brad left, Wade couldn't deny the truth in what he'd said to him; he was very blessed. The love and support of those around him was the only thing that made him believe that he *could* get through this.

Later that morning Wade was able to sit down with Alex and Jane and discuss his plans. He felt good about accepting their offer for him and Rebecca to stay with them. They were comfortable there, and it solved many problems. Wade insisted that he would care for Rebecca as much as he possibly could, but he would be grateful for Jane's help when he couldn't. And Alex was always in the center of helping with the children whenever he was around.

Wade also had long conversations with Elena's parents and siblings. Most of them lived in the area, and they very much wanted to remain involved in Rebecca's life. She was a blood relation to them and compensated for the loss of Elena in a way that he understood. They eagerly offered to help care for the baby once he got back into school, which would alleviate having so much of the responsibility fall on Jane. Wade also spoke with his own parents and siblings, and many of them too were more than happy to help with Rebecca. In truth, he had so many offers of help that he had to admit it was like the windows of heaven; there was not room enough to receive them.

With Neil's help, they were able to quickly collect the life insurance, and Wade was grateful for the help of his biological father in setting up a plan to use the money wisely. He paid for the funeral and headstone, and he paid Neil back for the burial plots. What little debt he'd had was paid off, and the rest was put away in a variety of accounts that would serve Wade the most favorably. He felt an overwhelming relief to realize that if he was reasonably careful he could actually live off the money until he was finished with school. And that was even leaving allowance for some recreation and being able to make extra purchases as needed. Not having to work meant that he could move less stressfully through school and still have time to be a somewhat decent father to his infant daughter. If nothing else, he was deeply grateful for the spiritual preparation that had prompted having such a good insurance policy. The money was a tremendous blessing, plain and simple.

Over the next few days, miracles fell into place as the emergency refund of Wade's tuition came through, and he was able to get out of his rent lease when the landlord heard about the situation. And somehow Neil made some connections and was able to miraculously get Wade registered at the University of Utah to continue his education. To Wade it felt as if Elena's death, the arrangements for his future, and the care of Rebecca had all been carefully orchestrated by divine hands. Everything fell together so neatly that he was left in awe, and he felt deeply grateful.

With the funeral behind him, Wade suddenly felt an aversion to shaving, and within a few days the beginnings of a beard were readily evident. Alex teased him about it, since it seemed to have some connection to enduring difficult times in life. There had been a time when they'd both been struggling for different reasons, and they'd both worn beards that had come off when circumstances had improved. Wade didn't know if he subconsciously connected his not wanting to shave with the grief in his life. He didn't really care why; he just didn't feel like shaving.

Ten days after the funeral Alex and Neil flew back east with Wade to pack up the contents of the apartment he'd shared with Elena. All of her things were carefully boxed up and marked so that they could be sorted through later. Wade had moments of crumbling with grief, and others of unfathomable anger. He understood the stages of grief and had to believe all of this was somehow normal, but he still felt like he was going to lose his mind.

With everything packed carefully into a rented U-Haul, the three men drove back to Utah where the contents were unloaded into Alex and Jane's garage. For a week their vehicles were parked on the street while a meticulous sorting process took place. With the help of Elena's mother and sisters, all of her belongings were quickly taken care of. While there were difficult moments, Elena's mother took the frank approach that it was better to do it now as opposed to having to dread doing it later. Many of her things that had no sentimental value went to Deseret Industries. Other things were carefully divided among her loved ones as keepsakes. Wade appreciated the way her family members always asked him if certain objects meant anything to him before they made decisions. They treated him as if he had been the most important person in Elena's life, and he couldn't help thinking how hard it would have been if their attitude had been different. At Alex's suggestion he used Elena's cedar chest to store all of the things he'd kept for himself and Rebecca that had belonged to her mother. The chest was put in Wade's room, while pictures of Elena and certain keepsakes were set out as constant reminders of the part she'd played in his life.

Once the material objects of Elena's life had been sorted and stowed away, Wade did a thorough sorting of his own belongings and streamlined them down to a minimum. The furniture he and Elena had been using hadn't been much to speak of, so he sold it at a yard sale, knowing he could buy more when the time came to be on his own again. What he didn't have in the two rooms in the house where he and Rebecca lived, he had stored in a handful of organized boxes in the garage.

On a night when he couldn't sleep, Wade found himself in front of the computer, looking at all of the digital pictures that he and Elena had been taking since they'd first met. They had both loved taking pictures, and there were literally hundreds of photos that documented the life they'd shared together. He programmed the computer to play them like a slide show, and he just sat and watched them all the way through, more than twice, before Alex found him there past three in the morning.

"What are you doing?" Alex asked.

"Watching a great movie," Wade said without taking his eyes off the screen. "I'm afraid it has a sad ending, however."

Alex looked over his shoulder and said, "Wow, there are some really great pictures. Aren't you glad you took them?"

"Yeah," Wade said, his voice cracking. He paused the computer, choked back the tears and said, "What are you doing up in the middle of the night?"

"I'm on my way to work," Alex said, and Wade took note of the scrubs he wore. It was difficult to keep track of his varying shifts.

"Lucky you," Wade said with sarcasm.

"I'll see you in about thirteen hours," Alex said and hurried out.

Wade continued the slide show, then fell asleep in the chair. He woke up to the sound of Rebecca crying on the monitor he had close by, and found the pictures still rolling. He closed the file and hurried upstairs to take care of his daughter, and as soon as she was back to sleep, he slept too. Her indifference to night and day suited him fine, but he knew that would change when school started.

After breakfast, Jane encouraged Wade to go to the temple while she watched Rebecca. He felt reluctant, thinking how he'd not been there without Elena since he'd married her. But Jane tearfully suggested that perhaps he could feel closer to her there than anywhere else. Wade took her suggestion and was glad that he had, even though his grief felt close to the surface, and he was prone to frequent tears. He felt no obvious manifestation that Elena was close to him, but he was vividly reminded of the blessings of the temple and eternal marriage, and he left feeling a distinct peace that promised to help carry him through.

The week before the term was set to begin, Wade had to admit his life was as organized and in order as it could be. He had settled into a fairly comfortable routine of caring for Rebecca, and he felt completely at ease in his brother's home as he settled in more deeply. But he still felt like his world had shattered. He continued to struggle with the ongoing grief of losing his wife, and often found himself crying when he was completely alone—usually in the shower or in bed at night. In spite of the peace that soothed his loss, being without Elena just felt all wrong, and he hated the loneliness of her absence. But all he could do was press forward, one day, one hour at a time.

Wade couldn't deny a keen aversion to social situations that would tempt his grief to the surface. He purposely missed the family reunion that he'd helped plan just before Elena's death, but then he'd seen most of those people at the funeral anyway. He finally realized he had to buck up and go to church, something he'd especially avoided for fear of having his emotions get out of hand, leaving him embarrassed or upset. He appreciated the kindness and support of ward members, but he hated the pity in their eyes, and he could well imagine many of them wondering how they might cope if it happened to them. He heard the same kind words spoken over and over to the point of becoming tedious. He had to remind himself not to be put off, but to appreciate that people simply wanted to express their care and concern.

Now that he'd officially moved in with Alex and Jane, his membership records were moved to that ward. Even though he hardly knew these people, they had been amazingly compassionate and supportive, but the genuine care and concern of others was often the very thing that prompted his tears to the surface. He hoped that all the crying he was doing would get the grief out of his system so that he could go to school and keep himself together. He'd never cried so much in his life, never imagined that a man could have that many tears inside of him.

When classes began, Wade had a difficult time being away from Rebecca for so many hours at a time. But the people who loved her—and him—were wonderful to work out babysitting schedules that allowed him to be with her every minute he could and still get his classes and study time in. He felt blessed to be able to get through his days as if nothing in the world was wrong, but he still struggled with unexpected tears here and there. Thankfully they usually showed up when he was alone.

On the one-month anniversary of Elena's death, Wade stopped at the grocery store after classes for diapers, wipes, formula, and some basic food items to contribute to the household. He picked Rebecca up from Elena's mother, and during the short drive home she became very fussy. By the time he got home she was screaming to be fed. Once he'd changed and fed her and got her to sleep, Jane had dinner ready. He hurried to eat, helped load the dishwasher, put in a load of laundry, then studied until Rebecca woke up again. He changed and fed her again, put the clothes in the dryer, then studied with her in his arms. He'd just gotten her down for the first stretch of the night when he turned around to see Alex and Jane in the doorway to her room. Jane was holding a box.

"Hey," Alex said, "we have a little something for you."

"Okay," Wade said and sat down in the rocking chair. Alex and Jane sat on the little love seat near the window.

"I told Jane I'd caught you looking at pictures on the computer more than once. This was her idea." She handed the box to Wade.

"I copied the files and got them printed up," she said. "There were a few that I thought were worthy of framing; pictures you should have sitting out."

"Wow," Wade said before he opened the box. There on the top of white tissue were four separate framed five-by-sevens. One was of him and Rebecca, one of him and Elena, one of Elena and Rebecca, and one that Alex had taken of the three of them together. Wade's eyes filled with mist that became tears.

He wiped them away and said, "Thank you. They're perfect." He took them out one at a time, looked at each one and set it aside before he removed the tissue paper. Beneath it was a very thick photo album. Each picture he'd had on the computer had been printed and put in chronological order, documenting the brief span of his life that he'd shared with Elena, and there were pages of pictures at the back with Rebecca in them that they'd taken during those first two weeks of her life. Wade let out a little laugh through his tears, then he hugged both Jane and Alex and thanked them again. Long after they left the room he sat and looked through the album. He kept it next to his bed, and he set the framed photos out on the end tables and the dresser in his bedroom. They were a poor replacement for his wife, but a fond reminder that she had been real.

The following Saturday he accepted an invitation from Brad and Marilyn to go to the temple with them, and after the session they ate lunch together in the cafeteria. He missed having Elena there so badly that it hurt, but he couldn't deny the peace of simply being within temple walls.

Rebecca was nearly seven weeks old when she began what Jane called a fussy stage. Every evening for about two hours, like clockwork, she would cry for no apparent reason, and nothing could soothe her. Wade's determination to care solely for his daughter when he was at home waned quickly on the fourth evening when the baby's fussing felt like a neon reminder that her mother was not around to share the burden. He had proudly refused Alex and Jane's offers to help with her while she fussed, but as he felt himself reaching a point of internal agitation that was almost frightening, he carried the crying baby directly to Jane's arms, admitting shamelessly, "I can't do it alone." A tearless sob escaped his throat as Jane took Rebecca into her loving arms. "I feel like she's crying for her mother, and I . . . I can't . . . do it."

"It's okay, Wade," Jane assured him while Alex looked on, holding a contented little Ruth in his arms. "Go put some headphones on or something and let me take care of her. It's okay."

Wade could only nod and walk away, but once alone in his room he had to cry for twenty minutes before he could force himself to study—taking Jane's suggestion to put some loud *Collective Soul* on the headphones to drown out the distant sounds of Rebecca crying. More than an hour later he was pleased to realize he'd finished up an ugly assignment just before he felt a tap on his arm. He pulled off the headphones and turned to see Alex, with Rebecca sleeping soundly in his arms. Without a word he shifted the baby into Wade's hands, and he immediately felt the peace of her tranquil presence in contrast to her horrible fussing earlier. Alex smiled at Wade and put a hand briefly to his face, as he might to one of his children. "Thanks for letting us help with her. Believe it or not, you're doing just fine. I've had moments like that with all of my kids, Wade—especially Barrett. He was so colicky and fussy that I wondered sometimes what we'd gotten ourselves into. And I had his mother around." He smiled again. "It's okay to admit that you can't do it alone. We're glad you're here."

Like a thousand times before, Wade could only nod in response, too overcome with emotion to speak. Alex left the room, and Wade held Rebecca close, breathing in her aura of serenity as she slept. He hoped that Elena could be aware of how thoroughly beautiful and precious their daughter was. And he hoped she wouldn't be too disappointed with the way he was fumbling through fatherhood without her.

* * *

The day that Rebecca was blessed in church, Wade struggled with a paradox of emotions. Surrounded by family, friends, and ward members, he couldn't deny how blessed he was. But it just didn't seem right to have such an event without Elena at the center of it. He felt certain she was close by in spirit, but that was still way too out of reach for his liking.

When Rebecca turned two months old, Wade felt proud of himself for the way he was managing to handle his grief more reasonably. Medical school was taxing at best, but he was managing to keep up with his studies, and Rebecca's fussy stage was easing up. Then Jane reminded him at the breakfast table that he'd overlooked something.

"Rebecca needs her two-month checkup. And that means her first set of immunizations."

"If you're going to specialize in pediatrics," Alex teased, "you've got to know this stuff."

"Or I can rely on Jane," Wade said, "who keeps track of everything two weeks ahead with Ruthie."

"That works," Jane said. "Do you want me to take her in? Elena took her to a different pediatric clinic than the one we use. I believe her sister recommended the doctor. But I can still do it; I'd be happy to."

"No, thank you," Wade said. "I'll do it." He'd purposely set up his class schedule with a couple of evening classes so that some afternoons could be kept open for just such needs. He found the paperwork from the pediatrician's office where Elena had taken Rebecca for her two-week checkup. He stared at the information while he pondered the memories of that day. Elena had taken her to the appointment while he had gone to lunch with Kirk. Elena had been alive and real and apparently perfectly healthy, while a time bomb had been within hours of going off in her brain. Wade felt a little sick as he thought about it and had to force his mind elsewhere. He called and made an appointment, then left for the day's classes.

When the day of Rebecca's checkup arrived, Wade felt awkward in the waiting room of the pediatric clinic. There were babies and children of many ages waiting to see one of three different doctors and a couple of physicians' assistants who manned the clinic. And every other child was there with a mother; some of them had the father along as well, but he was the only single father in the room. He concluded that he'd do well to get used to it.

Rebecca slept in her little seat while they waited, and he found his mind wandering until he heard a nurse call, "Rebecca Morrison."

Wade put the diaper bag over his shoulder and picked up the baby seat by the handle. He followed the nurse into an exam room, feeling a little foggy as he often did, while something in the back of his brain kept comparing the reality to what should have been.

"I'm sorry we'll have to wake her up," the nurse said, but her voice was soothing and tender, putting him at ease. He noticed that her name badge said Laura, LPN. "You'll need to undress her down to her diaper, and then we'll get her weight."

"Okay," Wade said, and she left the room. He undressed Rebecca and wrapped her in a blanket to keep her warm, and thankfully she seemed content and wasn't fussing. They waited several minutes before Laura came back in.

"Hello there, beautiful," she said to Rebecca as she took her from Wade and laid her gently on the scale. She smiled at Rebecca and talked to her as if she was the most important baby in the world. Then he remembered Elena telling him how the nurse at the clinic had been that way with the baby on the previous checkup. Was this the same nurse? Probably. But his thoughts were more with the irony that Elena should have been here. And he hated the fact that she wasn't.

Laura handed Rebecca back to Wade and wrote down the weight, commenting on how well the baby was growing according to the chart. She took Rebecca again and laid her down on the paper-covered exam table to put a pencil mark above the baby's head, and below her foot. She then picked the baby up, smiled at her and seemed to enjoy just holding her, as if she didn't want to hand her over any sooner than she absolutely had to. He couldn't help wondering if she'd chosen this line of work because she just liked to hold babies. While she momentarily seemed enthralled with Rebecca, she said casually, "It's not often we get the dads bringing babies in for this kind of thing, at least not alone. Is Mom working?"

Wade swallowed hard and counted to ten while he considered that he'd never taken Rebecca anywhere that had called attention to the unusual circumstances—except for church, and everybody there had already known. Laura seemed concerned by his silence, and he hurried to say what needed to be said, hating the tension. "Um . . . no. Rebecca's mother died about six weeks ago."

Laura gasped and met his eyes, as if to verify that he was serious. He found himself staring at her, perhaps silently daring her to diplomatically brush it aside with some empty words of sympathy and move quickly past the awkward moment. Then he saw her eyes moisten before she closed them and held Rebecca a little closer, as if she could give her just a small degree of a woman's love and a woman's comfort. Watching her, Wade felt tears spill down his face before he could think of holding them back. He was considering the distance to the box of tissues when Laura opened her eyes and looked at him again. He couldn't bring himself to feel embarrassed or ashamed to be caught crying, especially when her expression conveyed such perfect compassion. Compassion was different from sympathy he realized in that moment. She didn't feel sorry for him; she hurt for him. He could see it in her eyes. Suddenly the moment wasn't awkward at all, even though they were standing there staring at each other—complete strangers, both crying silent tears. He waited for the silence to be broken by some feeble attempt to console him. He'd heard it all a hundred times. He could imagine her telling him that it would get easier with time, that life could sure be tough sometimes, that trials could make us stronger. But she only said, "I don't know what to say."

"There's nothing to say," Wade said. "But thanks for caring."

Noises in the hall seemed to alert her to the fact that there was work to be done. She gave Rebecca another motherly hug, then reluctantly gave her back to him before she grabbed a couple of tissues, handing one to him. "Thanks," he said, and he noticed her wedding ring. He wondered why he would feel anything but indifference to realize she was married when he couldn't even imagine having any interest in moving on in that regard. But he couldn't deny the feeling; he was disappointed. He watched her while she measured between the marks she'd written on the table and wrote down Rebecca's length on the chart. Her dark blonde hair was long and slightly curly, and pulled back into a thick ponytail, with some shorter curls framing her face. She was average height and build, and her features were gentle. She wore scrubs with brightly colored frogs and lizards all over the shirt; the pants were bright green. On her feet were bright purple tennis shoes that went well with the prominent purple in the shirt. She had a little purple plastic frog hanging on a cord around her neck. She had clearly dressed to be a spectacle to the children who came in here. He found the concept charming and took a mental note to remember such tactics when he crossed the line to actually work as a pediatrician.

"Forgive me if I'm being presumptuous," she said, "but . . . I noticed your CTR ring. You're LDS."

"That's right," he said and waited for her to say something about how comforting it must be to know that he had forever with his wife. He'd heard that one a hundred times, as well.

Instead she said, "I'm sure those eternal blessings can bring some amount of peace, but it's got to be tough to think of getting through the next fifty or sixty years."

Wade was amazed to realize how perfectly she'd expressed how he felt. He just said, "Yeah, that about covers it."

Laura asked him some general questions about Rebecca's eating and sleeping habits, then told him the doctor would be in soon.

"Thank you," Wade said as she reached for the doorknob.

She hesitated and looked straight at him, reminding him of the emotional moment they'd shared while she'd simply been going about her medical duties. "She's a beautiful baby, and she's very lucky to have such a wonderful father."

Wade couldn't think of a response before she left the room, but once she was gone he had to face more tears. He was glad the doctor was slow coming in so that he could compose himself first. He checked Rebecca thoroughly while Wade paid close attention, longing for the day when he would be on the other side of this. The doctor declared her to be doing well, then said that he'd send someone in to give Rebecca her immunizations. Wade had forgotten they had shots to face. He was relieved when Laura came back to do the dirty deed. Rebecca screamed as any baby would, but Laura talked to her gently as if Rebecca could understand, and the moment it was done she took the baby from Wade, as if her maternal instincts required her to give some comfort for a minute as part of the procedure. She calmed the baby down before she gave her back to Wade, along with a tender smile.

"Thank you," Wade said.

"We'll see you again at four months," she said and left the room.

Wade got Rebecca dressed and buckled into her seat, grateful that a pacifier was keeping her quiet. He wondered if he should feed her something before they started home, but she seemed relaxed, and she fell asleep as he drove.

It wasn't until he'd been home a couple of hours that he realized his favorite little blanket of Rebecca's was missing. She had lots of blankets that were constantly circulating through the laundry, but this one was special. A thorough search only made him aggravated, but he didn't realize how much until Jane asked, "What's wrong?"

"Her blanket is gone," he snapped, looking behind the couch where he'd already looked three times.

"Which one?" she asked calmly.

"The . . . one with the . . . pink stars . . . and . . ."

"The crocheted edge?" she asked, and he nodded, realizing he was near tears. He felt Jane's hand on his arm and realized she was fully aware of how upset he was, even though he'd been trying to hold it back. "It's okay," she said. "We'll find it. Where did you last have it?"

He thought for a minute. "The doctor's office," he said and resisted cursing.

"Okay, well . . . things probably get left there all the time. I'll call and ask."

"Okay," he said, "thank you."

While Jane went in the other room to call, he went upstairs and kept searching in all the places where he took care of the baby, places he'd already looked more than once. Jane found him and said, "They said it's not there, but they'll keep an eye out and let us know. Did you look in the car?"

"Yes," he said.

"Wade," Jane moved closer and took his shoulders into her hands, "I know that blanket means a lot to you, but I don't think your emotion right now has anything to do with the blanket."

Wade wanted to swear at her as hot tears burned into his eyes. He couldn't speak as she wrapped her arms around him in a tight, sisterly embrace. "It's okay, Wade. We'll find the blanket, and we'll keep coping, and you can cry if you have to."

As if he'd only needed her permission, he slumped into a nearby chair and started to sob. She just sat close beside him, holding a box of tissues, and using one occasionally herself. While he cried he silently prayed to find some peace over losing a blanket. *I know it's a silly thing, Father, but that blanket means a lot to me, and I need to have it and hold it. Please.* His mind returned to this horrendous outpouring of emotion that he couldn't seem to get a handle on. He appreciated the way Jane didn't try to fill the silence. She just silently grieved with him until Ruthie woke up from her nap. A few minutes later, Rebecca woke up too. He heard the phone ring while he was sitting in the family room feeding Rebecca her bottle, but he ignored it as he usually did. This was Alex and Jane's home, and most of the calls were for them. But Jane brought the cordless phone to him, saying, "It's for you. It's the doctor's office."

As he took the phone, Wade wondered if they'd determined that something was wrong with Rebecca. "Hello," he said.

"Mr. Morrison?"

"Yes."

"This is Laura from the pediatric clinic. I just wanted to let you know that you left Rebecca's blanket here, and I have it."

Through the course of his mini breakdown he'd honestly forgotten about the blanket, but he couldn't express his relief to hear that it had been found—and that he hadn't lost his mind in not being able to locate it.

"Oh, thank you," he said. "I'll pick it up sometime tomorrow." As soon as he said it he realized he had classes during the hours the clinic would be open. He could ask Jane to pick it up, but she already did so much for him, and taking care of all these kids was more than a full-time job for her. And Alex would be working a day shift, as he was today. Maybe he could ask his mother.

"That would be fine," she said, "or if you prefer, I checked your address in the records. You're almost on my way home. I'd be happy to drop it off."

"Oh, that would be great," he said, unable to hide his enthusiasm, wondering if he could tell her that her effort was such an obvious answer to prayers that he almost felt tempted to start crying again.

Wade hung up the phone and went to tell Jane about the extra mile this Laura was going. Jane smiled and said, "The tender mercies of the Lord show up in strange little ways, don't they?"

Wade smiled back. "Yeah, they do. Thanks for holding me together, sis."

"It's okay, Wade. That's what family is for. I only wish I could do more."

Ruthie started to cry from where she was rocking back and forth in the baby swing, and Jane went to get her.

Wade had just gotten Rebecca to sleep against his shoulder when the doorbell rang. He ignored the quickening of his heart as he opened it to see Laura in her colorful scrubs and silly shoes.

"This *is* the right place," she said. "The house is so beautiful; it's hard to imagine people actually living in it."

"Yeah," he said. "It's my brother's home. We're living with his family while I'm going to school. They help a lot with Rebecca, so I'm grateful to say the least."

"Is it a family home?" she asked, touching the brick next to the door, and then the plaque there that identified it as a state historical site.

"Yes, actually. His family; not mine."

She looked confused. "But you're brothers?"

He laughed softly. "Half-brothers," he clarified.

"Oh, I see," she said, smiling. "Here you go." She handed the blanket to him, and he took it with his free hand.

"Thank you . . . so much."

"With that beautiful crocheting around the edge, I figured it must be sentimental. I didn't want someone else making off with it."

"Thank you," he said again, and then perhaps hoping to explain his overt enthusiasm over getting it back, he added, "Her mother made it."

Laura offered a sad smile and said, "It's beautiful."

"Yes, it is," Wade said. "Thank you again."

She smiled once more, and he couldn't help thinking she had a beautiful smile. "I'll see you at the next checkup," she said and turned to go down the steps. She turned back before Wade closed the door. "Forgive me," she said, "if I'm being presumptuous, but . . . is there anything I can do? I just can't stop thinking of how . . . tough this must be for you. I know I'm probably completely out of line, but . . . truly, if I could help in any way."

Wade breathed in her genuine concern and recalled Jane's words a while ago. *The tender mercies of the Lord show up in strange little ways.* He didn't feel at all awkward saying, "You're very sweet, Laura. And I don't think you're out of line. But honestly, we're doing okay. We have a lot of family around, and they're great. There's always a long line of people who love Rebecca and want to help with her, and we have every-thing we need. But . . . thank you." He held up the blanket.

"And thank you for taking the time to bring this back. It means a lot."

"You're welcome," she said. "Hang in there."

"Thanks," he said and watched her walk away. After he closed the door, he leaned against it and held the blanket close to his face, muttering into it, "Thank you, Lord."

* * *

Throughout the following weeks Wade realized he was having more good days than bad ones, as opposed to the other way around. He missed Elena so badly that it hurt if he pushed the pause button of life long enough to ponder reality. He couldn't say that he was growing accustomed to her absence, but he had learned how to cope with it. And he certainly hadn't gotten past the need to grieve, but it had ceased taking control of his life. He made regular visits to her grave, sometimes taking Rebecca along, but he never stayed long. Her spirit wasn't there, and he knew it, although he found a strange comfort in pressing his fingers over her name carved in granite. He also visited the temple whenever time allowed, unable to go for long without the peace and strength it gave him. He thought occasionally of what a tremendous blessing it was to have the gospel in his life, and to know all that he knew. It didn't magically erase his loneliness or heartache, but it gave him an understanding that blanketed his grief with comfort and made it possible to go on. Without that knowledge, he wondered how he would ever be able to feel hope again.

Being a father became easier as Rebecca began sleeping more at night, and she eased into a new stage of smiling and cooing. Wade found great joy in seeing her focus on his face and respond to his silly voices. She was beginning to feel like a real person with her own personality, and he looked forward to each stage of her progression.

Rebecca wasn't yet four months old when more than one well-meaning ward member suggested to Wade that he should get out and start dating. One elderly lady put it rather bluntly. "You need to get that child a mother, young man," she'd said as if his not doing so before now was somehow criminal.

After church Wade vented to Jane and Alex while they were working together to put Sunday dinner on the table. "I can't believe someone would be that insensitive. We're talking about a wife here, not a new vacuum or something. You don't just go out and get another one because you happen to need it."

"I'm sure she meant well," Jane said.

"I'm sure she did too; so did the other two people who suggested the same—albeit more tactfully. But it still ticks me off."

"Okay, so you know well enough that anger comes in spurts when you're grieving," Alex said, "but you've got to keep perspective. Obviously no one but you can know when you're ready to move forward. Just smile and say, 'Thank you for your concern,' and let it roll off."

Wade knew Alex was right, but it was easier said than done. When he didn't comment, Jane said, "I take it you *don't* feel ready."

"Ready for what? To replace Elena in my life? I can't imagine *ever* being ready for that. The very idea of even *dating* again makes me nauseous."

"So you're not ready," Alex said. "But again, you've got to keep perspective. Being alone can't be easy, especially after you've become accustomed to sharing your life with someone. You're not betraying Elena by moving forward—whenever it may feel right."

Wade felt suddenly weak and sat down as a memory took hold.

"What's wrong?" Jane asked.

It took Wade a moment to answer. "We talked about this; I'd forgotten, but . . . we did. At the time I mostly laughed it off. I didn't want to have a serious discussion on what I would do with my life after she died." He let out a humorless chuckle as her words became clear in his mind. "She told me I could laugh if I wanted, but one day I would be glad we'd talked about it. So here's that day." He shook his head. "It still doesn't seem real sometimes. This separation between life and death, trying to mix the memories with the present."

"And the future," Jane said, sitting close beside him while Alex leaned against the counter.

"So what did she say?" Alex asked.

"She told me that one of the hardest things for her to think about was leaving me alone. She said she didn't want me to be alone a minute longer than necessary, that I needed someone to take care of me." He chuckled again. "And she said if she had any pull from the other side she'd be looking for just the right woman, and pushing her in my direction."

"So, maybe she is," Jane said.

Wade made a scoffing noise and changed the subject as he stood up to mash the potatoes while Jane took the roast from the oven, and Alex got the dishes down so that Barrett could set the table.

Dinner with the family was pleasant, and once it was over and cleaned up, Wade played Batman Monopoly with Barrett, while Preston kept climbing on his lap and wanting to play, and Katharine regularly came to see who was ahead. Preston finally followed his sister to play dollies with her, then Wade and Barrett sneaked into the kitchen for big bowls of ice cream that they took upstairs to eat while Barrett analyzed why he'd won and Wade had lost.

"Face it," Wade said, "you were just lucky. You landed on the Bat Cave and Wayne Manor so you could buy them. And you're so greedy with the rent you charge."

Barrett laughed. "I just play by the rules, and you're going to have to live with it."

Wade laughed with him, wondering what he'd done to deserve having such a great friend—who was only eight years old.

CHAPTER 5

Over the next several days, Wade felt almost disturbed to find his train of thought steering toward the things Elena had said about him not being alone. He'd been thinking that he couldn't start dating until he'd stopped missing Elena, but now he wondered if he would ever stop missing her. He knew that he could never find anyone to replace her, but he wanted to believe there was someone out there who could fill the void she had left.

Wade took Rebecca to the clinic for her four-month checkup and another set of shots, and he was disappointed to find that Laura wasn't there. Her replacement wasn't nearly so tender or enthusiastic. He couldn't help thinking that Laura was the kind of woman he might consider taking on a date, but she was married.

It took another couple of weeks of pondering the idea of dating before Wade dared admit aloud to Alex and Jane what he was feeling. Then he asked his most pressing question, "Where do I start?"

"Well, there are adult singles functions," Jane said. "Dances and firesides and—"

"Okay, but . . . I don't have *time* for that. I already leave Rebecca too much as it is. Don't they just have . . ." he waved his hand impatiently, "mail-order brides or something?" Jane laughed, and he added, "Can't I just . . . make a list of what I want and order it?"

"And what would it say?" Alex asked.

Wade became more serious as he said, "Just like Elena."

He heard Rebecca cry on the monitor he had hooked to his belt and hurried upstairs to get her. That evening as he was bathing her, he watched her kick and giggle in the water and decided to just ask her what she thought. "What would you think about me finding you a new mother? She'd have to be pretty amazing. Not just anybody could raise a princess like you, in the way you deserve." Rebecca let out a happy squeal and splashed her hands and feet in the water, while her eyes stayed focused on his face as if she were hanging on his every word. "Okay, well . . . I'll see what I can do," he said. "But I'm not going out with any woman more than once or twice unless you approve of her. Got it?"

Again Rebecca made a happy noise, and Wade put his attention to getting her hair washed.

The next day Wade's mother called with good news. "Guess what?" Marilyn said.

"The big white envelope arrived," he said with certainty. He knew that his younger brother Brian had submitted his mission application, and they'd been waiting for the mission call to come in the mail.

"Yes!" she practically squealed. "We're all meeting here at six for him to open it. Can you be here?"

"I wouldn't miss it," he said.

"Good. We're having dinner too. I'm making tacos."

"How marvelous," he said. "Can I bring anything?"

"Just you and that adorable baby of yours."

"She goes where I go," he said and ended the call.

Wade enjoyed being with his family that evening, and he especially enjoyed the way they all fussed over Rebecca with so much love and adoration. Once again he was reminded of how thoroughly blessed he was to have been raised in such a loving family.

After the family had eaten and cleaned up the kitchen, they all gathered in the front room to watch Brian open the envelope. Wade recalled this event in his own life, and briefly pondered all that had happened since his mission. He'd come far; some of the changes had been good, others just hard. Brian had, at one time, shown a tendency toward rebellion—a direct result of the nightmare of discovering that their mother had once been guilty of adultery. But they had all come to terms with that now, and Brian was a great kid. His enthusiasm for serving a mission was evidence of that.

Brian pulled the letter out and scanned it before he grinned and announced, "Idaho."

"Are you serious?" their sister, Robin, demanded.

"No," Brian laughed. "But I had you all there for a minute." Everyone laughed and scolded him for teasing. He then said more seriously, "I'm going to England."

Everyone cheered, and Marilyn started to cry as she hugged Brian tightly. The family talked about the mixed feelings involved with Brian serving a mission. There was nothing more wonderful or exciting than to see him take this step, but they would miss him, and it was hard to think of letting him leave for two years.

For no apparent reason, Wade found his attention drawn to his older siblings, who were all married. Seeing them interact with their spouses left him feeling disoriented and consumed with a lonely ache. He was actually relieved when Rebecca became inexplicably fussy, and he had a good excuse to leave.

Wade kept too busy the next few days to give the dating issue much thought until he overheard a conversation at school about Internet dating sites. He'd toyed with them a little, prior to meeting Elena, but at the time he'd felt a lot more like socializing than he did now, and using the computer to meet women had felt like a waste of time. Now, his circumstances were much different. Curiosity pressed him to explore the sites later that evening after he had put Rebecca down for the night. He quickly realized the sites geared specifically to LDS people were more to his liking. He didn't even want to wonder if the women he might connect with shared his religion. That was simply a must. Impulsively he decided to register on two different sites where he posted some minimal information about himself, but he decided he felt more comfortable using an email handle as opposed to his name. Feeling cautious and wanting some degree of privacy, he felt no motivation at this point to actually include a picture of himself. Once he had full access to the sites, he started scanning through what seemed endless faces and information related to available women. Alex came into the study and stood behind him, asking lightly, "What *are* you doing?"

"Feels like shopping," Wade said cynically. "Pick a woman, any woman—and with any luck she might actually be what she claims to be when you meet her."

"Yeah, that would be good," Alex said and sat on the couch, putting his feet up. "So, does this mean you're feeling ready to start dating again?"

"This means that I feel like I should, not necessarily that I want to. Truthfully, I feel more like I'm looking for a mother for Rebecca, and I know that's not fair."

"Well, maybe it will actually take going on a few dates to get over feeling uncomfortable about the whole thing."

"Maybe," Wade said, but he didn't feel convinced.

"You don't *have* to use the Internet, you know. Aren't there any available women in your classes?"

"No one that's ever caught my attention."

"Okay. Maybe you should go to a singles ward."

"I would prefer going to church with you, thanks anyway." He sighed loudly. "You know, it really just feels . . . awkward. I want to be married, settled. But I don't want to do this. Maybe it *is* too soon."

"Maybe. Maybe not," Alex said. "I heard once that widowed people who had a good marriage were more likely to get married again more quickly." Wade turned to look at him. "If you look at it that way, your desire to be married again is a tribute to Elena and the love you shared with her. And you know she didn't want you to be alone."

Wade felt some food for thought settling in, but he only turned off the computer and said, "I think I need some sleep."

"Good plan."

"I'll see you in the morning."

"Actually, I'm leaving for work here in a few minutes."

"Lucky you," Wade said with sarcasm.

"Yeah, be glad your chosen field won't require shift work. You'll have occasional emergencies at odd hours, I'm sure, but you won't have to become nocturnal at odd intervals."

"Yeah, but think of all the adventure you get at the ER," Wade said, then told his brother good night.

Wade quickly developed a habit of spending a short while each day looking through the profiles of available LDS women, pondering the things they'd written about themselves and what they were looking for in a man. He finally emailed a few, just sending a simple anonymous note that suggested a desire to get to know these women better. Since his email address was barrettsuncle@yahoo.com he signed his letters simply, Barrett's Uncle. Within a few days, Wade could easily tell from the responses he got that he was way off base. The tone of their letters either put him off or felt tedious. He tried a few more and found one that he enjoyed some minimal communication with, then she let him know that she'd met someone she believed to be the right man for her.

Wade left the Internet singles scene alone throughout the course of the holidays. The first signs of Christmas appeared when Jane began putting together what had become a recent tradition. Since her son had spent many difficult months at Primary Children's Medical Center, Jane had taken on the yearly project of doing a Christmas tree for the Festival of Trees. The fully decorated trees, and whatever might go along with them in the form of gifts or decor, were donated, then auctioned, and all of the proceeds went to the medical center. The trees were also put on display for a few days before they went to the purchasers, and the event had become a very big deal for the Keane family since Barrett had survived leukemia. Wade actually helped some with the little ornaments that Jane was making. This year, her theme was the Nutcracker Ballet, and the tree would be covered with little ballerinas and nutcracker prince ornaments.

Wade enjoyed participating in the festival, and they were all pleased when Jane's tree brought in a fair amount of money. The family had a great time pitching in to see the project through, then once their obligations with it were completed, they all went to Temple Square to see the Christmas lights display.

Beyond that point, getting through Christmas and New Year's proved to be even more difficult than Wade had antici-pated, but as always he was grateful for the family love and support surrounding him, and especially for Alex and Jane and their children and the way they truly made him and Rebecca feel like part of the family.

Still, Christmas felt all wrong to Wade without Elena. How could he not think about last Christmas and the joy they'd shared together? And this year the only gift he could get for his wife was a beautiful wreath for her grave. It felt horrible and wrong, and he hated it. He found himself wishing he didn't even have to celebrate the holiday, then it occurred to him late one night as he was praying, that Christmas was the celebration of the very thing that could give him hope and peace over losing his wife to premature death. Looking at it from that perspective, he was able to find moments of joy as he worked to involve himself in the celebrations and not dwell too much on Elena's absence.

It was a delight to see all of the children taking in the holiday celebrations, and he loved showing Rebecca the pretty ornaments on the tree and the twinkling Christmas lights that would make her eyes sparkle. She'd reached a delightfully chubby stage with wrinkles in her wrists and ankles that looked like little bracelets. Her hair had remained dark like her mother's, and was long for a baby her age, even though it was thin in spots and looked rather silly. But Wade had gotten fairly good at pulling some of it into a little topknot with a tiny barrette.

They all had great fun putting Rebecca and Ruth side by side, or facing each other on their tummies, where they would make googly noises and sometimes make each other giggle. They quickly became dubbed "the twins," due to being almost exactly the same size, with barely any difference at all in the stages they achieved—although they looked nothing alike. Both girls strongly resembled their mothers, and what little blood they shared hadn't shown up in their physical appearance. Still, they were both adorable, and seeing them grow together was a joy. For Wade, being in his brother's home and a part of their lives was a silver lining in the clouds of grief over losing his wife. He wondered occasionally what it might have been like if he'd never discovered the truth about his paternity, and that Alex was his brother. How grateful he was for what had once been a horrible trial!

January brought dreadfully cold temperatures and a new semester. Adjusting to different, more difficult classes brought a new level of stress for Wade. The new year also brought Rebecca's six-month birthday. Jane threw a party halfway between the two girls' half-year marks to celebrate for both of them. The house was filled with relatives who doted on both babies and laughed hysterically as they were put side by side in their highchairs and given a piece of cake to demolish. As with every event and advancement in Rebecca's life, Wade couldn't help but wish that Elena were there to share the joy. He had to believe she was aware of their lives from the other side of the veil, but the longer she was gone, the harder it became to even imagine what it would be like to have her around. In the days that followed, Wade was taken aback when a new wave of grief overwhelmed him, and he almost felt as if he were starting over with the shock of losing Elena. He didn't understand it; he only knew he hated it.

Brian's leaving for his mission was a huge event for the family. Wade was a little startled by the depth of emotion that Brian and his parents all seemed to feel over his parting. He concluded that with Brian being their youngest, Brad and Marilyn were having a difficult time letting him go. And Brian had always been a sensitive kid with tender emotions. Still, their emotion tended to bring his own to the surface, blending the present challenge of letting his brother leave for two years with his grief over losing Elena.

Spending more time with his family also made Wade realize that it was difficult feeling like the odd one. Being the illegitimate child hadn't bothered him for a very long time, but somehow being the only one except the missionary without a spouse was tough to swallow. His older siblings had been married for years, and his younger sister, Robin, had gotten married soon after he'd married Elena. She too had a baby, a little boy who was a few months younger than Rebecca. And Robin always looked deliriously happy. With Brian gone, Wade just felt a heightened sense of being on the outside.

Barrett took a keen interest in Brian's mission and wrote him a letter the day after he left. He talked to Wade a number of times about going on a mission someday, and asked him many questions about his own mission, which he'd served in Africa. As always, Barrett was often around, making Wade smile at any given moment. It wasn't uncommon for Barrett to do his homework sitting next to Wade while he studied, and once in a while they would compare notes between medical terminology and third-grade grammar and math. But Barrett was fascinated with the big words that Wade was learning, and he always wanted to know what they meant and how to spell them. Alex commented more than once that his own mother's occupation had been transcribing medical records, and it was Alex's fascination with those words that first piqued his interest in medicine. Barrett declared that he would be a doctor someday, while Alex and Wade both encouraged him to keep an open mind and see how he felt after his mission.

Soon after Brian left for his mission, Alex's cousin, Susan, and her husband, Donald, returned from *their* mission. Susan was actually his mother's cousin, but they were very close. Since Alex and Jane had purchased their home from Donald and Susan, they shared an agreement that the older couple would live there as well for as long as they needed. Of course, there was plenty of room, and they were really great people. Wade enjoyed having them around. They adored Rebecca and were very kind to him, even though they were Alex's relatives, not his. Still, they weren't around for long before they left for an extended road trip to spend some significant time with each of their children who lived out of state. They planned to be gone for several months.

While Wade struggled to absorb all he was learning in school and deal with long hours of studying and rigorous tests, he couldn't begin to express his gratitude for the support system he'd been blessed with. Elena's parents and sister each had weekly time where they took Rebecca, wanting not only to help, but also to maintain a relationship with this child who was a part of their family. Wade's mother and sisters and Roxanne all helped as well, which eased his guilt somewhat for all that Alex and especially Jane did to help with the baby. Jane took Rebecca into her little flock of children as if she were more like a twin sister than a cousin to Ruthie. Her maternal instincts and experience were priceless to Wade. She had a way of guiding him without overstepping his desire to be the primary parent to his daughter. But Jane also seemed to understand the strain of his class schedule and how taxing it was. In that regard he was grateful to be living under the same roof with Dr. Alex Keane. No matter how busy Alex might be, he never seemed the least bit put out if Wade asked for some help or clarification with his studies. His encouragement and validation of how tough medical school could be didn't hurt either.

Perhaps taking care of Rebecca and getting through school wouldn't have been so challenging if it weren't for the emotional strain that continued to hover with him due to Elena's absence. His grief and loneliness were not eager to relent. He just didn't know what to do about it beyond getting up every day and pressing forward, saving his tears for the private times when he might have been alone with his wife.

Wade was surprised when Jane reminded him that he'd overlooked making an appointment for Rebecca's six-month checkup and shots. And for some reason this reminder threw him off. Of course he knew how old his daughter was. They'd had a party not so long ago. But facing the checkup brought to mind some facts he had trouble accepting. Had it been that long? Was she really that old? *Had Elena really been gone that much time?* After discussing it with Alex, he came to the conclusion that he'd subconsciously resisted the passing of time, not wanting to move too far away from his life with Elena, and the six-month anniversary of her death was likely the reason his grief had risen to a new level of demand. Whether that was true or not, it didn't change the bottom line. He had to keep going.

Wade dreaded Rebecca's shots and hated taking the time to even do the whole thing, as busy as he was, even though he knew it was important. It seemed like they waited forever while he looked around and watched the mothers with their children. As in past visits, there was only one other father in the room, and he was there with his wife and baby. Wade felt momentarily angry, cheated out of what should have been. He had to remind himself, holding Rebecca a little closer, that this was the path of his life right now, and no amount of anger would change it.

"Rebecca Morrison," a nurse called. Wade picked up the diaper bag and headed in that direction, pleasantly surprised to recognize Laura. He hadn't given her a second thought since she'd been absent at the four-month checkup. But suddenly this chore didn't seem quite so tedious. She smiled at him while he took in how different she looked from last time. Her hair was down instead of pulled back, and full of rich curls. This time her scrubs were *The Wizard of Oz.* The shirt was printed with characters from the movie, her pants were the color of Emerald City, and around her neck was some semblance of a necklace with plastic figures of the tin man, the lion, and the scarecrow. But the best part was her shoes: bright red and glittery, like Dorothy's ruby slippers.

"Hi," she said brightly, holding the door open for him to go into the hall where the exam rooms were located. "Look how big Rebecca is getting!"

"Yes, she is," he said and followed her into one of the rooms. "I like your shoes," he added as she took Rebecca from him, apparently wanting to give her a proper greeting.

"Thanks," she said. "Shoes can be a great conversation piece in a place like this."

The baby immediately started playing with the plastic figures hanging around Laura's neck.

"Oh, she's beautiful," Laura said, as if she'd never seen a baby before.

"Yes, she is," he said. "So you collect shoes?"

Laura laughed softly. "Yes, I suppose I do." She handed Rebecca back to Wade. "Undress her down to her diaper and I'll be right back."

"Okay," he said, and she left the room.

When she came back to get Rebecca's weight and measurements, she said to Wade while she worked, "So, what are you majoring in?" He felt confused, and she added, "The last time we talked, you said you were staying with your brother while you were going to school."

"Oh, I'm studying medicine at the U."

"Really?" she said, sounding impressed. "You're going for the MD then?"

"I am," he said.

"That's great. I'm rather fond of the field, myself."

"So I see. Maybe you can give me some pointers. I'm going into pediatrics."

"Really?" she said again, sounding thoroughly pleased. "You like kids, huh?"

"Yes, I do."

"Well, I'm not surprised. I'd say pediatrics would suit you." She laughed softly while Rebecca became enthralled once again with what was hanging around Laura's neck. "So, one day I could be working for you, then."

"Possibly," he said, "although I'm specializing in pediatric oncology."

She looked a little startled as she said, "That's very noble, but . . ."

"But what?" he asked when she hesitated.

"Cancer in children is pretty ugly stuff. I've seen very little of it, but what I've seen is haunting."

Wade followed her example of being straightforward. "So, you're wondering if my goal is naive, if I'm deluding myself into thinking I know what I'm in for?"

She didn't say anything, but Wade could see the truth in her eyes. He wasn't offended, but he did explain. "My nephew is a leukemia survivor. Not just the standard chemo for three years scenario; he had full-body radiation and two bone marrow transplants. The kid puked more than if he'd had bulimia. He couldn't swallow or even talk for months because of the radiation ulcers. His body was taken right to the door of death a number of times, and his spirit became completely broken. But he's alive because of the training and commitment of doctors who were able to look beyond the suffering and invest some hope."

Wade found her staring at him, much as she had when he'd told her his wife had died. Tears welled up in her eyes before she hurried to look away. Attempting to lighten the mood, he said, "Now I've made you cry again."

"I was in one of those crying moods anyway," she said. "Forgive me for being presumptuous."

"You weren't being presumptuous. If you haven't camped in a pediatric isolation unit, it's impossible to know what it's really like. But I'm grateful for the opportunity, and I know it awakened a gift inside of me."

She looked up again, her eyes shining with some kind of adoration. Wade felt his heart quicken, and he had to ask himself if it was simply the outpouring of her emotion—or something more. He reminded himself that she was married. But a quick analysis of his feelings made him realize that perhaps he was coming to a point where he might really be ready to consider dating again, as opposed to just forcing himself through the motions of writing silly emails to women. If nothing else, Laura could be an excellent prototype for what he was looking for. But he had to wonder if another woman like her might actually exist out there somewhere.

"That's great then," she said, bringing him away from his thoughts. "And your nephew is okay?"

"Oh, yeah. His little body went through a lot, and he may have complications come up throughout his life. But he's alive, and he's doing really well."

She smiled and finished what she was doing with Rebecca, then she asked, "And how are you?"

"I'm okay," he said. He appreciated her concern, but didn't necessarily like the attention being focused on him. He hurried to ask, "How are you?"

She looked surprised, perhaps hesitant. Then she smiled and said, "I'm having a good week. Thanks for asking."

She left the room while Wade wondered what a bad week might entail. The doctor came in to do the standard exam, then Laura came back to give the shots. Just like before, Laura held Rebecca after it was done and soothed her before handing her over to her father.

"It's good to see you," she said. "Take care."

"You too," he said, and she left the room. He got Rebecca dressed and made sure he had everything, even the blanket.

The following Sunday Wade went to a singles fireside. The speaker was good, and the refreshments were too. But he felt awkward and out of place and was glad to go home and be with Rebecca. He grudgingly decided to go to a dance the following Saturday, and Alex made him promise that he would ask at least three women to dance.

"I can't dance," Wade insisted.

"Then why are you going to a dance?" he asked, and Wade just scowled at him.

After supper Alex announced they were having a family meeting. Wade entered the family room with Rebecca to find all the furniture pushed back. Alex and Jane were dancing while the children looked on and cheered. He knew they'd actually once been partners on a ballroom dance team, but they could do just about any kind of dancing and make it look good. He enjoyed just watching them and cheered a little himself. Alex put on a different song and they *all* started dancing. Katharine and Preston held hands and wiggled adorably. Jane danced with Barrett, and Alex held Ruthie in his arms. Wade followed his brother's example and danced while holding Rebecca, making her laugh.

"See, you do too know how to dance," Alex said.

"I don't have to impress Rebecca," Wade insisted. "I'm the one who feeds her."

The next song Alex played was an old Bruce Springsteen song that Wade had always liked. *Dancing in the Dark.* Watching Jane and Alex do a fairly complicated version of the swing, he was intrigued to hear Alex say to his wife, "Remember when we danced to this song?"

"I remember," she said. "We *were* dancing in the dark, weren't we?"

"Did you have the lights turned out?" Katharine asked.

"No," Alex chuckled, "we were just kind of . . . lost."

The children looked confused, but Wade knew what he meant. The *dark* was metaphorical, and Wade couldn't deny feeling pretty lost in the dark himself at the moment.

At the singles dance the following Saturday, Wade kept his promise to Alex and he did ask more than three women to dance. He couldn't say the experience was miserable, but it wasn't exactly enjoyable either. Through some minimal conversation with other people who were there, he quickly realized that most of them were divorced, and only a few were widowed, or had never been married. The ones he met who were widowed were all much older than he was. He certainly wasn't opposed to marrying someone who had been through a divorce, depending on the reasons for it. In fact, he concluded that he would likely prefer someone who had been married before, since they would have some experience in marriage. Still, he couldn't help feeling like he was just groping in the dark, and he hated it. When they played that song Alex and Jane had been dancing to earlier in the week, he decided he couldn't stay another minute. *Dancing in the Dark* just hit a little too close to home. Elena had been a light in his life, and in her absence *everything* felt darker. And he *hated* it. He cried himself to sleep that night, certain that Elena had been the perfect woman for him, and he wasn't likely to ever find one who would even come close. But a few days later the loneliness drove him back into his search, and he returned to perusing the Internet for the future Mrs. Morrison. As futile as it felt, he believed it was better to do something than nothing.

Days passed with the same monotony, his only joy being the time he spent caring for his daughter. She started to crawl, and new adventures began, but since Ruthie had started a week earlier, Alex and Jane had already baby-proofed the areas of the house where the babies were kept corralled with closed doors and baby gates. Wade found it amusing the way Rebecca always crawled toward people, as if she wanted to socialize, while Ruthie was more drawn to toys. And one of Rebecca's favorite people was Barrett. She loved Katharine and Preston as well, but if Barrett was in the room she instinctively went to him, and he could always make her giggle. Wade felt perfect joy to see them interact and couldn't deny being grateful that they were all living in the same home. And gratitude was one of the few things that kept him standing.

Late on a very cold evening, Wade felt especially discouraged as he grudgingly spent a short while perusing profiles on the Internet singles sites before going to bed. He felt completely bored and borderline insane, wondering why he was wasting his time with this recently acquired habit. And then he saw Marina. Her dark hair and brilliant smile caught his attention, but reading her profile sparked something to life in him. She worked for a travel agency, taught fourteen-year-olds in Sunday School, and she loved hiking and camping, something that he also enjoyed but hadn't found the time for since he'd started medical school. She wrote that she loved children, had a fetish for collecting hats that she never wore, and her greatest weakness was spending hours in bookstores before she could actually decide on the perfect book that she could take home and get lost in. Wade loved what she'd written about herself, as well as the way she'd written it. For the first time since he'd begun this quest, he actually felt excited about the prospect of getting to know a woman.

Wade felt positive, perhaps even happy, as he wrote her a quick email, simply expressing an interest in getting to know her better. He even signed the letter with his first name. He said a little prayer as he clicked the Send icon, then he forced himself to focus on finding some information on the web that he needed for a class assignment.

Before going to bed, he checked his email, as surprised to find a message there from Marina as he was by the way his heart quickened when he saw it. He opened it to read:

Dear Wade,

I must say I was pleased to receive your note, which was refreshingly straightforward and charming. I would love to get to know you better, especially since you've said practically nothing about yourself on the

website. I'll look forward to hearing from you.
Marina

Wade read it three times, feeling like her message was the doorway into some wonderful, unexplored world. He quickly wrote back to tell her that he too enjoyed camping and hiking but hadn't had the opportunity for quite some time. He told her about being in medical school and his reasons for the specialty he'd chosen, and that he too taught teenagers in Sunday School. He felt a little nervous getting to the most important point, but he knew it needed to be addressed right up front. Since her profile made it clear she'd never been married, he found it a little difficult to explain his situation. He pondered how to say it, and then decided it really didn't matter. He just had to say it.

I've been married before. Her name was Elena, and she passed away very suddenly when our daughter was two weeks old. Rebecca is now seven months and looks very much like her mother. I would love to have you meet her. If you're interested in continuing this conversation with a widower attached to a baby, I'd love to hear from you.
Wade

He sent the letter and forced himself to go to bed, wondering what it might be like to actually have the companionship of a woman in his life again. The following morning he found a minute to check his email before he left for classes. Again his heart quickened to see Marina's name in the inbox. He printed the email since it was lengthy, and he didn't have time to read it right then. Over lunch he finally had a chance to pull it out and read it. She began by saying,

I would love to meet Rebecca, especially if that means I get to meet you too.

She went on to express compassion for his loss, then she wrote of an aunt who had passed away suddenly, leaving three young children, and how difficult it had been for the family. Her uncle was now happily remarried. She talked of how she loved working in the center of Salt Lake City, and how it was her habit after work each day to wander onto Temple Square, often taking a book with her to read for a while, but when the weather was cold, she would go into the Crossroads Mall and sit by the fountain in the basement. Reading was obviously a passion for her. She told him about her family, who all lived nearby, and cozy details of how she had been thinking of him as she'd gotten out of bed early, unable to sleep. She talked about her cat and her plants and how she loved scented candles and lemonade. She finished the letter by saying,

Would it be too forward of me to ask if I could fix dinner for you? Even though we've never met, I'm assuming that we would have much to talk about, and we could have a marvelous time. Without meeting and getting to know each other better, we obviously have no idea if this could ever turn into something romantic, but at the very least, I would hope that we could be friends. Let me know what you think.

Wade pondered her letter throughout the afternoon and talked to Alex about it when he met him at the hospital where he worked. Over dinner in the cafeteria he showed Alex the emails and asked his opinion.

"Well," Alex chuckled, "I'd wager if you showed up ugly and obese she'd certainly be taking the *friends* option."

"Maybe she will anyway," Wade said. "Or maybe once I meet her, *I* will prefer the *friends* option. She's obviously beautiful, unless the picture is very old or computer enhanced. Attraction is important, but it's clearly rhetorical for me to say that appearance is meaningless in the big picture."

"Yes, but you still have an advantage. You know what she looks like." Alex smiled. "I think you should meet her. What can it hurt? And hey, you've got Rebecca. You know what they say about a man with a baby."

"No, what?" he asked.

"Babies make great female bait."

"Is that right?" Wade asked, not certain if he felt amused or disgusted.

CHAPTER 6

That night and throughout the following morning Wade pondered the situation far more than he even wanted to. He felt a bit vulnerable and almost afraid to realize how much Marina was on his mind. He felt intrigued, and he wanted to meet her. His last class ended mid afternoon and he went home and made a couple of calls to travel agencies in the downtown area to find out what time they closed, then he impulsively decided to take Rebecca for an excursion to the mall. It was far from the first time he'd taken her shopping or just on a senseless jaunt for the sake of getting out of the house, just the two of them. Getting her out of the car at the mall, he felt sure he was dreaming to think that he could actually come across Marina so haphazardly, then he wondered if perhaps she'd mentioned her habits with the hope that he might try. If she was wanting to be found, it might not be so difficult.

Wade almost took the stroller out of the trunk but opted against it. Rebecca was at a stage of preferring to be carried, and she wasn't so heavy that he was uncomfortable with that if he shifted arms occasionally. With a minimally loaded, lightweight diaper bag over one shoulder, he carried the baby into the mall. Her eyes sparkled, and she made adorable noises as new sights and sounds confronted her. He loved that expression on her face, of taking in her world with such awe and fascination.

They went down the escalators to the basement where some fast food restaurants were located, and there was a lot of space to just sit. And there, the central focus was a pool of water with a fountain in the center. He noticed a few people sitting on the edge of the fountain, but no women on their own with a book. He felt a nervous fluttering in his stomach as he walked around a little, went up one floor, looked in some shop windows, then went back down, discreetly taking in the people around the fountain as he descended. His heart threatened to jump out of his chest when he clearly saw a dark-haired woman sitting on the far side, reading a novel.

"Oh help," he muttered, and Rebecca made a cooing noise as if to respond. "Do you think we're crazy, baby girl?"

Wade casually wandered to where he could get a look at this woman's face, then he concluded that this was just way too easy when he could see beyond any doubt that it was definitely Marina. She was dressed fashionably without being too showy. And there was no denying that she was beautiful. While he was wondering what he might say or how to approach her, Rebecca began to squirm as if she wanted to get down. Under any other circumstances he would have never put his baby down to crawl in such a place, but he couldn't resist when he knew that if he set her down close enough to Marina, he knew exactly what she would do. Sure enough, Rebecca went straight toward Marina's black platform boots with chunky heels.

Wade's heart was pounding as he watched Marina look down in surprise, then she laughed softly and took a quick glance around herself, searching for the negligent parent. Their eyes met for only a split second before she smiled, then focused again on Rebecca. Not wanting to appear too obvious, Wade hurried to say, "Sorry. She wanted to get down. She has a thing for shoes."

He picked Rebecca up and grabbed a baby wipe out of the bag to hurry and wash her little hands.

"She's adorable," Marina said, setting her book aside.

"Yes, she is," Wade said. "She looks just like her mother." He could see that Marina hadn't yet made any connection to the emails they'd exchanged. Unable to bear the suspense any longer, he tucked the dirty baby wipe into the bag and hurried to say, "Her name is Rebecca. She wanted to meet you." He saw the enlightenment come into her eyes, then she looked as if she might cry, looking first at the baby, and then at him. For a long moment their eyes connected, and he felt something change inside of him while he could clearly sense something changing inside of her.

"Wade?" she asked as if she didn't dare believe it.

He smiled. "Hello, Marina."

She let out a little emotional laugh, and then she hugged him. He returned the embrace with the arm that wasn't holding Rebecca, noting that she smelled good, and her forehead came to his nose—even with those platform boots she wore. He wondered if this was one of those romantic moments he might one day share with his grandchildren. She stepped back and laughed again.

"Wade what?"

"Morrison," he said and held out his hand.

She held it more than shook it as she said, "Marina Patterson." She laughed and added, "I can't believe it. How did you find me?"

"You told me where to find you," he said, and she let go of his hand.

She looked thoughtful, and he felt sure she hadn't done it on purpose. "Oh," she said, "so I did." Rebecca made some noise as if to remind them that she was there. Marina laughed softly and turned her attention to the baby. "May I hold her?"

"Of course," Wade said, and Rebecca went easily into her arms. "She's very social; she's always reaching out to other people."

"And perhaps she always will," Marina said, admiring Rebecca up close. Wade almost felt like crying as he watched them together. He felt a twinge of heartache to think of how Elena might feel to have another woman caring for her daughter. On the other hand, he felt some sense of joy to think that perhaps he and Rebecca might have truly found someone to fill the emptiness that had been left by Elena's absence. He told himself it was ludicrous to be entertaining such thoughts when he'd barely met Marina. But at least he was making progress.

"Oh, she's precious," Marina said, then turned to look at Wade. "This is a very nice surprise. I was thinking I would need to write to you this evening and demand to see some pictures of you and Rebecca, but now I don't have to."

Wade didn't comment. He felt fascinated with watching her as she cooed at the baby and touched her hair. To ease the silence, he said, "Her hairstyle is all the latest with girls her age."

Marina laughed and said to Rebecca, "Your daddy is just jealous because you're so beautiful that you get all the attention."

"You got that right," Wade said, and they both laughed. "Hey," he added impulsively, "have you eaten? Can I buy you some dinner?"

Marina smiled brightly. "That would be divine." He motioned toward the choices of fast food available and said, "Anything you want. It's on me."

"Oh, Mexican is my favorite," she said, and ten minutes later they were seated over a variety of Mexican fast food, while Rebecca sat in a high chair and ate Cheerios that Wade always kept in the diaper bag. They chatted so comfortably that Wade couldn't believe they'd only met just half an hour earlier. He fed Rebecca a bottle while he continued to eat with one hand. Once they were done eating, Wade took Rebecca in the restroom to change her diaper, then he met Marina again near the fountain.

"Are you in a hurry?" he asked.

"No, not at all," she said.

"Shall we . . . browse?" he asked and held out his free hand. She smiled as she took it, and they spent more than an hour wandering the mall and talking in a way that made him feel they were really getting to know each other, as opposed to pointless chitchat. There was only one moment when he felt some tension between them, and that was when he said something about Elena, and she seemed uncomfortable.

"Sorry," he said. "I guess I shouldn't go there."

She only smiled timidly and glanced down, which seemed to be an agreement. He made a mental note that discussing the dead wife while trying to woo the potential new wife was taboo. So he moved on to something else, and the conversation became easy again. Rebecca was fairly well behaved; Wade just had to change arms occasionally when she got heavy, and then he would hold Marina's other hand.

Rebecca was starting to seem restless with the activity when Wade's cell phone rang. Marina took the baby as he answered it, as if helping care for Rebecca came naturally.

"Wade," he heard his father say.

"Hey, Dad. What's up?"

"I wonder if you're in a position to help me out. I've got a flat tire, and my jack is broken. Alex is working and—"

"Sure, where are you?"

Neil told him a location that was about ten minutes away. "I'll be there in twenty minutes," Wade said and hung up. Then to Marina, "My dad's got a flat tire and a broken jack. So, you are welcome to come along, or we can say good night."

"I'd love to come along," she said, "if that's okay."

"It's more than okay with me," Wade said, and they headed toward the parking garage. It truly was nice to be holding somebody's hand.

Rebecca seemed more relaxed once she was in her car seat with a toy. Wade and Marina continued to talk as he drove, and they easily found Neil's SUV by the side of the road. Marina got out of the car when he did, and Wade said to his father, "Dad, this is Marina."

"I interrupted a date?" Neil asked, sounding appalled with himself as he shook her hand.

"Not really," Marina said. "We just met, actually. It's so good to meet *you*, Mr. Morrison."

Neil chuckled and winked at Wade. "Actually," Wade said, "it's Mr. Keane."

"But you can call me Neil," he said easily.

Marina looked confused, and Wade added, "I'll tell you later."

"It's a pleasure to meet you, Marina," Neil said, and she smiled.

"Why don't you wait in the car with the baby," Wade said. "It's freezing out here."

"You talked me into it," Marina said with a little laugh.

Once Marina was inside the car and Wade had his jack out to help with the tire, Neil asked, "You just met?"

"We've been exchanging emails," he said. "We just met face-to-face."

"She seems very nice," Neil said. "And she's very pretty."

"Yes, on both counts."

"So, I take it you're feeling ready to move forward."

"Truthfully, Dad . . . I don't know. I'm certainly enjoying her company. It's nice to have someone around; her letters have been nice, but . . . I guess we'll see."

"Well, if she sticks around for longer than a date, bring her over for dinner."

"That would be nice," Wade said and focused on the tire. It was changed in a few minutes, and Neil gave Wade a quick hug, thanking him for coming to the rescue.

Getting back in the car he found Marina talking in a silly voice to Rebecca, who was clearly amused. He grabbed the diaper bag and used a baby wipe to clean his hands. "I don't know what I ever did before I had a baby around," he said.

"Oh, these things are great," she said, putting the package back in the bag for him. "I keep them around all the time."

Wade started the car and pulled out onto the road, knowing he needed to address what had been said with his father. "I know you must be wondering, so I'll get straight to the point. Obviously, a father and son should have the same last name."

"But you don't."

"No, we don't."

"You look like him."

"He is my biological father."

"So, you were adopted?"

"Uh . . . no," Wade said, then he chuckled tensely. "Okay, this is a bit awkward. If we can get through this conversation and survive it, then we might have a reason to move on to a real date."

"I'm listening," she said gently.

"My family situation is very unique. For me, blended family takes on a whole new meaning. You see, my parents—by that I mean my mother and the father who raised me—had a pretty rough marriage to start with. When she couldn't get him to change his bad behavior, she left him for a couple of years. He straightened up; they worked things out. They've been very happily married and strong in the gospel ever since. The thing is . . . I'm what resulted from her leaving him."

She gasped softly as it sank in. "You're saying your mother had an affair?"

"That's right."

"And that . . . was your biological father?"

"That's right," he said again.

"Wow, that must be tough for you."

He shrugged. "Initially, yes. But now that I've gotten used to it, I'm very grateful for both my families. I've been very blessed. *All* of my parents are good people."

"That's nice. What do you mean . . . initially?"

"When I found out; it was only a few years ago. I was in pre-med, messing around with DNA, found out I didn't match up with the man I'd always believed to be my father. At first it was very tough; I was angry and horrified. But that's all in the past. It's good now. I can tell you for a fact that repentance and forgiveness are real. It's worked miracles in my life."

Marina smiled and took his hand. "That's wonderful."

"So, you still want to see me again?"

"I certainly do. Are you asking me on a date?"

"Yes, I believe I am. I have evening classes tomorrow. How about Friday?"

"That would be great. But why don't you come to my place for dinner? You can bring your favorite movie."

"Okay," he said, "that sounds great."

Wade took Marina to where her car was parked. She thanked him and kissed his cheek before she got out of the car, not giving him a chance to even get out and open her door. He made sure she got in her car and got it started before he left. Throughout the remainder of the evening he felt almost elated about the time he'd spent with Marina. But lying in the darkness that night, as he attempted to sleep, his feelings melted into something akin to despair. He missed Elena so badly that it hurt. He didn't *want* to be dating. He wanted to be married to Elena. He wanted to talk to her, to laugh with her, to hold her close. He had to take something to help him sleep, and he tried not to think about it during his morning classes. He had the afternoon off and was glad to find that Alex was home. They talked for nearly two hours while they kept the babies safe and happy. With Alex's insight and perspective he was able to see that dating Marina wasn't a bad thing, as long as she could accept that he wasn't necessarily ready to move beyond that point yet. Wade just needed some time, and he only had to communicate that to her. Hopefully, she would be okay with that. He debated whether to have a conversation with her, or to take care of it via email. He opted for the latter, figuring it would be better to get it out of the way before he saw her tomorrow. This way he could weigh his words carefully. He also didn't have to worry about being reduced to tears in front of her.

Checking his email he found a letter from her that helped soothe his concerns somewhat. She expressed how much she had enjoyed his surprise appearance, their time together, and her adoration of Rebecca. She also expressed compassion for the loss of his wife, and said it had been nice to meet his father. She included her address and phone number, and told him that dinner would be at seven.

Wade wrote back, honestly telling her how much he had enjoyed his time with her and that he was looking forward to their date. He then carefully told her that he was still struggling with grief over his wife's death, and while it was nice to have some companionship, he wasn't ready to move beyond that point, and wasn't sure when he would be. He came right out and said that if she was okay to keep their relationship at a level of casual dating, he would love to spend time with her. And if that didn't feel right to her, she needed to let him know. The following morning he received a response; she was more than alright with moving at whatever pace he felt comfortable with. Her words had an undertone of hope that when he was ready, great things might happen between them. His heart quickened as it received that message, but his spirit still felt too heavy over losing Elena to fully appreciate it.

Wade arrived at Marina's apartment with a bouquet of mixed flowers and a video of the very first *Star Wars* movie. The decor was modern and streamlined, with modern art on the walls. It felt a little strange to him, but left him intrigued. Dinner was nice, and he felt comfortable with her. He enjoyed their conversation, and he liked doing something as simple as helping her clear the table. They sat together and watched the movie, holding hands. When it was over they analyzed what made it a classic, and they committed to watching the other *Star Wars* movies, one a week.

Wade quickly developed a habit of talking with Marina every day, and he saw her three or four times a week. She met and spent time with both of his families and seemed comfortable among them. He met her family and spent some time with them. Her parents seemed like wonderful people. Lane and Julia Patterson took him and Rebecca in with open arms and open hearts, and he enjoyed being involved with them. Marina's interaction and help with Rebecca felt easy and natural. He'd only taken Rebecca to her place once, however, since it was far from baby-proof, and keeping her out of trouble there was way too stressful. But Marina seemed to love spending time at his place, and he was fine with that. He loved holding her hand, and he felt a sense of gratitude to not be alone in so many situations where it would be natural for him to have a woman at his side. He even took her to Kirk's house for dinner and was finally able to be with Kirk and his wife and not feel resentful or out of place because he was alone.

By the time they had viewed each of the *Star Wars* movies, they had graduated to where she occasionally put her head on his shoulder, and sometimes he put his arm around her. But that was as romantic as it got. A part of him wanted to ask her to marry him. He had every reason to believe they could make a good marriage, but he still had trouble balancing his aching for Elena and his belief that Marina could ease that ache.

Wade's attention turned elsewhere when Rebecca came down with a bad cold. He was grateful to have a doctor in the house when she became terribly ill with it, but Alex assured him she had all the classic symptoms of a virus, and no sign of any infection. Ruthie came down with the same symptoms at nearly the same time, so it seemed they'd both gotten it from the same place, which was likely from the other children, since Katharine had gone through it, and then Preston and Barrett. Wade was grateful for Jane's eager willingness to care for Rebecca while he attended classes, especially when he knew it couldn't be easy caring for *two* sick babies.

After a week of not sleeping well due to nighttime bouts with congestion and coughing, Rebecca woke up crying and wouldn't stop. After more than an hour of holding her while she cried in a way he'd never heard before, Wade was about to go wake Alex and get some professional advice when the doctor knocked at his bedroom door.

"What's up?" Alex asked, taking Rebecca from him.

"I don't know," Wade said, hearing the strain in his own voice. "You tell me. She feels hot."

"Yeah, she does," Alex said, talking loudly enough to be heard above the continued wailing.

"I gave her Tylenol more than an hour ago when she woke up, but she's still hot and obviously still hurting."

"I can't tell for certain without being able to look in her ears, but I'm guessing it's an ear infection. It's common for the congestion to be a precursor to this kind of thing. Get her in a tub of lukewarm water to bring the fever down." He handed her to Wade. "I'll be back in a minute."

Wade did as he was told and laid Rebecca on the bathroom rug while he ran the bath and undressed her. Alex returned and set some things on the bathroom counter. He stuck a digital thermometer in her ear and declared her temperature to be 103, then he stuck a medicine dropper in her mouth with some kind of reddish liquid.

"What is it?" Wade asked.

"It's a prescription cough syrup left over from a bad bout Katharine had a while back," he said. "This is a safe dose for Rebecca; it will ease the pain and help her sleep until you can get her into the clinic in the morning. The co-pay for the clinic will be cheaper than the ER, and I can't prescribe anything without officially seeing her. But if a patient called me in the middle of the night, this is what I'd tell them to do."

"Okay," Wade said and put Rebecca into the tub. He was relieved that just being in the bath soothed her somewhat. She continued to fuss, but it wasn't the constant crying she'd been doing. He knelt beside the tub and talked tenderly to her, while Alex sat on the closed toilet seat, silently keeping him company. Fifteen minutes later Alex took her temperature again, and it was 100 degrees. Wade took her out of the tub and got her dressed. Ten minutes later she was asleep in his arms.

"You're a genius," Wade said to his brother.

"Nah," Alex chuckled, "I've just seen a zillion babies in the ER in the middle of the night. It's usually ear infections or strep throat." He pressed a hand tenderly over Rebecca's little head. "These are the moments that make us grateful for modern medicine."

"Amen," Wade said and laid Rebecca in her crib.

"Do you need one of us to take her in tomorrow?"

"No," Wade said, "I'll just miss a couple of classes. I can manage. Thanks anyway."

"Okay. Good night, little brother." He moved toward the door.

"Hey, Alex."

"Yeah?" Alex stopped with his hand on the knob. "Thanks for everything you do for us. On top of free rent and babysitting and a shoulder to cry on, you pass out medical expertise too. I'm grateful."

Alex smiled and said, "We're family. It's a pleasure, Wade, truly. To be perfectly honest, we all dread the day when you and Rebecca will leave our home."

"Well, I think I dread that day too."

"You shouldn't. That's the day you'll be getting married to some amazing woman and starting a new life. Unless, of course, you can convince the new Mrs. Morrison to live with us too."

"Maybe," Wade said, "but I would think that eventually we'd wear out our welcome. I am more indebted to you than I could even begin to imagine."

Alex turned more directly toward him and put his hands on his hips. "No, Wade," he said firmly, "you are not indebted. It is no sacrifice to have you in our home and to help you get through this season of your life. But even if it were, I would not begrudge it. You saved my son's life, Wade." He lightened his tone. "That bone marrow has got to be worth five or six years' rent, at least." He chuckled, then left the room before Wade could tell Alex that his giving bone marrow had been no sacrifice. But maybe it didn't need to be said again, and maybe he understood Alex's point. How can you be indebted to someone who loves you when they give of themselves from the heart?

Wade called the clinic the minute they opened and got an appointment for an hour later. With another dose of cough syrup, Rebecca remained sleepy and free of pain. He felt relieved and comfortable when Laura was the nurse who came into the waiting room to get them. She wore scrubs with teddy bears all over the shirt, and teddy bear earrings. Her shoes were brown with a teddy bear actually drawn on top of them. Just seeing her made him smile.

"So, Rebecca's not feeling well," she said as they entered the exam room. He quickly explained the symptoms, what his brother had told him, and the medicine he'd given her. She made notes while he talked, then said, "So, your brother's a doctor too?"

"Too?"

"You're going to be a doctor, right?"

"Eventually. Yes, my brother's a doctor. He works in the ER at the U medical center."

She made an interested noise and took Rebecca's temperature, then she said, "And how are you? You look tired."

"Well, a sick baby has a tendency to interrupt your sleep."

"So I hear," she said with a tenderness that touched him, or perhaps it was longing. Did she have children? he wondered. He decided to ask.

"You have any kids?"

"Not yet," she said, and her smile seemed forced. He wondered if that was a sensitive topic for some reason. "When I *do* become a mother, I want to have a daughter just like Rebecca." She smiled again and left the room, saying, "The doctor will be here in a minute."

"Thank you," he said and then waited much longer than a minute. The doctor looked in Rebecca's throat and ears and firmly declared that she had infection in both ears. He prescribed an antibiotic, and something else that would relieve the congestion and help her sleep. Wade didn't see Laura again before he left, and he felt disappointed.

That afternoon Wade took a nap while Rebecca did. As soon as he woke up, he called Marina to give her an update and to cancel the date they had that evening. An hour later Jane found Wade to tell him that Marina had called her, insisting that she was bringing dinner over for the family, and she'd be there at six. She arrived with a large pot of homemade chicken soup with big noodles, a Jell-o salad, and a pan of brownies.

"You are so sweet," he said after he'd helped her carry the food into the kitchen from the car. "Thank you."

He kissed her forehead without even thinking about it, then she looked up at him with such overt admiration in her eyes that his heart quickened. He knew that look; he'd seen that look in Elena's eyes countless times. And he knew what it meant. *Marina was in love with him!*

"You're welcome," she said, and he had to wonder if he was in love with her, too. He certainly cared for her, but he found it difficult to bring the word love into it when he still felt so hopelessly in love with Elena.

Marina stayed through the evening and helped care for Rebecca while he got some studying in. He was grateful, and he told her so more than once, but he sensed that she was more than ready for the relationship to move forward, and he simply wasn't. Still, he didn't feel she was being impatient, and for that he was also grateful.

Rebecca quickly improved once the antibiotic kicked in, but three weeks later she came down with a fever again and became excessively fussy. Wade took her to the clinic and felt sorely disappointed when a different nurse took care of them. He asked about Laura and was told that she'd called in sick. He missed her funny shoes.

The doctor declared that Rebecca had strep throat and she was put on another antibiotic. All of the other kids except for Barrett came down with the same thing, and Wade hated the thought of his daughter having brought the germ into the house. Alex and Jane assured him that it was just one of those things and that they were in it together. Alex reminded him that Rebecca had gotten her cold from one of the other kids, but Wade still felt badly about the strep epidemic, even though he had no idea where she would have gotten it. Could have been from a cart at the grocery store, for all he knew.

Donald and Susan returned from their extended vacation and settled into living in the home that had once been theirs. Wade didn't know them all that well, although they'd always been completely kind and gracious toward him. He'd not lived in the same home with them for more than a few days before now, and wondered how the household dynamics might change with them there, but he quickly found that they were truly delightful people. They both made a fuss over Rebecca, along with the rest of the children, and were eager to help without being meddlesome. He even took opportunities to chat with them a few times and found their insight and compassion very touching.

Less than a month after Rebecca's strep throat, she got another bad cold that sent them to the clinic again. Laura was there, wearing scrubs with castles and dragons on them. She wore a purple dragon on a cord around her neck, and her shoes were purple with green laces. Rebecca was declared to have a virus and sent home. She felt better within a few days, but she got a new bout of sniffles a week later. After being awake with her stuffy nose part of the night, Wade commented at the breakfast table, "She sure has been getting sick a lot lately. It's getting really old. Am I doing something wrong?"

"No," Alex said immediately, then Wade saw Alex and Jane exchange a cautious gaze.

"What?" Wade demanded.

"Nothing," Alex said, but he reached over to feel Rebecca's neck, and under her arms. Wade knew he was checking to see if the lymph nodes were swollen, but he didn't like the implication.

"What?" Wade repeated impatiently.

"Kids get strings of viruses all the time," Jane said. "I'm sure it's nothing."

Wade looked at her, then at Alex and insisted, "Tell me what you're thinking."

"Jane's probably right. It's likely just what it seems—a string of viruses. But I would feel better if you'd take her in and get a CBC."

Wade's heart quickened. "A complete blood count? Why?"

"Because we have a certain paranoia around here, Wade. Just make sure, okay?"

Wade felt a little nauseous. "You're thinking about the leukemia, aren't you? Is that what happened? He kept getting sick?"

"That's right," Alex said. "So we'll all just feel better if you make sure nothing else is going on, okay?"

"Okay," Wade said and made an appointment, not wanting to admit how ill he felt at the very idea of something possibly being horribly wrong with his little girl. He gained a fast, hard empathy for what Alex and Jane must have felt to discover that Barrett had cancer, while he told himself he was just being cautious and that he didn't need to panic.

At the clinic he was grateful to see Laura and her *Wizard of Oz* ensemble. She looked pleased to see them as well, although she expressed concern for yet another visit. Without preamble he said, "This is one too many illnesses in too short a time. I just need someone to humor me and do a CBC, just to make sure nothing's going on."

"Okay," she said, meeting his eyes, her concern showing clearly. She looked like she wanted to say something tender, but she only moved toward the door, saying, "I'll take care of it."

A few minutes later as she drew the blood from a screaming Rebecca, Laura said quietly, "You're thinking of your nephew—leukemia symptoms."

"I just need to make sure," he said. She gave him a wan smile and left the room.

Wade took Rebecca home and got her down for a nap, oblivious to the classes he was missing while his mind wandered between concern for his daughter and formless thoughts of Laura and her gentle concern, which felt somehow personal. Was she that way with every young patient and concerned parent? Most likely, he reasoned.

When the call came from the clinic, he answered it, his heart pounding. He was relieved to hear, "Hi, this is Laura." She added quickly, "Everything's fine. Her blood is perfect."

Wade heaved a deep sigh and felt like crying. "Oh, thank you," he said. "You're really very good to us, you know."

"That's not hard," she said, and a long silence followed.

Wade was surprised to have a clear thought form in his mind, seemingly out of nowhere. He wanted to tell her that he thought she was an amazing woman, and he hoped that her husband was treating her the way she deserved. The very idea felt completely ludicrous given the measure of their acquaintance, so he forced the thought away and simply said, "Thank you again, Laura. I hope you have a marvelous day. You deserve it."

"Thank you," she said, sounding mildly emotional. "You too. Give Rebecca a hug for me."

"I'll do that," he said and ended the call, but he kept thinking about Laura until that evening when Marina came by to once again share the sick child vigil with him so that he could catch up his homework and make some headway in keeping up with the classes he'd missed due to Rebecca's illnesses. Fortunately he'd made some friends who were willing to email notes they'd taken, and he also had a couple of professors who were very compassionate to his being a single father.

Donald and Susan left on another mission, and Wade actually felt sad to see them go. But he admired their commitment to serving and wondered if he might have the opportunity to grow old with someone that way.

Wade exchanged regular letters with his brother Brian and enjoyed the unmistakable evidence of his spiritual and personal growth. He was serving in a tough mission, where the work didn't come easy, but Brian's convictions were firm, and he was doing well overall. Wade couldn't help but think of his own mission, and he felt a little stunned to realize how much his life had changed in the years since.

He facetiously said to Alex, "Hey, how come you never wrote to me when I was on my mission?" Since they'd not known of each other's existence at that time, the question was ridiculous.

Alex looked a little stunned, then he chuckled. "You didn't give me your address."

"Okay then," Wade said. "In that case, I forgive you."

Wade continued to enjoy the company of Alex and Jane's children. A day rarely passed when Preston didn't track him down and ask him to read a story, and Katharine often coaxed him to her room to see what she'd built from Legos, or to show him a picture she'd drawn. They were adorable kids, and he loved them, but he was most especially drawn to Barrett. A day never passed when they didn't talk for a few minutes and keep up with each other's lives, and at least once a week Wade took some time to do something with him, even if it was just to play a board game or put a puzzle together. Sometimes they went shopping and took Rebecca. Barrett loved the baby and was gifted at making her smile and keeping her happy. They had to be the cutest little cousins in the world.

Rebecca was eleven months old when Wade realized that he'd been living in his brother's home for a year. He and Elena had come after he'd finished classes in June in order to be there for Barrett's baptism and to stay until after the baby came. Oh, if he'd only known at the beginning of last summer how the summer would end! He was struck by a new wave of grief as he pondered how long Elena had been gone, but something in this bout of sorrow felt different. He truly was tired of being alone and found himself asking why he wasn't doing anything about it. He then asked himself if he loved Marina, and he knew that he did. He wondered if he loved her enough to be a good husband to her, to love her the way she deserved, and he was surprised to realize that he did. He truly did. She was a good woman who shared his beliefs and took good care of him and Rebecca. And it was time he did something about it.

Following a lengthy conversation with Alex concerning his feelings and plans, Wade called Marina at work and was surprised to hear how utterly pleased she was to hear from him. Then he realized she always sounded that way. He was struck by how absolutely patient she had been through these months they'd been dating while they'd become completely comfortable as friends, spending huge amounts of time together, but never discussing any kind of romantic feelings or commitment.

"Hey," he said, "I want to take you out to dinner—a nice dinner."

"Really?" she asked and laughed softly. "That sounds wonderful."

"Well, I know we've gone out a lot, and we spend a lot of time together, but . . . I think we need a *real date*. What do you say?"

"I can't wait."

"Then how about tonight?"

"Okay."

"I'll pick you up at seven."

Marina looked stunning when he met her at the door. She was wearing a deep blue dress and matching high-heeled shoes. Little was said between them as he drove to the center of the city and parked beneath the Joseph Smith Memorial Building.

He wondered if she sensed the changes that he was feeling, but neither of them seemed to want to comment. As he opened the car door and helped her out, he said, "I have reservations upstairs, but we have a little while. How about a walk?"

"Okay," she said eagerly, and they wandered through the building and onto the beautiful grounds east of the Salt Lake Temple.

They sat down at the edge of the mirror pond directly in front of the temple before he took both her hands into his and said, "Before we go to dinner there's something I need to say. Well, a couple of things, actually. First of all, I want to thank you for being so patient with me. You have been a great blessing in my life, Marina, and I know it probably hasn't been easy waiting for my broken heart to heal."

She looked down quickly, but he saw the truth in her eyes. It *hadn't* been easy for her and he knew it. Meeting his eyes she asked, "And is it healing?"

"Slowly, yes," he said. "I believe it is." Her eyes filled with obvious hope before he added, "I need to tell you that I love you, Marina. And I should have figured it out a long time ago."

The relief in her eyes was immediately followed by a rise of moisture there. She laughed softly and touched his face. "I love you too, Wade."

He smiled in return. "Yes, I know you do. I've seen in it your eyes, felt it in all the things you do for me and for Rebecca." He touched her face as well, and then he kissed her. He felt no guilt, no betrayal of Elena when he'd almost expected to. In truth, kissing Marina brought something to life inside of him that he had thought he could never feel again. He *did* love her. And he knew beyond any doubt that the course he had chosen was right.

Easing back from a meek but lengthy kiss, he found tears spilling over her face. He wiped them away and gave her another quick kiss, murmuring softly, "It's okay, Marina. Perhaps your patience has finally paid off."

She smiled, and he took her hand, urging her to her feet. "It's time for dinner, I believe," he said, and they went back into the Joseph Smith Memorial building and up the elevator to the top floor. They were seated at a table near the window where the view was incredible.

After they had ordered, Wade said, "I want this to be a celebration dinner, Marina. So before we go any further, there's something I want to give you."

"Okay," she said cautiously, with curious eyes.

Wade reached into his pocket and pulled out the little box. He popped it open in front of her and just said it. "Will you marry me?"

She gasped. She looked at the ring he'd picked out earlier that day. She looked at him. Her eyes sparkled with tears, and a smile filled her countenance. "Yes," she squeaked, then more firmly, "Of course, yes."

Wade couldn't hold back a little laugh as he took the ring out of the box and slid it onto her finger. "Your mother told me what size to get; if it doesn't fit or you don't like the style, it's exchangeable."

She laughed softly as she lifted her hand to look at the ring, clearly pleased. "Oh, it's beautiful, Wade. It's perfect." She looked at him. "Everything's perfect."

They both stood up in the same moment as if they mutually felt the need to eliminate the table between them. Stepping around it they met with a long, tight embrace, and then he kissed her again, oblivious to anyone else in the room who might be observing.

Throughout the remainder of dinner they made tentative plans, and Wade couldn't deny feeling as happy as she seemed. Alex was waiting for him when he got home, wanting to hear how it had gone.

"Perfect," Wade said, and then he laughed. "We're getting married in August so we can take a honeymoon during the break between semesters."

Alex grinned. "Wow. That's wonderful. Do we get to have Marina move in with us then?"

"Actually, I'll probably be moving in with her." Wade shrugged. "You can't have everything. But don't think you'll be getting rid of us. I'm still going to need day care. Marina wants to keep working until we have another baby, and I'm fine with that."

"You look happy," Alex commented.

"Yes, I believe I am."

They talked for a long while before Wade went up to bed, feeling more content than he had since the night Elena died.

The following Sunday Wade invited Marina to go to church with him, and later he heard through the grapevine that some people were apparently not pleased with his dating so soon after his wife's death. After hearing the gossip he said to Jane, "Is there some kind of committee I'm supposed to consult or something? Some people thought I should have remarried within a week; others think ten years is too soon."

"Obviously," Jane said, "everyone has their own opinion, and you just need to let it roll off. You're the only one who knows what's right for you. Don't let the judgmental attitude of other people make you judgmental."

Wade had to admit, "Okay, you got me there."

Jane just smiled.

CHAPTER 7

Wade quickly found himself in a whirlwind of wedding plans. He told Marina to just do whatever she wanted. He'd been married before, but this was her first wedding and her last, and he wanted it to be according to her every wish. Her mother had apparently put money aside for Marina's wedding, and she had very distinct ideas and big plans, so he left them to it.

He was surprised one afternoon when he was out with Marina ordering the wedding cake by a call she got on her cell phone. He was glad they were in the car and not in the bakery they'd just left when he could actually hear Julia yelling through the phone. Marina calmly argued with her mother for more than ten minutes before she hung up, and he asked, "What was that all about?"

"Oh, she just has these fits sometimes. It's not a big deal."

"That didn't sound at all like the mother I've gotten to know over the last few months."

"Well, I guess she's been on her best behavior for company," Marina said. "Don't worry about it."

Wade sensed that Marina felt embarrassed by her mother's behavior and didn't want to talk about it, so he changed the subject. A few days later they were at her parents' home to have dinner and to go over wedding plans. Since Marina was the oldest, the house was full of younger siblings, ages seventeen down to twelve. Including two at college, there were seven children altogether.

Wade was surprised to find the entire evening absolute chaos. Every visit prior to this had given him an entirely different impression. Marina's mother was sharp with the kids, impatient with her husband, complaining that Marina did nothing to help with the family when Wade knew that she actually did a great deal, especially considering that she hadn't lived at home for a few years.

After they left, Marina said to him, "Sorry about that. It can get pretty crazy sometimes."

"Apparently I'm not company anymore," Wade said satirically, wondering if his previous visits to their home had been subject to some kind of playacting for his benefit. The idea left him uneasy.

"Apparently not," she said and took his hand.

As the wedding drew closer, Wade became increasingly uneasy over the behavior he saw in Marina's family. He kept telling himself that it was Marina he loved, and Marina he was going to marry. But he still felt unsettled.

* * *

Rebecca's first birthday brought a great mixture of emotions for Wade, but he dealt with his grief privately and felt completely confident about moving forward with his life. Before the anniversary of Elena's death he would be married again, and he knew in his heart that was a good thing.

Rebecca's party was a huge success, and just being surrounded by so many people who loved them reminded Wade of how thoroughly blessed he was. Marina's family had been invited, but they weren't able to make it for reasons that weren't quite clear. However, he felt immensely relieved by their absence and concluded that wasn't a good sign.

The following week Wade took Rebecca in for her one-year checkup and shots. Laura greeted them with her usual smile, and she was enthusiastically thrilled to see Rebecca. Wade loved watching them interact, and he loved the way that Laura kept saying how beautiful and precious the baby was. Then she turned to him and asked with genuine concern, "And how are you doing?"

"I'm great," he said. "I'm getting married next week."

For a moment he almost thought she looked upset, but she quickly turned her attention to Rebecca, and he felt sure he'd imagined it. "That's wonderful," she said. "So Rebecca will have a mother again."

"That's right."

Laura held the baby close. "Well, she's a very lucky woman, whoever she is."

The visit proceeded as normal, with a good report on Rebecca's growth and health. Then Laura gave her the immunizations, after which she held her and gave her comfort. Before leaving the room she said with a smile, "Congratulations. I hope you're deliriously happy."

"Thank you," he said, sharing her sentiment exactly. But that night another drama occurred with Marina's parents, and he went home feeling concerned and frustrated. As usual when he needed a sounding board, he sought out Alex. He found him in the study, reading.

"Can we talk?" Wade asked and closed the door before he sat down.

"Sure," Alex said, setting his book aside. "What's wrong?"

"Nothing . . . particular. It's more a . . . general problem."

"Okay, I'm listening."

"How long were you and Jane engaged?"

"Too long," Alex said. "She wanted to get married in the temple and I refused to go to church because I was angry with my father. You know this story. It took me a long time to come around."

"Okay, but . . . how long before you knew she was the one for you?"

"About five minutes," he said, and Wade was surprised.

"And you *knew?*"

"Let me put it this way. Even if I had been temple-worthy at the time, we wouldn't have run right out to get married that first week. A certain amount of wisdom and propriety should precede a marriage, for obvious reasons, although I've known of many good marriages that happened in a hurry. I think we both knew very quickly that we were meant to be together. If circumstances had been different we might have gotten married right away. Why? Are you having doubts?"

"I don't know." Wade groaned and stood up to pace the room.

"Talk to me," Alex said.

Wade sighed and sat back down. "I've barely met members of Jane's family. Are they good people?"

"Yes," Alex said. "I mean . . . they're not perfect; nobody is. Her sister had a strong aversion to me in the beginning, but we've gotten over that. Her parents were always very good to me, even when I was being a rebel. What are you getting at?"

Wade looked directly at him. "Marina is amazing, Alex. I love her, and she loves me. But you've heard the adage that when you marry someone, you marry their family. And I'm not so sure I want to marry this one."

"I see," Alex said.

"Before we were engaged they just seemed to be . . . a great, average family. But since we've started planning the wedding, I cannot believe the issues that have come up." He gave an ironic chuckle. "Makes me grateful for the home I was raised in. I never imagined that people living under the same roof could be so . . . *cruel* to each other. I am amazed at the . . . manipulation, and . . . controlling behavior, and . . . the *contention*. I can't believe the way they treat her sometimes, and the way she's always dragged into the drama, like she's supposed to fix it or something. It's like now that we're engaged nobody's holding back for the sake of appearances."

"Well, that's a good thing. Better that you see it now, I think."

"Yes, but what do I do about it?"

Alex thought for a minute. "I think my concern would not be so much the kind of family Marina comes from, as her perception of it. Does she think this is normal?"

"For the most part I think she sees the problems; we've talked about it. But she's still very . . . shall we say, accustomed to it? And whether or not she recognizes the problems, the reality is that she was raised in a home with rampant dysfunction."

"So, you're what? Concerned that when it comes to dealing with life and solving problems, she's going to revert to what she was raised with?"

"Yes, that's exactly what I'm afraid of. Where do you draw the line between logically assessing the character traits and background of a person when choosing a spouse, and the feelings you have for each other?"

Apparently Alex had to think about that one even longer, then he started talking about all the struggles that he and Jane had been through together. They were fairly compatible and had both come into the relationship with reasonable communication skills. But the challenges they'd faced had certainly propelled weaknesses to the surface. He talked about struggles he'd seen in the marriages of other people he knew. He told

Wade that he and Jane had often discussed the challenges their siblings and friends had encountered in their relationships, and how those challenges might be avoided in their own.

"Wade," he said, leaning his forearms on his thighs, "look at me." Wade lifted his head and met Alex's gaze. "Do you know beyond any doubt that this is the woman God wants you to marry?"

Wade took a sharp breath as the question struck him deeply. He leaned back and rubbed the side of his face. At his hesitance, Alex clarified, "Take everything else out of the mix. Just based on your personal experiences with Marina, and the things you've felt, answer the question. You prayed very hard about this decision before you proposed to her; you told me so. Is it right or not?"

"Yes," Wade said firmly, "I know it's right."

"There you have it. That knowledge will carry you through whatever difficulty may arise in the future. I don't think marriage is necessarily meant to be easy. It's meant to help each of us reach our greatest potential. And if you can do that for her, and she can do that for you, then it's a good match. Given her background, you may need some extra help. Counseling isn't a bad thing. And maybe Marina needs a husband who has been through just enough personal struggle to be willing to tackle the problems head-on. If the two of you remain committed to the marriage, above all else, taking a righteous approach to all that you do, there isn't any problem you can't overcome."

"You really believe that," he said.

"I really do. And if you want my advice about the family . . . I'm assuming you want advice or you—"

"Of course."

"If I were you, I would have a very frank conversation with Marina right now about your feelings on what you've seen in her home. Make it clear that you will not tolerate manipulation or contention in your home. Promise her that you will never treat her the way members of her family have treated her, and that you expect the same in return. Establish ground rules for being able to bring things up without creating a rift. You ought to be able to say to each other, 'This doesn't feel right to me,' or 'Maybe we need some help to solve this one.' Is that making sense?"

"Yes," Wade said, feeling more calm.

"And I would also take one particular scripture, memorize it, recite it, make it your mantra."

"Okay, what?"

Alex chuckled and turned to the computer next to where he was sitting. "I don't know. I have to look it up." He waited for the monitor to come on, then typed in a couple of key words before he said to Wade, "Okay, there's a few different versions of this in the scriptures, but in Mark, chapter ten it reads, 'For this cause shall a man leave his father and mother, and cleave to his wife.'" He turned to look at Wade. "Once you exchange vows with her, *you* are her family. That doesn't mean you can't do everything to maintain *healthy* relationships with extended family members, but whatever may be going on in the family she leaves behind should never be allowed to have influence within your marriage. Decisions are to be made between you and Marina, based on healthy, appropriate behavior. What's right and true should be more important than what's easy or comfortable. And neither of you should ever side with or choose extended family over each other. There. That's my advice. Take it or leave it."

"I think I'll take it," Wade said and let out a deep breath. He felt Alex's words sink deep into his heart, and he appreciated the definition he'd given to a healthy boundary. He knew he could simply never live with a wife who would choose to side with her family rather than her husband. He prayed that Marina could understand that and respect it.

"Okay, I feel better. I might actually be able to handle this."

"Good," Alex said.

"I know it's not going to be easy, but I know it's right."

"There you have it. If you know it's right, you can do just about anything."

The following evening Wade had a long talk with Marina, taking Alex's advice very seriously. He was pleased and relieved to hear her talk about her observances of the challenges in her family and how she didn't want that in her own home. She said she appreciated his attitude of taking it head-on and being open about it, and she promised that she would never let her family come between them, even if it meant alienating herself from them if it became necessary. Under normal circumstances, Wade would have thought that such drastic measures would never become necessary. But given the dramas he'd seen Marina's mother create, he had to wonder if it might eventually come to that. He felt sure that when it came time to do his residency, moving out of state for a few years might be a good thing for them.

As the final wedding preparations came together, Wade was confronted with a couple of incidents where he felt so thoroughly angry with Marina's mother that it took everything he had to avoid a heated argument. Julia just had a knack for rubbing him the wrong way with behavior that was so clearly manipulative and disruptive he could feel nothing but appalled. He talked with Marina about it. She seemed embarrassed but assured him it was mostly due to the stress of the wedding. He reminded himself that in a matter of days Marina would legally and morally be *his* responsibility and they could end all of this havoc. But he feared that might be easier said than done.

Two days before the wedding, Marina's sister Jamie threw a big party at her house for both families to get to know each other better before the wedding took place. Wade liked Jamie, and he liked her husband, Luke. But when he arrived at their home early to help with the preparations, he felt disconcerted to observe dynamics between them that were a little too much like Julia and Lane Patterson. He relaxed when his own family began to arrive, and they all had a great time. While relatives took turns looking out for Rebecca, he and Marina mingled among their families, introducing people to each other and enjoying their company. He caught sight of his father and step-mother sitting with Jane and Alex, visiting quietly, and he took Marina by the hand to join them.

"I hope you're having a marvelous time," Wade said, and they all smiled toward him.

"Did you get enough to eat?" Marina asked.

"More than enough," Alex said. "Thank you."

"It's marvelous to see you so happy," Neil said to Wade, and Marina smiled up at him.

"Amen to that," Roxanne said. "And we're looking forward to having Rebecca at least through part of your honeymoon."

"You and Mom are going to have to fight over her, I guess," Wade said, glancing at his mother on the other side of the room, visiting with one of Marina's brothers. As always, at such gatherings he was grateful for the forgiveness and healing that had made it possible for both of his families to be together with no animosity or hard feelings.

"What about me?" Jane asked.

"Oh, you get her far too much," Wade said. "I think you need a break."

"I think I'm going to miss her," Jane said.

"Me too," Alex added.

They all chatted for a few minutes before Roxanne reminded Neil that they needed to get home since one of her daughters was bringing her children over to spend the night. A few minutes after they left, Jane said to Alex, "Maybe we should get home as well and see if the babysitter is still alive." Wade knew they'd chosen to come without the children in order to relax and enjoy the evening more.

Alex asked, "Do you want us to take Rebecca home and put her to bed or—"

"And who might this be?" a woman's voice interrupted, and they all turned to see Marina's mother, Julia. Wade knew why she'd not been officially introduced to some members of his family. He'd preferred to avoid anything that might initiate even the smallest drama. She added in a syrupy voice, "You haven't introduced me to your friends."

Wade said with no hesitation, "Actually, this is my brother Alex and his wife Jane."

They exchanged cursory greetings, then Julia said to Wade, "But I thought I'd met all of your brothers."

It only took a second for the tension to rise. Marina looked astonished, perhaps embarrassed. Wade felt angry. He was grateful when Alex hurried to say in a light voice, "Actually, I'm his other brother." Wade tossed him a silent endorsement before he added, "I'm from the side of the family we don't readily admit to."

"Oh?" Julia said as if she had absolutely no idea what he was talking about. Wade's anger increased, knowing that Julia had been clearly informed of the situation. He hoped that Alex knew him better than to think that he would be marrying a woman in a couple of days and not have told her family about his unique circumstances.

As if to directly verify his assumption, Marina said to her mother, "We told you all about that, Mom."

Julia looked perfectly confused. "About what?"

Wade and Marina exchanged a discreet glance before Wade turned to Julia and said, "Allow me to remind you. We shared a lengthy conversation about a time in my mother's life that left me born into an unusual situation."

"Well, I must have misunderstood what you meant," she said, as if Wade had done something wrong. She looked at Alex as if he'd sprouted fangs or something. Then she looked at Wade the same way. "Are you trying to say then, that your *mother*," she made it sound like a dirty word, "had an . . . *affair*," she whispered, then pointed to Alex, "with this man's *father?*" Another dirty word. "And I assume that the older gentleman who was here would be your father?"

"That's right, and that's exactly what I mean," Wade said with no apology. Alex looked openly proud of him as he went on to say, "And if you misunderstood our previous conversation, then why do you suppose we spent so much time talking about forgiveness and repentance? Exactly what did you think I meant?" Wade's voice remained steady and calm, even though he felt extremely ticked off.

"Well, I don't know what I thought," Julia said, acting as if she'd been told her daughter was marrying a terrorist. "I just . . . never would have imagined that . . . such a thing could ever happen in a Mormon home." She shook her head with disgust. "Are all of these people going to be at the wedding . . . in the . . . temple?" She whispered the last as if the idea were somehow blasphemous.

"Yes, they certainly will," Wade said firmly.

"Mother," Marina said, "there will not be anyone in the temple who is not worthy to be there. We're talking about something that happened more than twenty-five years ago, and it has nothing to do with us."

Julia said in a voice that was loud enough to carry through most of the room, "If you actually go through with this wedding and marry this man, then it certainly does have something to do with us."

"Mother," Marina said again, her voice low and firm, "I certainly am going through with this wedding, and *all* of Wade's family will be there. If you have a problem with that, you would do well not to attend."

Julia looked horrified that her daughter would say such a thing, but Wade felt proud of her. Julia shook her head and made an emotional noise as if the world had just ended, then she made a dramatic exit up the stairs. Marina's father tossed a harsh glare toward Marina and Wade as if to blame them for whatever the drama might be, then he followed his wife up the stairs.

"Come on," Wade said, taking Marina's arm to lead her out the front door. Alex and Jane followed.

Once outside, Marina said, "I am so sorry about that." The apology was obviously meant to include all of them.

"You didn't do anything you need to apologize for," Alex said.

"Please tell me," Wade said to Marina, "that I am not losing my mind. We *did* make the situation very clear to her, did we not?"

"Yes, we did," Marina said, now crying. "I don't know why she does things like that sometimes. It's like she just . . . wants to make a scene, like she's been . . . thinking of ways to make the worst out of a situation. I should have seen it coming."

Jane put an arm around Marina, saying softly, "If you think it would be better for us not to come to the wedding, then—"

"No!" Wade said firmly. "I'm not getting married without the people there who are most important to me—from both sides of my family."

"But what if Marina's mother doesn't come?" Alex asked. "The mother of the bride needs to be there."

Marina became more emotional. She muttered a quick, "Excuse me," and hurried back into the house.

"Well, that was fun," Wade said with sarcasm.

"I certainly see what you mean," Alex said.

Jane put her arms around him with a tight hug. "It's going to be okay, Wade. You hang in there. You have good instincts. You'll know what to do."

"Thanks, sis," he said. "I guess I'd better get back in the ring and see if I can salvage the evening."

"Good luck with that," Alex said and gave him a hug as well before he and Jane left. They offered again to take Rebecca, but Wade felt prone to keeping her with him. He uttered a quick prayer, took a deep breath, and went back into the house, hoping this was not an omen for his future.

Wade quickly realized that Marina was upstairs, behind closed doors with her parents. Occasionally he could hear her mother's raised voice, but everyone just tried to ignore it, and thankfully it was impossible to tell what she was saying.

Gradually, his family slipped away, giving him hugs and saying they'd see him at the temple in a couple of days. When there was no one left but Jamie and Luke, Wade changed Rebecca into her pajamas and fed her the bedtime bottle, wondering how long he would have to wait—or if he even should. Jamie and Luke were working on cleaning up the mess, chatting a bit as they moved between the family room where he was sitting, and the kitchen area nearby. Rebecca fell asleep, and Wade was ready to ask Jamie to tell Marina to call him, when he heard the door come open upstairs. He laid Rebecca on a blanket spread over the carpet while he realized that Lane and Julia had stormed out of the house without saying good-bye to Luke and Jamie, who had gone to a great deal of work to host this event. He turned to see Marina gazing at him, her face showing clear evidence that she'd been crying—a lot. He felt both grateful and concerned when Luke and Jamie made a gracious exit.

"It went well, I take it," he said with obvious sarcasm.

"We need to talk," she said and sat down.

"Okay." He sat to face her. "I'm listening."

"My mother is *really* upset."

"I caught that. But why exactly? Is it because you're marrying an illegitimate heathen? Or is it because she has to be in the temple with people who aren't ashamed to admit that they once made some mistakes?"

"I don't know," she said and started to cry again.

"Oh, I think you know," he said. He kept his tone gentle and compassionate, in spite of how angry he was feeling. "We've talked about this, Marina. I've been around your mother enough to know what's going on."

"Well then you explain it to me," she said with a terseness that took him off guard.

"Okay," he said, "I will. Your mother's history would indicate that she enjoys being the center of attention. She creates drama so that she can revel in it. You've told me yourself she does that. Is that not true?"

"Yes," Marina admitted.

"You've also admitted that she has some control issues; she's very skilled at manipulating a situation to her liking. Is that not also true?"

"Yes," she said firmly.

"Okay, so that's that. She's found an aspect of my life that helps her achieve those purposes. I don't really care *why* she does it, Marina. I only know that I am not going to stand by and allow her to say hurtful things to me, or you, or members of my family because she wants life to be a soap opera."

Marina lifted her eyes to his, then quickly glanced away. She almost looked afraid, and he wondered why. He understood when she said, "I hate to even ask you this, but . . . under the circumstances . . . maybe it would better if . . ." She hesitated too long.

"If what?" he demanded, knowing he wasn't going to like it.

"Maybe we could just avoid any problems if . . ." He saw her visibly draw courage while his insides started to smolder. He knew what was coming and it made him sick. "Perhaps it would be better if your *other* side of the family . . . didn't come to the wedding."

Wade swallowed hard. He prayed that he could keep from shouting. He counted to ten, then to twenty. There was only one thing he could say. "I can't believe you would even ask me that." She said nothing, wouldn't look at him. "Let me get this straight," he said, proud of himself for the even tone of his voice when he felt like breaking something. "You have just admitted that you know your mother's behavior is inappropriate, but you're asking *me,* the man you are supposed to be marrying, to tell certain members of my immediate family that they are not welcome to attend my wedding for the sole purpose of making your mother less uncomfortable. Am I clear on that?"

She didn't answer, but he could feel the truth in her aura. And he couldn't believe it. Recalling the way she'd put it, about having his "other family" absent, he had to ask, "Does this mean it's okay for my mother to attend, even though she once committed adultery? But it's not okay for my biological father and his other children to be there? Is that because the family I was raised in has all present appearances of being a normal, good Mormon family? Is that because my *other family* is difficult to explain?" Again her silence confirmed that his assumptions were correct. And that's when the anger came out, even though he did well at keeping his voice low enough to prevent being overheard or waking Rebecca. "How dare she do this to me! How dare *you* do this to me. You promised me that you would never let your family come between us, even if it meant alienating yourself from your family. Obviously that was an empty promise."

Now she looked angry. "So, what are you saying? It's okay for my mother not to come to the wedding?"

"Is that it? She threatened not to come if certain members of my family are there?"

"She just doesn't want any ill feelings in the temple," Marina said, as if that explained everything.

"The only ill feelings would be hers, and that's her problem. She's trying to manipulate you, Marina. If you tell her you won't stand for it, she'll back down. She wouldn't miss her daughter's wedding over this."

"I wouldn't bet on it."

"How could you? No one's ever stood up to her before now. That's about to change. I will not give in to this, Marina. I am not going to ask some of the people I love most in this world to stay away from my wedding to appease her syco-phantic drama. I won't do it. Plain and simple. It's not open for discussion."

Marina's anger suddenly became so vivid it left him stunned. "So, you're telling me I should alienate my mother, but you're not willing to alienate *your* family for my sake? Who is taking sides, Wade?"

Again Wade had to count to ten . . . twenty . . . thirty, praying as he did. He managed an even, but tight, voice as he said, "This is not about taking sides, Marina. It's about what's true and right. Your mother's behavior is clearly dysfunc-tional. You sit there and admit it, and then you ask me to condone it."

She stared at him with defiance and anger in her eyes, and a horrible reality settled into him. His conversation with Alex about this very thing came back to him with clarity. He wanted to be grateful that it had come to this before the wedding, instead of after, but he felt more angry that it hadn't come to this long before their relationship had ever come this far. He felt surprisingly calm and suddenly void of anger as he said firmly, "You have a choice, Marina. It's either me or your mother. What's it going to be?"

"What are you saying?" she asked, sounding more appalled than concerned.

"I think it's pretty clear."

"You cannot expect me to get married without my mother there."

Wade felt as if a fifty-pound weight had just been heaved onto his chest. He looked at her as if through a fog. He couldn't believe what he was hearing, couldn't fathom what it meant. He asked himself some silent questions, and the answers were immediate and firm. He wondered what he was supposed to learn from this, but that question was far too complex to consider in the heat of the moment. For now, he knew what he had to do, and he knew he had to do it quickly and get out of here before he fell apart.

"Well," he said and swallowed hard, "that would be much easier than getting married without the groom there." He took hold of her left hand and slid the ring off her finger.

"What are you doing?" she demanded, her eyes flaring with panic.

"I'm taking the ring back," he said and stuffed it into his pocket as he came to his feet and put the diaper bag over his shoulder

"Wade?" His name erupted on a sob. "You can't be serious." She sobbed again as she stood up.

"That's what I was just thinking about you," he said, surprised at his own composure. Before picking Rebecca up he turned to face her directly. "You sit there and talk about the spirit that should be among the people attending a temple marriage. As it is, I could never be in the same room with your mother there and feel any kind of peace. But worse, I could never be in the same room with you there and feel any kind of peace after what you just said to me." Absorbing her horrified expression, he realized that he didn't want to have to dread trying to discuss this with her ever again once he left the room. He took a deep breath and said, "Listen to me, Marina, and listen carefully. I'm not going to repeat it. You promised me you would never let her come between us, and you just did. You broke a promise to me, and if the conversation we just had is an indication of what the dynamics of our marriage would be like, then you must know I can't live with that. I am who I am. And I will not live the rest of my life as part of a family who will look upon my circumstances with disdain and condemnation. I thought that you and I could stand against such problems together, but you just made it perfectly clear that you are not capable of doing that. Goodbye, Marina."

He carefully picked up Rebecca, hoping he wouldn't wake her while Marina just stood there, looking as if the power had just gone out in the middle of playing a movie. As he moved toward the door she seemed shaken from her stupor. "Wade, please," she said, following him, "we need to talk about this."

"There's nothing to talk about," he said. "In case you missed it, the wedding is off." He walked out the door without looking back, and couldn't resist slamming it, if only to put a solid exclamation point on what he'd just done. While he buckled Rebecca into her seat as she miraculously remained asleep, he kept expecting Marina to tear out of the house and argue with him. But he was grateful she didn't. He drove toward home feeling stunned and horrified over what had just happened. He didn't regret his decision and knew he never could. But how could he not grieve the loss of what he had believed would be the love to fill this hole in his life, for the rest of his life?

The shock stayed with him as he went into the house and tucked Rebecca into her bed. He was grateful that everyone else had gone to sleep; he had no desire to discuss any of this tonight—not even with Alex.

CHAPTER 8

After crawling into bed, the shock finally subsided, and Wade felt much as he had when he'd realized that Elena was dead. Marina was lost to him. He'd loved her, trusted her, believed in her. And now he was alone—again, still.

Wade took something to help him sleep when he realized his head would never stop spinning. He woke to daylight and the sound of his cell phone ringing. He staggered to find it clipped to his belt. Seeing Marina's number he turned the phone off and went back to bed. A few minutes later he heard the house phone ringing. Even though he had a phone on the bedside table, he ignored it. Most calls were for Jane or Alex anyway, but if it was Marina, he had no desire or need to talk to her. He groaned when he heard a knock at his door, and Alex called, "Are you awake?"

"No," Wade said.

Alex opened the door, his brow furrowed, the cordless phone in his hand. Wade mouthed, *Who is it?*

Alex replied noiselessly, *Marina.*

Wade shook his head vehemently. Alex looked concerned but spoke into the phone in a voice that sounded completely natural. "Apparently he can't get to the phone right now. I'll tell him you called." He turned off the phone and said to Wade, "I take it things didn't go well last night after we left."

Wade made a scoffing noise. "That would be an understatement."

"So, you're not talking to the bride the day before the wedding?"

Wade groaned and pulled the covers over his head, saying through them, "There's not going to be a wedding."

A moment later Alex pulled the covers from over Wade's face, demanding quietly, "Did I hear that right?"

"I took the ring back. I told her it was off."

Alex sat on the edge of the bed, looking horrified. "Are you okay?" he asked.

Wade looked away as tears burned into his eyes. He'd long ago gotten over being too proud to cry in front of his brother. He just said what first came to his mind, "I was too angry to tell her that she broke my heart. And if I talk to her I won't be able to say anything except that I hate her for it."

"I can't believe it," Alex said. "Tell me what happened."

Wade cried silent tears and wiped them with the sheet while he repeated the horror to his brother. When there was nothing more to say, Alex just repeated, "I can't believe it."

Wade made a dubious noise. "Yeah, well . . . I'm afraid it's true. I get to spend the day calling everyone on my invitation list to tell them it's off."

"We can help with that."

"Thank you. I'm not sure I can live through answering the 'why' a hundred times."

Alex said, "We're glad to do anything we can."

"As always," Wade said with chagrin. "You and your sweet wife sure do a lot of keeping me together."

"We love you. Truthfully, the silver lining in this for me is that you and Rebecca won't be leaving. And I know Jane would agree with me. She's been dreading it, crying every day. Barrett too."

"You just say things like that to make me feel better."

"No, I do not!" He playfully slapped his shoulder, which eased the pall for a moment, then he said solemnly, "Marina will be calling back. There are arrangements that must be undone."

"I'll send her an email," Wade said. "So, if she calls tell her to check her email. I'll do it now. They can post a sign at the reception center for anyone who might get missed with a phone call." Wade sighed at the enormity of all of the undoing that had to be done today. And the price attached—in more ways than one.

"Tell me, big brother, why do you suppose I have felt all along that this was right, only to be led to this point and be kicked off a cliff?"

"Whatever may or may not be right is contingent upon a person's free agency. Marina made a choice that you can't live with, a choice that broke a promise she made to you. And that promise was not unclear or passed over quickly, according to what you told me."

"No, it was not. I'm absolutely certain she understood my meaning and how important it was to me. So, if God knows the beginning to the end, He knew it would come to this."

"Yes, I'm sure He did."

"So . . . why? Why did it have to come this far? Why did it have to turn into such a . . . mess?"

Alex sighed. "I can't answer that, little brother. But I would bet that one of these days, when you least expect it, you'll understand. Or maybe the why is more important for Marina's growth than yours."

"Right now being the object of Marina's growth makes me want to . . ."

"Kick a chair?" Alex asked facetiously.

Wade recalled the first time he'd ever seen Alex truly angry, and probably the last. They had believed that Barrett would die, and Wade had put him through some horrible stress. And Alex had kicked a chair across the kitchen. "Yeah," Wade said, "I think I'd like to kick a chair."

"Come get some breakfast and you can have at it." Alex stood to leave the room. "Send her that email first, and then find that guest list. You have all the contact information in the computer, right? Didn't we use a label program for that?"

"Yeah, we did," Wade said. "I'll get it. Thank you, Alex."

Alex gave him a wan smile. "We're family."

Wade got up and went straight to the computer. He was glad not to find an email from Marina. He didn't even want to respond to anything she had to say at the moment. He hurried to make a written clarification of the words he'd said the previous evening, then he stated what he would do and the calls he would make to undo the arrangements, making it clear that the rest was up to her and her family according to arrangements they'd made—things he had no idea how to undo. He knew there would be money lost on many things that couldn't be undone at this point. But it seemed a small price to pay in contrast to the marriage that he could now see he'd almost fallen into. In spite of the grief, he felt deeply grateful. He felt hurt and angry, but he felt relieved too. He tried to focus on the relief as he sent the email to Marina and printed off the contact information for friends and family who had been invited to the wedding. Thankfully, his guest list hadn't been nearly as long as Marina's, and he knew that family members could help spread the word through relatives and friends.

Wade left the printout on the study desk and went upstairs to find Rebecca just waking up. He lost himself in the happiness that always radiated from her in the mornings, as if being well rested with a new day before her was truly blissful. She was such a joy to him! He felt grateful that he hadn't married into a family that would have probably subjected her to many trials.

Once they were both dressed, Wade took Rebecca to the kitchen, where Jane immediately wrapped him in a tearful embrace. "I'm so sorry," she said.

He just hugged her back and said, "Thank you. I'm just grateful it came up now and not next week."

"I know," she said, wiping at her tears, "but it's still horrible."

"Yes, it is," he agreed firmly. "But Rebecca's happy this morning, so I think we should all follow her example."

"Excellent idea," Jane said and pulled the orange juice out of the fridge.

Breakfast proceeded as normal while Wade kept thinking of last night's encounter with Marina, and he began to fume. He couldn't believe it! How could she have just . . . thrown away everything they'd shared over something so petty?

"What's wrong?" Alex asked, nudging him.

"It's that obvious, eh?"

"Yeah," he chuckled satirically, "it's that obvious. You look like you could kill something."

"I'm pretty ticked off."

"Better angry than sad, sometimes," Jane said. "At least when I feel angry I have energy. And we need energy to get through a day like today. You just have to be careful not to let your anger make you do or say something you regret."

"So take it out on us," Alex said. "Go ahead." He dramatically motioned to an empty kitchen chair. Wade didn't even hesitate before he stood up and kicked it across the room. Jane gasped. Alex laughed. Wade chuckled and sat back down to finish his breakfast.

"It's a start," he said, then smiled at Rebecca who looked adorably perplexed.

Then the phone rang. Wade felt knots in his stomach as Alex reached for it, glancing at the caller ID. "The fireworks begin," he said facetiously just before he pushed the button to answer it.

"Hello, Marina," he said. "I'm afraid Wade's not available. When will he be? Well, next month sometime, I think. Yes, I'm quite serious. He's sent you an email that should cover anything that might have been overlooked." Alex sighed and was obviously listening with a patience that was made comical by the dramatically impatient faces he made. "Marina," he finally said as if to interrupt her, "there is nothing you, or anyone else, can say or do to change it now. His reasons for calling it off are not impulsive or unreasonable. I know this is difficult for you; it's difficult for Wade too. But it's just the way it is. I need to go now. We've got a lot of phone calls to make."

He ended the call and turned to look at Wade just as his tears fell. Hearing Alex's words put the reality front and center. He stood and left the room, saying, "Yeah, I think I prefer being angry. But I think I need a good cry first."

Wade locked himself in his bathroom and cried long and hard. He took a shower and cried some more, then he said a prayer, read from the Book of Mormon for ten minutes, and went to face the undoing of a dream. By the time he got downstairs, Alex showed him the guest list with red marks next to the people he'd called, and blue ones next to those that others had agreed to call for them. There were only about a dozen names left. Alex declared that answering machines helped the process go more smoothly, then he offered to finish making those calls while Wade used his cell phone to cancel the tuxedo order, the flowers, and the honeymoon reservations—all of which had deposits that would be lost. He called his mother and talked to her for a while. He cried while she consoled and encouraged him. Neil called a few minutes later to offer his support and to let him know that he'd canceled the wedding luncheon he'd arranged. Of course a deposit had been lost there as well, but since none of the food preparation had begun, it wasn't as bad as Wade had expected. They discussed what else needed to be done, then Neil said, "I'm proud of you, son. I know it took courage, and it's not easy, but I really think you did the right thing."

"Thank you, Dad. I don't know what I'd do without you." Neil had a way of appropriately getting into the middle of a problem and solving it at moments when Wade was too grief-stricken to think clearly.

A couple of hours later, he sat down with Jane and Alex to evaluate what they'd done, and the wedding was declared officially canceled from their side. There had only been two people they'd been unable to reach or leave a message with, and Alex had given those numbers to Wade's mother, who would keep trying. She said she would go to their homes and leave notes on their doors if she had to.

"Okay," Alex said, "now on to the next stage of the problem."

"What?" Wade demanded, wondering what he'd overlooked.

"Well, Dad and I talked about it and realized we have a big problem. You have several days off and nothing to do and nowhere to go. So here's the deal."

Jane was smirking, and Wade wondered what was coming. "You need to pack for you and Rebecca and meet us in the driveway at two o'clock." He glanced at his watch. "That's about ninety minutes."

"What on earth are you trying to pull?" Wade demanded.

"Here's the equation, kid," Alex said. "Two SUVs, five kids, five adults—two of those being grandparents who love to help take care of the five children; ten pieces of luggage, two strollers, and our very efficient stepmother who has the itinerary and reservations all taken care of."

Wade chuckled. "Don't you have to work?"

"I called in some favors and some vacation days. It's all good."

Wade couldn't hold back a burst of laughter. "Where are we going?" he asked, even though he didn't care. The very idea of not having to sit around and think about the honeymoon that didn't happen felt completely glorious.

"Oh, it's perfect," Jane said with enthusiasm. "Tonight we're staying at the Excalibur in Vegas. They have great stuff there for kids. Then we've got two nights with two family suites at a hotel across from Disneyland, and three nights in San Diego, where we will go to the zoo, the beach, and Sea World, and we'll spend Sunday there and find a church. Then another night in Vegas at some new place on the way home. And if you're wondering how she got these reservations at such short notice, chalk it up to a miracle."

Wade laughed again. "Where do I sign up?"

"Just get packed," Alex said, and Wade hurried from the room. Alex called after him, "Don't forget your camera!"

Ninety minutes later Neil and Roxanne arrived and started helping load the luggage scattered in the driveway into the two vehicles. Roxanne had the children in giggles as she told them how much fun they were going to have, and she recited her seating plans for the drive so that she would have a turn riding with each of the kids. When she saw Wade, she wrapped him in a tight, motherly hug, and he had to fight tears. He was so blessed!

Alex recorded a message on their answering machine that said, *The wedding is off. We're not answering the phone for a week or so. Have a good day.* On the door of the house he left a note that read the same thing and asked a neighbor to take it down in a couple of days, along with picking up the mail.

When everything was packed and ready to go, Neil gathered everyone around and offered a beautiful prayer on behalf of pressing forward and having a safe vacation. The kids ruined Roxanne's plans when they all insisted on riding with Grandma and Grandpa. She just laughed and helped get Barrett, Katharine, and Preston all situated in the backseat of their vehicle. Alex and Wade got the baby seats secured in the other vehicle, and Jane insisted she preferred the backseat where she could keep the babies happy and enjoy a good book. Alex tossed Wade the keys and said, "You get the first shift."

They got in, and Alex pulled out a CD that he stuck in the stereo right after Wade turned on the engine. *"Collective Soul,"* Alex said histrionically, and Wade laughed. Alex knew the band was Wade's favorite, and Alex was pretty fond of them as well. He then added something he said often. "Nothing wrong with some good, clean rock and roll." Wade recognized it as one of their older albums, but one of his all-time favorites. Alex put the music in the front speakers and turned it up loud as Wade backed out of the driveway. He obviously knew that Wade liked it loud, especially when he was dealing with rough emotions—something he'd done a lot of in the last year.

The adults all laughed when the babies responded to the music and started bouncing up and down in their seats and giggling. Rebecca did some patty cake and Ruthie mimicked her. On the freeway Wade and Neil made a game out of passing each other every few minutes, which made Katharine and Preston laugh and comically wave at their parents as they went past. Wade laughed too. He couldn't think of a better way to spend a non-honeymoon.

Twenty minutes into the drive, Wade's mind turned to the lyrics of the song on the stereo. It was one of his favorites, and he knew it by heart. But it suddenly took on poignant meaning. And the dense rhythm of the chorus seemed to express the anger he was feeling.

Why drink the water from my hand, contagious as you think as I am? . . . Why follow me to higher ground, lost as you swear I am? . . . Turn your head, now baby, just spit me out . . . December promise you gave unto me, December whispers of treachery. December clouds are now covering me, December songs no longer I sing.

When the song ended Wade started the track again, saying to Alex, "Okay, so it's August, not December, but it still fits."

"I'd say," Alex said, making it clear their thoughts had been in the same vein.

"Do you think he wrote it after he'd called off a wedding?"

"Something like that. He obviously knows how it feels."

This time they both sang along, so loud and obnoxious that it made Jane laugh. They moved on to the next track, and a few bars into it, Alex said, "Ooh, this is a good one too." He started it over, and Wade listened to the lyrics he knew well as they took on new meaning.

Give me a moment; got to get this weight up off my chest. Don't feed me sorrow; pain is a poison I digest . . . Find yourself another soul to hold. Off upon my journey I must go . . .

They listened to that track three times, singing along. Then Wade felt his anger melt into gentle grief. He shed a few tears while Alex kept a hand on his shoulder, then he turned the music up louder and just kept driving.

* * *

The impulsive family vacation ended up being a glorious success, even if keeping the "twins" happy was often a great feat. Wade was glad to be able to return home knowing that they'd been off having a wonderful time while he'd passed the anniversary of Elena's death. He was also glad to be able to get back into school, if only so he could stay busy enough to avoid thinking about his loneliness, which often triggered tears or anger. Over the next several weeks, the grief of losing Marina merged into his grief over losing Elena. The result often left him lost and spinning. But more than wishing that he and Marina could be happily married, he ached to have Elena alive and well, sharing with him the life they should have lived together. Still, Marina had become a big part of his life. They'd spent hundreds of hours together. She had truly become like a part of the family. He watched Rebecca becoming more steady on her feet and recalled how she'd taken her first steps into Marina's arms. And now Marina was just . . . gone from their lives. Vanished. As good as dead.

Weeks stretched into months while Wade struggled to keep up good grades, and he counted every step that was getting him closer to that medical degree. He reached the point in his education where rigorous classes and studying were replaced by rotations in clinics and hospitals, which often meant bizarre hours and a new set of challenges. He became even more grateful for the army of family members who were so eager to help with Rebecca so that Jane didn't bear the entire brunt of her care—even though Jane never complained. He was also grateful not to have to be working an outside job when his rotation schedules could be difficult to work around at times.

The holidays were in some ways better than the year before, and in some ways harder. Again he purchased a beautiful wreath for Elena's grave and was grateful when Alex suggested that perhaps the whole family could go with him to put it there. They all hovered in the cold for several minutes, talking about some good memories, and discussing their gratitude for the true meaning of Christmas and the hope that Christ offered in the face of life's struggles.

Celebrating Christmas had many bright moments for Wade, but it marked the passing of time. Rebecca was growing. Life was going on without him. Rebecca's hair filled in and became thick, retaining its dark color, so much like her mother's. She started saying a few words, the first being Daddy, which thrilled Wade—except that she called Alex Daddy, too. But then she called Jane Mommy. All of the other kids did, so it was perfectly natural. Wade really didn't mind. He was just grateful to have Jane and Alex love him and his daughter so much.

Rebecca's favorite word was "don't," and she said it forcefully over many silly things. He was glad to see that his daughter had a straightforward way about expressing her opinions. She also loved to play in the snow and go shopping, both of which Wade indulged her in regularly. The two of them occasionally went to the mall where there was an indoor carousel; it became her favorite place to go, and sometimes Barrett went along.

Kirk called the week after Christmas to see how Wade was doing. He phoned once in a while to check on him, and Wade was grateful. But his repeated offers for Wade and Rebecca to come to dinner were always politely declined. The time he'd gone with Marina had been nice, but now the memories of that just made the situation even more uncomfortable. Wade simply had a hard time with the idea of seeing his longtime friend happily married, while he was still on his own. Perhaps one day he might feel differently.

Wade heard nothing from Marina, but he did get notified that he was being sued by her parents for the expenses of the wedding that had not been refundable. Alex told him that was the stupidest thing he'd ever heard, and then an attorney basically told him the same thing. He had the attorney send them a letter clearly stating Wade's point of view, that he already *had* covered expenses that had been his responsibility, and that the elaborate wedding plans had been Julia's desire, not his or

Marina's. The letter also stated the reasons for the breakup. In appropriate legal jargon the letter basically invited them to contest it in court, but made it clear they would only be setting themselves up to have a judge throw the case out. Wade heard nothing more about it.

In January, Rebecca turned eighteen months. She was able to go into the nursery at church, and she absolutely loved it. She wasn't one of those kids crying for her daddy; she loved being with the other kids and hardly noticed he was gone. Wade liked that about her. He could see the makings of a self-confident and well-balanced woman. And Wade actually got to sit all the way through a priesthood lesson for the first time in months.

Taking Rebecca in for a standard checkup, just to make sure she was growing normally and all was well, Wade was glad to learn that she didn't need any more immunizations for a few years. He hated those shots and the way she would scream. But he did look forward to seeing Laura. He entertained a brief fantasy about having her work for him someday; she'd actually mentioned it once. Then he thought that considering she was married, it wouldn't likely be wise to see her on a regular basis.

When she appeared and called Rebecca's name, he was delighted to see her attired in apparel with the theme of Mickey and Minnie Mouse. She was even wearing mouse ears on her head. They exchanged a smile, and Rebecca immediately reached for Laura, drawn to the mouse faces on her scrubs. Laura laughed and handed the chart to Wade as she took Rebecca, saying, "Hello there, little lady. You're getting so grown up." She said to Wade. "And more beautiful every time I see her."

"Yeah," Wade said and followed her to the exam room where he set the chart on the counter. Laura seemed content to just let Rebecca play with the plastic Minnie Mouse hanging around her neck. "We went to Disneyland last summer. She has a couple of Minnie toys that she loves."

Laura laughed softly and set the baby on the exam table, then she took the headband from her own head and put it on Rebecca's saying, "Do you want to look like Minnie Mouse? You're much prettier than she is."

Rebecca giggled and pulled the ears from her head, then tried to put them back on Laura's. Wade just enjoyed watching them together, trying not to think about the heartache he felt over the absence of a good woman in his life—and in Rebecca's.

While Laura was getting Rebecca's weight, she asked casually, "So, how is the new Mrs. Morrison?"

"What?" Wade asked, taken off guard.

"Last time you were here, you told me you were getting married soon. I was just wondering how—"

"I called it off," Wade said abruptly, feeling both touched and upset that she'd remembered.

Laura turned to look at him in a way that reminded him of that first visit when he'd told her of Elena's death. She looked as if she might cry, while her eyes silently questioned the reasons. He hurried to say, "It's a long story."

"I'm sorry," she said, focusing again on the baby.

"Thank you," he said. "But it was for the best."

"Is there anyone else, then?" she asked, sounding so genuinely concerned that he wanted to hug her.

"Just Rebecca," he said, trying to sound cheerful.

Laura smiled and finished what she was doing. Since there were no shots, she didn't come back in after the doctor had declared that Rebecca was in perfect health. For some reason Wade felt especially lonely that night, but he forced his mind to other things.

A few days later Marina called him out of the blue. At first he feared they were going to have an ugly conversation, but she actually expressed regret for going back on her word, saying that she understood why he'd done what he'd done. She apologized for her parents' behavior, mentioning the legal threats as well as the drama related to the breakup. He kindly accepted her apologies and asked her how she was doing. She didn't sound enthused about life, but she told him she was fine and dating someone. She ended the conversation by saying that it was likely better it had turned out this way, that their backgrounds were probably just too different.

You got that right, he answered silently, then said aloud, "I would agree with that."

He was glad to feel that they'd ended on friendly terms and that there were no hard feelings. But he still missed her, and he missed Elena, too. Bottom line, he was tired of being alone, but after what had happened with Marina he felt even more hesitant to embark onto the dating scene than he had been before. So he just tried not to think about it and stayed busy. Between doing medical rotations and caring for a toddler, staying busy was not a problem.

A distraction from the loneliness issue came when Brad, the father who had raised him, called to ask if Wade could come over, and it would probably be better if he didn't bring Rebecca.

"Okay," Wade said. "What's up?"

"We can talk when you get here. And would it be possible for Alex to come with you? Any time is fine. We're not going anywhere."

"I think he's off work at six. I'll find out and let you know."

Wade felt uneasy as he left a message for Alex, who called him back a while later. He was glad to come along but also admitted to being baffled. Jane gladly offered to watch Rebecca, and Wade picked Alex up at the hospital when his shift ended.

In the car, Alex asked, "Did he say anything about what they want?"

"Not a clue, but he did sound pretty somber. Something's wrong; I can feel it."

"I'm just wondering why they want me there."

"Maybe it's a family thing; maybe everybody will be there," Wade said.

"Okay, but . . . that still doesn't explain them wanting me there."

They drove mostly in silence to the home where Wade had been raised. They arrived to find only Brad and Marilyn there. Brad answered the door, giving them each a hug before he motioned them into the front room where Marilyn was huddled at one end of the couch, wrapped in a blanket, looking as if she'd been crying. Wade and Alex each hugged her before they sat down, and she said, "Thank you for coming, both of you."

"What's up, Mom?" Wade demanded.

Brad said, "Your mother wanted to talk to you first, Wade, before she told the others."

"Okay," Wade said warily, then gave his mother a penetrating stare. She'd often told him she felt closer to him, more comfortable with him. But this was scaring him.

"I got a mammogram a few days ago," she said, and Wade inwardly cursed at the same moment his every nerve tightened. He tossed a sharp glance toward Alex and saw his own fears reflected in his brother's eyes. Then Marilyn added, "They found a significant lump, something that there had been no sign of a little more than a year ago when I had the last mammogram. They've done a biopsy. It's cancer."

Wade felt stunned. He recalled his conversation with Alex following Elena's death about cancer being an epidemic. It was like a plague. He felt angry and hurt and scared. But mostly, he was in shock. It took ten minutes of expressing those emotions back and forth before the conversation could go on.

When the dramatics faded into silence, Alex said quietly, "I'm still wondering why you asked me to come along. Not that I mind being here, I just—"

"I want a second opinion, Dr. Keane," Marilyn said. "I've been given very frank advice on what I should do. I want to know what you think."

"I'm not a specialist, Marilyn."

"But you've had some firsthand experience with cancer."

"Leukemia is a whole different ball game," Alex said. "Your cancer is localized, but in many ways that's better. It's operable; it can be removed."

"Okay," Marilyn said. "So, when I'm being told that it should be removed surgically—and immediately—you would agree with that?"

"Absolutely," he said. "Get it out of you and do it fast."

Marilyn swallowed carefully and took a deep breath. "Okay. Now . . . I've had these words going through my head . . . things they told me. I think I understand, but I need you to help me make sure I've got it right."

"Ask away. If I don't know something, I'll find out."

"They told me they needed to do a . . . lumpectomy. Is that the right word?"

"Yes. That means they would just remove the lump and the margins around it to make certain they got it all."

"They talked about margins," Brad said, "but I'm not sure I understand that."

"That's simply the area around the lump. They want to take the tissue surrounding the lump, and they'll test it to make sure that the marginal areas have no cancer. If they do, then they'll have to go back and remove more."

Marilyn said, "They told me if they get in there and it looks bad, they could do a partial mastectomy, or a complete mastectomy. Am I saying that right?"

"Yes. And that means they will either remove some portion of the breast, or all of it."

"Okay," Marilyn said after taking another sharp breath. Then she got a little teary. "I appreciate your time, Alex. This is all taking some getting used to." She seemed hesitant, perhaps embarrassed.

"It's fine," Alex said. "You *do* need to understand what you're up against and explore your options. With Barrett's leukemia we did a lot of talking and studying to try to be prepared. It's far better than going into it blind. Ask me anything you like. You're not going to embarrass me, and Wade's in medical school. He can handle it. Let's talk."

Marilyn said nothing, but Brad did. "I'm a little lost on what they told us about the lymph nodes. Apparently that's a big deal, but it's not making sense to me."

Alex leaned his forearms on his thighs. "The lymph nodes absorb infection in the body; that's why they can become enlarged or sore sometimes when people get an infection. They will also absorb cancer cells if the cells have traveled into the bloodstream. When cancer like this is removed, they remove lymph nodes as well to test them for cancer. If the lymph nodes have no cancer, then that's the best possible report. That means it hasn't traveled. In that case they sometimes do chemotherapy or radiation treatments anyway, just as a precaution, but it's not likely to be so intense. If the lymph nodes have cancer, then we know it's gotten into the bloodstream, and it could have traveled elsewhere in the body. Depending on how many of them have cancer cells determines how intensely it needs to be fought. That's when chemotherapy and/or radiation are mandatory to hopefully kill it wherever it might be hiding. The radiation would probably be done in the area where the cancer was removed, and the chemotherapy is administered into the blood-stream to work through your entire body. The side effects can be nasty—for some people more than others—but it saves lives."

Wade listened to Alex offering his frank and educated oratory while he watched the reactions on his parents' faces. He felt increasingly sick to his stomach but didn't know what to do about it. He was grateful beyond words for Alex being here. Not only did he have the answers, he just had a way of taking a problem on and solving it. He'd survived some pretty ugly medical horrors with a loved one; surely having him around through whatever lay ahead was a good thing.

After Brad and Marilyn had seemed to assimilate what they'd heard so far, Marilyn went on to say, "Next question. They're telling me I also need to have my ovaries removed, that there's a connection. I think I understand why, but I would like you to explain that to me—if you know."

"I do actually," Alex said. "I know great developments have been made since I did my residency, but the basic principles are the same. I did spend some significant time in oncology. There are many different types of cancer, Marilyn; they feed on different things. Obviously they have determined that the type of cancer you have is fed by female hormones. If they remove your ovaries, then your body will stop producing those hormones and give the cancer less opportunity to grow."

"Okay," she said. "Why not take the uterus too? Obviously I'm done having children, even though I still haven't fully reached menopause, I guess; I don't need it anymore."

"In my opinion," Alex said, "you should just have them take the uterus at the same time. I would think that leaving it there is pointless. It may never give you any trouble, but it might. That's an opinion. You might ask someone who deals more with such things."

Brad then asked Alex if he knew anything about the oncologist and surgeon they'd been recommended to see. Alex had heard good things about both of them, and had actually worked with the surgeon a few times as he'd turned ER patients over to him, and had then checked with him for progress reports. They talked for a while longer, discussing more about the possible side effects of the treatments, should she need them, and what to expect concerning the surgeries.

After sharing more hugs, they left the house, and Wade asked Alex to drive. The emotion he'd been struggling to keep in check wasn't going to be held back much longer. In the car, he cried and raged while Alex just listened.

"My mother doesn't deserve this, Alex."

"I know. Barrett certainly didn't deserve leukemia. Obviously it's not some kind of punishment from God or something; it's just life."

"Well, it stinks."

"Yes, it does. But don't go putting the cart before the horse. We don't even know how bad it is yet. Cancer research progresses continually. The chances are much higher that she'll survive than not. The fact that she had a good mammogram a year ago suggests that it isn't likely to be too far advanced, but we'll just have to see." He took Wade's hand. "Whatever happens, little brother, we're in it together."

"Yeah," Wade said with sarcasm, "another adventure for you to carry me through."

"I'll get even one day. Besides . . . you know what they say?"

"What do they say?"

"He ain't heavy, he's my brother."

They exchanged a poignant glance and drove home in silence.

CHAPTER 9

Marilyn's surgeries went well, and Wade was grateful to have Alex around to communicate with the surgeon about the details. They had done a full mastectomy, feeling that it was the best precaution. Only a couple of the lymph nodes ended up showing any signs of cancer. They didn't consider this terribly serious, but still enough of a concern to follow up on carefully. The oncologist recommended a chemotherapy regime and some minimal radiation to help ensure that the cancer would be completely eradicated. Marilyn told the doctor she needed to think about it, and once again she wanted a lengthy conversation with Wade and Alex. This time she asked Jane to come as well. She asked about their experience with Barrett, and the quality of life through such treatments as opposed to the ability to extend life. Alex assured Marilyn that the suffering she would endure with her chemo would be minimal compared to Barrett's experience of full-body radiation and a bone marrow transplant. He also said that in spite of how horrid it had been to see Barrett suffer, he was alive today because of what he'd been through, and it had truly been worth it. Jane agreed wholeheartedly. Alex suggested to Marilyn that this was a decision she and her husband needed to pray about, and surely the Spirit would guide them to the right answer. His personal opinion was that she should follow the advice of a good oncologist who had a great deal of experience in saving lives.

Less than a week later, Wade got another call from his father. Brad wanted him to come over, this time alone. He only said that his mother was upset. Wade felt especially concerned when his father said, "I'm warning you, however. She didn't want me to call you or anyone else, so she might not be happy to see you."

"Okay," Wade drawled and hurried to his parents' home. His father met him at the door with a hug and led him into the master bedroom without any explanation. When they entered, Marilyn turned slightly to see who was there, then she settled back into a comfortable position, mostly beneath the covers, her back to the door. "What are you doing here?" she asked, sounding completely unlike herself.

"Dad called and said you were upset." Marilyn gave Brad a subtle scowl but said nothing. "What's up, Mom?"

"I've made the decision not to do the chemo or radiation. That's all."

"You're not going to tell him the rest?" Brad said. She scowled at him again. "You should know better than to think we're going to keep any secrets, my dear. And don't try to tell me that I don't have cause to share this with Wade after what you said."

"What did she say?" Wade demanded.

"Tell him; I don't care," Marilyn said. "Just . . . tell him and leave me in peace."

Brad was clearly angry as he said to Wade, "She said that with any luck the cancer would come back hard and fast, do its job, and get it over with."

Wade didn't even attempt to hold back how that made him feel. "What in the world is that supposed to mean?" he demanded, moving closer to his mother. She only squeezed her eyes closed and turned away. "What's going on, Mom? What is this sudden death wish?" Still she said nothing. He said to his father, "Is she depressed, or what? Get her some Prozac or something. This is ludicrous." And to his mother, "Don't you dare do this to me, Mom. I've lost my wife. And a fiancée too. You cannot expect me to lose my mother as well." She looked at him then, but still said nothing. "You have to do everything you can to fight this. You have to live to see Rebecca grow up. She needs her grandmother. Are you hearing me?"

Tears rose in Marilyn's eyes as she said, "Forgive me, Wade . . . but I just don't have any fight left in me." She rolled over and turned her back to him. "I need to be alone."

Brad motioned Wade toward the hall. They left the room and closed the door behind them. In the family room Wade said, "So what do you know that I don't know?"

They both sat down before Brad said, "You know that your mother teaches Relief Society once a month."

"Yes."

"Well . . . last month, before we found the cancer, she taught a lesson on eternal marriage. She was nervous about it but came home feeling like it had gone well. She told me that at the end she felt compelled to say that she'd made some stupid mistakes in her life that could have destroyed her marriage, and she was grateful for repentance and forgiveness and the gift of the Atonement. We've all heard her say it a hundred times. And we know she says it very beautifully. She said she bore testimony of the power of repentance and the need to make that a part of marriage."

"Okay," Wade said, wondering where this could be headed.

He watched his father pick up an envelope from the end table and realized that he'd taken that seat for a reason. "This came in the mail yesterday." He reached across the coffee table and handed it to Wade. The envelope had Marilyn's name and address typed on it, and nothing else on the outside except for the stamp with a local postmark. Wade felt uneasy and wary as he pulled out a one-page letter, typewritten, single-spaced. At the top it said, "Dear Sister Morrison," and at the bottom there was no name or signature.

"Anonymous?" Wade asked before he started to read.

"I can't imagine that anyone would *dare* put their name to something like that," Brad said.

Wade groaned. "This has to do with me, doesn't it."

Brad only said, "You're not going to like it."

"Well, thanks for the warning," Wade said with sarcasm and began to read. Apparently a sister in the ward, who had been present during his mother's last lesson, had been highly offended by the things she had said. She was basically saying that Marilyn had a lot of nerve standing up there and preaching about the sanctity of marriage after the things she'd done in her life. It stated that when everyone knew the truth, she was a fool to think she could get away with such hypocrisy. The letter also said that it wasn't right to allow members of the Church to believe that they could make such choices, commit such horrible sin, and still have a good marriage and receive the blessings of the temple. The woman writing the letter ended by saying that Marilyn's punishment would be up to God, but until judgment day came, she should be more careful about what she dared teach the other sisters with her hypocritical example.

Wade was so thoroughly stunned that he had to read it again to believe it was real. A particular sentence jumped out at him, and he had to read it aloud, as if that might help him believe it really was there in black and white. "'It's disgusting the way you so boldly declare your sins and boast about them to women who are trying to do what's right.' I can't believe it."

"I would add my vote to that."

Wade felt so furious he had to stand up and start pacing. "Who would do something like this? Who would have such a ridiculous distortion of the gospel to . . . to think that such an attitude had anything to do with it?"

"That's the million-dollar question," Brad said. "The problem is that we don't know *who*. And that means it could be anyone. Your mother asked me how she's ever supposed to go to church again, wondering which of the women smiling at her is secretly responsible for this. She called the bishop and asked to be released as a teacher. She told him it was because of the cancer, but last week she told me she wanted to keep teaching, that it was important to her, and that she felt sure she could manage." Brad let out a weighted sigh. "She tells me that she doesn't want to live in a world any longer where she will never be allowed to be forgiven for her past, where people can be so heartless and cruel."

Wade shook his head, contending with a rise of anger and grief. He looked again at the letter. "Boldly declared? Boasting?"

"Now, we both know that your mother has never been anything but completely humble and penitent about what happened. What this woman is saying is simply not true. There is only one aspect of this situation where your mother feels no shame—publicly or privately."

Wade felt the sickness in him heighten, and he had to sit down. "Me."

"That's right."

Wade groaned and pushed his hands through his hair. "This is my fault, isn't it?"

"By no stretch of the imagination is this your fault, Wade."

"Oh, I think I could believably stretch it that far," he said, hearing the anger in his own voice. "Until I found out the truth, no one else knew. Now everybody knows. Why? Because

I made it clear that I was not going to be ashamed of my existence, and I was not going to pretend that I didn't belong to two families."

Brad's voice was kind and tender as he said, "Wade, that decision was a good one. You talked to us about it at the time. You were concerned about the impact on your mother. She meant it when she said that it didn't matter. She was more concerned about your being able to come to terms with all of this. She figured that publicly acknowledging her past was a small price to pay for your being able to find peace over who you are. And I agreed with her. I still do."

"Well, I'm not sure I do," Wade snarled. He thought for a couple of minutes about past events, trying to piece them together before he stated firmly, "It was the wedding, wasn't it?"

"What?"

"When I married Elena. That's when everybody realized I had a brother that no one had ever met before; he was the best man. I didn't go out of my way to tell people he was my brother, but I didn't try to hide the fact, either."

"It doesn't matter, Wade."

"It *does* matter!" Wade countered. "My mother would prefer to die than have to face this kind of . . . garbage." He slapped the letter.

"She's not going to die, Wade. She's a strong woman, and she will come to terms with this. We can't go back and change what's past, and we are not going to regret the choices we've made in trying to come to terms with all of this. You just need to go in there and tell her what matters and what doesn't." He shrugged and gave a subtle smile. "For some reason she takes things better from you than from me. Maybe it's because my brain has been fried by all that time I spend in front of television sports."

Wade gave him a dubious glare, then said tenderly, "You're a good husband and a good father, and you can quote me on that."

Tears sprang to Brad's eyes, and he motioned with his hand. "Go talk to your mother."

Wade sat on the edge of his mother's bed and held her hand while he told her how much he loved and respected her, and how grateful he was for the choices she'd made in her life that had been such a good example to him. "I've said this before, Mom . . . we both know you made some bad choices, but you followed them up with some really good ones. You're a good woman and you deserve to be happy. Don't do this to yourself because of one person's distorted opinion."

"You're very sweet," she said, "and I love you, but . . . I just need some time."

"Okay," he said and kissed her before he left the room. He talked with his father a while longer before he went home.

Just inside the door Alex asked, "So, what's up . . . if you don't mind my asking?"

"The scribes and Pharisees are alive and well," Wade said, and then they sat down together so Wade could explain. Alex was almost as angry over it as Wade.

"You know," Alex said, "when my father left us—for your mother," he added as if Wade might not know how it had played out, "one of the hardest things for me was the way people on the outside judged the situation. The things some people said to my mother just pushed me over the edge. It took me twenty years to come to terms with the fact that people are human and imperfect, and we have to keep our focus on the fact that this is Christ's church. But it still ticks me off."

"Yeah, me too. But there's not much we can do about it."

Jane joined the conversation and gently reminded both of them of something she'd taught Wade once before. "Don't allow the unfair judgment of others to make you judgmental in return."

Alex let out a comical sigh and motioned toward Jane as he said to Wade, "She always does that—says something wise and perfectly Christian just when you're enjoying a good wallow in self-righteous judgment."

"I know," Wade said, going along with him. "She's always ruining our fun."

"You guys are so weird," Jane said and left the room.

Later that night Wade lay in the darkness, futilely trying to sleep. He prayed for direction in being able to help his mother get through this, and he couldn't deny needing some help himself. The circumstances surrounding his birth hadn't bothered him for quite some time. But it was bothering him now. He questioned the way he had handled it, but he had to agree with what Brad had said. Wade had made the decision to embrace both of his families and not be ashamed of his birth; it had come through much fasting and prayer and he'd known it was right. But how could he cope with his mother's present struggles?

Wade finally slept and woke the next morning with the thought that he'd overlooked something very important. Glad that it was Saturday, he called Neil right after breakfast. "Are you busy?" he asked.

"No, you need a babysitter? It's been far too long since we've spent some time with Rebecca."

"No, but thank you. I just wanted to talk to you. I can certainly bring her, even though she's not very conducive to a peaceful conversation."

"I'm sure we'll manage," Neil said. "It'll be good to see you—both of you."

As Wade pulled up in front of his father's home, he couldn't help recalling the first time he'd come here—something he hadn't thought about for a very long time. He'd recently discovered that the man who had raised him was not his biological father, and he'd come to this house in search of the man he belonged to. It had taken several minutes to gather enough courage to go to the door, and Alex had answered it. The rest was history—a history he was deeply grateful for. He could never regret being a part of both of his families, or the difficult circumstances that had made such a thing possible. But he sure regretted his mother's present situation. He just didn't know what to do about it.

Once Wade and the baby were inside, Neil and Roxanne both made a fuss over Rebecca. The child preened with comical femininity when Roxanne told her how pretty she looked, making them all laugh. She did look rather adorable, Wade concluded. The red plaid jumper with black tights and a black turtleneck looked absolutely perfect with her dark hair and rosy cheeks.

When they'd been there a few minutes Roxanne said to Rebecca, "Let's go make some cookies while Daddy and Grandpa talk, shall we?"

Rebecca ran to the kitchen with a giggle. Roxanne winked at Wade and followed after her.

"Come along," Neil said and guided Wade into the den. He closed the door, and they sat down. "It's good to see you. I know school keeps you busy."

"Yes, it does, but we should still get together more often."

"That's life. I'm glad you're here now. What can I do for you? You need money?" he asked, sounding slightly facetious, but his expression made it clear he'd write a check if Wade asked him to.

"No, Dad," Wade chuckled, "I don't need money. I hope I have a *little* more character than the kid at college who only comes to visit when he needs money."

"Oh, much more character," Neil said with a proud smile—a smile that clearly expressed the love Wade's father had for him. How could he not be grateful for that?

The silence made it evident that Wade had to get to the point. "Uh . . . I woke up this morning and realized I'd overlooked telling you something very important. I've known for a couple of weeks, and I should have told you sooner, or maybe I thought Alex would have told you, but he thought I would have told you, and . . . anyway. I'm here to tell you."

"Okay," Neil drawled.

Wade just said it. "My mother has cancer."

Neil's expression immediately betrayed that he was shocked and upset. There was a time when Neil had been very much in love with Wade's mother, even if their relationship had been completely inappropriate. That was all very much in the past. These days they interacted amicably when their paths crossed relating to any significant event in Wade's life. But Wade knew they cared about each other as friends, and this had to come as something of a shock.

"How bad is it?" Neil finally asked.

"Not too bad, actually," he said and went on to explain the diagnosis, the surgery, the low presence of cancer in the lymph nodes, and the oncologist's recommended treatments.

"So, she's going to be okay?" Neil asked and wiped a hand over both sides of his face to brush away a couple of tears.

"Relatively speaking," Wade said. "At this point she's refusing to do the chemo and radiation."

Neil looked shocked once again. "Why?" he demanded. "Why wouldn't she do everything she possibly can to extend her life?"

Wade sighed. "The answer to that is difficult," he said, his voice cracking.

Neil's expression turned intense and concerned.

"She doesn't want to live, Dad. She's depressed."

Wade went on to explain what had happened, not surprised by Neil's fury on Marilyn's behalf. He got emotional as he expressed his regret over the choices he'd made that continued to bring grief into her life, but Wade countered him by saying lightly, "Careful there, Dad. I'm the consequence, remember."

Neil sighed and gave Wade a tender gaze. "That's the paradox in all of this, you know."

"I know," Wade said, and knew what Neil was going to say, but he let him say it anyway.

"I'm grateful every day to know that you are my son."

"And I'm grateful every day to know that you're my father. Like many times before, I need your advice."

"What?" Neil asked, as if he would gladly do anything to help Wade.

"She's depressed, Dad. I don't know how to help her see perspective. There have been dozens of times when people have ridiculed her over this and she's come to terms and let it roll off. Why not this time? I've been depressed, but it was over present circumstances, and I got over it. But *you* know what it's like to *really* be depressed. That makes you an expert."

Neil made a scoffing noise. "I can't very well go over there and start chatting with her about it, now can I?"

"No," Wade said, "that likely wouldn't be a good idea. But you're still an expert."

"That was a very long time ago, and just because I survived it doesn't make me an expert."

Still, Wade prodded his father with questions about his own experiences with depression, and the things he'd learned through countless hours of intense counseling. They shared lunch and warm cookies with Roxanne and Rebecca, while Neil caught Roxanne up to speed, and she became involved in the conversation. Wade left feeling like he'd had a great education on depression, and a firm conviction that the best thing he could do for his mother was to simply let her know, as often as possible, that he loved her, that he accepted her no matter what her state of mind might be, and that he would not judge whatever she might be struggling with, because he simply couldn't see life through her eyes. He went straight to her home, stopping along the way to buy her a bouquet of mixed flowers. Rebecca's antics made her smile more than the flowers, and he stayed a long while, just spending some time with her, and not trying to convince her of anything except that he loved and admired her.

Two days later Brad called Wade to say, "Your mother's decided to get the treatments. She's still pretty upset over what happened, and I know it's bothering her much more than it should, but she has agreed that she's not going to let someone's opinion shorten her life."

Wade admitted his relief, then asked, "What made the difference?"

Brad chuckled. "Well, I know your visit the other day helped. She told me after you left that she could never regret having you in her life, and she *did* want to live to see Rebecca grow up. But the clincher was the visit she got yesterday. I think she's made a new friend."

"Who?"

"You'll never believe it."

"I'm waiting."

"Roxanne Keane stopped by with homemade bread and a basket of all kinds of those little things that women love." Wade couldn't help smiling as Brad went on. "Once your mother got over the shock of getting a visit from your father's wife, the two of them went in the bedroom for about three hours. I can only tell you I heard a lot of chattering and laughing and crying, even if I couldn't hear what they were saying. After Roxanne left, your mother told me she was going to do the treatments. Roxanne took her to her appointment this morning, and they went out to lunch."

"Unbelievable," Wade chuckled. But when he stopped to think about it, he wasn't really all that surprised. Neil had been right when he'd said it wouldn't have been appropriate for him to visit personally with Wade's mother, but he and Roxanne were the kind of people to find a way to solve a problem. And now Roxanne and his mother had apparently become friends. The miracle of forgiveness, he thought.

Later he called his father's house, and Roxanne answered the phone. "I hear you've been busy," he said to her.

"Having a marvelous time, actually," she said, as if her visits and support to Marilyn were purely selfish. "Your mother is a wonderful woman, Wade."

"Yes, I know. And so are you. Thank you. I don't know what you said to her, but it's obviously helped."

"It's a pleasure, Wade, truly."

They chatted for a few more minutes, and she told him she had a sister who had survived breast cancer, which had given Roxanne some insight and perspective. And Roxanne herself had been through some personal challenges in her life that had been mixed with depression. She was vague about the details, but it really didn't matter. She was the right person who had been willing to reach out at the right time. Roxanne then put Neil on the phone. He told Wade it had been Roxanne's idea, and she'd genuinely enjoyed her time with Marilyn.

"Apparently they have a lot in common," Neil said.

"That's not such a surprise," Wade said, but the situation was still ironic—Neil's wife being friends with the woman Neil had once had an affair with. Of course, Roxanne wasn't the woman Neil had been married to at the time of the affair, but with all that Wade had heard about Alex's mother, Ruth, he wouldn't have been at all surprised to have her reach out the same way, were she still alive. *The miracle of forgiveness.*

Wade kept in close touch with his parents while Marilyn endured the side effects of chemotherapy, and she continued to struggle with the implications of the anonymous letter she'd received. But at least she was fighting her cancer, and she was functioning for the most part.

Brad told Wade that they had seriously discussed moving to a new neighborhood where the past was not known by others, but Marilyn had insisted that she wasn't going to allow something like this to drive her from the home where she'd lived for nearly thirty years, and away from many people in the neighborhood who were truly good friends. Still, Brad mentioned to Wade that she *was* allowing the issue to keep her from hardly going out of the house. She'd stopped going to church, and rarely went anywhere at all except to get her chemotherapy and radiation, and Roxanne came to take her to those appointments at least once a week. Wade felt immensely relieved that his mother hadn't given up; he wanted her to live for a very long time.

When Wade expressed to his father once again his regret over his own choices that may have contributed to this situation, Brad said, "You can't take accountability for this, Wade. You can't. You know you did the right thing, and we have to give the matter to God. And truthfully, I think there is more to this depression than this issue alone."

"What do you mean?" Wade demanded, wondering what else might be going on.

"Wade," Brad said gently, "there are things close to her heart . . . and that's where they need to stay. I'm not saying this to arouse your curiosity or deepen your concern. I'm telling you this is more complicated than the issues you're aware of, and you need to let it go. Just . . . pray for her, and keep doing what you do. She'll be fine."

Wade struggled with subduing his curiosity *and* his concern, but he did as his father had asked. He just hoped that whatever the problems were, they would sort themselves out. And as always, he kept his mother in his prayers.

* * *

Alex was in the middle of a night shift when Becky, one of the nurses, said to him, "If you're finished with that broken leg, there's a patient in room four who requested you."

"Really?" he said.

"They asked if you were on duty, and were utterly thrilled when I said you were. They've only been here a few minutes."

She handed him the chart, and his heart quickened with dread. It said Marilyn Morrison.

"What are the symptoms?" he asked, wondering if this had something to do with her ongoing cancer treatments.

"Nausea, vomiting," she said. *That could be chemo,* he thought. "Fever." *Infection; low immune system from chemo. Maybe just the flu gone bad.* "Severe chest pain," she added, and Alex rushed to room four. *Something else is wrong; likely unrelated to cancer.* Becky came right behind him, telling him what they'd already done.

"Hello there, gorgeous," he said brightly, not wanting Marilyn to sense the depth of his concern.

"Oh, you really are here," Marilyn said with a wan smile, clearly in pain.

Alex kissed her cheek and squeezed her hand. "Hello, Brad," he said, shaking his hand quickly.

"We're glad you're here," Brad said, upset and concerned. "I've never seen her in such pain, not even in labor."

"She's been vomiting?" he asked while listening to her heart.

"Yes," Brad said, "but I think she's emptied out now."

"I'm still really nauseous," Marilyn said and moaned.

Alex said to Becky, "Get some morphine and Phenergan into her, stat."

Becky left the room. Alex asked some questions, listened to her lungs, and prodded gently in a few places on her abdomen.

Becky came back and gave Marilyn the medications while Alex wrote some things down on the chart. He then said to Becky, "On top of the CBC, get me a CMP and an ultrasound. And I want it as quickly as possible."

"I'm on it," Becky said, opening the door. He stopped her and requested a couple of other tests that came to mind. He hoped that meant he was being inspired.

He was glad that the ER was relatively quiet, which allowed him to sit with Brad and Marilyn for a few minutes. While Brad held tightly to Marilyn's hand, he said, "Is it her heart, Alex?"

"Maybe," he said, "but my hunch is no. I'm guessing it's her gall bladder, but only the tests will tell for sure. If that's what it is, then we're just going to send her right down to surgery and get it removed. It's really not a big deal." He took Marilyn's hand again, saying gently, "You should start feeling better in a few minutes, and we'll figure out what's going on."

"Thank you," she said and squeezed his hand. He could already sense her relaxing from the medication. "You were always such a good boy." Alex wondered if the morphine was taking effect and bumbling her memories. Then she added, "You don't remember, do you?"

"Remember what?" he asked and glanced at Brad, who obviously knew what she was talking about.

"You know our families lived in the same ward."

"Yes, of course," he said. That was where his father had met her, and they'd gone on to have an affair that had caused an enormous amount of grief for a great many people. But that was all in the past, and they'd long ago gotten past being upset over it.

"When you were ten, I was your Primary teacher."

Alex thought about it for a minute, then chuckled. "Oh, my. So you were." He chuckled again. "That's weird."

She just smiled and repeated with a slurred voice, "You were always such a good boy."

Alex said to Brad, "She should be pretty relaxed now, and we can hopefully get it all figured out before she has any more pain. I'll talk to you when the tests come back."

"Thank you, Alex," Brad said. "Or should I call you Dr. Keane while we're here?"

"Alex is fine," he said with a smirk and left the room.

A while later he reported to Brad that the problem was indeed Marilyn's gall bladder. He'd already spoken with a surgeon on the phone, who would be arriving at the hospital soon to take care of the matter.

"They'll be prepping her for surgery in a few minutes, and then she's officially not my patient any more, but I know this surgeon well. He'll keep me informed, and I'll check on her before I go home. If you have any questions later, feel free to call me—anytime."

"Thank you," Brad said, and Alex left to care for another patient.

His shift had nearly ended when Becky handed him the phone. "It's the OR, about Mrs. Morrison."

"This is Dr. Keane," he said into the phone. He was then told that Marilyn's gall bladder had been gangrenous. The surgery had gone well, but she was being taken to ICU for observation. Since the chemo had depleted her immune system, the surgeon was worried about a number of possible problems.

Alex got off the phone and resisted the urge to curse. He knew Marilyn's emotions were fragile right now, not to mention those of everyone who loved her. Her cancer had been coupled with some pretty intense emotional challenges, and he couldn't help being concerned.

As soon as Alex's shift ended he went to the ICU and found Brad there, looking deeply troubled. Marilyn was still unconscious following the surgery. Brad hugged Alex and thanked him for coming, then they sat and talked quietly. Alex answered his questions, hating the need to list all the possible problems that could result.

"Have you called any of the kids?" Alex asked, wondering if Wade knew about this yet.

"I didn't see any reason to wake them in the middle of the night," Brad said.

"Well, it's morning now," Alex said. "If it's okay with you, I'll tell Wade. I need to call home anyway and let Jane know I'm going to stay here a while."

"It's really not necessary for you to stay," Brad said.

"I'm just going to grab a bite to eat," he said, "and then I'll come and sit with her while you do the same. I'll stay until you get some reinforcements here."

"Thank you," Brad said and teared up.

Alex went to the nurse's station and explained his connection to the Morrisons. He gave them his pager number, and they promised to let him know if anything changed. He then found a phone to call home. Jane answered, and he explained the situation, then she took the phone to Wade.

Wade was just pulling Rebecca out of her crib when Jane appeared, handing him the phone. "It's Alex," she said, looking cautious.

"Hello," he said.

"Hey, little brother," Alex said, sounding somber. "I'll get straight to the point. Your mom is in the hospital; I told Brad I'd call you."

"What's wrong?" he demanded, setting Rebecca loose. She ran down the hall in search of Ruthie, as she always did.

"It's her gall bladder," Alex said. "It has nothing to do with the cancer. They came in the middle of my shift and asked for me. She just came out of surgery."

"Surgery?" he said. "And you're calling me *now?*"

"It was routine, Wade. Your dad didn't see any reason to wake his kids in the middle of the night."

"Is she okay?"

"For the moment."

"What is that supposed to mean?" Wade demanded, hoping Alex knew his anger wasn't directed at his brother. He could tell something wasn't right, and this conversation was taking way too long.

"She's in ICU, Wade. The gall bladder was gangrenous. They need to keep a close eye on her. I'm afraid a number of things could go wrong. Or she could be fine."

Wade forced himself to remain calm and asked, "What could go wrong, Alex? Give it to me straight."

"Hypotension can be a problem, or renal failure. And . . ."

"And?"

"And there's a very high chance of septic shock; I don't have to tell you what that means."

Wade cursed under his breath. "Okay, I'm coming. You'll stay till I get there?"

"Of course."

"Thank you, Alex."

"I'm glad I was here. I really think she'll be okay."

"I hope you're right," Wade said and ended the call.

He went to find his daughter, and Jane met him in the hall. "I'll take care of her. Get to the hospital."

"Thank you," he said and kissed her cheek. "You're an angel, as always."

CHAPTER 10

Wade found Alex and Brad sitting at his mother's bedside. Brad stood and embraced him tightly. "You okay?" Wade asked.

"A little shaken," he admitted. "Now that you're here, I'd like you to help me give her a blessing. The others won't be here for a while; they live farther away."

"It would be an honor," Wade said and moved to his mother's side, taking her hand into his. She opened her eyes and gave him a weak smile.

"She's still pretty groggy from the surgery and the pain medication," Alex said, "but she does remember being my Primary teacher."

"Really?" Wade chuckled and glanced at Alex before he looked closely into his mother's face. "You hang on, Mom. I mean it."

"It's not up to me," she said weakly.

Wade touched her face, and his voice broke. "I love you, Mom. Next to Rebecca, you're the most amazing woman in the world."

She smiled again. "You're just saying that because you haven't met the most amazing woman in the world yet."

"Not this world, anyway," Wade said, missing Elena so badly it hurt.

After the blessing, Marilyn fell asleep, and Alex went home to do the same. But he insisted that Wade call if anything changed.

While Marilyn slept, Wade left the room and called Neil to tell him what was going on. He was concerned and insisted that Wade promise to keep him informed. After Wade ended the call he couldn't deny feeling a little disconcerted over the situation related to his parentage. Since the most recently related issue had come up for his mother, the whole thing had been bothering him a lot more than he'd wanted to admit. But he pushed the uneasy feelings away and focused on the present. At least it was Saturday, he concluded, and he could stay as long as he needed to without neglecting his obligations related to his present rotation at a family practice clinic. He felt doubly relieved for a day off as he pondered the long hours he'd spent following a doctor around who was condescending toward medical students and somewhat lacking in a compassionate bedside manner. But Wade had no choice but to learn all he could from the situation, while he prayed that he would get another rotation assignment sooner rather than later.

The following day Marilyn was showing no sign of improvement. The risks were still very high, and Wade felt utterly terrified that he was going to lose his mother. His siblings came and went for brief visits, but Wade could hardly tear himself from her bedside. Brad was often there as well, taking turns with him at getting something to eat, and talking quietly with Marilyn when she was awake. After hearing the doctor's report, Wade called Alex and asked if he'd call their father, then he and Brad sat side-by-side, saying nothing. While Wade prayed silently, with all his soul, he wondered if Brad was doing the same.

The room phone rang, startling both of them. Wade stood up to answer it, noting that his mother stirred slightly from the sound.

"Wade?" Neil said.

"Yes."

"How is she?"

"The same," Wade said, feeling a deep relief just to hear Neil's voice. In spite of the closeness he felt with the father who had raised him, he couldn't deny a certain bond with his birth father. Both of these men had been great examples to him, but they were different enough in personality that they offered him different strengths.

"Are you okay?"

"Not really, but thanks for asking."

"Are you going to be there for a while?"

"I'm not going anywhere," Wade said. "Why?"

"Is Brad around?" he asked, and Wade felt taken aback.

"He's right here."

"Could I talk to him?"

"Okay," Wade said and held the phone toward Brad. It was one of those moments when his circumstances felt strange and almost unreal. Looking at the man he'd grown up believing was his father, he said, "It's for you."

"Who is it?" Brad asked.

Wade could only answer, "It's my father."

Perhaps if Wade's parents had been divorced and he'd been raised by a stepfather, the situation might not have felt so bizarre. These two men had crossed paths a number of times on Wade's behalf. They'd both come to his wedding, some birthday parties, and they had both stood in the circle when Rebecca had been blessed. And most of the time Wade hardly gave the odd circumstances a second thought. He'd become accustomed to it, and so had everybody else involved—for the most part anyway. Brad didn't look upset, or even surprised as he took the phone.

"Hello," he said, and it was followed by a lot of listening, a few "okays" and "yeses," and finally a very kind, "It's alright,

Neil. I understand. It's not a problem. I'm sure Wade will be fine with that, but it's really not necessary. Okay, we'll be here. Thank you." He handed the phone back to Wade, saying, "He wants to talk to you again."

"Yes," Wade said into the phone, resisting the urge to insist on knowing what these two men might have been talking about.

"I've asked Brad if he would mind if I came to visit your mother," Neil said, alleviating Wade's curiosity. "There are some things I've felt the need to say to her, and I can't let her go wishing I would have said them."

Wade wasn't prepared for the way tears overtook him, hard and fast. Maybe it was the way he'd said *let her go.* "Okay," he said, wiping a hand over his cheeks.

"I want you to be there; it's more appropriate that way, and . . . I just want you to be there."

"Okay," Wade said again and sniffled.

"I'm on my way in just a few minutes."

"I'll be here," Wade said and ended the call.

He turned to Brad and asked, "What isn't necessary?"

Brad sighed loudly, then he glanced toward the bed. Marilyn appeared to be asleep, but they both knew she'd been drifting in and out. Brad took Wade's arm and guided him into the hallway, where he spoke quietly. "He wants some time to talk with your mother. He wanted you there so it wouldn't appear inappropriate. I told him that wasn't necessary."

Wade just stared at him, wondering what to say, feeling more uncomfortable than he'd felt since the day he'd discovered he had none of this man's DNA.

"What's wrong?" Brad asked.

"There are just times when it's so . . . weird."

"Yes, it is . . . probably more for you than anybody else."

"I don't know about that." He looked at the floor, still feeling tense. "This has got to feel pretty weird for you."

"Wade, listen to me." He looked up as Brad went on. "Did you expect me to be upset or feel jealous because this man wants to have a conversation with my wife?"

"She *did* live with him for a couple of years," Wade said, as if Brad might not have known that. "Obviously what happened between them has got to make you uncomfortable. A child did result. She was married to you at the time."

Brad sighed again. "Maybe it's time I shared something with you that I've never said to anyone but your mother. Most people could never understand how all of this feels from my perspective. But, you know how it feels after you've gotten through a trial, and then you're actually grateful for it because you realized how much you've learned or gained?"

"Yes," Wade said. He knew the concept well, and he certainly had some personal experience with it.

"There was a day," he said, his eyes almost sparkling, "when you were about three, and your mother was pregnant with your sister, and I looked around at my life and realized that we had done it. We had taken an ugly marriage and a dysfunctional family, and we had created a home that was full of love and peace. Not perfect, by any means, but pretty darn close in my opinion—especially compared to what I'd grown up with. I remember the moment like it had happened today, Wade. There were three points that stood out very clearly. The first was the stark contrast to the moment when I'd realized your mother had left me. The hurt and anger I'd felt in that moment were beyond comprehension, and it took me a very long time to come to a place of humility and regret—and accountability. The second was that I felt this almost desperate desire to find Neil Keane and thank him."

Wade felt his eyes widen and his heart quicken. Brad chuckled and looked down as he folded his arms. Then he looked again into Wade's eyes. "Your father, Wade, taught me how to be a decent human being. He taught me the power of appreciation, and love, and mutual respect. If I had been willing to give those things to your mother to begin with, she never would have given him a second glance. Now, I would be a fool to believe that your mother doesn't have tender feelings for a man who once gave her everything I couldn't give her. It's not about the intimacy they shared, Wade. That's just a byproduct and has absolutely nothing to do with our present circumstances. He made her feel *valuable*. I made her feel *worthless*."

"That's all in the past."

"Yes, it is. Thanks to your father."

"He had an affair with your wife."

"Yes, he did. I'm not condoning their sin, Wade, and I'm not trying to justify it or excuse it. But I do understand it. You see, I learned that Satan is most powerful when he plays on unfulfilled needs. Every human being needs to feel loved and secure; they need to belong and feel connected. Why do you think kids turn to drugs, gangs, immorality? Most of them are futilely trying to meet an unfulfilled need. Of course, there will always be people who willfully commit sin, but there are many who are just wandering in those mists of darkness, struggling to fill what is missing inside." He gave a humorless chuckle. "My wife would not have started sleeping with another man if he hadn't first filled all else that was missing in her life because of my neglect and abuse."

"Abuse?" Wade echoed, certain that was an exaggeration.

"I never physically hurt her, but I said awful things to her. I had . . ." his voice cracked, and he struggled for composure, "I had knelt at an altar with her and promised to *honor* her. I didn't do that. It took me a long time to figure it out, but I was the one who broke covenants first. But hypocrisy and pride are much more difficult to define in this life than other, more visible sins."

Wade was thoughtful through a minute of silence while his father struggled again for composure. He felt compelled to say, "I understand what you're saying, and I admire your attitude more than I could ever tell you. But having an affair was not the way to solve the problem. Surely there were other options."

"Yes, there are always other options, Wade, and I would never recommend such a choice to anyone, because I've seen the consequences she has suffered up close and personal. Again, I'm not condoning her choice, but I have compassion for it."

"And you took her back," Wade said with admiration. "You're an amazing man."

Brad looked mildly angry. "Truthfully, Wade, I have a hard time with that."

"With what?"

"With your . . . thinking that I'm some kind of a hero because I took her back and forgave her. My regret for the events that preceded her leaving make me sick to even think about. She forgave *me* for *that.* But neither of us will ever forget."

"They say we should forgive *and* forget."

"Yes, they do, but I'll tell you my personal theory on that. I don't believe the human mind is really capable of *forgetting.* I think the word *forget* probably has many meanings that our language cannot define, just as the word *love* has many different types and aspects. I believe that forgetting is symbolic. When we forgive, we let go, we stop holding it against the offender. But how can we learn if we forget? If I forgot how I once treated your mother and the regret it caused me, how could I ever keep myself in check by treating her the right way now? If I forgot that she once left me for another man, how could I make certain that I never go a day without making sure that she is so loved and secure she would never have any desire or need to look elsewhere? If we *forget* how can we protect ourselves from further injury? But by forgiving, by truly giving the matter to God, we achieve a level of *emotionally* forgetting the offense. It doesn't hurt anymore; it just makes us more wise. I will never forget the joy I felt when she came back to me. How can I appreciate that joy if I can't remember the contrasting grief? Her coming back to me was a miracle, Wade; it was the parting of the Red Sea in my life. But Neil lost her that day, and I know for a fact that the loss was deep and hard for him—which is one of many reasons why I think it's good for him to have some time to talk to her. Now, if Neil were arrogant or belligerent about any of this, I would have still forgiven him, and I would have still been grateful for what I learned through these struggles, but I wouldn't likely be anxious to have him visiting with my wife. If she had an ex-husband who was difficult, I would do my best to protect her from those difficulties. But you and I have both seen much evidence of Neil's humility and penitence over this. And I'm glad he wants to come and talk to her, because I think she wants to talk to him too. Maybe if circumstances had been different, there wouldn't be the need for such a conversation, but—"

"What circumstances?"

Brad said gently, "They share a son. Don't you think they've ever just wanted to *talk* about that?"

The tears that Wade had barely been keeping back overtook him once again. Brad gave a wan smile and wiped them away, as if Wade were still a child.

"What was the third?" Wade asked.

"What?"

"You said there were three points; you only told me two."

Brad smiled. "The third was this stunning realization that in spite of all my weaknesses and stupidity, God in his tender mercy had given me an incredible gift." His smiled broadened. "He gave me you."

A little burst of surprised laughter came through Wade's tears just before Brad hugged him tightly. Wade returned the embrace, murmuring against his father's shoulder, "I'm not ready to lose her, Dad."

"Neither am I," Brad said, crying as well. "We can only hope for the best and accept God's will."

They both cried a few minutes before Brad urged Wade back into the room where they found Marilyn apparently sleeping. But when Brad took her hand, she opened her eyes and gave him a weak smile.

"How are you feeling?" he asked and kissed her brow.

"Not so bad," she said, but her weakness was evident.

The nurse came in to check her, and Brad said, "We're going out to the waiting room for a while. Do you need anything?"

"No, I'm fine. Thank you." She looked into her husband's eyes and added tenderly, "I love you, Brad. You're so good to me."

Brad smiled and kissed her hand. "It's the other way around, Marilyn. And I love you too. I'll check back a little later."

Wade walked by his father's side back to the ICU waiting area where his siblings, Lance and Sadie, were sitting. As they sat nearby, Sadie asked, "How is she?"

"The same," Brad said. "Hey, why don't I take the two of you downstairs and buy you some lunch."

"Oh no," Wade said. "Go next door to Primary Children's. The food is much better there."

"Okay, I think we'll do that," Brad said and rose to his feet.

"You go ahead," Sadie said, "I'm going to sit with Mom for a while."

Brad glanced toward Wade before he said, "Let's go eat first, and then you can. Now's not a good time."

"Why not?" Sadie asked, sounding suspicious.

Wade wondered how his father would handle this, but he didn't sound at all concerned or embarrassed as he stated matter-of-factly, "Wade's father is coming to visit her; he'll be here soon. We need to give them some time."

Wade saw Lance and Sadie exchange a startled glance, and he knew what was coming. All of his siblings had come far in accepting the fact that their family had some bizarre dynamics, but Lance and Sadie were the two who had struggled with it the most. Just his luck it would be them here at this moment. But then, maybe that wasn't a coincidence. Maybe they *needed* to be here.

"*You* are Wade's father," Sadie said.

"One of them," Brad said and chuckled. Glancing at Wade he added, "How *do* you keep track?"

Wade only shrugged and said, "Just do."

Brad turned back to face the others as Lance said, "Let me get this straight. We're going to go eat so we can give our mother some time with the man she once had an affair with?"

Brad appeared to be baffled over their concern. "Is that a problem?" he asked.

Sadie said, "I should think the problem is obvious."

Brad leaned toward her and said gently, "What do you think might take place? Are you concerned that given an hour alone together they might immediately do something wrong?" He made a scoffing noise. "If you know your mother at all, you know that the very idea is ludicrous." His eyes took in both Lance and Sadie. "I know your mother's heart, and I trust her completely. But even if I didn't, given the big picture here, I think she's more than entitled to a conversation with this man. Besides," he motioned toward Wade, "your brother will be there too. I'm certain he'll do a fine job of chaperoning his parents."

"Very funny," Wade said with light sarcasm, but they exchanged a warm smile, and Wade felt his love and admiration for this man growing deeper.

"Come on, let's go," Brad said, and they all walked toward the elevator. Wade noted that Lance and Sadie apparently had nothing more to say, and the silence became tight. Wade waited with them even though he would be staying. The ice was broken when Sadie said quietly, "I'm sorry, Wade, if I said anything to . . ."

"It's okay," he said. "I know it's all pretty weird, but hey, it's life, right?"

"Yeah, it is," Lance said, also sounding compassionate. "I must admit I never really stopped to think how it must be for you to have two fathers. You must feel torn sometimes."

"Torn, no," Wade said, and the elevator door opened to reveal Wade's *other* father.

Neil smiled at Wade as he stepped off, and they shared a common embrace. His siblings had certainly met Neil on a number of occasions, but this moment felt more significant for some reason, and Neil was well aware of their scrutiny.

Neil then turned to Brad, and Wade felt close to tears to see them not only exchange a firm handshake, but also a heartfelt embrace, and neither seemed eager to let go. Wade leaned toward Lance and Sadie, saying softly, "Now, that's what I call a miracle. How can I feel torn when both of my fathers are such incredible men?" He chuckled and added, "That's what you get for living the gospel, eh?"

Lance and Sadie said nothing, but their expressions made it clear they'd both just gained some perspective. As Brad and Neil stepped back from each other, Wade noted they both had tears in their eyes. Neil shook Brad's hand again, saying, "Thank you for allowing me a short while. It means a lot to me."

"It's not a problem," Brad said. "Take all the time you need."

Brad got onto the elevator with Lance and Sadie. Wade and Neil walked slowly toward Marilyn's room.

"How are you, son?" Neil asked.

"Worried. How are you?"

"The same. She's way too young to die; I'm praying she doesn't leave us yet."

"That would be the consensus," Wade said, his voice cracking.

At the door to her room, Neil blew out a harsh breath, and Wade could tell he was nervous. "Okay," he said firmly, "you'll hold me together, right?"

"I'll do my best," Wade said, not certain what to expect.

In the room Wade moved to his mother's bedside and took her hand, wondering if she was asleep. She immediately opened her eyes and gave him a weak smile. "Hey," he said. "You doing okay?"

"Yeah," she said and shifted in the bed.

"Are you up to company?" he asked. "There's someone here to see you."

Wade's eyes shifted to Neil as he tentatively moved to the other side of the bed. Marilyn turned to see who was there. Her surprise was evident, but something else was evident as well. Relief. She didn't have to say a word for Wade to know that she was glad for this opportunity.

"Hi there," Neil said, taking her other hand.

"Hi," she said.

"I was hoping we could talk for a few minutes. Are you up to it, or would another time be better to—"

"Now is fine," she said. Neil smiled and moved a chair close to the bed. Once he was seated he took her hand again and looked directly at her. Wade eased back and sat down himself, while something warm sprouted inside of him to see them together this way. *His parents.* Beyond a few words exchanged in a group counseling session following Wade's suicide attempt, he'd only seen them politely acknowledge each other in passing at family events.

"Marilyn," Neil said, visibly nervous, "there's something that's rolled around in my head ever since I realized that we had a son. I need to say it, and I hope that you'll hear me out."

"Of course," Marilyn said, seeming more alert than she'd been since she'd come into the ICU, even though her voice betrayed her weakness.

"Do you remember the day you left me?" he asked, and her brow furrowed, more with concern than confusion.

"Of course," she said. "It was one of the hardest days of my life. I was so worried about you."

"Yes, I know you were. I think that's what kept you from leaving long before then. You knew my inner demons, even better than I did at the time. You weren't afraid of them, but I was. And you knew that too. Somehow, you kept them at bay. But I think we both knew that you would only be able to do that for so long."

Wade saw understanding in her eyes. She knew exactly what he was talking about.

"The day you left me, Marilyn, I woke up, and you were packing. I started crying like a baby, begging you not to go. Do you remember?"

"Of course," she said again, and tears leaked from the corners of her eyes.

"For months you'd struggled with whether or not you should go back, and I think a part of me believed that you never would, that you would always stay with me, that eventually you would agree to divorce him and marry me. In the months after you left me, I wondered a thousand times why that morning was different from any other; I wondered what suddenly made you in such a hurry to abandon me. I remember so clearly what you said, because I went over it again and again, trying to figure it out. You said that it was as if something or someone had kicked you out of bed. You told me you felt that if you spent one more hour away from your family, you would lose your last chance for redemption." Neil leaned a little closer. "Do you remember?"

"I remember," she said, and more tears came. An inkling of regret tinged her voice as she added, "But if I had just stayed a few more days . . . it would have been so—"

"Different?" he finished for her, and she nodded slightly. "That's just the point, Marilyn. How many days was it before you realized you were pregnant?"

"Three," she said without hesitation.

"And if you had stayed with me for three more days, what do you suppose would have happened?"

Again Marilyn didn't hesitate; it was evident this issue had haunted her as much as it had him. "I would have divorced Brad, and I would have married you, and—"

"And it would have been all wrong," he interrupted.

Wade felt his heart jump at the implication, and he had to press a hand over his mouth to hold back a rise of emotion. He couldn't even imagine how his own life might have been if such a thing had been different.

"You can't possibly regret going back to Brad and the life you've lived since," Neil said.

"I don't," she said firmly. "But I regret the suffering you went through after I left."

"We couldn't have had it both ways."

"I know, but . . ."

"Marilyn, listen to me," he said with firm tenderness. "It took me years to figure it out, but now I know . . . and you need to know . . . if you had stayed with me, it would have been a disaster for all of us."

"But you were . . . so good to me, Neil. You were—"

"I was good to Ruth, too," he said, and Wade swallowed hard on hearing Alex's mother mentioned. "It took a lot of counseling to understand, Marilyn. But I left Ruth because I felt unworthy of her. Somewhere inside I didn't believe I had the right to be happy. If you had stayed with me, I have absolutely no doubt that I would have eventually reached the same point. I would have unconsciously sabotaged our relationship, and I would have moved on, leaving more damage and destruction behind me. It was your leaving that forced me to a point so low that I had no choice but to face my inner demons or die. You need to know how *grateful* I am that you left me that day, and I cannot begin to express how grateful I am that Wade was raised in *your* home. I know your decision to leave took a lot of courage, and I'm absolutely certain it was from that moment—when you were kicked out of bed and started packing—that both of our lives were finally put on a path to making right everything we had done wrong."

Neil sighed and added, "I know that in spite of the way we were living, that you never stopped praying—something I just felt too ashamed to do. And I truly believe, Marilyn, that your prayers were answered; you were guided to what was best for all of us. It's like the story of the woman at the well in the New Testament."

She looked curious, and he went on. "When Jesus met her there, He knew—and He told her—that she was living with a man who was not her husband." Wade's heart quickened already at the analogy. It wasn't the first time that a story from the New Testament had taught him a great deal in regard to this situation. "She was clearly not living the way she was supposed to, but Jesus didn't condemn or ridicule her. He taught her and expressed His love for her. But I think the most amazing aspect of this account is the evidence that *she* knew He was the Savior. Some might say that a person living in sin would never feel the Spirit, but I believe that this woman did, that *you* did—because the desires of your heart were to correct the mistakes and do what was best. Just like the woman at the well, God had compassion for you. He guided you back, Marilyn. You were praying, and you were listening, and we were both blessed for it."

Wade saw his mother's countenance take on a positive, peaceful quality. He didn't know if her silence was the result of weakness, of emotion, or of simply being left speechless—perhaps all three. She smiled and cried fresh tears, and Wade couldn't keep from crying himself. He felt overcome by the poignancy and irony of what his parents had gone through, the choices they'd made, and the very fact of his existence.

"There's one more thought I have on the subject," Neil said. "Soon after I discovered that you and I had a son, I was lying in bed, putting all the pieces together, thinking about that day you left, and the irony of how it had all worked out." He chuckled softly, but tears rose in his eyes. "Oh, Marilyn, I can't explain how I know, but I know; I know it beyond any doubt. You said it was like someone or something kicked you out of bed; you knew you had to leave then. I believe that, somehow, it was our son."

Wade sucked in a sharp breath the same moment Neil glanced toward him. A rush of warmth encompassed him as Neil looked again into Marilyn's eyes and added firmly, "His life had begun, and his spirit knew which home he needed to be raised in."

Marilyn laughed softly through her ongoing tears. "I believe you're right," she said, as if the idea had never occurred to her before. "It's not such a surprise." She turned to look at Wade. "He always had a strong spirit and a good heart."

Neil turned to look at Wade as well, and he felt terribly conspicuous while tears ran steadily down his face. They both smiled, then turned to look at each other in the same moment. "Yes, that's true," Neil said. "He's an amazing young man, and I am grateful beyond words to have him in my life. And I'm grateful for all that I was forced to face and to learn. But at the same time, how can I not feel sorrow for the grief I brought into your life?" Tears rolled down his cheeks. "Oh, Marilyn, I'm so sorry. I know you've forgiven me, and I know it's in the past, but I . . . just had to say it . . . one more time. I am *so* sorry."

"You're a good man, Neil," she said, squeezing his hand. She turned to look at Wade. "I always saw you in him, Neil, and I learned to remember the good, and to let go of the heartache and pain, once I knew that all was forgiven." She looked again at Neil. "I'm so glad you came. I want you to know that . . ." new tears came, "I never stopped caring; I never stopped worrying, or wondering. And I wished so many times that you could have known you had a son, that I could have somehow shared the joy he brought into my life."

Neil smiled at Wade. "He's making up for that now."

Wade saw his mother's head droop suddenly, and he rushed to her side. "You okay?" he asked, taking hold of her hand.

"Just . . . tired . . . I guess," she whispered.

"Don't you die on me now, Mom," he cried. "I need you."

Marilyn looked up at him. "I'm not going to die . . . not yet, at least."

"How do you know?" he demanded.

She smiled. "I just know. Everything is going to be okay." She turned again to Neil, barely able to keep her eyes open. "Thank you . . . for coming . . . and for everything. Thank you for being such a good father to Wade."

"Thank you for raising him to be such a fine young man," Neil said. He rose to his feet, keeping her hand in his as he bent over and pressed a tender kiss to her brow. "You take care now," he said, "and I'll see you at Rebecca's birthday party, if not sooner."

"Okay," she said, and lifted Neil's hand to her lips. He smiled at her once more and left the room.

Wade held his mother's hand for another minute, until he knew she was asleep, then he slipped into the hall and found his father there, tears streaming down his cheeks. Wade just hugged him tightly, not knowing what to say, but words didn't feel important.

When Neil remained emotional, Wade said gently, "That can't have been easy."

Neil shook his head. "I really loved her, Wade."

"Still do, apparently."

Neil showed a wan smile and wiped at his tears. "How could I not love her, Wade? She's your mother. I have not been pining for her all these years. My thoughts and feelings are not inappropriate; I hope you know that."

"Of course I know that."

"But . . . how can I not hold a place in my heart for her? We were lost and confused and went about things in all the wrong ways. You know that."

"But losing her was hard for you," Wade said tenderly.

Neil nodded and hurried away, going into a men's room down the hall. While Wade felt certain his father was having a good cry, he went out to the waiting room and sat down, feeling a little stunned. There were a couple of other people there, but they were on the far side of the room, talking quietly. Wade put his elbows on his thighs and pressed his head into his hands, while an unsettling realization came over him. Since he'd first learned the truth about his paternity, he'd gone through many degrees of shock and grief, and he'd gained much understanding; he'd done a great deal of healing. But the reality was still there, and stopping to consider it could still be tough to swallow. His very existence was the product of a great deal of sin and dysfunction. Of course, he had the blessing of knowing that, in his case, the present circumstances were as positive as they could possibly be. Neil and Roxanne were happily married, and so were Brad and Marilyn. They were all good and righteous people, who honored their covenants and lived the gospel fully. But the consequences of their past challenges and mistakes would never go away. As hard as Wade had tried to reconcile his existence with the bizarre circumstances, he had to admit that a part of him still didn't want to accept it. He found himself wondering about certain aspects of the situation that would likely be better left buried. But still, he couldn't help wondering.

CHAPTER 11

"You okay?" Wade heard, and looked up to see Neil standing beside him.

"Relatively speaking," Wade said, and Neil sat down. "How are you?"

"Oh, the same way I get every time these old wounds open up. Intellectually I can add up the facts. It's in the past, I paid the price as far as I could, and I gave it to God. But emotionally . . . it sometimes just . . . knocks me flat. Knowing how messed up I was, I don't see any other possible path that could have gotten me from there to here, and in that respect it's difficult to feel regret." He shook his head. "I guess sometimes I just . . . feel a little shaken by . . ."

"What?" Wade pressed gently when he hesitated too long.

Neil sighed loudly. "I guess I could summarize it as . . . the injustice of life. Brad, Marilyn, and I were all raised in homes that had varied types and degrees of problems, but it left us all just . . . so messed up, to put it quite frankly. Not one of us had the skill or the appropriate self worth to go about solving our problems the right way. I want to say that I wish I could go back and do it again with the knowledge I have now, but that's the big irony of life, isn't it? Even if we could go back, we'd probably do the same stupid things over again, unfortunately."

Wade listened to his father with growing emotion. He managed to keep it in check until those last few words hit a sore spot. Neil took note of his tears and asked, "Did I say something wrong?"

Wade shook his head and swallowed hard. "I want you to say whatever you have to say, Dad."

"But?" Neil said. "Come on, tell me the rest."

Wade could only shake his head. His father was on to him, but he was too choked up to speak. Neil's voice was tender as he asked, "Would it be anything like the statement you made the first time you came to dinner at my home?" Wade glanced toward him, not certain what he was referring to. Neil clarified, "It was something to the effect that you hated having your existence referred to in the same sentences with words like guilt, and regret, and sin."

Wade looked away, and his tears increased to hear his own feelings expressed so perfectly. He'd forgotten he'd said that, but it was certainly how he felt—then and now.

"Wade," Neil said, putting a hand on his shoulder, "I could never regret your existence—never!"

"I know that," he said, and wiped his face on his shirtsleeve. "And I'm the only one involved in this situation who doesn't have any accountability, you know. I didn't choose this."

"But you're suffering for it."

"I'm not suffering. I have the blessing of two families, two fathers."

"Yes, you do. And I have the blessing of *two* sons, when I'd thought I only had one. But that doesn't take away the flip side of the coin, now, does it, son?" Wade didn't comment, and Neil added, "Sometimes this whole thing feels like a tangled mass of wires, some negative and some positive, and where they cross each other, they spark and shock me with emotions that I don't know how to handle."

"Yeah," Wade said, "that about covers it."

They sat in silence for several minutes while Wade's mind wandered—and wondered. He finally turned to his father and said, "Can we just . . . pretend for a few minutes that the relationship between my parents was not something wrong and shameful and . . ."

"And what?" Neil urged.

Wade let out a sardonic chuckle. "I want to know how you met, how you fell in love. You're my *parents*. But you were both married to someone else, and it just feels wrong to even . . . imply that it might have been . . . romantic or . . . tender."

Neil sighed loudly. "Can I explain something to you?"

"Please," Wade drawled almost sarcastically, hoping his father knew he was more frustrated than angry.

"People will get nowhere in trying to understand sin or overcome it by pretending that the sin itself is ugly and distasteful. The very nature of sin is that it brings pleasure and enjoyment. It's the consequences of sin that are ugly and distasteful. Satan lures people in with the enjoyable aspects of a situation, without showing them the long-term outcome. Why would anyone be tempted to commit sin if sin itself was miserable? There was a always a degree of guilt woven through my relationship with your mother, and no one knows the consequences better than those of us who are directly affected by them. Still, I cannot romanticize what we shared because it would eradicate the price we paid. The world is full of such attitudes, and it creates a great deal of grief and havoc. I've talked all of this through with Roxanne, and even with my children. I even talked to Ruth about it before she died."

Wade felt surprised, but maybe he shouldn't have been. He knew that Neil had repaired his relationship with the wife he'd cheated on and left behind; he knew they'd become friends, and that she'd helped him through some tough times. He'd simply never thought about the possibility of them actually discussing the feelings behind the affair he'd had that surely would have hurt Ruth deeply.

Neil went on. "It's not important how we came together, Wade. It was a series of bad choices that were put away when my membership in the Church was restored after being excommunicated. But in spite of my mistakes, I believe that you were meant to come when and how you did—even if that sounds like a complete paradox." He took Wade's hand and squeezed it. "You've blessed many lives and caused a great deal of healing, just by your existence."

Wade made a dubious noise and looked down. "I don't know about that."

"You are a miracle to me, Wade. I thank God every day that he would be so merciful as to give me such a gift as you. You're like a shining star that rose out of the mire of my past life." Wade looked into his father's eyes, marveling at the intensity he saw there as he added, "You must know, Wade, that the dynamics of my relationship with your mother have nothing to do with your value as a human being. No matter how base the circumstances surrounding the conception of a child, that child is of equal value in God's eyes. He is no respecter of persons."

"I know that," Wade said. "I really do. But . . . it's still nice to know that you loved her, and she loved you. And for me . . . it means something to know that I'm the product of love, even if I'm also the product of sin. And I want you to know that I thank God every day that He led me to the truth so that I could have you in my life, and have Alex as my brother. Between the two of you, I manage to stay upright."

"We're family," Neil said.

"Yes, I know, and that's why . . ."

Brad approached with Lance and Sadie, and Wade felt a little taken aback without knowing why.

"Everything okay?" Brad asked.

"Yeah," Wade said, "she's resting. The nurses know we're out here if anything changes."

Brad said to Lance and Sadie, "Why don't the two of you go sit with your mother."

"Okay," they both said, then Lance stepped forward and held out a hand toward Neil. "I don't believe we've *officially* met, even though we've crossed paths a few times." Neil stood and shook his hand. "I'm Wade's brother, Lance, and this is our sister, Sadie."

While they shared some friendly greetings, Wade wondered what the lunch conversation might have entailed. Could it have been anything like the one Brad had shared with him just a while ago? Lance and Sadie were so genuinely kind to Neil that Wade knew something must have been said to give them a new perspective.

Wade's brother and sister left to sit with their mother, and Brad said, "Do you mind if I join you?"

"Not at all," Neil said, sitting back down.

Brad said, "Did your visit go well, then?"

"I think so," Neil said. "Thank you again."

"It's not a problem," Brad said, and in the ensuing silence, Wade wondered exactly what he was supposed to do, sitting there with both of his fathers.

Wade finally said, "She did tell me she's not going to die yet."

"Well, that's good." Brad chuckled. "Let's hope she's not just being overly optimistic." His eyes took in both Neil and Wade as he added, "If nothing else, perhaps this has given us the opportunity for some healing."

"I believe it has," Neil said, his voice cracking.

Wade wasn't sure if he preferred having this conversation stay in tense chitchat, or become deep and emotional. Either way it felt difficult. He knew it was destined for the latter when Brad added, "I wonder if it would be alright if I take this opportunity to say something."

"Of course," Neil said, but Wade could tell he felt anxious. But then, Brad looked fairly nervous as well.

Brad's nervousness became more evident as he cleared his throat and said, "This is not easy, but . . . I have to admit there's something I've always wanted to say to you."

Neil responded in a voice that was both facetious and cautious. "I'm certain there have probably been a lot of things you'd like to say to me that we wouldn't want Wade to hear."

Brad chuckled tensely. "I admit that's true. But that was a long time ago. And vice versa." Neil looked confused, and Brad clarified, "You know more than anyone how badly I treated Marilyn back then, and I'm sure you would have liked to tell me what you thought about that."

"Okay, I admit to that," Neil said lightly.

"I guess I just wanted to say that . . . while we all have many regrets . . . I'm grateful every day that Marilyn came back to me, and that she brought Wade with her. There were times when I almost felt guilty for finding so much joy in being Wade's father, when you didn't even know he existed. For that, I'm sorry."

Neil's smile was sad as he glanced at Wade. "I'm glad to have him in my life now. I'm sure it's better he was raised as he was."

Silence fell again, but neither Brad nor Neil seemed to want to leave. It occurred to Wade that they might actually want to talk without him there. Coupled with a sudden weariness of the topic, and far too much food for thought, he stood abruptly. "I need some time, if that's okay. I'll catch up with you later."

Each of his fathers stood and hugged him tightly before he hurried away. He called the house, and Jane told him that Elena's mother had picked up Rebecca and wanted to keep her overnight. He asked if Alex was there, and she told him that he'd traded a shift with another doctor, and he was working. Wade called the ER and was told that Dr. Keane was in the middle of a trauma, so he just left a message. Wade wandered around a little and discreetly peeked into the ICU waiting area to see that Brad and Neil were still there talking. He went to his mother's room and sat with Lance and Sadie while Marilyn slept. They asked how he was doing, but nothing came up about the bizarre conversations that were tumbling through Wade's head.

Less than an hour after Wade had called the ER, the phone rang in Marilyn's room, and Sadie answered it.

"Hello," he heard her say. "Is this Alex? Mom told us you took good care of her, and she got better service than she's ever gotten in an ER. Dad said it was good you'd made the diagnosis quickly, and you were quick to give her something for the pain. I just want you to know we're grateful." She listened for a moment, then said, "Well, thank you anyway. Even if you were just doing your job, you do it well. Here's Wade."

She handed him the phone. "It's your brother," she said, as if it were the most natural thing in the world.

"Hey," Wade said. "How did it go?"

"What?" Alex asked.

"The trauma."

"Oh, fine. She'll be okay."

"Saving lives again?"

"Occasionally."

"So, what damage did you undo today?"

"Just pumped about thirty sleeping pills out of this woman's stomach. She wanted to die today, but chances are she'll be glad she's alive one day up the road. What did you need? How's your mom?"

"The same," he said. "But I could really use a conversation with a doctor."

"Not a big brother?"

"Well, there're some of those around, but not the right one."

"They're in the room, and you're being diplomatic," Alex guessed.

"That's right."

"Okay, I have a dinner break coming up. How about if I meet you at the usual place in about twenty-five minutes?"

"I'll be there," Wade said. "Thank you."

Wade greeted Alex with a hug just outside the cafeteria at Primary Children's. Once they had their food and were seated across from each other, Alex asked, "So, what's up?"

"I just spent some time listening to some pretty amazing conversations. One of them was between my parents."

"Your parents?" Alex asked, clearly needing clarification.

"My mother, and our father."

Alex showed surprise. "Really? How did this come about?"

Wade went on to tell Alex the whole story, and some of the things that had been said. He couldn't hold back tears as he repeated certain aspects of their conversation that had left him so thoroughly humbled and in awe. But he just discreetly wiped his tears, really not caring what anyone around them might think. They were in a hospital where children were sick and dying; he knew well enough that people cried in here all the time.

Wade also told Alex about the conversation he'd shared with Brad, prior to Neil's visit. They both agreed that Wade had two amazing fathers, and again Wade found tears on his face. He wondered if his fear over losing his mother was spurring them on more readily.

"And," he said, "after that, *both* of my fathers sat and talked." He repeated the gist of what had been said there, while Alex's amazement grew, then Wade concluded, "They were still up there talking last I checked."

"Amazing," Alex said.

"Forgive me," a feminine voice said, and Wade turned to see familiar scrubs that were rather silly. His heart quickened unexpectedly as he looked up to see Laura's face, clearly concerned. Her hands were tucked into big front pockets.

"Hi," he said and stood up.

"I know I'm being nosy," she hurried to say, "but . . . seeing you here, I just have to ask if something's wrong with Rebecca."

It took Wade a moment to grasp her meaning. Then it dawned on him—the combination of his tears and being at this hospital. "Oh, no," Wade said, "Rebecca is fine, and you're not being nosy. I just . . . meet my brother here for lunch occasionally. He works next door, but the food is better here." He motioned toward Alex. "This is my brother."

"Hi," they both said at the same time.

Before Wade could explain to Alex who this woman was, she added, "So everything's okay?"

He knew she was questioning the fact that he'd been sitting there crying; it wasn't the first time she'd seen his tears. He just said, "My mom is in ICU; it's a little touchy. We don't know which way it will go."

"Oh, I'm sorry," she said and seemed to mean it. "Is there anything I can do?"

"Oh no, but thank you."

There was a moment that felt slightly awkward until Wade asked, "So . . . what are you doing here?" It was Sunday, and he knew she worked at a clinic that would be closed today.

"Just . . . stopped in to check on a little patient."

"You're doing rounds for the doctor?" Wade asked lightly.

"No, I just . . . wanted to see him, and see how his mother is coming along." Wade wondered if she wore the scrubs just to make the child feel more at ease. "He came into the office a couple of days ago with a high fever and fluid in his lungs."

"Pneumonia?" Wade said.

"Very good," she drawled and smiled, making his heart quicken again.

"That's not a real tough diagnosis, now is it," Wade said.

She smiled again. "Okay, well . . . I hope your mother comes through, and I'm glad Rebecca is alright." She nodded toward Alex. "It was nice meeting you." Then she hurried away.

"Who was *that?*" Alex asked while Wade watched her go. Before he could answer, Alex kicked him gently and chuckled as he added, "The future Mrs. Morrison?"

"No!" Wade insisted.

Alex chuckled again. "I haven't seen you that ga-ga since the night you introduced me to Elena. Maybe you should keep an open mind."

Wade was surprised at the chagrin in his own voice as he said, "She's married."

"Oh, I see," Alex said, clearly disappointed. Wade knew how he felt. "Who is she, anyway?"

"She works at the pediatric clinic where I take Rebecca."

"She's really married?"

"She really is," Wade said. "So, unless you want me to follow in my father's footsteps and—"

"No, I do not!" Alex said firmly, then changed the subject. But Wade didn't hear what he was saying. Something raw and deeply painful oozed out of some deep, hidden cavern within himself, suddenly demanding to be acknowledged. A tangible pain gathered in his chest and between his eyes just before new tears overtook him.

"Wade?" Alex said, startling him. "What's wrong?"

Wade looked hard at Alex then hurried from the cafeteria, knowing Alex would have to clear their table. But if he stayed another second he'd be making a complete fool of himself. He'd already been caught crying, but his tears had been quiet and discreet—and that was no longer possible. He rushed out of the hospital through the huge revolving door and quickly found a place where he could let the tears flow without being observed. He put a hand over his mouth to maintain some degree of control. While he wept, he had to ask himself the possible reasons behind such an unexpected outburst. As his silent questions received noiseless answers, his emotion increased. He had no idea if Alex could find him, and he wasn't sure he cared. But he was only there a few minutes before he felt Alex's hand on his shoulder. "What is it?" his brother asked gently.

Wade fought for composure while Alex waited patiently. He finally managed to say, "I think that . . . something just . . . rushed out of denial, and it scared the . . . heck out of me."

"You were going to swear, weren't you," Alex said lightly in an attempt to ease the mood.

"Yes, actually."

"Well, I commend you for your self-discipline." More seriously he said, "So, what is it that scared the heck out of you?"

Wade felt his stomach tighten. "Maybe I *am* following in my father's footsteps." His voice broke with new emotion. "I think I'm in love with a married woman." He chuckled without humor. "You said it yourself. I'm ga-ga when she's around. Is this some . . . sick . . . genetic thing, or something?"

"No, it is not. That's the most ridiculous thing I've ever heard."

"Then explain it to me, Alex," Wade insisted hotly. "My parents met and fell in love while they were each *married* to somebody else. It's nice to know they loved each other, but it was *wrong!* I don't have to tell you that there was a time when I *hated* them for that choice, Alex."

"But you've come to terms with that now."

"Maybe not as much as I thought I had. And now I'm doing the same thing. Without even trying, I'm doing the same thing. I have no business thinking about her the way I do, or—"

"Whoa, whoa. Hold the phone," Alex said. "Are you trying to say you've had inappropriate thoughts about this woman?"

"No! Just . . . I think about her, wonder how she's doing. I find myself *wishing* she was single."

"Okay, well . . . before you get all upset and uptight over this, you need to consider something very important. Your feelings do not determine your character, Wade. It's what you do with your feelings, how you act on them, that determines who and what you are. You have a choice to encourage the thoughts and feelings, or to fight them and pray for help to put them where they belong. And maybe there's a reason for the way you feel; maybe there's something to be learned from it. As long as you hold to your covenants, you have nothing to be feeling guilty or upset over." Alex sighed and added, "And maybe it's time you got over being gun-shy enough to put Marina behind you and start dating or something, instead of pining over a woman you can't have."

Wade heard the words, then he felt them penetrate. And he had to say, "Ouch." He sighed. "You always have a way of telling me the truth—even when it hurts." He faced Alex firmly. "You really think that's true? You think what happened with Marina has made me afraid to . . ."

"I know it's true," Alex said, not waiting for him to finish. "It's understandable, but you've been alone way too long, in my opinion."

Wade said nothing more, but he couldn't argue.

CHAPTER 12

Alex went back to work, but Wade wandered idly while his mind tried to catch up with all that he'd seen and heard and felt in the last several hours. He finally went back to his mother's room and found no family members anywhere around. A nurse told him they'd just left a few minutes earlier. Marilyn stirred at the sound of his voice, and he scooted a chair close to her bed.

"Hi," he said, taking her hand. "How're you doing?"

"I'm okay," she said. "How are you?"

"Just worried about you."

"I'll be fine," she said. "Where's Rebecca?"

"She's with her other grandma. I'm sure they're having a marvelous time."

Marilyn smiled, then her eyes became distant. "It was good to talk to your father," she said. "Perhaps we needed some . . . closure."

"Perhaps," Wade said, and couldn't resist adding, "He was out in the waiting room talking to your husband for quite some time." Her eyes widened. "Yes, I'm serious."

"Who would have dreamed . . ." She sighed, then squeezed his hand. "What your father said earlier, Wade . . . when he was here. It's true, you know. I can see that now. You were the reason I had to go back."

"Oh, I don't think it was just for me. Your going back affected a great many lives."

"I know but . . . it was your life on the line at the time."

"And yours, and both of my fathers."

"They're good men, Wade. Both of them."

"Yes, they are."

"I don't know how I could have been so blessed, with all I've done wrong in my life, to be loved by two such men. They've both had their problems, as you well know, but they've come so far."

"Yes, and so have you and I," Wade said. "And I don't think you should wonder why you are so blessed." He kissed her hand.

"I don't regret having you in my life, Wade. I know I did some stupid things, but I can't regret all that I learned and gained. I hope that doesn't make me sound like a wicked person."

"Not at all," he said. "It's like I've told you before, you made some bad choices, but you followed them up with some really good ones. And I love you for it. I know it took a lot of courage to go back, and it was hard. Dad told me that . . ." She looked confused and he chuckled. "Actually, *both* of them told me how hard that time was—for Neil when you left him, and for Brad those first months after you came home. I guess it's okay if I use their names to keep them straight."

"Of course," she said. "And yes, it was hard." She tightened her hold on his hand and smiled. "But there was a moment . . . when all the hurt and bitterness I felt toward Brad just . . . vanished. I had fallen completely out of love; sometimes I even hated him. Even though he was trying so hard, and I knew that going back to him was the right thing, I wasn't sure if I could ever really love him again. But there was a moment when it all came together for me, and I realized that I loved him more than I could ever comprehend. You were about three minutes old," she said, "and he held you in his arms and wept, and right there in the delivery room he verbally thanked God for giving him such a miracle as this beautiful son. Then he looked at me and told me how much he loved me, and he thanked me for making him the happiest man alive."

Wade wiped tears from his face and once again kissed his mother's hand. He could never tell her what that meant to him. So he just smiled at her, and she smiled back before she said, "There's something I want you to do for me."

"Okay. Anything."

"At home . . . in that old dresser in my bedroom . . . if you pull out the bottom drawer all the way, there's something underneath it. I want you to get it out, and you'll know what to do."

"Why don't you just wait until you go home, since you're not going to die."

She smiled again. "Oh, I'll be going home. But *you* need to take care of this, and I think the time is right."

"Okay," he said.

They talked a few more minutes before she fell asleep. He kissed her brow, as his father had done earlier, and hurried out to his car. The need to see whatever might be under that drawer was suddenly stronger than anything else. He checked his cell phone and found a message from Elena's mother, repeating what Jane had told him, that they were going to keep Rebecca overnight, and they'd gotten her things from Jane.

At the house, Wade opened the door with his key and went straight to his parents' bedroom. The bottom drawer slid out easily, then only resisted slightly when he removed it. And there beneath the drawer was a large, rectangular box, about three inches deep. He lifted it out and blew the dust off, then coughed. On the box was simply written, "For Wade."

He sat down on the floor, right where he was, and carefully lifted the lid. The contents were covered with a layer of tissue paper, but on the top was a white envelope with his name on it, written in his mother's hand. Inside Wade found a lengthy, handwritten letter from his mother. It began by saying that he might be reading this following her death, or at a time when she had guided him to it, and then she went on to say that he may or may not have realized by then that his life was not as it had always appeared. In tender, loving language she wrote of the circumstances surrounding his birth, including many things that he'd heard spoken just today by herself and the two men who loved her. Wade couldn't keep from crying as her love for him filtered off the pages, and he couldn't help wondering how he might have felt to read this following her death, or not knowing the truth prior to that moment. The very idea was chilling. She concluded the letter by stating his father's name and some very minimal information about him that might help Wade find him, followed by a request to give Neil the contents of the box if he could actually locate him. Wade set the letter aside and carefully folded back the tissue paper. He gasped, then laughed, then cried some more as he found a carefully organized collection of memorabilia from his own life. On one side of the box was a photo album filled with photographs that documented Wade's life from infancy, through childhood, his high school graduation, his mission. The final pictures were taken when Wade had received his bachelor's degree, and Neil was in some of them. Next to the album was a neat stack of papers that he shuffled through. He found photocopies of certificates and awards. There were several pictures he'd drawn, mostly done in crayon, spanning a number of years, as if she'd kept a piece for his father at every stage. He found one done at age six that made him laugh, and he pulled it out for another purpose, certain his father would never miss it—and he'd certainly understand. After perusing the contents carefully, he tucked the letter in his pocket, put the lid on the box and drove to his father's home, calling from his cell phone to make certain he was home.

"What's up?" Neil asked when he answered the door.

"I have something for you," he said and led the way to the family room. Neil followed and sat down on the couch beside him. Wade kept his hands over the box and asked, "So how did it go with Brad after I left?"

"Good." Neil smiled slightly. "I think we all did a lot of healing today. Even though it was hard in some ways, it was still good."

"Yeah, I know what you mean," Wade said.

"What have you got there?"

"My mother told me where to find this, and she said I would know what to do with it. There was a letter for me inside, telling me everything on the chance that she might have passed away without my knowing the truth." He gave an ironic chuckle. "I'm glad I didn't have to wait that long to discover the truth, or to discover it while I was dealing with losing her."

"Amen to that," Neil said.

"Anyway, the letter ended with a request to find you and to give this to you." He set the box on Neil's lap and removed the lid. "Souvenirs," he said proudly, and Neil gasped as he realized what he was looking at. There on top was a crayon drawing of a zebra, and in his mother's handwriting in the corner, it said, 'Wade, age three.'

Neil lifted that paper, then another, and another. He gasped again as it seemed to sink in more fully. Then Wade opened the cover of the photo album and heard an emotional noise come out of his father's mouth as he saw baby pictures of Wade.

"Apparently she got double prints," Wade said.

"I can't believe it," Neil muttered and turned the page. He struggled with tears as they looked through the album together, and Wade talked about memories triggered by many of the pictures.

After they had looked through everything in the box, Neil smiled and said, "When I got home this afternoon, after talking with your mother and Brad, I told Roxanne that one of the difficult consequences of all of this for me was the fact that I had not been able to see you grow up. Now I feel like I didn't miss quite so much." He sighed. "Tell her thank you . . . for me."

"Tell her yourself," Wade said. "You'll see her at Rebecca's birthday party, remember?"

"I hope so," Neil said.

The following day Wade wasn't terribly surprised to learn that his mother had made a miraculous turnaround; she was going to be fine. He couldn't help wondering if there had been some greater purpose in this brief but traumatic illness. Given the healing that had taken place, for himself as well as his parents, he couldn't possibly chalk it up to coincidence. A few days later she came home from the hospital, and he took Rebecca to see her. They had a marvelous visit and he couldn't help noticing that she didn't seem depressed, even though she was still coping with chemo and radiation. He hoped that she was finding peace with whatever might have been weighing on her.

The ongoing treatments were difficult for Marilyn. She felt quite ill off and on, but mostly weak and tired. When the treatments were finally completed, the family had a big party, and he could see that she was doing well emotionally, and with time she would physically recover from the strain of the treatments. But she'd not gone to church since the arrival of that letter, and it made Wade sick at heart. Talking to his brother about it, Alex reminded Wade of a time when Jane had struggled with her faith when they had believed Barrett would die.

"But in her heart, Jane's testimony was always there. And eventually she came back to it. Your mother knows the Church is true, and she knows Jesus is the Christ. Be patient with her. I really think that eventually her desire to be an active part of that will override her hurt."

"I hope you're right," Wade said and just kept praying for her.

* * *

Wade found Barrett sitting on his bed—reading from the Book of Mormon. *What an amazing kid,* Wade thought.

"Hey there, buddy," Wade said, and Barrett smiled as he set the book aside. "I haven't got to see you much lately."

"You needed to be with your mom," Barrett said as if he completely understood. "And Dad told me how hard it is to get through rotations."

"Yes, it sure is," Wade said and sat on the edge of the bed. "But I've missed you. What have you been up to?"

Barrett talked for a while about what he'd been doing with his friends, the books he'd been reading, since he loved to read, and he told Wade about a funny video he'd watched at a neighbor's house.

"I have something for you," Wade said with exaggerated pride as he lifted the piece of paper he'd been keeping discreetly out of Barrett's view since he'd come into the room. Showing Barrett only the back that was blank, he said with aplomb, "I found it in a box of stuff that my mom kept from when I was a kid. And I just knew I had to give this to you, but you have to promise you'll always take good care of it. It's *very* old. I drew it when I was six; that makes it more than twenty years old."

"Wow," Barrett said. "That *is* old."

Wade chuckled and turned the paper around, saying exuberantly, "Ta dah!"

"It's Batman!" Barrett said, then he laughed so hard he nearly fell off the bed.

"My artwork isn't *that* bad," Wade said.

"I'm not laughing over *that,*" Barrett said, but he kept laughing too much to explain. He finally managed to say, "It's pretty good for being six. But you really *did* like Batman when you were a kid."

"Still do," Wade said.

"That is so awesome!" Barrett said, wearing a big grin and holding the paper up to look at it closely. "I think I need to frame it like you framed the one I gave you."

"I'll even buy the frame," Wade said. "I think giving each other pictures of Batman kind of makes us like . . . blood brothers, or something."

Barrett gave him one of those humorously disgusted looks he was famous for. "No, I think that was the bone marrow. Duh."

Wade just laughed and hugged him.

* * *

Wade did his best to stay busy enough that he didn't have to think about the truth Alex had confronted him with. But he was once again struck with the passing of time when he realized he'd been living with Jane and Alex for more than two years, and his daughter's birthday was approaching. Rebecca was talking now, saying new words every day, and her hair had filled in thick and dark, so much like her mother's. She loved loud music in the car, playing with Jane's shoes, and her favorite movie was *Charlie and the Chocolate Factory.* Her favorite things to say were a fair imitation of Willy Wonka saying, "Ooh," and "Know why? Know why?" She was adorable, and he loved her more than life, but she needed a mother. He felt sick to death of being alone, but horribly reluctant to trust his instincts enough to venture into the dating world again. As always, when approaching any disconcerting detail of his life, Wade found the opportunity to talk it through with Alex. He talked about the fear he was feeling to be able to discern whether a person was what they appeared to be, or if they would hold up to the integrity they might claim to have. Alex reminded him that he not only had some practical experience on the matter, but he had the gift of the Holy Ghost to guide him.

"You do your best to live close to the Spirit. It will guide you. But you're never going to find a wife by sitting around being scared."

They talked for a long while about the concerns he had from his own experience—and that of other single adults he'd come in contact with. He couldn't deny that there were some unique challenges related to dating in the twenty-first century. He felt sure there were struggles unique to single adults who had been married previously, but he knew that youth were also faced with equivalent challenges. The world was filled with evil influences that couldn't help but intrude into the course of trying to find a suitable mate. With images of casual sex and a complete lack of morals coming from all sides, it could be a constant struggle to keep righteous standards clear and strong—which was the very reason that standards were perhaps more important than they had ever been.

Combined with his own negative experience, Wade also admitted that he was almost afraid to even put himself into the dating scene at all when he'd heard so many horror stories. He knew there had to be good people out there, searching the same way he was searching, but he felt afraid of being able to navigate his way through the maze in order to find the right person.

When Wade mentioned that he feared dating or marrying someone with baggage, Alex made an interesting point. "In my opinion," he said, "there's not likely any human being who doesn't have baggage and/or dysfunction in their life. The trick isn't finding someone without those things; the trick is finding someone who knows how to deal effectively with overcoming those things. Do they look at their weaknesses realistically, strive to address them and overcome them? I would be most concerned about a person's level of self-awareness and her problem-solving and communication skills—and of course those things need to coincide with living the standards of the gospel."

Alex went on to say that Wade should pray for discernment, pay attention to his feelings, and use his brain. Wade couldn't deny that he was right, but he had to admit feeling concerned. Still, he had to say, "I know I just need to get over my fears and move forward. It's time; I know it is."

"So, it's back to wife shopping, eh?" Alex asked.

"Looks that way."

Wade pondered his need to move forward over the next few days. He was distracted from the issue when his mother called to say, "Do you have plans Sunday?"

"Nothing unusual, why?"

"I was wondering if you and Rebecca might be willing to come to church with me."

Wade felt taken aback. "We'd love to, but . . . may I ask why? Is this a special occasion?"

"The occasion is that I haven't been to church for a very long time, Wade. I've realized that . . . well . . . I guess one bad apple doesn't spoil the whole tree. There are a lot of good people here who have always been kind and accepting of me, and I need to keep perspective. I know I need to go back to church, and I know I need to find a way to come to terms with the reasons that have kept me away. I'm not quite sure yet how I'm going to do that, but . . . when I told your father I wanted to go but felt nervous, he suggested there might be strength in numbers. Whether you like it or not, you're the child who is closest to these issues for me, and . . ." she started to cry, "and you're one of my best friends, and . . . I would just like to have you there."

"It would be an honor, Mother," he said, "and for the record, I *do* like it."

"Like what?"

"Being the child who is closest to the issue. I am grateful for the outcome—most of the time anyway. But there are few people who understand those mixed emotions the way you do."

She sighed deeply. "You are such a joy to me, Wade."

"And the other way around, Mother. I'll see you Sunday."

When the day came, Wade picked Marilyn and Brad up at the house and drove the short distance to the building where they attended church. His mother was visibly nervous as they entered the chapel, and he felt certain she was wondering which person in the room had been the one to send that judgmental, condemning letter. But Marilyn was here, and he knew it had taken great courage. He felt proud of her.

They sat on one of the side benches, and he quickly spread out a coloring book and crayons on the bench to keep Rebecca entertained. A Ziploc bag full of Cheerios didn't hurt either.

As the meeting began, Wade couldn't help wondering if the woman who had written such disparaging things to his mother might be present. He actually felt angry, and had to remind himself of something that Jane had said more than once, that it was important not to judge when others were judgmental. He prayed that the anger could be lifted, and he found himself wondering what kind of pain or heartache a person might be suffering that would allow her to be so easily offended by something that made her uncomfortable. Obviously it was impossible for him or any other human being to know the heart of a person, even if that person's behavior might be appalling. He recalled hearing once that charity was the ability to separate a person from his or her actions. In the middle of the sacrament song he leaned over and whispered his thoughts to his mother. She smiled at him with tears in her eyes, then she squeezed his hand tightly.

As the testimony portion of the meeting began, Wade was surprised when his mother was the second person to stand and walk to the pulpit. He exchanged a glance with his father, who obviously hadn't expected this either.

Marilyn began by expressing appreciation for the meals that had been brought into her home throughout the course of her cancer treatments, and during her time in the hospital. She then said that spending some time in ICU had a way of making a person ponder what was truly important in life. She expressed gratitude for the Atonement, and for her personal relationship with the Savior that had nothing to do with anyone or anything else in her life. She stated that her reasons for attending Church meetings and living the gospel were because of that relationship and commitment to keeping His commandments, that she'd gotten off track a bit in that regard but was determined to make some positive changes.

Marilyn then became too emotional to speak for about half a minute, but when she did, her voice was firm with conviction even though her tears continued. "I need to say . . ." She pressed a tissue beneath her nose, then continued. "How very grateful I am for the healing power of repentance and forgiveness. I am grateful for the Savior's example in His acceptance and compassion for the sinners, even though He could never condone the sin. I am grateful for the depth of what He taught when He invited any person without sin to cast a stone at the woman taken in adultery."

Wade's heart began to pound as he recalled this analogy coming up before in their lives; it had been a huge step in his own healing, and he waited anxiously to hear what else she would say, while the chapel seemed unusually still.

"Today we don't cast stones, we use words. But it still amounts to the same thing. I just want to say how grateful I am to all of you who have accepted and loved me in spite of my past mistakes. You will never know how much your compassion means when the consequences of my past actions will always be a part of my life. So . . . thank you."

Wade inhaled deeply, drawing her words into his spirit. She had surely been inspired. Without saying anything negative at all, she had put the situation of one person's negative judgment neatly into perspective.

Marilyn's eyes shifted toward him and his father as she added, "I'm grateful to have my son Wade here with us today. I want him to know that I *do* have a testimony of the gospel, and of the healing power of the Atonement. Without it I would not be here. I want him to know how much I love him, and that no mother could ask for a finer son. And I'm grateful to my good husband for standing by me unquestionably through many difficulties. He's a fine man and I love him dearly."

Marilyn then concluded her testimony and returned to her seat between Brad and Wade. Brad put an arm around her shoulders and kissed her cheek, while Wade took her hand and squeezed it tightly before he pressed it to his lips. She looked toward him, and he mouthed silently, *I love you, Mom.* She smiled and silently told him that she loved him too.

When sacrament meeting was over, Marilyn said that she needed to go home; she was just too tired to sit through the other meetings. He knew she was still struggling with the long-term effects of her cancer treatments, but he suspected her time at the pulpit had been emotionally draining. Before they got out of the chapel, however, seven different people stopped to tell her how much they appreciated her testimony, and how they loved her. One woman even said that Marilyn was an inspiration to her.

Later that day, Wade drove home with Rebecca, pondering the miracle of this day. It got better late that evening when Brad called to tell him that the bishop had called Marilyn with an anonymous message from a sister in the ward, apologizing for her misjudgment and unkindness. Marilyn was glad not to know who the offender was; it didn't matter. She was just grateful to have it resolved and to feel that she could press forward without this dark cloud hanging over her.

The very next day Wade forced himself to sit down at the computer. He decided that the Internet was the easiest approach to the dating challenge, considering his time and personal issues. But not a single woman's profile intrigued him enough to want to write even one lousy email. Again he talked his feelings through with Alex, wondering if it was fear holding him back. Alex offered to give him a blessing, and Neil came over to help him. In it he was told that someone special had been set aside for him, and it was time for him to move forward with faith until the time came when he would know beyond any doubt she was the right woman to entrust his heart to, as well as the raising of his children. Wade felt better after that, and then he focused on celebrating Rebecca's second birthday, which included a family excursion to the zoo. Barrett loved the zoo.

He felt decidedly reluctant to take Rebecca in for her two-year checkup. The very problem was that he wanted to see Laura, but the feelings associated with his desire were difficult to acknowledge—or to know what to do with. He'd prayed almost daily for his feelings to be tempered, but truthfully nothing had changed. If anything, he'd only thought about her more than ever, and he found it difficult to weigh such thoughts and feelings with the choices his father had made. Perhaps he was being given a lesson in empathy, but he didn't even have to wonder if he would ever make the same choices. He just wouldn't. Few people knew the heartache of such things more than he did. He simply couldn't do it. He concluded that if he didn't get a handle on the way he felt soon, he was just going to have to start taking Rebecca to a different clinic. And with any luck he'd never see Laura again.

When it came time for Rebecca's appointment, the child ended up in one of those moods that let Wade know why they called this stage the terrible twos. Seeing Laura made his heart quicken, but Rebecca's antics made it impossible to pay much attention, which he considered a blessing. He reminded himself that she made a great prototype for what he was looking for. He went home with a fresh determination to get serious about easing this ongoing loneliness, but it was two days later before he got to the computer.

Going onto the site that he liked best, he first went to where new profiles were posted. And what he saw made his heart pound and his mouth go dry.

"It can't be," he said to the empty room, glad no one was around. He let out a noise of disbelief. He read it. Looked at it. Read it again. Relief washed over him as he realized his feelings hadn't been off base or wrong at all. He'd just been too stupid to pay attention to what they were really trying to tell him. Still, he couldn't believe it. He stood up and paced the room while he attempted to accept the change of circumstances in his head. It was a *miracle*. Or was it? He reminded himself that perhaps it was too good to be true, and he needed to be careful.

Again he had to look closely, certain it was just an uncanny look-alike, or that maybe he hadn't read the profile closely enough. But there it was. Only her first name was there. Laura. Laura, who worked at a pediatric clinic because she loved children. In the section where she'd written what she was looking for in a man, it said she wanted someone who was genuinely strong in the gospel, not just pretending to be to impress a woman. She wanted someone who wasn't afraid of the words dysfunctional and emotional, and who was not ashamed to cry. She was looking for someone who liked to talk and read, and she hated television sports. On her hobbies it said that she loved to sew, and she enjoyed all kinds of dancing; the waltz and the swing were her favorites, even though she'd not done either for a very long time.

Wade felt absolutely ecstatic and at the same time scared out of his mind. He couldn't deny that he'd been intrigued with her from their very first—and extremely memorable—encounter. But she'd been married! How long had she *not* been married and he'd never bothered to take notice? He read her profile again and felt like she was talking to him, then he told himself that he could very well just be fantasizing or delusional. Surely it *was* too good to be true. Struggling with this inner battle, he printed out the profile and took it to Alex. He found his brother in Barrett's room, reading with his son. Wade sat down and joined them, then he hugged his nephew tightly before he was tucked into bed.

Wade and Alex went down the hall to the little TV room where they could be alone. While Alex was picking up toys, Wade said, "Have you ever had a moment in your life that felt like the parting of the Red Sea?"

Alex looked thoughtful while he established some manner of order, then he said, "Yes, I suppose I have."

"Like what?" Wade asked.

"Oh, that's easy. Of course, if a moment is like the parting of the Red Sea, it certainly should be memorable."

"Well . . . yeah." They both sat down.

Alex smiled. "When Jane came out of that coma," Alex said. "I'd spent so many weeks holding her hand while it seemed like I would never see her come back to life and then . . . suddenly, she was there. Awake, alive, real. It was incredible."

Wade smiled and Alex went on. "I bet you could guess the other one."

"When *Barrett* came back to life," Wade said.

"That's right. There were many miracles that preceded and followed that moment, but . . ." His voice cracked. "When he looked up at me and spoke for the first time in months . . ."

"What did he say?"

Alex chuckled. "He asked if we could go to the zoo."

"Of course." Wade chuckled as well.

"Is there a point to this conversation?" Alex asked, putting his bare feet up on the coffee table.

"My father . . . Brad . . . he told me the day my mother came back to him . . . it was like the Red Sea parting. I've thought about that, and . . . I guess it would be a moment when everything that felt wrong suddenly became right, but at the same time, it must have been frightening for those people. Brad said they had many challenges after that, but it was still a miracle."

"Okay . . . yeah," Alex said, as if he sensed that Wade wasn't getting to the point.

"I just had one of those moments," Wade said, and his heart quickened just to think of what he'd discovered.

"Really?" Alex's intrigue was evident.

Wade just went ahead and said it. "She's not married, after all."

Alex looked disoriented, then astonished. "The nurse? The one you were ga-ga over?"

"That's the one."

Alex chuckled. "How do you know?" Wade handed the paper to his brother, and Alex started to read. "Wow," he said and chuckled again. "You know . . . she just didn't . . . *act* married. I mean people put off vibes, and she seemed . . . available. I think she was acting a little ga-ga over you too."

"Really?" Wade asked, wishing he hadn't sounded so overtly eager.

"Really," Alex said and smiled.

"Am I deluding myself to think that everything she's looking for could be me?" Wade asked.

"Only on one count," Alex said.

"What?"

"She likes to dance." He smiled and lifted his brows. "You need dance lessons, buddy."

"Okay," Wade said, "I can agree to that."

"Ooh, you must be in love. You've always resisted dance lessons before."

"I *am* in love," Wade said matter-of-factly.

Alex looked at him askance and said, "So what made you think she was married?"

"The first time I saw her, she was wearing a wedding ring. Since then I don't think I even bothered to notice; I just took for granted that she was married. But . . . she's incredible, Alex. She's given Rebecca all of her shots, kept track of her growth, and cuddled her when she fussed." Wade felt compelled to add, "And she's seen me cry."

"Really?"

"The first time I went in . . . she asked if Rebecca's mother was working; she said not many dads came in alone for checkups. When I told her what had happened, I started to cry, but I was too depressed to be embarrassed. And she cried too. And then . . . I remember just . . . watching her. It was like . . .

she held Rebecca a little closer like she could . . ." Wade's voice cracked. "Like she could just . . . give her even a little bit of a woman's love. She's been like that ever since. Every visit. She remembers us, asks how I'm doing, fusses over the baby like we were family."

"Wow," Alex said again. Then he laughed. "So, what are you going to do about it?"

"I don't know," he said, feeling decidedly nervous. "Truthfully, I feel scared out of my mind. After what happened with Marina . . . how can I know if my feelings are valid? Or if my instincts are just totally screwed up?"

"I think that nobody can answer those questions but you, little brother," Alex said.

Throughout the next day and a half Wade pondered the situation concerning Laura, and he even prayed about it, not wanting to do something stupid. He feared blowing it with a woman who seemed so amazing, but he was more afraid of finding out that perhaps she wasn't as amazing as she appeared.

At breakfast he was helping Rebecca with her scrambled eggs when Jane asked, "What's on your mind? You're like a million miles away."

"I want to ask a woman to go out with me," he said, wondering if it might be good to get a female opinion, since Alex was at work. "But I have to admit I have some trust issues after what happened with Marina."

"I would assume that most of the single people in your age group would have trust issues."

"That's likely. So what should I do about it?"

"Is this the girl you found on the Internet?" she asked. "The same one who works for Rebecca's doctor?"

"Your husband tells you everything, doesn't he," Wade said lightly.

"If there's a reason for him to keep something in confidence, I'm sure that he does."

"Yes, I know you're right. It's okay. Yes, that's the one."

"So . . . write her a letter. Isn't that the advantage of this Internet thing? I mean . . . she doesn't have to know your name or anything, right?"

"I suppose not. I'm registered on the site under a handle, no picture."

"What is it?"

"Like my email address. Barrett's uncle."

"I like it," she said and laughed. "Okay, so write her a letter. Get to know her a little that way, and then go from there." Her face lit up, and she added, "Hey, this is like that movie."

"What movie?" he asked and could see her struggling to remember.

"Tom Hanks. Meg Ryan." She snapped her fingers. "She owned a bookstore and he put her out of business while they were writing to each other on the Internet and—"

"*You've Got Mail?*" he asked.

"That's it. In the movie he figured out it was her and started seeing her while he was writing to her, and she didn't know it was the same man." Jane smiled mischievously. "It was very romantic."

"Okay, but . . . couldn't that be construed as dishonest?"

"It doesn't have to be. Just be careful what you say and how you say it, and . . . well . . . you don't have to be writing and go out with her at the same time. Just . . . start writing and see what happens."

"Okay, I think I will," he said.

"And make sure you save the letters," Jane said and smirked. "Someday you may want to show them to your grandchildren."

"Yeah, we'll see," Wade said dubiously.

Throughout the day Wade contemplated simply taking the step of writing a letter to this woman. After he got home and spent some time with Rebecca, he took her with him to the study and worked on composing a letter. He went over it carefully, and in spite of several interruptions from his daughter, he felt good about the finished draft. He wanted to make Laura laugh and leave her intrigued, but he wanted to be completely honest without sounding too corny. He hoped it would work.

Dear Laura,
First of all let me say that I'm not very good at this kind of thing. I thought I had it figured out once, but a bad experience has left me leery. However, I was impressed with what I read about you, and I would very much like to get to know you better. For the time being I would prefer to remain anonymous for reasons that are difficult to explain, but I hope you'll understand. If a time comes when you find out who I really am, I hope you will be forgiving of my cowardice. I want to ask you a hundred questions, but one is probably good for starters. Which character on Sesame Street do you relate to the most, and why? If you have any desire to continue this conversation, I would love to hear from you.
Most sincerely,
Barrett's Uncle

Taking a deep breath he clicked the Send icon. Then he tried to forget about it and kept busy. He did some studying, cleaned up Rebecca's room, and washed the dinner dishes. But for all his efforts, Laura's face was foremost in his mind.

CHAPTER 13

After he had bathed Rebecca and put her to bed, Wade went to the computer, telling himself it was ridiculous to think he'd get a response so soon. But there it was. An email from Laura. His heart quickened to the point of being annoying as he waited for the file to open.

Dear Barrett's Uncle,
I enjoyed your letter very much. So, yes, I would like to continue this conversation. Your letter felt more honest and unweird (is that a word?) than anything I've received in a long time. I can respect anonymous, but you've got to be fair and tell me more about yourself. In answer to your question, it is without a doubt Cookie Monster who is most like me. Why? Because he eats everything in sight, but he has so much fun doing it. I'm working on the fun part. So, I have TWO questions for you. Why do you think Oscar the Grouch is so grouchy? And who is Barrett?
Until next time,
Laura

Wade laughed aloud, deciding he liked this as he hurried to write a response.

Dear Laura,

If *unweird* isn't in the dictionary, it should be. Maybe we could put together a petition or something. So you want to know more about me. Well, I'm a pretty boring person. I'm going to school at the U, and I'm twenty-eight years old. You're going to have to guess if I'm still in school because I'm a slow learner, or because I'm pursuing a profession that takes a lot of years in school. I was married for about a year, but I'd rather not get into that right now. I grew up in this area and served a mission in Africa. I was the only male in our household who didn't appreciate sports. I preferred to read a book, so I grew up the oddball of the family, but they're a good family. I'm not feeling photogenic so I'm not sending you a picture of myself just yet, but I will tell you that I'm six foot two, with brown hair and hazel eyes. By the way, I think you're beautiful. I printed your picture off the Internet and hung it on my bedroom mirror. It makes me want to be a better man. Does that sound corny? Now, to answer your questions. Oscar is clearly grouchy because he's rattling around in that garbage can, wondering what to do with his life when there's no Mrs. Grouch. If you think there's some hidden metaphorical meaning in my answer, you're probably right. Barrett is my nephew.
Waiting with breathless anticipation,
Barrett's Uncle

Wade sent the letter and went to bed, feeling like a man in love. And not feeling guilty for it.

The morning was crazy, and he didn't have a chance to check his email. He didn't get to the computer until late evening, but there it was.

Dear Barrett's Uncle,
So Barrett is your nephew. Ask a stupid question and you'll get a stupid answer. Let me rephrase that. Is Barrett your only nephew, or is there some reason that you would choose his connection to you as your email handle? I've never heard the name before as a first name, but I like it. I can't help being curious.

She went on with a fairly lengthy letter, analyzing his theory on Oscar the Grouch, and sharing details of her hobbies of sewing and making useless things that create clutter. She also talked about collecting things that collected dust. She talked about loving ice cream and rain and autumn leaves. She wrote that she would bet he was more the type to be committed to a grueling education, as opposed to being a slow learner, and she ended by saying that she would go to sleep imagining his hazel eyes. She signed the letter, *Tenderly, Laura.*

Wade read her letter three times before he wrote back, admitting right off,

I love reading your letters, Laura. I think if Oscar the Grouch could read your letters, he would be a little less grouchy, but I don't know his email address. I love hearing the details of your life and wish that I could just walk into it and stay there, but that surely sounds presumptuous and forward. So consider such statements a fantasy, not a proposal. You asked about Barrett, and I am only too happy to tell you about him. I have many nieces and nephews, but he is absolutely one of my favorite people. He's smart and funny and quite good-looking. I appreciate your questions about my connection to Barrett, because declaring myself as his uncle has deep meaning for me. However, explaining that meaning to you is getting pretty personal. So, I may be remaining anonymous for the time being, but I'm going to tell you something that I don't spread around easily. I don't like people knowing, mostly because they tend to make a big deal out of it. Barrett and I share a special bond because a few years ago he needed a transplant in order to survive. I was a perfect match. So there's your answer. There's a little of me inside Barrett, and watching him come back to life left a whole lot of Barrett in my heart. You're right that it's not a common name. Barrett is his father's middle name, because he was named after an ancestor, so Barrett was actually the family surname for generations.

Wade went on to tell her some funny stories about Barrett, avoiding anything specific about the leukemia, since Laura knew that Rebecca's father had a nephew who had survived the disease. He talked about his theories on life and love and the power of finding peace with yourself. She wrote back and expounded on his theories in a way that made him feel as if she knew him inside and out. Letters went back and forth for several days, at least one a day, each one becoming longer, more deep and personal, while Wade managed to avoid any information that might give her a clue to the fact that she already knew him.

She wrote cryptically of a recent event in her life that she was struggling with a great deal. She talked in generalities about grief and trauma, but she admitted that she wasn't ready to share the details yet of whatever had happened. He found himself regularly praying for her, that she could find peace over the struggles in her life.

Wade was surprised to get a call from Marina, and even more surprised that she went from asking how he was doing to asking if they could go out.

"Why?" he asked. "And don't say for old-time's sake."

"I miss you, Wade," she said, and he resisted the urge to say something horribly rude. "Maybe I made a mistake."

"Maybe you did," he said, "but it's too late."

"What do you mean?" she sounded panicked.

"I'm seeing someone," he said and figured that having Laura's picture on his bedroom mirror and making visits to the doctor's office could fall under that category.

"I see," she said. "Is it serious then?"

"It could get that way," he said.

"Okay, well . . . if it doesn't work out, then . . . call me and—"

"Marina," he interrupted, "what we had is gone. What happened was tough for both of us, but once I came up for air I knew it was the best thing. We are just not compatible. And that's okay. It's good to hear from you, and I wish you all the best, but I think it's better if we just keep this the way it is."

She got off the phone quickly, and he knew she was crying. But it only took him a minute to remind himself that he absolutely knew what he'd told her was true. It was time to move on.

When Wade told Jane and Alex he was ready for some serious dance lessons, they made arrangements to use the church cultural hall.

"So," Alex said when they were ready to begin, "she said she loves to dance; the swing and the waltz are her favorites. Is that right?"

"That's right."

"Well, we're starting with the hardest first. The swing, in my opinion, is more relaxed and spontaneous, while the waltz is more of an art form."

"Maybe this is a bad idea," Wade said.

Alex chuckled. "Oh, you're not getting out of this, little brother. Dancing is to life like . . . like," he snapped his fingers as he struggled for an adequate metaphor, "like . . . frosting is to cake. So pay attention."

Wade smirked and had to bite his lip to keep from chuckling. His brother obviously took this dancing stuff very seriously. "Okay, I'm listening."

"Wade," Jane said, moving between him and Alex, "if a woman likes to dance, and you make the effort to indulge her in that, she'll notice—trust me."

"Give him the brief version of Dance Theory 101," Alex said.

Jane smiled at Wade then began, "Dancing is as old as time, Wade. It's a silent expression of emotion. There are as many kinds of dance as there are emotions. For ages, people have danced before going to battle, in celebration and victory, and for the purpose of wooing."

"Wooing?" Wade echoed as if it were a foreign language.

"Yes, wooing," she said and laughed. She turned to Alex, "That really is a silly word."

"Just get on with it," Alex said and laughed as well.

"The swing is fun and energetic; it's a dance of joy and laughter. The tango is passion. The rumba is flirtation. And the waltz is love, Wade. It's metaphorical of the relationship between a man and a woman. The man leads and has control, but it doesn't work if the woman isn't trusting, allowing herself to be led. She's not going to let him lead if he isn't trustworthy, and he can't lead if she's defensive or resisting. Is this making any sense?"

"Yes, actually," Wade said, a little in awe that it could actually be so deep. But he felt more intrigued as Alex took over.

"With both of these dances you mirror each other, so a man does everything exactly opposite of a woman. So you're going to stand behind me while I dance with Jane, and you can imitate my movements."

"Okay," Wade said dubiously. Alex held up his left hand and Wade did the same. Jane put her right hand into Alex's, and put her left on his shoulder. Alex counted out the steps and took them slowly while Wade tried to mimic him, feeling horribly awkward. After a minute he said, "Just . . . do it for a few minutes and let me watch, so I know what I'm trying to do."

"Fine," Alex said lightly and moved toward the CD player, motioning for Wade to join him. He showed him which track to play, then said quietly, "You know what's the greatest thing about ballroom dance, little brother?"

"I'm sure you're going to tell me," Wade said with mock chagrin.

Alex smirked and whispered, "Eye contact. You don't have to say a word to let her know exactly how you feel." He tightened his gaze on Wade and spoke softly, as if he didn't want Jane to overhear. "In the ER I'm surrounded by these women—nurses and receptionists—and they all sit and chatter about how unromantic the men are in their lives. Between my mother's tutoring and ballroom dance classes, I was smart enough to figure out that it doesn't take a whole lot of effort to appease that need in a woman. If a man would just realize it's not that hard to put a little romance into the life of the woman he loves, the world would be a much better place. Dance isn't the only way to do that, but it's a good one. Watch and learn, little brother."

Alex moved toward Jane. Wade pushed the button on the CD player. He watched Alex hold his hands up in silent invitation. Jane smiled as she stepped toward him and wordlessly answered it. Their feet began to move at exactly the same moment, perfectly mirroring each other with a simple waltz step that Wade actually believed he might be able to handle. Recalling what Alex had said, he took note of the way they were gazing at each other as they danced. From the first time Wade had seen Alex and Jane together, he'd been well aware of the love they shared, and he'd certainly seen them dance before. But he'd never consciously stopped to ponder what Alex had now drawn his attention to. Alex was looking at Jane as if she were the most important person in the world to him. Of course, she was. But how many people take for granted such things as a good spouse? Wade would give his right arm to have a woman in his life that he could love the way Alex loved Jane. Her expression clearly reciprocated her love for Alex, but she almost looked as if she might melt into the floor. Wade imagined dancing with Laura that way, watching such an expression on her face. His insides fluttered, and his heart quickened, and suddenly learning the waltz was very appealing.

When the dance ended Jane pressed a tender kiss to Alex's lips, as if she just couldn't resist. Then she hugged him tightly. Alex glanced toward Wade, wearing a self-satisfied smirk.

Wade took on the dance lessons with more enthusiasm while he mimicked Alex's movements and learned to count out the three-quarter time of the waltz step. When Alex declared that he had it down, he said, "Now you can try it with a partner."

"Oh," Wade said as Jane stood in front of him, and he felt decidedly nervous.

"I'm not going to bite," Jane said, holding her hands up. "You can even step on my toes, and I'll still love you."

"That's reassuring," Wade said and took her right hand into his left. He put his right hand to her back as she set her left on his shoulder.

Alex adjusted the position of Wade's hand on Jane's back, saying, "Your hand needs to be where the amount of pressure you use will guide her the direction you want her to go . . . because you're leading and you need to act like it."

"Yes, sir," Wade said humorously, and Jane smiled at him.

Alex then adjusted Wade's left hand, and the way it was holding Jane's, while he explained how it wasn't just a place to put their hands, it was a tool to guide his partner. Alex counted the steps and they tried it. Wade fumbled a few times, but they just laughed and kept at it. He was grateful for the comfortable relationship he shared with Jane; she had been a sister to him since the day he'd met her. Alex finally turned on the music and they kept at it until Wade actually felt like he could do the waltz without making a fool of himself. They took a break, then went back to it, since Jane insisted that only practice would make him comfortable enough to be able to do it without having to think about it. He was beginning to feel like that might be possible when Alex nudged him and said, "Sit this one out, kid. I'm going to dance with my wife."

Wade sat down and watched with fascination as they put some embellishment into the waltz, making it clear they'd once competed doing this. The song ended that they'd played over and over, and Alex said, "Let it play."

Jane laughed as the music began, and they immediately moved into a complicated rumba. Wade recognized it as a dance they'd done for a floorshow he'd seen them do together about the time he'd met Elena. He had a moment of nostalgia over his memories, then his thoughts turned to Laura. Perhaps learning the rumba could be worthwhile as well. What had Jane said? *The rumba is flirtation.* But it looked a little too complicated for him. Maybe he'd do well to stick with the waltz for the time being.

A few days later they had another dance lesson, and it only took a minute for Wade to be able to waltz effortlessly with his sister-in-law. He even managed to guide her through a graceful dip and a couple of extra spins, which made her laugh. He thought of Laura and felt impatient to get beyond this stage of writing letters and hiding behind the Internet.

With the waltz well learned, Alex and Jane taught Wade the swing. With the lessons he'd gotten so far, he picked it up rather quickly. They pointed out the difference between the rock-and-roll swing and the disco swing, and played both kinds of music so he could try it both ways. Once he had the basic steps mastered, Jane taught him some simple embellishments that were easy to learn and a lot of fun. She assured him that most women who knew the basic swing could respond to his lead and handle the steps without much trouble.

As some maintenance dance lessons progressed, letters continued back and forth between Wade and Laura, and his heart became steadily more invested. When he admitted that her letters had become an addiction that made his days easier to get through, she admitted to feeling the same way. He told her he wanted to meet her but felt afraid of taking a step that could shatter any pleasant illusions they might be holding about each other. She agreed with that too, but made it clear that she considered life too short to hold back out of fear. She said that they could never really be sure if a relationship would work through letters alone, and if it wasn't going to work it would be better to find out and move on. She signed that letter, *With love, Laura.*

Wade pondered the situation all through a Sunday, then he sat down to write his next words very carefully.

Dear Laura,

I want you to know that it took great self-discipline not to address this letter to Barrett's Aunt. Maybe it's irrelevant to keep myself from doing it if I go straight to telling you about the temptation. Truthfully, my logical side is telling me that a man can't make life-altering decisions through letters alone. Written words can be carefully premeditated, and you don't

know what I'm really like, any more than I know what you're really like. On the other hand, the letters we've shared have given me insight into a woman with many qualities I admire. Be assured I'm not the kind of man to propose to a woman based on written words alone, but I still want you to know that it's tempting. Rather than doing something so ludicrous, I propose that we take this to the next level. I want to talk to you face-to-face, Laura. I want to hold your hand and confess my deepest secrets to you. I want you to trust me enough to do the same. I want us both to believe that no matter how we might have been hurt in the past, we can trust each other with such confessions, and maybe, just maybe, there could be something for you and me beyond this moment. I would like to say let's meet tomorrow, and maybe I'll change my mind, but for the moment, I have to say that there's something I need to take care of before I reveal myself to you. One of these days I'll tell you everything, and I pray when that day comes you will be forgiving of my methods.
With love, Me
P.S. I'm learning how to dance.

Wade read the letter through and sent it with a prayer. The next morning he called the pediatrician's office to make an appointment for Rebecca. When they asked the reason he just said that he wanted her checked to make certain everything was okay. He spent some hours at the urology clinic where he was doing his present rotation, grateful that this particular doctor was easygoing and willing to offer some flexibility on getting his hours in. After leaving there he picked Rebecca up for the appointment. Jane teased him a little as she sent him out the door, her final comment being, "Tom Hanks has nothing over on you."

"I don't know," Wade said. "He had somebody writing the script for him. But I do have Rebecca. She make's great female bait."

"Let me know."

"Of course," he said and hurried to meet the appointment.

As Wade checked in and paid the co-pay, it occurred to him that Laura might not be here. In nearly two years she'd only not been there once, as far as he could remember, but knowing his luck, she'd be out today. They'd waited about ten minutes when he heard the name of a different patient being called. He looked up, and the nurse at the door was not Laura. His heart sank, and he felt utterly depressed, then he reminded himself that there were three doctors in this clinic, and they each had a nurse. Not two minutes later Laura appeared and called someone's name. Wade felt so giddy he had to suppress an audible laugh.

They waited for another fifteen minutes while Rebecca played with a little boy near her age, and Wade tried to be interested in a magazine. Just the thought of seeing Laura made his insides flutter. He pondered their letters, their encounters, and the way she made him feel, and he prayed this was not just a path to more disappointment. He became so caught up in his thoughts that he was startled to hear, "Rebecca Morrison."

He looked up to see Laura standing in the doorway, and it took great will power not to just sit there and gape at her. Today she wore pink pants and there were pink pigs all over her shirt. Her necklace had five little piggies. Her shoes were white and pink striped canvas. He quickly grabbed the diaper bag and Rebecca. Laura smiled at him as he approached, saying warmly, "Hello, Rebecca's father."

"Hi," he said and followed her to the exam room.

"How are you?" she asked, as she always did. He felt heady just being with her.

"I'm well. How are you?"

"The same," she said brightly and closed the door. He noticed the absence of the wedding ring and wondered how long it had been gone while he simply hadn't been paying attention. He wanted to kick himself for being such an idiot. "So, what are we seeing Rebecca for today?"

"Rebecca is fine," Wade said, ignoring his own heart rate, praying that he wouldn't blow it. "But you could put down that she has a cold or something if it will appease the insurance company." Laura looked up at him startled, and he hurried to add, "I figured a co-pay was a small price for the opportunity to see you . . . to ask you something."

She didn't look as disconcerted as he'd expected. He hoped that was a good sign.

"Okay," she said and took Rebecca from him. "My goodness, she's getting so big."

"Yes, she is."

"So, you need a little feminine advice?" she asked.

"No," he said, "I was wondering, since . . . you're not wearing that ring anymore, if . . . well, I need to know if you'd consider going out to dinner with me."

Now she looked utterly astonished. "You're serious," she said incredulously.

"Hey, I took care of the co-pay at the front desk."

She smiled slightly and looked away. "That *is* serious. If you didn't have insurance, what would you have done?"

"I would have just had less money to spend on dinner. This way I can afford to take you anywhere you want. How long has it been since you went out for a nice dinner, Laura?"

She looked at him again, and her expression reminded him of the moment he'd told her his wife had died. His question had struck something inside her; he just didn't know what. He might wonder if she wasn't ready to be dating, except she'd been advertising on the web. Instead of answering him, she said, "Now, that's not fair. You know my name but I only know you as Mr. Morrison, a.k.a. Rebecca's father."

"It's Wade," he said. She smiled but said nothing. He added, "So, what do you say, Laura? Would you go out with a guy like me?"

"Yes, I would, actually," she said, and he smiled.

"But *will* you?" he asked.

"Well . . ." she drawled, "I am very impressed with the co-pay thing. I don't think anyone's ever gone to this much trouble to ask me out." She laughed softly, seeming almost shy when she'd never seemed that way before. "Sure, why not?" She looked more at Rebecca and the shyness went away. "Will Her Majesty be going with us?" Rebecca reached for her father, and he took her back, knowing she could get heavy after a few minutes.

"Not this time," he said, hoping it didn't sound presumptuous to assume they might go out more than once. "I did say a *nice* dinner out. She prefers grilled cheese sandwiches or macaroni and cheese." Laura laughed again, and he added, "How about tomorrow? If that doesn't work, then—"

"Tomorrow would be great," she said.

"Great." He laughed himself. "And where exactly should I pick you up?"

Laura wrote on a corner of the paper covering the exam table and tore it off, handing it to him. "There's my phone number and address. How about seven?"

"I'll be there," he said. "And thank you."

She laughed again, and he left the room, resisting the urge to let out a loud whoop once he was in the parking lot.

"Did you hear that, *Your Majesty?*" He laughed. "I'm going on a date. She probably likes you more than she likes me, but it's a start."

He buckled her into her seat and started to drive. Rebecca said from behind him, "Moozah, Daddy, moozah."

He laughed and turned on the stereo, noting in the mirror as the loud rhythm began that she was bouncing and clapping. He knew how she felt. His favorite band had come up with a more recent song that jumped into his heart in that moment.

Oh, I'm newly calibrated, all shiny and clean . . . Let the word out; I got to get out. Oh, I'm feeling better now . . . Oh, I'm happy as Christmas. All wrapped to be seen. I'm your recent acquisition . . . The world's done shaking me down.

At home, Wade walked in the door and set Rebecca free; she ran off to find the other children. Alex stepped out of the study, wearing scrubs. He'd obviously just gotten home from work and had been waiting for him.

"How did it go?"

Wade just held up the little piece of paper he pulled from his pocket, but he couldn't help grinning.

"What's that?" Alex asked.

"Address and phone number. We have a date tomorrow at seven." Wade laughed. "You don't know where I could get a babysitter, do you?"

"You don't even have to ask," Alex said and laughed with him.

* * *

Laura watched Rebecca Morrison and her father leave the exam room, then she had to close the door and just be alone. With everything that had happened in her life recently, all that she had been struggling with internally, she had trouble accepting that she might actually be given something so positive. She wasn't prepared for the wave of tears that crashed out of her, but it felt good to cry as opposed to feeling as if her grief and fear and anger would just mill around inside of her eternally, eating her alive.

Pondering feelings she had been unable to deny long ago, Laura had to convince herself that she really did have a date with this man she had admired for nearly two years. As silly as it sounded, Rebecca Morrison was her favorite patient. The visits were few and far between, but she'd always felt herself light up to see the name on the chart. And Rebecca's father just had a way, without hardly saying anything at all, of brightening her day a little. Having lost his wife he had a bit of a lost puppy look that had always been a weakness for her. But at the same time she'd never sensed a hint of self-pity or bitterness. His love for his daughter was readily evident, and she just had a good feeling about him. She prayed that her instincts were on better track than they used to be.

Wade. His name was Wade.

Realizing she would either be missed or get caught crying, Laura hurried to subdue her tears and compose herself. But as she went back to work, she couldn't help smiling. She had a date with Wade Morrison.

* * *

Wade had no trouble finding where Laura lived. Pulling into the driveway, he couldn't help thinking how quaint the little house was, and how it suited her. The front yard was small, with a couple of large trees. The house was brick with a big porch. It looked old but well kept.

He felt nervous as he knocked at the door and uttered a little prayer that this would go well. She answered the door, looking pleased to see him. Her hair looked more curly than usual, and she wore a black dress, simple but elegant.

"Hi." She opened the door wider. "Come on in. I just need a minute."

"No problem," he said and watched her walk toward the kitchen, which he could see through a doorway, then she turned the other direction and disappeared, her heels clicking on a hardwood floor. The house was small, but he liked the mood she'd created. The front room in which he stood was decorated with a great deal of personality and was very cozy, with a unique flair that combined many different kinds of things—some homemade, some not. He couldn't help thinking that as beautiful as it was, it would be a nightmare to let Rebecca loose in such a room.

When Laura came back, declaring that she was ready, he couldn't resist saying, "Wow. You look great. Not that scrubs don't suit you or anything, but . . . you really look great."

"Thank you," she said. "It's nice to have a reason to put on something besides scrubs."

"Your shoes, however, look way too normal." She laughed and stepped outside.

Wade watched her lock the door and put the keys in her little black purse before he walked her to the car and opened the door for her. Pulling out onto the road he said, "So, you don't have any food allergies, do you?"

"No," she laughed softly.

"Any strong aversions?"

"As long as it's not too out-there ethnic, I can take just about anything."

"Great," he said.

"So, who is watching Rebecca?"

"My brother and his wife," Wade said.

"You're still living with them, then?"

"That's right. It works out nicely while I go to school. As you know, they have a large home. And they're great people. It gives Rebecca some stability."

"That's good, then," she said.

Nothing more was said, and Wade hated the tension. He decided to take it head-on. "So, I guess a first date is prone to all kinds of awkwardness no matter how old you get."

He was relieved to see her smile. "So . . . ask me anything you want. Maybe we can break the tension down a little."

"Okay," he said. "Do you think Huggies or Pampers are better for little girls?"

She looked surprised, then she laughed. He went on. "I can't talk about the latest movies because I haven't seen any, and I can't talk about what I've read because it would probably bore you to tears. Studying medicine sometimes bores me to tears. Although you would at least probably understand what I was talking about, considering your career. I could talk about the kids' shows on public television, or we could analyze why a two-year-old girl who has no comprehension of social expectations far prefers that everything she owns is pink or purple, and is obsessed with digging her aunt's shoes out of the closet and wearing them around the house. The higher the heels, the better."

Laura laughed again. "Those all sound like invigorating topics, actually. I could especially get into analyzing shoes."

Wade smiled, making the connection. "So you could."

"I could talk about what's on TV because I watch far too much of it, and while I try to avoid what's yucky, the rest is usually stupid. I can't talk about movies unless they can be rented, because I never go to theaters. I could analyze the full spectrum of frozen and fast food that make up a menu for one."

Wade absorbed the underlying message and couldn't find any humor. He met her eyes, then looked back at the road. "It's okay," she said. "You don't have to say anything. I really don't *want* to talk about my pathetic and lonely existence. For the first time in many weeks I'm *not* feeling sorry for myself, and I don't feel lonely—thanks to you. Now I just have to wonder if being so candid will make you feel less awkward with me—or more."

"Oh, definitely less," he said. "I prefer not having to guess what someone is thinking—or feeling." He smiled at her. "I'm glad to know that I could help, because I was certain you couldn't be doing this for any reason beyond feeling sorry for *me.* "

"I've never felt sorry for you," she said, and Wade wanted to stop the car and hug her. Not only because he knew that what she'd said was true, but also because she was actually talking about it.

"I know," he said. "And I appreciate that. I'm not sure how to explain why, but I do."

A moment later she asked, "How did she die?"

Wade shot her an astonished glance, then looked back to the road. "You don't really want to talk about my wife."

"Yes, I really do. Don't you like to talk about her?"

"It's not that. I just . . ."

"What?"

"I didn't really think it was good . . . protocol . . . for a date—to talk about the dead wife."

"Would you prefer trying to ignore that she was once the center of your life?"

Wade swallowed carefully to remain composed, feeling startled by the emotion she'd just provoked. "No," he said, "but the last woman I was . . . close to . . . seemed to prefer it that way."

"How did she die?" Laura repeated.

Wade pushed a hand through his hair. "Um . . . it was a cerebral hemorrhage."

Her voice was tender as she said, "No warning, then."

"Nope. She got up to feed the baby and I was watching her, sitting there in the rocking chair, and I thought how beautiful she looked. She put Rebecca back in the bassinet and got into bed. We talked for just a minute then went back to sleep. I woke up to the baby crying, and I thought Elena was just exhausted, so I got up and changed the baby's diaper." He paused and sighed. "Elena was already cold."

Wade pulled into the parking lot of their destination and put the car in park. He turned to look at Laura and found the same compassion in her eyes that he'd seen the first time he met her. He was surprised to hear her ask, "What did you talk about?" He hesitated, and she clarified, "You said you talked for a minute. Do you remember what was said?"

"I remember it like it was this morning."

"If it's too private to share, then—"

"No, it's okay," he said, amazed by this conversation—and the way it was making him feel. "I told her I loved her, and asked her if she knew how happy she'd made me. She said it was the other way around, that she could never ask for anything more than what she had right there in that room." He looked away and forced a steady voice. "She said that her life was complete . . . and then she fell asleep and never woke up."

He felt Laura take his hand and looked at her fingers holding his before he looked at her face. "How have you survived?" she asked. "I've always thought how . . . strong you seem. You've been an inspiration to me."

Wade let out a dubious chuckle that eased the mood a bit. "That shows how little our paths have crossed. I've never felt strong. For months I cried every time I got in the shower. I would fall asleep crying and wake up crying. And then I'd just force it all down and take care of my daughter and get through my classes. But I've been very blessed. We were staying with my brother when it happened. I was going to medical school back east, but we'd come home for the summer so she could have the baby here, where we both have family. Their help and support has been priceless. And the life insurance was good. If I'm careful I can actually get through medical school without having to work, and I can have enough time to actually be a father to Rebecca."

"That's great," she said. "Most people our age don't have good life insurance. You must have been inspired."

"Yes, I know we were. And I guess that would really be the answer to your question. I've survived because I absolutely know it was her time to go. In fact, I knew before I married her that her life would be brief. And she knew it too. We just . . . did our best to make the most of it."

"Incredible," she said, her voice reverent. "But that doesn't make you miss her any less."

"No, it doesn't, but . . ." He turned to look at her, unable to believe this was real. For the first time since he'd found Elena dead, he felt truly alive.

CHAPTER 14

"I think that's probably enough on that topic for now," Wade said. "Let's talk about . . . what's on TV or something."

"No, let's go with analyzing little girls and shoes."

"And big girls and shoes?" he asked and got out of the car. As he opened Laura's door and took her hand to help her out, he added, "Thank you."

"For what?"

"For asking. Most people either don't want to talk about it, or they say really stupid things that are meant to make it all better. Your understanding means a great deal."

After they were seated and had ordered, Wade said, "I do not even know your last name, Laura."

"It's Dove."

"Dove. How charming. Laura Dove. And is that your ex-husband's name?"

"No, it's my maiden name. The marriage was annulled; it didn't last long."

Wade felt a little taken aback. He stopped to ponder what that meant. He'd seen the ring on her hand the first time he'd met her. If the marriage hadn't lasted long, then . . .

"How long have you been single?" he asked.

"It'll be two years come November," she said, and Wade almost choked. It took all his willpower not to scream or stand up and kick the chair. *Nearly two years?* All this time she'd been single while he'd been enduring and struggling and secretly harboring thoughts of her. How could he have been so stupid, so blind?

"Is something wrong?" she asked.

Wade swallowed hard, forced a smile, and said, "No, I'm fine. You want to tell me about it?" She looked hesitant, and he added, "Fair is fair."

"You got me there," she said and drew a deep breath. "It's easy to look back now and see that there were warning signs. They were subtle, but still there. And I chose to ignore them. The problem was a combination of naiveté on my part, and the fact that he was a very good actor. Once we were married he became a completely different person, almost overnight. He was controlling and obnoxious. And when it became clear that he had no interest in even attempting to work on our problems, I kicked him out and filed for an annulment. We only lived as husband and wife for a little more than a month, but it was a nightmare." She sighed and looked down. "I think it was hardest for me to exchange vows over a temple altar, believing it was forever, and then to turn around and realize that it wasn't even going to last a moment. It took a lot of fasting and prayer to come to terms with the fact that I could not take away his free agency, and it was not right for me to hold on, as much as I wanted to. I learned that the reality of a temple marriage is in the way two people love and respect each other and are committed to caring for each other. I got married in the temple, but it was not a temple marriage. So, once the annulment was legal, I did everything I had to in order to apply for a cancellation of the sealing as quickly as possible. While that way certainly isn't the norm, I was very blessed to get permission to have it done. It's over, like it never happened—except for the way it's changed me. You don't go through that kind of loss and betrayal without having some scars."

"I would agree with that," he said, and Laura caught something in his eyes. Experience.

"Tell me about it," she said.

"What?"

"Your loss and betrayal, your scars."

"We were talking about you," he said.

"Now we're talking about you. Was your marriage not good?"

"Oh, my marriage was very good. We had a few hiccups to iron out, but overall it was about as good as they come, I think."

"Then you must be talking about the fact that you were almost married last year."

"That's right. In a nutshell, I think I too ignored some signs. Overall, I think she's a really great person. She just had some challenges that I couldn't live with. Truthfully, I became concerned when I began to see the kind of family she came from." Laura tried not to bristle at that, wondering what he might think if he knew the truth about *her* family, then he added, "But I wasn't so much troubled by her family as I was by her perspective of it. We talked very frankly about it, and I had every reason to believe that she could see the dysfunction and she wouldn't allow it to bring negative influences into *our* family. But then an incident came up where it became very clear where her loyalties were, and that she would side with her family over me—or more accurately, she would side with what was comfortable, as opposed to what was right and true. And I knew I couldn't live with that. So I called it off—two days before. And yes, it left some scars."

They focused more on their meal, and Wade was pleased to see how Laura seemed to be thoroughly enjoying the experience. He thought of what she'd said about frozen and fast foods. He wanted to invite her to come to the house for dinner when Jane was cooking. All in good time, he thought, wishing he could eat every meal with this woman for the rest of his life. He asked himself if he should feel afraid to be opening his heart so fully to her, and to be investing hope that she might be everything she seemed to be. But he couldn't deny that his instincts—and his logic—were telling him nothing negative. He knew now what bad instincts felt like, and this wasn't it. He concluded that his mind and his spirit were both doing quite well with this, and his heart . . . well, his heart was lost. He loved her and he knew it. In a way, he knew he'd fallen for her the first time she'd looked into his eyes while he'd been crying over Elena's recent death. And he'd only grown to respect her and care for her more with each encounter over these past couple of years. He prayed that his feelings would not set him up for a fall, that this would be the beginning of forever.

"So," he said, wanting to know everything about her, "I take it with all the time you spend alone in front of the TV that you don't have family around here."

"No, they're mostly in Nevada. I came here to go to school and loved it, so I decided to stay. I bought the house as soon as I was able to after getting out of school. I like having roots."

"Roots are nice," he said.

"So, where are you from?"

"Here," he said. "Most of my family is all around here. I'm pretty firm on settling close by; I really want to work at Primary Children's Medical Center. That's the goal, anyway. I can get my degree at the U, but then I'll have to do some time out of state to get through my internship and residency. That's just temporary, though. I want to live here. I love it here."

Laura saw him smile and returned it. She wanted to point out all that they had in common so far, but she felt certain he already knew. And it wasn't just a matter of preferences or personalities. They both knew betrayal and disillusionment.

They both cared about and understood the effects of dysfunction in a relationship. She asked herself if what she was feeling could be real and right and good. She asked herself if, at this point, she could pinpoint a single warning sign in his character. And all the answers pointed to a firm belief that she *could* trust him, trust that he was all that he seemed, that her instincts were in firm harmony with the love she felt for this man. And yes, she did love him. It seemed ridiculous, but on the other hand, she knew she had fallen for him the first time he'd brought Rebecca into the office. She'd been at the point of just trying to come to terms with the fact that her marriage wasn't going to make it. And she had looked into Wade Morrison's eyes and had wished that Randall could have possessed the same tenderness and character she had seen brilliantly through that first conversation. Through their brief visits over the last couple of years, she had seen in Rebecca's father evidences of integrity and values and a sensitive heart. There had been no reason for her to believe that he might be trying to deceive or impress her. He'd been a grieving widower in a doctor's office, completely candid—vulnerable but forthright.

Laura had allowed herself to indulge in hope when she'd ended her own marriage, but she hadn't been able to bring herself to say or do anything to indicate her interest in him, fearing it would be inappropriate. And her disappointment upon learning of his engagement had actually sent her into one of those downward spirals of depression that had been difficult to snap out of. To this day she couldn't believe how much she had cried over thinking that this man, who was practically a stranger, was lost to any possibility of a future. She'd railed at herself for being so silly, to even be fantasizing about a future with a man she hardly knew. And then when he'd told her it had been called off, her joy had been a stark contrast. But again she'd told herself that it was ridiculous to think that he would ever give her a second glance. When he'd shown up with the purpose of asking her out, she'd been ecstatic and stunned. Even now, sitting across from him, feeling so thoroughly comfortable and at ease, as if they'd been the center of each other's lives for all of their lives, she kept having to tell herself that it was real. Rebecca Morrison's father truly was looking at her as if she was the most beautiful thing he'd ever seen. If it was a dream, she prayed to never wake up.

Through the remainder of the meal they stuck to small talk: her job, his schooling, and Rebecca. Wade loved the way she *wanted* to talk about his daughter. She laughed at his funny stories about her, and she readily admitted that Rebecca was one of her favorite patients, and she always looked forward to seeing her.

"So that's it," Wade said, "you're only going out with me so you can worm your way into spending some time with Rebecca."

"It's working, isn't it?"

"Yes, it is," he said. "So, I have a proposition for you. First I should ask if you're busy on Saturday."

"Nothing important, why?"

"Well, about once a month I take Rebecca to the mall in Sandy where they have that indoor carousel. She loves it. We get popcorn and have lunch, go to the toy store, and buy her something new to wear. It's a tradition. Would you like to come along?"

Laura felt so giddy she had to fight to keep from laughing aloud. "I would love to," she said.

"Good." He smiled. "We'll pick you up about ten."

"I'll look forward to it."

As they left the restaurant and walked outside, Laura commented on what a beautiful night it was. Wade suggested they take the long way to the car, which included going across the street, down the block and back again. Laura liked the long way, especially how he held her hand as they walked. They talked casually through the first part of their walk, then silence fell again and remained until they approached the car.

During the silence Wade pondered what he was feeling. His mind went back to the countless times he'd wondered why he'd had to endure the relationship with Marina only to have it end in such an ugly way. And now he knew. It had been a lesson in comparison. He'd felt attracted to Marina, had enjoyed her company, he'd been comfortable with her. But he'd never felt so intensely drawn to her as he did to Laura. He'd felt intrigued with Marina, but never so thoroughly captivated that he had to struggle to keep his thoughts where they belonged. He'd told himself that his feelings for Marina had simply been different from what he felt for Elena, that he could never expect to love another woman the way he'd loved her. Now he knew that he'd simply never loved Marina the way he should have. He'd been prepared to settle for the relationship, believing they could make a good marriage. And if she'd not chosen to be so enabling to her mother's dysfunction, maybe they could have. But it never would have been what it should have been. And now he knew the difference. Now, he didn't even have to question if this was right for him. He felt a passion and intensity toward Laura that had *never* been there with Marina. He also realized that in the last few hours he had done something he'd never been able to do before now. He had put his feelings for Elena to rest. He loved her; he always would. But something had let go; something had filled the hole she'd left in his life. No matter how hard he'd tried in the past, he'd always found himself comparing Marina to Elena, all the while knowing it wasn't fair. But he didn't feel that way anymore. Comparing his experience with Marina with what he was feeling now had somehow allowed him to let go of any discontentment he might have ever felt in the future. And he was grateful.

"So, we're back to that awkward thing," Wade said when the silence grew long.

Laura leaned back against the car and looked up at him. "Silence isn't so bad."

"I guess not, but . . ." Wade wondered if he should say what he was feeling. His concern about being too bold or scaring her off was unmistakably overridden by his present thoughts and feelings. He felt as if they'd eat him alive if he didn't express them. "Laura," he said, "there's something I want to say, but . . ."

"It's okay. Just say it."

"I want to say . . . I don't know how to say that . . . I didn't believe I could ever feel this way again."

Laura's heart quickened. Could it be possible? Did he really feel about her the way she did about him? It was one thing to see it in his expression, and another thing entirely to hear him express it.

Wade watched her eyes grow wide. "I think you just did . . . say it."

"So I did." He glanced down and chuckled, then met her eyes again. "Is that too much for a first date?"

"We've had several dates," she said. "They were just . . . less formal."

Wade smiled, but he wished he had some idea of what she was thinking about his recent confession. He was relieved when she spoke, especially when she said, "So I'll just follow your example and say that . . . I don't know how to tell you that I've *never* felt this way before."

"I think you just did," he said, while he attempted to accept what that meant. And without even bothering to wonder whether or not he should, he took hold of her chin and pressed his lips over hers. Her response was eager, and he wrapped her in his arms in the same moment she took hold of his shoulders. Their kiss was brief and unassuming, but filled with hope and promise. He felt something inside of him come back to life, something that had died when Elena had. Something he'd never felt with Marina.

"Oh," she said when he drew back, "I think you found an excellent way to get past that awkward thing." She lifted her lips to his, and he kissed her again.

"Yeah, I think I did," he said. "But maybe I should take you home before it *really* gets awkward." She smiled shyly as if she'd caught the implication, and he helped her into the car.

Laura hated the silence that once again descended, and the way they kept drifting in and out of this horrid awkwardness. And she hated the path of her thoughts as she realized that his kiss had triggered a mixture of memories and emotions. She hated having to guess what he was thinking, and speculate over whether or not he was a good man, or just a good actor. She had to ask herself what he was after and why. And while she scolded herself for being so mistrusting, she had to remind herself of how many times trusting a man had put her into difficult—and even hurtful—situations.

Realizing she would never get any answers if she didn't start probing, she carefully chose some words that she hoped would crack the barrier a little. "This dating after you've been married can be tough."

"Yes, it can," Wade said, feeling as if she'd read his mind. He hoped they were talking about the same thing, and far preferred to have such things in the open as opposed to guessing. When she said nothing more, he added, "So, do you want to say it, or do you want me to say it?"

"Sometimes I can be a little too straightforward . . . to the point of embarrassing myself, or the people around me. Maybe you'd better say it . . . so we won't have to wonder where we stand."

"Okay, but maybe we're not thinking about the same thing."

"And maybe we are. Just say it."

Wade cleared his throat and did just that. "It's hard to stop with a kiss when you've been in a relationship where you didn't have to stop." He glanced toward her. "Is that what you were going to say?"

Laura looked at him, wishing she could gauge the motives behind such a statement. Then she looked out the window, hating what past experience had done to distort her thinking. Why couldn't she just take him at face value? Trying to buy some time and ease the tension, she said, "No, I was going to say that I think Huggies and Pampers are probably a toss-up." He laughed, and she told herself to just cut to the chase. "Actually . . . I think it would be better if I don't say what I want to say. Instead, I would like to ask you something, and I'm assuming that you'll be honest with me."

"Do you think I would be honest about telling you I'll be honest?" he asked, wanting to get past this hovering sense of mistrust. At moments he felt like they were completely connected and open, while at others he could almost believe she was terrified of him. And maybe he was terrified of her. How could he say that he just wanted to be able to spill his every thought and have her do the same, without judgment or fear?

Laura thought about that question in regard to her experience so far with him, separate from anything else in her life. She answered firmly, "You've never given me any reason not to trust you."

"Well, that's something," he said with a dubious chuckle. "But it's not like you have a lot to go on."

"Actually, I do," she admitted, recalling her own reasoning in regard to their previous encounters. He would have had no reason to put up any smokescreens with a nurse who was giving his daughter shots. "Yes, Wade, I believe you'll be honest with me."

"Okay, that's a start. I will be honest, Laura. Ask me anything you want."

She took a deep breath. "Alright. And after you answer the question honestly, I'm going to tell you why I'm asking it."

"Okay."

"I need to know exactly how you feel about moral issues in dating. Since you don't know how I feel about it, you have no choice but to tell me how you really feel, not what you think I want to hear. You see, you really don't know if my reaction when you kissed me was genuine or just baiting you. So tell me where you stand, and we'll see if we have any reason to go out again."

"You already told me you'd go with me and Rebecca on Saturday."

"Maybe I'll change my mind if I can't get what I want out of this relationship. Since you've kissed me, and we've shared deep confessions about our past loves, I assume we have a relationship."

"Yes, I would think so."

Wade digested what was being said and abruptly pulled the car into an empty parking lot next to an office building. He put the car in park, unfastened his seatbelt, and turned to look at Laura. She looked a little startled but returned his gaze boldly.

"Baiting me for what?" he asked.

"While I am likely stating a gross generalization, I've come to find that most people in our situation fall into one of two categories. Do you know which one I fall under? Am I a woman who will stick to my values regardless of how badly I've been hurt or how lonely I may be? Or am I a woman who has been so thoroughly disillusioned and betrayed that I just don't care anymore? Am I hoping you will be decent and respectful, or that you won't be opposed to spending the night with me? If you can't give me what I want, Wade, then we have nothing more to talk about. So tell me where you stand."

Wade looked at her long and hard, vacillating between a deep respect and a touch of anger. But maybe that would depend on what kind of woman she turned out to be. In that moment, he honestly didn't know. And perhaps that's what bothered him most of all. He tried to tell himself that his instincts about her had been good, and he found it difficult to believe she wouldn't be a woman with values. But his own history had taught him that battered emotions could drive a person to do things they might not normally do. Did he simply *want* her to share his convictions? Or did he feel some tiny degree of guilt in realizing there was a flicker of temptation inside of him to answer this intense attraction he felt? But he knew where he stood, and he didn't even have to question or weigh it. He did however feel compelled to give her some perspective on the ultimatum she'd just thrown at him. In one agile movement he pushed a hand into her hair and pressed his mouth over hers with a kiss that was brief but clearly indicative of how she made him feel.

"Is that your answer?" she asked breathlessly, looking into his eyes while he kept her head held tightly in his hand.

"No," he said. "That's to let you know that my answer isn't the easy one; it has nothing to do with any lack of attraction or desire. My answer is that my covenants with God are the most important thing in my life, Laura. They are the only things that hold me together and keep me going. My personal convictions regarding intimacy within marriage are deeply ingrained for reasons that you could not possibly comprehend, knowing as little about me as you do. I do not believe in any intimacy outside of marriage beyond a kiss. Period. And I will put that above your feelings or mine. If you are the kind of woman who is hoping I will spend the night with you, then we have nothing more to talk about. But now that you know exactly where I stand, you tell me how I'm supposed to know that whatever you say next isn't just telling me what I want to hear, or would like to believe."

Laura looked into his eyes as he spoke and felt the conviction of his words rush into her heart. She felt more breathless from his words than she had from his kiss. But he was right. How could he believe that she agreed with him completely? And truthfully, she couldn't deny that the recent course of her thoughts left her feeling somehow unworthy of such an incredible man. Before any response could form in her mind, a burst of unexpected tears overtook her. Her momentary temptation to feel embarrassed by her emotion was immediately squelched by the memory of their first encounter, when they had faced each other, both crying without shame. He watched the tears spill down her face and asked gently, "Is this disappointment or relief? Tell me, and I'll believe you."

Laura only shook her head, unable to speak. A moment later she found her face pressed to his shoulder and his arms around her while she cried like a child, cried like she'd wanted to cry for days, even weeks, but had been unable to do so. Why now? Here she was, on a first date, blubbering all over the place, releasing tears that had felt frozen and stopped up until this moment. What was it about Wade Morrison that inspired her to be so thoroughly open, so vulnerable, so completely at ease? Did he have any idea how he had just restored her faith in the human race? How he had proven to her that God was indeed mindful of her? That prayers were heard and answered? That life was not just a meaningless endeavor?

Wade wasn't certain what had just happened to motivate this, but he felt privileged and undeniably grateful to be the one holding her, escorting her through this grief, whatever its source may be. He thought of her letters, her vague allusions to struggling with grief over some recent event, and he wondered what had happened in her life. He wanted to know her heart and soul, to ease her every pain, to never let her go.

When her crying finally quieted, he expected her to ease away, but she kept her head against his shoulder while she held to his arm with both hands as if he'd just saved her from drowning.

"Are you okay?" he asked gently, pressing a kiss into her hair.

"I'm better now, thank you," she said, but she still didn't move. "I should probably feel embarrassed, but I don't."

"And you shouldn't. How *do* you feel?"

"Safe," she said. "And most definitely relieved. But it's a relief more deep and complex than you could ever know."

"I could never know because I couldn't understand, or because you'll never tell me?"

She was quiet, then subtly tightened her hold on his arm. "Maybe I'll tell you one of these days, and then I guess we'll see if you can understand."

"Okay," he said, and she felt him tighten his arms around her, conveying a silent acceptance and security that filled her every nerve with peace.

Laura's thoughts started to spin with the conversation that had led up to her emotional outburst. Now that she'd gotten past her biggest concerns, she wanted nothing more than to just talk to him forever; to share her deepest fears and dreams, and to hear him do the same. She wondered where to begin, or if she should just let the silence stand for the time being.

Wade answered that question when he said, "You said that after I answered the question honestly, you would tell me why you were asking it. I'd really like to know."

"Okay, but . . . I have a confession."

"Alright."

"If I tell you there's a little bit of disappointment mixed in with the relief, would you think less of me?"

"No, I would think you're human, and I would know I'm not the only one suffering from some severe temptation."

She drew a contented sigh and had to say, "I love the way you can say things like that as if it's no big deal to talk about it. If people would talk about such feelings more, I think it would be a lot easier to navigate through the world we live in."

"I could agree with that," he said. "But I went through a harsh education on frankly discussing things that some people might consider embarrassing or sensitive."

"I'd like to hear about that."

"Another time," he said. "You still haven't told me your reasons for asking which category I fall into."

Laura sighed but kept her head against his shoulder. Not only did it prevent her from having to look at him while she talked about sensitive issues; she also never wanted to relinquish the warmth and security she was feeling.

"I don't know how much time you've spent circulating in the LDS singles scene," she said. "I've probably spent too much time there."

"A little," he said. "I was usually just too busy with school and taking care of Rebecca."

"Well, I had a few bad experiences, and I've talked to a lot of women in my position who have shared their experiences with me. It seems there are both men and women who have pretty much let go of their values as a result of whatever they've encountered through the course of their lives that's put them into a position of dating at an age when they should be married. Of course, being female, I can only speak for how it is from my side of the fence, but it's not uncommon for a guy to throw out some comment to gauge how a woman will react. It's often to the effect of, 'I can't believe what some women are willing to do. One woman I went out with wanted . . .' And then he fills in the blank. Sometimes it's vague, sometimes downright crude. If a woman is horrified or disgusted, then he pretends to be equally horrified or disgusted. But if she says something to indicate to any degree that she might be that kind of woman, if she leaves even the smallest opening, even if it's silence in an attempt to avoid the topic, he keeps pushing until she finds herself in a situation where she has to get downright rude to get rid of him. And after it happens a few times you sit alone and start to wonder what the world is coming to if members of your own church are confronting you with stuff like that. I'm sure there are decent guys out there, and I'm sure they're confronted with similar challenges from women who have lost themselves somewhere in the casualties of this war between good and evil.

"So I was sitting there at dinner tonight and realized that I couldn't help wondering if sticking to my convictions was really worth it. What I was really thinking earlier was that, in spite of what I know is right, a part of me wanted you to spend the night, and if you wanted this relationship to remain chaste you'd do well to leave me quickly at the front door. But I didn't want you to think that I was just throwing out some comment like that to see how you'd react. I didn't want you to think that what I wanted and what I would actually do would be the same." She paused, then added, "Are you shocked and disgusted by my blunt honesty, Wade?"

"Not in the slightest. I'm grateful for it, Laura. I have no desire to muddle through ten or twelve dates trying to figure out where we stand and what we believe in."

She laughed softly. "I think we've just about gotten to an emotional level of the tenth or twelfth date."

"Yeah, I'd say we have." He drew a long, slow breath. "And the feeling is mutual, if it's any consolation."

"What feeling?" she asked.

"What I want . . . as opposed to what I would do."

She tightened her hold on him as if she appreciated the validation, but she was quick to say, "A consolation perhaps, but a little frightening." She finally eased away and looked at him almost fiercely. "Forgive me if I'm being too blunt, Wade, and forgive me if I'm repeating myself, but with the way I feel, I need to be very clear. It seems that when a person becomes disillusioned with marriage, it can be difficult not to let religious values suffer. I've worked very hard to hold to those values, but I know a lot of people who haven't. Out in the world it's apparently become acceptable to go to bed together on the first date, and when you stir severe loneliness and some depression into the mix, it can be easy to wonder why it would matter. I'm sorry if this is coming across somewhat obnoxious, but . . . I've become more disillusioned by dating men who have turned away from their values than I was by having my husband turn out to be a jerk. But I never felt for any of them the way I feel about you, and in spite of what I believe in my heart, I'm not sure I have the fortitude right now to resist such a temptation." Her gaze tightened on him. "I'm begging you not to make it a temptation. I feel very fragile right now, Wade, for reasons I would be happy to share with you some other time . . . if you're interested. I would love to talk to you all night, but . . . right now . . . I just need you to take me home."

"Okay," he said, wishing he could tell her how much he admired and respected what she'd just had the courage to say. He pulled the car back onto the road, taking her hand into his while he drove in silence, just letting the conversation settle into his spirit. He pulled the car into her driveway and put it in park before he turned more toward her and said, "For the record, Laura, I agree with you completely, and I appreciate you stating it frankly, because I hate guessing games. I want you to know that I meant what I said; I haven't turned my back on my values. I promise you that you will never have to worry about that with me."

She smiled, and he hurried to get out of the car before he gave in to the urge to kiss her long and hard and make a hypocrite out of himself. He walked her to the door, gave her a quick kiss on the cheek then stepped off the porch before he said, "May I call you?"

"Anytime," she said and smiled. "Thank you, Wade . . . for everything."

"A pleasure," he said and hurried to the car before he gave in to the urge to go back and kiss her again.

* * *

Laura closed the door and locked it before she leaned back against it and drew a deep breath. Never in her life had she experienced anything like what had just happened in the last few hours. She'd gone out on a lot of first dates, and very few second or third ones. But less than three hours with Wade Morrison had taken her to a level she'd never experienced through a dozen dates, or even in marriage. She'd never felt so comfortable and secure, so calm and at peace, even with the man she'd once trusted to make her happy for a lifetime. In truth, she'd never imagined that a man could understand her so completely, accept her so thoroughly. And she didn't even have to wonder if he was being genuine with her. She'd seen and felt false diplomacy and manipulation all her life. And this wasn't it.

Ambling into the bedroom, she took off her shoes and tossed them in a corner, then her eye was drawn to the computer, and a wave of confusion—even heartsickness—washed over her. It had become a habit to come through the door and check her email, an experience that had daily come to leave her breathless with anticipation and eagerly soaking up every word this man wrote to her—and she didn't even know his name. She would even go so far as to say that it had almost become her reason for living. Now, she couldn't help wondering what torturous trick fate had played on her. Through these many months of being alone, her every effort at dating and getting to know single men had ended in disappointment or disgust. And now she had found two different connections that both felt so right and good. She felt afraid to turn the computer on, not certain what to do. Instead she got into her pajamas and brushed her teeth, pondering her feelings carefully, then she went to her knees beside the bed, earnestly thanking God for the profound evidence of His blessings in her life this day, the tender mercies that He had shown her, and she couldn't hold back the tears that came with her expression of gratitude. She'd not cried for weeks—until Wade Morrison had walked into the clinic yesterday. And now she couldn't stop. She then prayed fervently to know what to do concerning her present situation. *Please help me handle this with integrity and with the best interest for my future.*

Laura got up off her knees, wondering how she would ever cope if both of these men ended up being a dead end. But she couldn't think of that now. Now, she only knew the step that had to be taken in this moment. But it wasn't going to be easy. She turned on the computer and found no letter from the other man in her life. She laughed softly at the thought of Wade Morrison being *the man in her life.* She asked herself if such an idea was delusional, but in her heart she knew it wasn't. Her time with him had been more real than anything she'd ever felt. She wasn't going to quibble over it. She considered it a miracle, and she intended to jump in with both feet, and prayed she didn't end up the fool—again.

CHAPTER 15

During the drive home, Wade pondered the enormity of the evening. The conversations, the kisses, the tears, the confessions. And the love and respect he felt for her. A burst of laughter leaped out of him, immediately followed by warm tears in his eyes. Perhaps the loneliness was finally over.

Wade came into the house and locked the door behind him. He found Alex and Jane in the front room. She was sitting at one end of the couch with his head in her lap.

"How was Rebecca?" he asked.

"An angel, as always," Jane said.

"How was the date?" Alex asked, smirking.

"Oh, I don't think I'd call it a date," Wade said. "I'd call it more like . . . exploring a heartfelt and healthy relationship 101."

"Really?" Alex chuckled. Jane looked confused. Of course, Alex always understood him without even trying. "So . . . forgive the comparison, but . . . you didn't get this emotionally deep with Marina on the first date?"

Wade chuckled. "I *never* got this emotionally deep with Marina."

"Wow," Jane said. She obviously understood *that*.

"So now what?" Alex asked.

"Right now I'm going to call her; with any luck the date isn't over yet. And then, if my luck holds out, I'm going to marry her. Good night."

He hurried down the hall, but not before he heard Alex say to Jane, "Wow."

Wade slipped into Rebecca's room and pressed a kiss to her little head before he hurried to get ready for bed, then he called Laura from his bedroom. He was surprised to find her number busy, and wondered who she might be talking to. Then he wondered if she might have dial-up Internet. He read in the Book of Mormon for a few minutes and tried again, glad to hear it ringing.

Laura was surprised to hear the phone ringing only a minute after she disconnected the Internet. No one ever called her—especially not this late. She glanced at the clock, then the caller ID, confused when she read *Alexander Keane.*

"Hello?" she said, certain it was a wrong number.

"Hello," she heard Wade say. She wondered where he was calling from but didn't bother to ask.

"Oh, hi," she said, and Wade was glad when she sounded pleased to hear his voice. "When you asked if you could call I didn't really think it would be tonight, but I'm glad you didn't wait until tomorrow. That's so far away."

"Exactly what I was thinking," he said. "It was busy or I would have called sooner. I can't help wondering who you might call."

"No calls. I was just checking something on the Internet," she said, and he felt proud of himself for second-guessing her. But he pressed forward with his most prominent thought. "So, tell me, Laura, why you are very fragile right now? You said you'd tell me if I was interested. I'm interested."

Laura felt a little taken off guard. She'd actually forgotten that she'd admitted such a thing. "It's kind of a long story," she said.

"I'm not in any hurry, but . . . if you're not comfortable with—"

"I don't mind talking to you about anything, Wade. I'm just not sure you'd want to hear about the trauma in my life. I'm not one to whine and complain; or at least I try not to be."

"I know that. Telling me about your struggles isn't whining."

"Okay, well . . . I have to go back a little." Laura attempted to put herself in a frame of mind that wouldn't take her too close to the emotion involved with this story. "In junior high I became part of a group of girls. There were four of us, and we had three things in common. We went to the same school, we belonged to the same religion, and we all came from family situations that were . . . less than ideal for a number of different reasons. We've been close ever since. These women are more important to me than my own family members for reasons I'll get into some other time. We ended up all over the country, but we all keep in very close touch. Those of us who are left, anyway. About five years ago Fiona was killed in a car accident."

"Whoa," Wade said. "That's got to be tough."

"Yeah. You just don't expect to have to attend the funeral of a peer you love that much when you're still in your twenties. I don't have to tell you that."

"Was she married?"

"Engaged. But that's where it gets weird. Rad—that's her fiancé—ended up marrying another girl in the group, Tina. So we all go to Fiona's funeral, and then Rochelle and I go to Rad and Tina's wedding, and within weeks we realize that Tina is as lost to us as Fiona. We could see signs, but Tina never admitted to anything until she ended up in intensive care because he'd knocked her down the stairs."

"Good heavens," Wade muttered. "Is she okay?"

"Relatively speaking. This was a couple of years ago. She was five months pregnant, and the baby died. While she was on life support her husband put on a show that could have

won him an academy award. Rochelle and I were the only ones
who could see through him. We knew Tina, even better than
her own family. But he had everyone so convinced that Tina
was some psychotic manic-depressive that by the time she came
around, her confessions of his ongoing abuse didn't fly. The
charges she pressed were dropped, and he ended up with
custody of their two-year-old son."

Wade gasped, feeling physically ill. "That is unbelievable."

"Yes, it is, but it happened. Now, you have to understand
that just about the time Tina ended up in the hospital, I was
trying to get my marriage annulled because this man I had
believed to be so wonderful was in actuality a very good actor
as well. Rochelle had just become engaged, and the whole
matter of seeing her two best friends going through these
nightmares with their husbands kind of threw her. I told her
she couldn't just assume that the man she was engaged to had
problems because we'd had problems. She concluded that she
needed to do some serious praying about him, instead of going
with her romantic inclinations and rose-colored glasses. She
prayed and started paying close attention; we talked about
warning signs, indications of problems and . . ."

"What?" he asked when she hesitated.

"Are you still with me here? Sometimes I think I get talking
about stuff like this and . . ."

"What?" he repeated.

"I can't see you so I don't know if your eyes are glazed over
with all this psychobabble kind of stuff."

"They're not, I promise. If you must know, I'm pretty good
with psychobabble. Keep talking. I'm with you."

"Well, so . . . Rochelle started having very frank conversations with her fiancé, and it was amazing how quickly he got
defensive over certain things that she'd just taken for granted
were not a problem. Turned out he had a serious porn habit,

which he declared to be 'no big deal,' among other challenges. So she called the wedding off but became so thoroughly disillusioned and disgusted that she stopped going to church and started sleeping around. I've tried countless times to convince her that just because a group of girls raised in dysfunctional homes were attracted to losers, doesn't mean that all men are that way. But she's become firm in her own beliefs. So, while Tina was recovering from nearly dying and losing custody of her son, and I've been recovering from my own brand of marriage gone bad, Rochelle has been out living it up, and, by far, doing better than either myself or Tina—at least from all outward appearances. We talk regularly, as always, and more and more Rochelle is telling me that this religion stuff isn't all it's cracked up to be, and I'm constantly hearing about the advantages of casual sex. And then the real whammy happened last month, and I'm still struggling with it." Those last few words came out with a tremor.

"What?" Wade asked warily.

Laura coughed to avoid sobbing and just said it. "Tina overdosed on a combination of several prescription drugs."

"Is she okay?" Wade asked, feeling more and more sick on Laura's behalf.

"Yeah, she is," Laura said, her voice still quavering. "She's better than she's been in years. She's dead."

Wade sucked in his breath, then put a hand over his mouth when some unfavorable words came to his mind, and he didn't want them escaping. His eyes and throat became hot while he could hear evidence that Laura was crying, and attempting to do it quietly. He finally composed himself enough to speak, but he could only squeak out, "I don't know what to say."

"There's nothing to say," she muttered. "I'm the only one left. Rochelle is physically still living, but she's committed spiritual suicide, and I don't even know her anymore. How am I supposed to talk to her about trying to deal with the challenges of life while remaining faithful and sticking to what you know is right in spite of living in a world where it's so easy to do what's wrong?" She took a deep breath. "So . . . I go to work and I go to church and I keep my house meticulously clean and do my laundry and eat frozen dinners and cold cereal and I rent movies and pray to God night and day that I can be stronger than the voices in my head that are . . ." Tears overtook her, then she forced a tense chuckle. "I can't believe I'm saying all of this to you. In spite of how far I believe we've come in the last few hours, I still have trouble believing this is real. How do I know you won't just . . . just . . . use it against me, or . . . never talk to me again, or . . ."

"How *do* you know, Laura?" he asked.

She sniffled loudly. "I don't know, but . . . I really feel like I can trust you . . . that you are what you seem."

"I won't ever do anything to hurt you, Laura. I can't give you any good reason to believe that, but I swear to you that it's true."

"Okay," she said, her voice open and warm.

"What are the voices in your head telling you, Laura?"

"Well, I'm not schizophrenic or anything."

"I know what kind of voices you're talking about. I once had a very close relationship with such voices."

"You did?" she asked eagerly.

"Some other time," he said. "Right now we're talking about you."

She sighed loudly. "It's like I'm being given three choices, Wade. I can keep doing what I'm doing, but for what? Or I can take Rochelle's path . . . or I can take Tina's." While Wade was trying to think of something to say that didn't sound trite or patronizing, she chuckled with no sign of humor and added, "Now I'm sounding like a martyr."

"No, you're not. I know a martyr when I hear one. But I need you to promise me something."

"What?" she asked skeptically.

"If you are ever—*ever*—seriously tempted to follow either Tina or Rochelle, I want you to talk to me first. If I can't save you, then you're going to have to take me with you." She said nothing, and he went on. "I don't think you really want to follow either path, but sometimes it just feels like there's no other way to be free of the pain. And those voices in your head are very good at convincing you there are no other options beyond utter destruction—one way or another. There are no words to describe that kind of desperation, but when your own head is lying to you, Laura, you have to reach out and let someone save you."

Laura felt stunned to hear her own thoughts being expressed so clearly. She felt so completely validated, so thoroughly understood. And she wondered what he'd been through to give him such perfect empathy. She didn't know how to ask, but did manage to say, "It's not easy to find someone who understands that kind of desperation." He said nothing, and she added, "But you understand it, don't you."

"I do," he said. Wade only wondered for a moment if he should tell her, but he could find no reason to keep secrets from this woman. In fact, he wanted her to know everything. It was easy to say, "And I've got the scar in my wrist to prove it."

Laura felt her chest tighten and her heart soften. *He understood her!* He had known pain in his life, and he was willing to talk about it. She'd only dreamed that such a man existed. She was trying to think of anything remotely appropriate to say when he added, "I think I'm the one sounding like a martyr."

"Not at all," she said. "I was just . . ."

"Thinking you should date someone who is more emotionally stable?"

"No," she laughed softly. "I think you're probably a lot more emotionally stable than I am. It's just nice to talk to someone who doesn't believe experiencing pain in life has to be a broken leg."

"Or having your appendix removed?"

"Yeah," she said gently. And a moment later she added, "Wade, can I say something that might sound a bit . . . bold, or . . . presumptuous?"

He chuckled. "I thought we'd gotten past that being a problem."

"Well, this is different."

"Okay."

"I just have to say that . . . the timing of . . . your asking me out . . . I want you to know that it restored something in me. And I'm grateful. Even if I never saw you or talked to you again—I would be forever changed."

"And how is that?" he asked, sensing that the conversation they'd had in the car earlier was somehow connected to this.

"The last several days have been really tough for me, Wade. It started on Tina's birthday. Of course the grief is still fresh, but most of the time I still feel like I'm in shock, like it's not real. But on her birthday I missed her so badly I felt like I just wanted to be with her, whatever the cost. I talked myself out of that with some chocolate ice cream and a chick flick. Then Rochelle called and nearly had me convinced to take a vacation and come and stay with her so she could line me up with some of her friends. I can only imagine how that might have gone, or maybe I can't. Like a typical sitcom episode, I would assume. Naive disillusioned girl goes to visit her worldly friend in the city, and the plot hinges on whether or not she will go over the edge. And in the world's eyes, ending up in bed with a stranger would constitute some perverse version of a happy ending." She sighed. "So I talked myself out of that with Chinese food and general conference videos. But I'd heard the talks before, and those people are happily married, you know. So beyond going to work, I've prayed a great deal that God would just give me some reason to keep believing in Him, to keep going. I'm not a sign seeker, but I let Him know I needed something to hold on to. But it feels like I've been praying for that for such a long time, and it just didn't seem to be getting through, so I spent a lot of time pondering the choices and . . ."

"Don't stop now," he said when she hesitated. "I'm still waiting to hear how the timing of our date fits into all of this."

"You know I just admitted to emotional eating."

"I noticed that," he said. "Did you want me to be shocked or disgusted or something?"

"Are you?"

"No. I like chocolate ice cream and Chinese food—not necessarily together."

"I can't believe what I've admitted to you in the last few hours. What is it about you that makes me just . . . pour out my heart and soul as if I've known you forever?"

"Maybe you have," he said. "But don't be thinking this is all one-sided, Laura. I admitted that I tried to end it all with a box cutter. Emotional eating is several steps above that, in my opinion. You're trying to change the subject. Get to the point, Laura."

"Okay, well . . . when you asked me out, my initial reaction was like . . . I couldn't believe it. Here's another confession. I've admired you since I first met you. And I couldn't believe you'd actually asked me out. Then when I was laying in bed last night, you got all mixed up in those choices that have been haunting me. Without even trying, I realized that I was person-ifying the choices in you. I know that's not fair to you, but that's where my head has been. Even though my convictions have remained true to this point, I admit they've been wavering. Truthfully, when I asked you to consider which kind of woman I was, I wasn't sure that I knew myself. I knew what kind of woman I used to be, what I *want* to be, but I felt—still feel—so utterly attracted to you, that if you'd been willing, I can't help wondering if I would have gone for it. I would have hated myself in the morning, but I had to wonder if I could have resisted. I was praying for God to give me an exit to save my soul, and at the same time wishing for an opportunity for destruction. There you were, and I could look at you and see three doors. Door number one: sticking to what's right. But that seemed like such a lonely door. Door number two: this guy will give you the opportunity to try life on the other side. Door number three: either way he'll break your heart, and a package of sleeping pills will solve every problem."

Wade listened with growing awe and horror. He could never adequately express his gratitude for her candor, for the evidence of her humanness, as well as for her convictions that were obviously a lot stronger than she believed. Emotion crept into her voice as she continued. "I guess that's why I fell apart when you said what you did. God did hear my prayers, Wade. You might as well have said, 'God loves you, Laura, and He sent me here to prove it.'" She sighed again, long and deep. "I don't know where all of this will lead, Wade. After everything you know about me, I can't imagine any man ever wanting to see me again, but no matter what happens, you have changed me. You have strengthened me by your convictions, and I will forever be grateful for them—because they saved me."

"You know what?" he said. "I really don't think you could have gone through with it. If I'd thrown myself at you and begged on my knees, I don't think it's in you to throw away what you believe in. I think your spirit is stronger than you realize. You would have slapped my face and told me where to get off."

"Maybe. I'd like to think so, but . . ." Her words faded. Wade was silent a long moment, and she asked, "Have I scared you away?"

"Not by a long shot. I'm just . . . overcome, Laura. You are the most amazing woman I have ever met."

Laura repeated that in her mind, certain he must have said it wrong, or that she'd misunderstood. She hurried to ask, "Did I hear you right?"

"I don't know. Did you hear me say that you're the most amazing woman I have ever met?"

"That's what I heard. But shouldn't you have added something like, 'Beyond Elena, of course?'"

"Elena was an amazing woman, Laura. Make no mistake about that. I appreciate the way you started the evening out by allowing me to talk about her. She will always be an important part of my life; she will always be Rebecca's mother. And I will always love her. I am not going to make comparisons between my deceased wife and any other woman in my life, because it's that whole apples vs. oranges thing, or maybe it's more like comparing a river to an ocean. Both beautiful, both amazing, both with a very distinct purpose. But beyond comparing. Elena was a woman almost without fault—not perfect, mind you—but a good woman. However, you have to understand that given the life she'd lived, she had no cause to be otherwise. She was raised in a good home; in fact, if you add up the ingredients of a positive, functional family, they just about had it all. She never had any cause for her faith to be tested. Instead she died to test mine. I always admired Elena for her values and convictions, but I wondered occasionally how strong she might be if she had been called upon to face what many people in this world have to face. My sister-in-law used to be much like Elena. She too grew up in a good home. Her convictions were firm and strong—until life knocked her flat."

"What happened?"

"Her son got leukemia. She sat by his side while he endured months of unspeakable suffering for the purpose of saving his life, and then she believed he would die anyway. My brother tells me there was a day when she screamed and swore, and she threw the scriptures at him, telling him she didn't believe anymore. Eventually she came back to herself, and she admitted later that she'd never known until then the meaning of the trial of one's faith. In my opinion, it's not so tough to hold to religious values and convictions when everything's going okay. How much faith do you suppose it took for the Saints to go west? But more important, how much faith do you suppose it took to keep from denouncing their faith after they'd buried a loved one in the snow and had their feet cut off from frostbite? I'm telling you that you're an amazing woman, Laura, because you're not afraid to admit that it's not been easy, that you're human, that you struggle with temptations, that you don't always handle life perfectly, but you still turn to God for the answers. And I think you have a lot more faith than you believe you do. You are an inspiration to me."

Laura couldn't speak. She had a hand pressed over her mouth while tears rolled down her face, and it took everything she had to keep from sobbing audibly.

"Laura? Are you with me?" She couldn't answer, and he repeated. "Laura?"

"Yeah," she whimpered. "Just . . . give me a minute."

"It's okay, Laura," he said. "You can cry if you need to. Take as long as you need. I'm not going anywhere."

He relaxed his head on the pillow and kept the phone to his ear while minutes passed, and he heard an occasional sniffle. He thought of her losing a friend to suicide only a month ago and her confession that she'd hardly been able to cry over it. He couldn't imagine the grief she had rolling around inside of her. And grief was something he understood.

She finally said, "Sorry. I haven't been able to cry for weeks. I've watched sappy movies and listened to sad songs just trying to get myself to cry, but it's felt all clogged up inside of me ever since Tina's funeral. And now . . . you just have this way of saying things that . . . get it started, and it won't stop."

"Glad I could help," he said, and she laughed softly.

"So, are we still on for Saturday, or have you reconsidered?"

"We most certainly have a date Saturday. My only problem is that Saturday is too far away. And what might I reconsider, Laura? Any human being in their right mind would be a fool to look at these hours we've spent together and not do everything in their power to make it last a lifetime."

Laura's heart quickened at the implication. "So . . . the question would then be whether or not we're in our right minds?"

"Probably," he chuckled. "It's getting late and we should get some sleep, but . . . I just want to say that . . . my heart is with you in your losses, Laura. I can't take away the pain, but I really wish I was there right now, because I would like to just give you a long, tight hug."

She laughed softly. "That would be nice, but . . . it's probably good you can't. I think I'd have a hard time letting go. It's safer this way."

Wade agreed, but avoided discussing the reasons. "Okay, but . . . let me clarify something. A hug is not romantic, and it's not intimate. I'm a firm believer in the power of a hug. It's the kind of embrace you get from a friend, a parent, a sibling—sometimes a stranger—with no expectations or implications, just a simple expression of concern, support, and acceptance."

"That sounds nice," she said.

"Well, for now we'd better get some sleep. What time do you have to leave in the morning?"

"About eight-thirty," she said. "I have to be there before nine."

"You'd better get some sleep. I'd better too. I'll call you tomorrow, if that's okay."

"That would be great," she said. "And I'm looking forward to Saturday."

"Yeah, me too," he said.

Wade reluctantly ended the call, but he could tell that Laura was reluctant to say good night as well. And her reluctance left him comforted—and less lonely than he'd felt for a long time.

Wade had trouble falling asleep as his mind relayed all that had happened since he'd picked Laura up at seven o'clock. He grieved with heartache on her behalf, and was left in awe at the closeness he felt to her. This was not intrigue or simple attraction. He'd not just fallen in love with this woman. He *loved* her, heart and soul. There was no question as to whether or not he should risk his heart to her. It was already lost.

Somewhere in the middle of the night, a thought occurred to him that made him gasp. Finding any effort at sleep pointless, he went quietly downstairs and into the study where he turned on the computer, glad for cable Internet that didn't make him wait to connect to his email. He gasped again to see a message from Laura—a message that had come through less than half an hour after he'd dropped her off this evening. He held his breath as he opened the email and began to read.

Dear Barrett's Uncle,
Something's happened in my life that I need to share with you, but it's not easy. Funny how I feel that we've become so close through our exchange of letters, which makes what I have to say so difficult. You see, I've met someone who has changed my life very quickly.

Wade took a sharp breath and leaned back. He had to read that last sentence twice to believe what it said. Then he forced himself to read on.

> Actually, I met him a long time ago, but he asked me out and we spent the evening together. It's difficult to put into words what's happened to me through the course of an evening. I can only say that I've never met anyone like him. He's changed my life and restored my hope in ways that I could never describe. I feel that I can be completely honest with you, and so you'll understand when I say that I really believe he is the answer to my every prayer. I am hopelessly in love with him when I had believed that I could never fully open my heart to love again.

A combination of laughter and sobbing came from Wade's throat, then the screen went blurry as hot tears filled his eyes. *He couldn't believe it.* It was minutes before he got control of his emotions enough to keep reading.

> I know it sounds insane to say such things after one date, but the time we spent together feels equivalent to several dates according to my previous experiences. Even though you and I have never met, I still believe that what we have shared through letters constitutes a relationship, and I cannot in good conscience carry on with this relationship when I will now be seeing him exclusively—or at least that's the way it seems at the moment. Of course, I'm only assuming he feels the same way, and I can only hope that he does. If it doesn't work out, you might

just hear from me again. I want you to know that
your letters and your interest in me have made a
huge difference in my life at a time when I very
much needed them. You too have been an answer to
my prayers, and I'm grateful that you contacted me.
Truthfully, if this man I've fallen for has any degree
of the warmth and sensitivity you have shown to me,
he would be practically perfect, or at least perfect for
me. I wish you every possible happiness in your
future.
God bless always,
Laura

Wade had to keep wiping at a steady flow of tears as he read
the letter, then he read it again before he leaned back in the
chair and cried like he hadn't for months.

"I did hear someone in here," Alex said, and Wade actually
let out a little scream.

"Oh, you scared me to death," Wade said, wiping at his tears.

"What's wrong?" Alex asked firmly, moving into the room.

Wade felt embarrassed, even though Alex had certainly seen
him cry a great many times. He countered the question by
asking, "What are you doing up this time of night?"

"I was hungry. Sometimes this shift work is a killer. I can't
get my body clock to ever work quite right. I saw the light on
when I came down the stairs. What are *you* doing up this time
of night? And why are you crying?"

Wade motioned to the computer screen and said, "She
dumped me."

"Already?" Alex asked, sounding concerned.

Wade stood up, needing to find the box of tissues that he
knew was in the room. He said to Alex, "Have a seat. Read it.
I'll just sit over here and try to accept it."

Making himself comfortable on the couch, tissues at hand, Wade watched his brother read the letter. It was only thirty seconds before Alex turned toward him, his expression astonished.

"Keep reading," Wade said.

Alex read on, occasionally chuckling with disbelief, then he leaned back in the chair and sighed. "Wow," he said.

"You say that a lot lately."

"Your life these days is like . . . wow. That is . . . incredible."

"Yes, it is. So, what am I supposed to do about it?"

"First of all, you'd better come clean."

"Yeah, I'd better. And fast."

"And then you'd better bring her over for dinner."

"Okay. Given the tone of that letter, I don't think I'll have to talk her into that—unless of course she changes her mind once I come clean."

"Good luck with that," Alex said and stood up. "Come on. Let's find something to eat. We've lost sleep for lesser things."

"That's true," Wade said. "I'll be there in a minute."

He printed the letter and turned off the computer before he followed Alex to the kitchen for a long brother-to-brother talk over leftovers. After he'd given Alex a brief overview of how the date had gone, he said, "Tell me again how you met Jane; tell me about your first date. I don't think I ever heard about that."

"Okay," Alex drawled. "Well . . . I first saw her in the restaurant where I was moonlighting as a fill-in on rare occasions. She was with some chauvinistic jerk who'd been drinking. I rescued her when he refused to give her the keys to his car. She left without my knowing her name or anything about her. I couldn't stop thinking about her. And then two days later we were paired up on that ballroom dance team. It was so miraculous to me that I actually started believing in God again." Wade gave him a startled glance, and he added, "Well . . . I don't think I ever stopped believing in God, but maybe I'd stopped believing that He would take any notice of me."

"Wow," Wade said.

"What?"

"Laura said something to that effect; that the way we'd come together was evidence that God had heard her prayers."

Alex looked impressed. Wade went on to say, "Tell me about your first date."

"Well . . . we saw each other at rehearsals, but we couldn't find a time when we were both free until Saturday—that was a week after we'd first met at the restaurant. I took her to breakfast, and then we walked around the mall for hours, had lunch. We just talked and talked— not about the weather and politics kind of stuff. It was like . . . her beliefs, my beliefs." Alex tightened his gaze on Wade. "Why are you asking me this? It's ancient history. What does it have to do with you?"

"You and I have always been so much alike. You told me that you and Jane fell in love very quickly, but I don't think you ever told me how it went exactly. Maybe I just need to hear some validation that I'm not crazy."

"Well, I don't know what you're looking for exactly, Wade, but I told Jane I was in love with her about five minutes into that first date. Before the day was out I had unofficially proposed."

"Unofficially?"

"We weren't ready to get married. She wanted to get married in the temple, and I was inactive. It was four years before we got to the altar. But I knew my feelings wouldn't change, and they never did. I only loved her more every day."

"So, you think it really is possible to know that quickly if you've found the right one?"

"Absolutely. You have the gift of the Holy Ghost, Wade. As long as you're using your brain too and not ignoring the logical side of the situation, you're perfectly entitled to know. You don't need me to tell you that." He chuckled. "So, is she the one?"

"Yes," he said immediately. "I just hope she thinks that *I'm* the one. But I think we're off to a good start."

Wade forced himself back upstairs to make an attempt at getting some sleep. He read the letter again and got on his knees to give thanks for this miracle in his life, and to ask for guidance in pressing forward in a way that wouldn't ruin the progress they'd made.

He finally fell asleep about four o'clock and woke feeling bright and energetic in spite of minimal sleep. He got Rebecca dressed and went down to breakfast, where Barrett and Katharine were eating Cheerios.

"How long till school starts, guys?" Wade asked, putting Rebecca into her highchair.

"A week and two days," Katharine said with enthusiasm.

Then Barrett said, "Your date must have been pretty good. I haven't seen you with a smile like that since Rebecca was born."

"Really?" Wade said and laughed. "Yeah, it was good."

"Are you going to marry her?" Barrett asked with his mouth full. Katharine seemed indifferent, which was typical.

"I think there's a very good possibility of that," Wade said, "but let's keep that a secret for the moment."

Jane walked into the kitchen and said, "Good morning. Have you asked her to marry you yet?"

Barrett gave Wade one of those comically disgusted looks. "A secret, huh."

Wade just laughed and said to Jane, "Not just yet. Give me a few minutes."

"Hey," Barrett said as if he'd just remembered very exciting news, "I have something to show you. Come here, Katharine," he said to his sister.

Katharine jumped out of her chair as if she were equally excited, and the two children stood back to back in their stocking feet. "Look at that," Barrett said. "Look at that. I'm taller than Katharine."

Wade looked closely and declared, "You sure are! Woohoo!" He cheered and applauded, and Jane joined him. Rebecca laughed and clapped to imitate her father. Wade and Barrett shared a smile that was worth any amount of conversation. They both knew how dramatically Barrett's growth had been stunted through his bout with leukemia, and he'd been smaller than his younger sister ever since. The fact that he was catching up meant much more than his simply getting taller. Barrett was healthy and growing; he was alive, and that alone was a miracle.

"That's awesome, buddy. Before you know it, you'll be taller than me and your dad."

"Give me a few minutes," Barrett said, just the way Wade had said it earlier.

Katharine looked pleased with her brother's accomplishment as she sat down to finish her breakfast. She and Barrett didn't have much in common, but she'd always been Barrett's biggest cheerleader in overcoming his illness. Wade felt deeply grateful for his place in this family as he returned to helping Rebecca with her breakfast.

With Jane's help Wade was able to leave a little early to take care of something before he went to the clinic where he was presently doing a rotation. At 8:20 he knocked at Laura's front door. Just seeing her face brighten when she saw him sent his heart flying. She wore scrubs with Care Bears printed on them, and her shoes were baby blue with white ribbons instead of laces.

"Hi," she said and opened the door wider, but he remained on the porch, knowing he could only stay a minute.

"Good morning," he said and handed her a red rose, partially in bloom. "The florists aren't open this early. This is from the rose garden at the house. The bush is probably a hundred years old."

"How beautiful," she said, putting it to her nose. "Thank you." She smiled. "It's good to see you."

"You too." He smiled back. "I know you have to go, and I won't keep you. I just thought you could maybe use a hug to get you through the day."

"And what about you?" she asked.

"Well, the nice thing about a hug," he said, wrapping her in his arms, "is that it usually works both ways."

Laura felt his arms come around her, and strength rushed into her. She felt rejuvenated and replenished and full of life. She reminded herself that he'd defined a hug as nothing romantic or intimate, but she couldn't help relishing his masculine presence. She loved the feel of his beard against the top of her face, and the subtle male aroma that hovered around him. She loved the way he held to her as tightly as she held to him, and the way he looked into her eyes and smiled as he drew back.

"Hey," she said, "have you got plans this evening?"

"Nothing that being with you wouldn't preempt," he said, and she laughed softly.

"I was thinking earlier how nice it would be to have a good reason to cook something. I actually like to cook, but never consider it worth doing for myself. Would you take pity on me and come over for dinner?"

"Sounds marvelous," he said. "I'd love to. Except for the pity part."

"Bring Rebecca," she said.

"Actually," he drawled, "she has a date with her grandparents. Elena's parents have this monthly movie night with a bunch of the grandkids. They'll be picking her up at five."

"Next time then," she said, and he loved her alluding to a future together. "Is seven okay?"

"Perfect. I'll see you then." He kissed her brow. "You have a good day now," he said and hurried down the steps and to his car.

"Thank you," she called as he got in. He waved and drove away.

Wade couldn't hold back a burst of spontaneous laughter as he headed toward the clinic. Everything in his life had changed—in a heartbeat. After losing Elena the way he had, he never would have believed he could feel so happy.

CHAPTER 16

Laura went to work feeling like an entirely different person. Something inside tried to convince her that it was too good to be true, that surely the presence of a man in her life could not have had such an enormous impact so quickly. But she reminded herself this wasn't just any man; this was Wade Morrison. She'd never known anyone like him.

Any doubt she might have had on that count was erased when a dozen roses were delivered to her at the office. They were white and red intermixed, and just looking at them took her breath away. The other girls fussed and speculated, asking if she'd been keeping a secret. She just said, "Maybe," and left it at that. The card read,

> *Laura,*
> *The florist is open now. Here's to door number one. Maybe it's not so lonely after all.*
> *Wade*

Laura felt so overcome with emotion that she took the card with her into the ladies' room and had to cry for a few minutes. What was it about him that had opened the floodgates? It was as if all of her grief related to losing both Tina and Rochelle had been unreachable until Wade had touched something in her that had unlocked the barrier. For the first time in months she was feeling something beyond helpless and numb. But it felt good.

* * *

On a late lunch break, Wade went straight to the pediatric clinic. He said to the girl at the desk, "Hey, is it possible to talk to Laura for a few minutes? It's personal."

She smiled. "That would depend on whether or not you can give me the magic word."

"And what's that?"

"That would be if your name is the same one on the card that came with the roses. Since the roses made her smile, I'm assuming she'd probably want to see the guy who sent them. And the name would be . . ." She signaled for him to fill in the blank.

"Wade," he said.

"That would be the right answer," she said and motioned for him to follow her. In the hall she said, "She's overdue for a break, anyway. Actually, she's always overdue for a break. Wait in here. I'll get her."

"Thanks," Wade said, and she closed the door. He sat down in an exam room where he'd come many times with Rebecca. He prayed again that this conversation would go well, and he kept praying while he waited.

* * *

Laura was making some notes on a chart when Sally said, "Hey, you look like you could use a break."

"I'm fine," Laura said.

Sally came closer and whispered, "Trust me when I tell you that you need to take a break in exam room one." Laura looked at her astonished, feeling her heart race even before Sally grinned and added, "The man who sent the roses."

"Oh," Laura said breathlessly. "Maybe I do need a break."

"Make it a long one. I'll get Sue to cover for you. It's pretty slow at the moment anyway."

"Thanks," Laura said and hurried to room number one. She hesitated as she took hold of the knob, looking at the number on the door, struck deeply by the coincidence. She took a deep breath and pushed the door open to see him sitting with his ankle crossed over his knee. He was wearing slacks and a button-up shirt and tie. Of course he'd been dressed the same way this morning, but she'd been too distracted at the time to notice just how good he looked. Just seeing him took her breath away. "Hi," she said and pointed to the number on the door before she closed it. "I opened door number one, and here you are."

Wade grinned. "It must be a sign."

"It must be," she said and leaned against the counter since he remained sitting. "So, what can I do for you, Mr. Morrison?"

"Well," he said, "there's something I need to tell you, and it can't wait. I was praying you could take a break. So . . . I'll just say what I have to say, and then you can decide if you still want anything to do with me."

"Okay," she drawled skeptically. He stood up and leaned against the exam table, folding his arms over his chest.

"I know time is short, so I'll just get to the point." He took a deep breath. "Do you remember, a long time ago, when I told you my reasons for going into pediatric oncology?"

"I do," she said, confused over the topic.

"Do you remember what I told you?" he asked. "Not that I'm expecting you to; I'm just asking."

"Something about . . . a relative . . . a child in your family . . . who had leukemia."

"That's right," he said. "My nephew; he's an amazing kid, Laura. I feel a special bond with him. My giving him some of my bone marrow is the least of it."

Laura watched the expectancy in his expression and felt sure she was supposed to grasp a meaning deeper than his words. Something felt vaguely familiar about what she was hearing, and she tried to remember what else might have come up in their prior conversations here at the office. But it eluded her.

"Laura," he said, his gaze intent, "my nephew's name is Barrett." He paused, then added, "It's not a terribly common name."

Laura felt her heart react before the meaning settled into her brain. Then she found it difficult to breathe.

Wade watched the confusion on her face melt into enlightenment. His heart threatened to beat right out of his chest while he waited for a reaction. She looked at him as if she'd never seen him before. Her chin quivered. She bit her lip. She opened her mouth as if to speak, but nothing came out. Wade just kept his gaze connected with hers, giving her time to piece it together—and to decide whether or not she might feel angry or betrayed. She opened her mouth again, her voice squeaking as she said, "That was . . . *you?*" Wade nodded. "All those . . . letters, and . . . it was *you?*"

"Oh, Laura," he said with fervor, "when I saw your face come up on that website, the hopelessness in my life did a U-turn. I couldn't believe it. All this time, I thought you were married. I saw the ring on my first visit, and just assumed beyond then that you weren't available." He shook his head. "But I've been intrigued with you from that very first visit, Laura. Long before I could consciously accept that I was ready to move beyond Elena's death, I was thinking of you and looking forward to every visit here, feeling guilty because I thought you were taken. I kept telling myself that I just had to find a woman like you, that you would be my prototype. And then . . . there you were. But I was scared out of my mind . . . that you might not be what you appeared to be, or if you were that you wouldn't feel the same way about me. I told you my reasons for remaining anonymous in that very first letter. But truthfully . . . I never expected our letters to become so deep and meaningful . . . and so quickly. And when I asked you out, I kept expecting something to happen to contradict the woman I'd come to know through those letters. But what happened between us last night has left me so thoroughly in awe that I can hardly breathe when I think about it." He saw her start to cry, and while he worried over the reasons, he pressed forward. "I never dreamed that it was possible to have such a profound emotional intimacy with a woman, ever, let alone in one day. I love you, Laura. And I pray that you will understand why I had to get to know you this way, because now that I *do* know you, I can't imagine how I ever survived without you."

Wade felt like his head was in a guillotine, waiting for the blade to fall as he watched her squeeze her eyes closed and press a hand over mouth, while tears rolled steadily down her face. Was she relieved or displeased? Angry or glad? When she said nothing he just came out and asked, "Are you disappointed in me, Laura?"

She shook her head, and something resembling a laugh came out of her mouth, then turned into a sob before she covered her mouth again. Wade moved toward her, deciding to take what little he had to go on and assume she was okay with this. He touched her face, and she opened her eyes in response, looking up at him. When she moved her hand again, she was smiling, even though the tears kept flowing. "It was your face I saw when I read those letters," she said. "But truly, I never imagined, never would have dreamed . . . it was you." She touched his face as he was touching hers, as if to accept the reality of what existed between them. "Last night . . . I almost felt angry that I had to choose." Her eyes widened as if she'd thought of something horrible. "The letter I sent . . . last night. It was . . ."

"Incredible," he said. "I read it in the middle of the night; couldn't sleep. And I cried like a baby."

Laura felt overcome with all she was hearing, seeing, feeling, and all that it meant. Drained of strength she took hold of his arms as if he could keep her from falling. She found her forehead against his bearded face while she breathed in the scent of him, an aroma that had already come to represent comfort and perfect security. Her mind attempted to fully accept that the man she had come to love through his letters was the same man she had come to love, little by little, over the last couple of years. It was a miracle!

Wade took in the evidence of her acceptance, and relief filled his every cell. He wanted to take her in his arms, hold her impossibly close, and kiss her on and on. But this was neither the time nor the place, and he sought instead to ease the tension. "Now that you know the truth," he said, "I'm hoping we're still on for dinner this evening."

"Of course," she said, looking up at him.

The moment was so completely perfect that he simply couldn't leave without kissing her. The connection of their lips was even more magical than it had been the night before. The confessions and emotion they had shared gave substance and profound meaning to the tender fervor being ignited between them.

"I'll see you at seven," he said and hurried from the room before he did or said anything to diminish the power of the experience.

Laura watched Wade leave, and just like two days ago she had to close the door and sit down, crying like a baby. She'd never felt so blessed, so loved, so happy in her entire life. When she finally got control of herself and walked down the hall, the roses from Wade were sitting there, reminding her that it wasn't a dream. He was everything she'd ever longed for, and he loved her. Surely life could be no better than this!

* * *

After work, Laura stopped at the grocery store, enjoying the opportunity to buy an entirely different variety of foods. She felt purpose in even the simple task of buying groceries, then taking them home and setting to work in the kitchen while she listened to a CD. She couldn't remember the last time she'd bothered to put music on except in the car. It had either been the TV or silence; no wonder she'd been depressed. While she worked, her eye kept being drawn to the roses in the center of the table, and her heart felt warmed. And the rose he'd given her this morning was in a little bud vase on the kitchen windowsill. She paused for a moment to stop and smell it, then smiled at the analogy.

When the green salad was in the fridge and a chicken rice dish was bubbling in the oven, Laura got cleaned up and changed into jeans and a silky burgundy blouse. She set the table with candles, found an appropriate CD that she left on continuous play, and wondered how long it had been since she'd actually felt some joy and purpose in what she was doing within the walls of her own home. The doorbell rang at two minutes after seven, and butterflies came to life inside of her as she went to answer it. *I'm not dreaming,* she thought when she saw him standing there, holding a sack.

"Hi," they both said at the same time, and she motioned him inside, closing the door behind her. "I forgot to thank you for the roses earlier; they're beautiful. And the note was very sweet. It made me cry."

"I'm glad you liked them," he said, then handed her the sack. "This is kind of an emergency preparedness kit."

Laura opened it and laughed to see a carton of gourmet ice cream—chocolate. "Thank you," she said, "although I don't think you should encourage my bad habits."

"Actually, I was thinking you could just eat this for fun and replace your emotional eating with something else."

"Like what?" she asked lightly, heading toward the kitchen, motioning for him to follow.

"Like me," he said as she opened the freezer. She peered around the freezer door to see that he was serious.

While she rearranged the freezer enough to make the ice cream fit, she ignored her quickened heart rate and asked in a steady voice, "Are you saying that I should just call your number like a crisis hotline every time I feel the urge to give in to my vice?"

She closed the freezer and found him watching her closely. "I'm saying that I love you, Laura. And I would consider it a privilege to be there for you through any crisis that life might throw at you."

As Laura realized he really meant it, she was immediately overcome with tears. She turned her back to him, saying softly, "You've only been here three minutes, and I'm crying again."

"Tell me why," he said, taking hold of her shoulders, turning her to face him. He wiped her cheeks with his fingers and added more softly, "You must never be ashamed of your tears, not with me."

"How can this be happening?" she asked, her voice barely audible.

"I think they call it a miracle, Laura. It's one of those moments in life when everything that's seemed all wrong is suddenly right, when all the events that made no sense suddenly do." He pressed his fingers over her hair. "It's that moment when you realize the suffering wasn't in vain because God knew what He was doing all along."

Laura gave in to the urge to touch his face, as he was touching hers, as if they could both come to accept that this was real. "It must be a miracle," she said, "because I can't think of any other explanation. It's like water has turned to wine." He smiled, ever so subtly, while his eyes seemed to take her in, reflecting her own awe of the moment. She moved her hand to touch his hair and saw her fingers trembling. She pressed her fingers lightly over his beard, thinking of how she'd once wanted to touch it a long time ago, standing in the doctor's office when she'd been fighting to suppress her attraction to him.

"I love you too, Wade," she said. "I think I fell for you the first time I saw you cry."

"That was the day we met," he said, as if she didn't know. "I think I fell for you that day too. Even though I didn't feel ready yet to even have such thoughts, I was still having them. I was disappointed when I saw your wedding ring, and then I just assumed you were married after that." He knew he was repeating himself, but perhaps he needed to in order to grasp the reality.

"What have we been doing all this time?" she asked, laying her head against his shoulder as she'd done in the car the previous evening.

Wade put his arms around her the same moment her hands went behind his back. "Learning to appreciate this moment," he said. "Maybe it has something to do with . . . the miracle coming after the trial of your faith."

"Maybe," she said, savoring how right it felt to be in his arms. She wanted to hold him forever. She chastised herself for the temptation that flitted through her, then she reminded herself that a temptation was nothing to feel guilty for—as long as she didn't act on it. He kissed her quickly on the brow and took a step back, as if he too were consciously resisting the enticement of being so close.

"Maybe we should eat," she said, and he smiled. She loved the way he smiled.

"Can I help?" he asked as she took a dish out of the oven.

"No, it's ready. Just have a seat."

"Candles," he said. "How nice."

"Well, it's too light this time of year for them to be very effective, but I still like them."

After the food had been blessed, she said, "I can't stop thinking about what you told me earlier, about the letters . . . being from you." She laughed softly, timidly. "I still can't quite believe that the Rebecca's father I've known for two years is the same man who wrote all those beautiful letters to me." She laughed again. "For that matter, I find it difficult to believe that either of those men—*both* of those men—are sitting here having dinner with me."

"Well," he said, "if it makes you feel any better, I'm still finding it difficult to believe that you're available, that you wrote all those beautiful letters to *me,* and that you actually seem to like me."

She smiled, then her eyes became thoughtful. "Hey, this is . . . like that movie."

"You've Got Mail," he said. "Yes, that's come up before. I was hoping you'd be as forgiving of me as Meg Ryan was of Tom Hanks. Actually," he took her hand and smiled, "I think our version is more romantic."

"I would definitely agree with that," she said, returning his smile.

Wade thoroughly enjoyed the meal, hardly believing she could be such a great cook and so beautiful and amazing too. He encouraged her to talk about the friends she had lost, to remember the good times. She did, but he sensed that she'd not yet begun to properly mourn Tina's death, and he felt concerned. But there would be time for that. She asked him to share memories of Elena, and he loved the way he could feel completely comfortable talking about her.

"So, how is Rebecca?" she asked when they came to a lull.

"She's great. She's just one of the twins."

"Twins?"

"The family I'm living with . . . they had a baby girl two weeks before Rebecca was born. Ruth is her name, after her grandmother who has passed away. We call her Ruthie. The girls are precious together. We just refer to them as the twins."

"How delightful," she said. "I'm looking forward to Saturday. I miss Rebecca."

"Really?" He chuckled. "So, I was right. All of this attention is just your way of getting to my daughter, right?"

"I am very fond of her, but I don't think she'd look good in a beard."

"Not likely."

"I love your beard, by the way. I've always taken notice of men with beards. Some men look good in them, and some don't. On a scale of one to ten, I'd say you're like a . . . twelve in that beard."

He chuckled self-consciously. "So . . . will you still love me if I shave it off?"

"Maybe," she said and laughed.

"My brother and I have a running joke about beards. At one time we both stopped shaving while we were each going through some pretty intense struggles. When things got better the beards came off. Elena never saw me with a beard. I stopped shaving after I lost her. I didn't really think about it until my brother commented. But one of these days, I may just decide . . . to become a new man."

"Warn me," she said and reached across the table to touch it. "It's . . . irresistible."

He smiled and turned to press a kiss into her hand before she pulled it back to continue eating. When they were finished with their meal he said, "There's something I want to tell you, Laura, but I didn't want to spoil your appetite."

"And why would it do that?" she asked.

"Well," he drawled, "this is one of those conversations that I feel is necessary before I get too comfortable with anyone new in my life. And when you know certain things about me, if you still want to hang around with me, then I can relax and know there are no secrets. I have a strong aversion to secrets. Surprises can be nice, but that's different. That's like wondering what Rebecca's going to get me for Christmas." He chuckled. "But secrets . . . I don't like secrets."

"So, you're going to tell me all of your dark and dirty secrets?"

"I am," he said.

She leaned forward eagerly, as if she couldn't wait. She surprised him by saying, "I like this. Can I go first?"

Wade chuckled and motioned with his hand. "Go for it."

"You probably didn't think I could have any more after what I've told you so far."

"That chocolate ice cream thing is the clincher," he said.

"Oh, you haven't heard anything yet," she said. "For years I didn't want anybody to know certain things about my . . . upbringing. After a while I got very good at talking about it, because I . . . well, I didn't like secrets. If people can't handle what I've come from, that's their problem."

"Hear, hear," Wade said and laughed softly.

"What's funny?"

"Do you think there is anything in this world that we don't think the same way about?"

"Maybe," she said. "Anyway, I grew up in a very poor neighborhood in the Vegas area. My father was semi-active in the

Church, my mother wasn't active at all. She was antagonistic and drunk most of the time. There was a great deal of yelling and screaming in my childhood, and us kids even got knocked around once in a while when Mom really got set off. My siblings are all living at different levels of dysfunction. Some hide it with self-righteousness; others hide it with booze or drugs. Me, I just take psychology classes, devour self-help books, try a new anti-depressant every so many months, and try to keep a respectful distance from people who share my blood. I've worked very hard to overcome my dysfunctional upbringing, but sometimes I fear that it will haunt me forever. In my own defense, I've never succumbed to the substance abuse or immorality that runs rampant in my family. Still, I feel like a lost sheep most of the time. So . . . there, that's it. Those are the skeletons in my closet. And I already know about one of yours."

She took his hand and turned it over, pushing up the sleeve of his shirt to look at the wrist. He asked, "How did you know it was my left wrist?"

She touched the scar almost reverently. "You said it was only one wrist, and you're right-handed." She met his eyes but didn't let go of his hand. "But you didn't tell me what drove you to do such a thing. Was it losing Elena?"

"No." He shook his head. "I could have never left Rebecca that way. It was long before I met Elena. And it all ties in to the big fat skeleton in my closet." He sighed and leaned back, keeping his hand in hers. "And before I tell you this, I have to admit that this is the issue that ultimately came between me and Marina."

"Marina?"

"The woman I almost married last year."

"Go on," she said, with nothing but compassion in her eyes.

"I grew up in the model Mormon family. My parents were good people who lived the gospel. We had family home evening and scripture study and prayer. We all felt loved and secure. I followed the example of my two older brothers and went on a mission, then I continued my education, working toward my goal to become a doctor. And then one day the world came to an end for me. The rug was pulled out from under me, and I landed flat on my back."

Wade watched her concerned expression and felt hesitant to say it. Was it the reaction of Marina's family that made him feel ashamed and uncertain? He reminded himself that it was a part of who he was, and he wasn't going to let it remain unsaid. He leaned forward and wrapped her hand in both of his. "Laura," he said, "I want you to meet my family, but I can't do that until you understand that my family situation is extremely unique—especially within the parameters of normal Mormon expectations."

She looked confused. "You just told me that you grew up in the ideal Mormon home."

"Or so I had thought," he said. "I have eight siblings, but there is not one of them that's full-blooded. They are all half siblings, and they were raised in two different households. I have three parents—specifically, there are two men I call father."

"A divorce?"

"No, divorce would have been easy," he said. "You see, my mother got married, had three children, then left her family and had an affair before she went back to her husband and had three more children." He saw her eyes become enlightened even before he clarified, "I'm the one in the middle. I'm the child conceived in sin. But I didn't know about that until I was nearly twenty-five."

"Good heavens," she muttered. "How did you find out?"

"I was taking a genetics class; decided to have some fun with DNA testing. In a nutshell, when I asked my parents why the DNA didn't match, they told me the truth. My father—the man who raised me—admitted to having treated my mother badly, driving her away. She admitted to her bad choices and was completely penitent. She'd been excommunicated and had worked her way back. They're both amazing people, shining examples of overcoming ugliness and making something good out of it. But I couldn't see that at the time. I felt betrayed, lost; I didn't know who I was or where I belonged. I found my real father; he'd had no idea of my existence. I was so utterly lost and angry that one day I tried to end it all. My brother found me. He's a doctor. He stopped the bleeding and took me to the hospital to stitch it up. Later he told me I didn't know what I was doing, that I'd done a poor job of slitting my wrist, and I wouldn't have died from it. But he also told me it was my state of mind that concerned him. If the blood had started to clot, would I have done something else? Maybe, I don't know. I'm glad he found me when he did. The next day he checked me into a suicide crisis center. Things got better after that. But the reality is that my existence in itself is rooted in scandal, and the grief still follows my parents—and me. I have worked hard to come to a place where I can comfortably be a part of two families and not feel ashamed of the reasons for that. I'm happy to say that my relationships with all of my parents have healed; they're all amazing people. They all made some bad choices, but they all followed them up with some really good ones. I want you to meet them, but we talk openly about all of this, and you need to know what's going on. My mother has recently gone through a new set of struggles related to this, which we'll get into another time. I want you to meet my siblings, most of all Alex. He's not only my brother; he's my best friend."

"And which side of the family is he from?"

"Alex and I share the same father; we met a few years ago. I don't know what I ever did without him. Actually, you met him briefly at the hospital."

Laura nodded, then looked at him as if she'd never seen him before. He felt nervous, fearing she would now think less of him, and his hope for her acceptance would be shattered.

"Wow," she uttered, shaking her head.

"What?"

She smiled. "Do you have any idea how . . . *refreshing* it is . . . to talk to a man who doesn't believe that the ideal conventional Mormon family is the norm? While it's an ideal worth striving for, unfortunately many of us have had to settle for less and make the most of it."

Wade breathed a huge sigh and couldn't resist saying, "You are amazing, Laura Dove."

"No, *you* are amazing, Wade Morrison. Just look at us. We've both spent our lives trying to do the right thing, and struggling to understand and navigate through all the ugliness of the world around us."

He smiled and squeezed her hand. "I'm beginning to think that you truly understand me."

"Do I?"

"Don't you?"

"Maybe." She tipped her head. "So are there any other skeletons in the closet?"

"No, this one's so big there isn't room for any more," he said, and she laughed. "How about you?"

Laura looked down, completely sober in an instant. "Come on," he said. "We've come this far; surely we can handle another skeleton."

"I struggle with depression, Wade."

"Okay," he said. "Is it chemical or situational?"

Laura looked up at him, amazed to hear a man actually know the connection—and the difference.

"Truthfully, I think it's both, but I've spent years trying to figure that out. I've tried just about every antidepressant on the market, and I've struggled to deal with the side effects and adjustments. The way it's ongoing implies that it's chemical, but my life hasn't been free of depressing incidents, by any means." Wade was thoughtful until she insisted, "Say something."

"I'm just thinking," he said.

"Okay, but . . . are you thinking that you'd rather not hang around with a woman who—"

"No!" he protested. "I was thinking of how my encounters with you at the office would have never given me a clue that you were struggling with something like this."

"Well, work is . . . structured. I love it. I feel confident and secure there. I come home and feel lost. I work very hard to force myself through it, to function, but sometimes I fear it will overtake me. You need to know the truth. Wherever you and I end up, I don't want you to suddenly be faced with wondering what the heck is going on. And I truly wonder if a man might be wise to avoid any kind of relationship with a woman who—"

"Laura," he interrupted gently, "as long as we are honest with each other about our challenges and struggles, there is nothing we can't work through. If you were in denial and couldn't see the problem, I might be concerned, but . . ." He hesitated and touched her face.

"But what?"

"I think I'd like to prove that it's situational. I'd like to make your life so wonderful that you'd never have cause to be depressed again."

"What a nice thought," she said. "A bit naive and idealistic, perhaps. But a nice thought."

"Well, it's something to aspire to."

He insisted on helping her clear the table. She put the food away while he rinsed dishes and put them in the dishwasher.

"You look like you've got some experience with that," she said.

"Oh, I have my chores," he chuckled. "Alex and Jane won't let me live there without earning my keep." He leaned back against the counter and dried his hands on a towel before she took it from him to do the same. "Dinner was wonderful, Laura. Thank you."

"A pleasure," she said, repeating his words from the previous evening. "I didn't even think of dessert, but that ice cream you brought sounds pretty good right now. What do you think?"

"Sure, why not?"

"Have a seat." She motioned toward the front room. "I'll be there in a minute."

Wade made himself comfortable in the little front room, then he noticed her CD collection and stood up to look closer. "Unbelievable," he muttered.

"What's unbelievable?" she asked, coming into the room.

"You have at least twenty of the same CDs I own." He pulled out one of his favorites. *"Collective Soul?"*

"Oh, yes," she said, and he stopped the stereo to replace the CD. He found the track he wanted and pushed Play, turning up the volume. She smiled as the beat filled the room. Then she looked confused as he held out a hand. "What?" she asked, almost looking afraid.

"Dance with me," he said.

"You dance?" she asked, slipping her hand into his. Then she remembered that in one of his letters he'd said he was taking dance lessons.

"A little. But I didn't learn until my brother convinced me it would improve my social life."

"And did it?"

"We're about to find out," he said and urged her into a simple rock and roll swing. She fell into step with him so easily that he silently blessed Alex and Jane for their tireless lessons.

"Ooh," he said, guiding her into a turn and then back again, "I think this is my theme song."

Oh, I'm newly calibrated, all shiny and clean . . . Let the word out . . . Oh, I'm feeling better now. Break the news out . . . Oh, I'm happy as Christmas . . . The world's done shaking me down . . . Oh, I'm feeling better now.

She laughed as they danced, and he laughed with her, feeling a perfect happiness that was compounded by seeing the evidence of *her* happiness. When the song ended he started it again, and they kept dancing. When it ended again she changed CDs, and he noticed it was an older album done by the same band. The last time he'd listened to this CD had been the day he'd canceled his wedding. She found the track she wanted as she said, "Speaking of theme songs, this one's mine."

"Okay," he said, and they started dancing again.

"Or at least it is now," she added. Laura knew the lyrics well and didn't have any trouble picking out the ones that suited her now.

Today she dresses for the change she faces now. And the storm that's raging, a safe haven she has found . . . Her imagination has started stretching wide, and her new conviction no longer will she hide. The same love she gives, she requires . . . So she gathers rain to wash and cleanse and make her whole again.

Laura had to keep telling herself this was real. She couldn't remember the last time she'd danced, couldn't believe how good it felt, couldn't recall the last time she'd listened to these CDs that were among her favorites. And here was this man who had declared his love for her, continually surprising her with the increasing joy he brought into her life every hour.

CHAPTER 17

Wade and Laura danced until they were both exhausted, then they sat together on the couch, eating ice cream out of the carton with two spoons, since Laura insisted it tasted better that way.

"You know," she said, "I'm going to have to get over this emotional eating thing before I get older and my metabolism changes."

"Is this emotional eating?" he asked and took a bite.

"Yeah," she said. "The emotion of the day is . . ." she laughed, "bliss."

"How delightful," he said and put a spoonful of ice cream into her mouth.

When they'd had their fill of ice cream and it had gotten dark, Laura turned on a lamp and said, "If you have some more time, there's something I'd like to share with you."

"Okay," he said eagerly, and she left the room.

Half a minute later she came back holding some books of various sizes. She handed them to him, and he realized they were journals. He looked up at her in question, wondering over her purpose, surprised to think that she would want him to read her journals—even with the depth of confessions they'd shared. She sat at the other end of the couch and said, "On Monday, after you'd asked me out, I was . . . stunned. When I came home that night, I seemed to remember writing about our previous encounters in my journal. Knowing Rebecca's age and the timing of the usual baby visits, it wasn't too hard to find the right dates. I want you to read what I wrote. It's not much, really. But maybe it will help you understand why all of this feels so amazing to me."

"Okay," he said, "if you're sure."

"Of course. I've already poured my heart out to you; there's no reason why you shouldn't read my journals."

"I feel honored," he said, pressing a hand over the book lying on top. It had a blue velvet cover.

"The places are marked with those removable tape flags," she said, pointing them out as she reached over to open one of the books to the first marker. "Just . . . read between the flags."

"Okay," he said again but just looked for a moment at her written words, thinking how beautiful her handwriting was, and how marvelous it was that she kept a journal. It was something he wished he was better at.

"That first paragraph isn't about you, but you need to read it to understand," she said.

He nodded and began to read. The paragraph was a brief, disparaging summary of her quickly crumbling marriage and her husband's appalling behavior, and how it had made her feel. It sounded like a difficult yet brave moment in her life when she had snapped herself out of denial. His name was obviously Randall, and Wade felt immediately angry on Laura's behalf. Then he went on to read,

My own grief was diverted today by an encounter at the office. While I was weighing and measuring a beautiful two-month-old girl, I commented to the father about the fact that he had brought her in, and I asked where the mother was. He told me she had died six weeks ago, and it

took every bit of courage I had not to crumble right there on the spot. I wanted to just hold that baby and never let her go, as if I, of all people, could somehow make up for her losing her mother. Then I looked at this guy and he was crying.

Wade looked up at Laura to find her watching him closely, biting her lip. He thought of this moment from his perspective, and how well he'd remembered it all this time. Now it all felt marvelously eerie.

He read on.

Truly, a man was standing there crying, and I wanted to take HIM in my arms and never let him go, as if I, of all people, could somehow make up for him losing his wife. I remember his wife quite well, for some reason. Much of the time the children and their parents all blend together, but I remember that the baby looked like a miniature of her mother, and we talked about babies seeming to bring a little bit of heaven with them. She told me she felt sure that her little daughter could see angels. I wonder now if this precious little girl can still see her mother.

Wade put a hand over his mouth as sadness crept a little too close for comfort. Once he had composed himself he looked up again and asked, "You remembered her?"

"Yes, I still do. For some reason she left an impression."

Wade squeezed his eyes closed, and his emotions crept closer to the surface.

"What?" she asked gently.

Wade knew he couldn't share his thoughts now without falling apart. He just said, "Some other time," and continued to read.

Just the thought makes me cry, just like I cried when I was standing there in the exam room with a complete stranger. I'm sure my own emotions probably have a lot more to do with what's going on in my own life, but I couldn't help thinking that if I had died six weeks ago, Randall probably wouldn't be crying. Later I was actually excited to realize this sweet father had left the baby's blanket behind. I called him, then dropped it by on my way home. I was glad I didn't have to lie when I said it was almost on my way. He was so glad to get it back in his hands that I could almost imagine he'd been crying over misplacing it. His wife had made it, crocheted those pretty little edges. How sweet is that? For some silly reason I can't get his face out of my mind. Better his than Randall's, I suppose, when I feel so betrayed and angry with him.

He stopped where the little tape flag had been placed. He turned to her and said, "I *had* been crying over losing the blanket. Your calling me and bringing it over was an answer to prayers, truly."

She laughed softly. "And I thought it was just an excuse to see you again."

He smiled at her, and she said, "Okay, turn the page. Read what I wrote the next day."

I haven't been able to stop thinking about this guy crying over his wife's death while I was holding his baby. There's something about it that has suddenly made my decision very clear and easy. I can't stay with Randall. He will never change. He will never love me the way I deserve to be loved. I'm filing for an annulment, and I'm doing it today. Enough of this! I know it's going to be ugly, which is all the more reason I need to get it over with. I find myself praying for Rebecca (that's the baby's name), and for her

*father, even though I don't know his first name, and I
can't remember his last. Maybe I should look it up. For
the time being, I'll just pray for Rebecca's father. I wonder
if he's as lonely right now as I am. I wonder if it's harder
to lose a spouse to death, or to have them turn from Jekyll
to Hyde on the honeymoon. I think I might prefer death.
At least the love would remain pure. But maybe Rebecca's
father wouldn't agree with me. I'd like to talk to him
about it, but I doubt he'd appreciate having some silly
nurse calling to say, "So what are your thoughts on death
vs. divorce?" In my opinion, it stinks either way, and it's
not fair. But what do I know? According to Randall, I
know nothing.*

Wade had to reread that paragraph to fully absorb it, and
then he found himself crying—but grateful not to have to feel
embarrassed over it.

"What is it?" Laura asked, taking his hand.

"You know how they say that grief comes in stages?"

"Yes."

"Well, I think this is one of them." He shook his head and
wiped his tears on his sleeve. "I just . . . think about . . . how it
was back then, and . . . I don't know how I got through it.
You're right. Either way it stinks, and it's not fair." He turned
to look at her and smiled. "But then . . . if we hadn't gone
through it, we wouldn't be sitting here together."

"That's true," she said and wiped at his tears with her
fingers. "I didn't intend to make you cry."

"It's okay. You like men who aren't ashamed to cry. I'm just
trying to impress you."

"It's working," she said. "But you'd better read the rest and
get it over with."

"Okay," he said, and she took that book from him before
she opened the second one to the indicated spot. And he read,

Little Rebecca is six months old. I was so excited when I got to see her again that I had a hard time not jumping up and down. That would have been a spectacle in the waiting room! I wasn't too disappointed to see her father either. He wears a beard, a very nice one. I've always liked beards. I should look up his first name. He's going to medical school to be a pediatrician. I think he'll make a good one.

"Now here," she said, turning the pages for him to a date that was some weeks later.

Rebecca has an ear infection. Poor little thing. Her father looked pretty frazzled. I was tempted to offer to walk the floor with her through the night so he could get some sleep, but he probably would have threatened to call Social Services or something. I hope she gets feeling better quickly. I hate to see sick babies. That makes my job pretty pathetic. Okay, I love to see them get better, and those healthy baby checkups are a hoot. I love my job! And I can easily say that Rebecca Morrison (I remembered her last name this time) is my favorite patient. I wish I could see her more often, but I wouldn't want her to get sick again. And to tell the truth, I think I have a crush on her father, or maybe I just sense his broken heart, and something in me wants to believe that I could heal it. Or maybe he could heal mine. It's a nice thought, but purely fantasy. Still, a good fantasy and a carton of ice cream aren't such bad company. Better than a bad husband or a date with some loser who acts like we should be playing out some sick TV sitcom.

Again Wade felt tempted to cry, but he managed to force it into a chuckle instead. "You had a crush on me when she was six months old?"

"That's what it says, and I never lie to my journal. Well, I never lie anyway, but I don't mince words with my journal."

"What was I thinking?" he asked. "We could have had three more children by now."

She laughed at the exaggeration and pointed out, "You thought I was married."

"I know. I was an idiot."

He turned to find the next entry she'd marked, and she said, "I don't think you're going to like this one."

Wade took a deep breath and drawled hesitantly, "Okay."

"And I really debated showing this one to you; it's actually kind of embarrassing, but . . . we've gotten past that, right?"

"I should hope so," he said and began to read.

My fantasy has been shattered! I'm crying like a baby, feeling like a fool, and realizing how horribly pathetic my life is. Rebecca is a year old now. She's healthy and growing and beautiful, and her father is getting married again. Didn't he realize through our total of twenty minutes of interaction through the past year that I had fallen for him? That's what you get, Laura, for sitting around indulging in senseless fantasies while you do nothing to go out there and make any real life happen. You're pathetic! And now you have to admit, my dear self, that you've allowed your heart to be broken once again, which is completely ludicrous. How can someone break your heart when they never even knew they were holding it? I don't even know his first name. Why do I keep forgetting to look it up on the records? Maybe I don't really want to know.

Wade slammed the book closed as if he could slam the door to his memories of how deeply Marina had hurt him. Of course, he was glad he hadn't married her, but he wished he'd never fallen in love with her. He wished that he had been paying better attention, that he and Laura could have ended each other's loneliness and misery a long time ago. And even though he understood the reasons, and that this was how it needed to be, he still didn't like it.

He turned to look at her but didn't know what to say. She looked concerned, almost scared. Reading what little he'd read about Randall, he wondered if she believed he would lose his temper. The thought made him sick. He took her hand into his and kissed it, then he urged her closer and put his arm around her, pressing his lips into her hair. "Where was my head, Laura? We should have been together a long time ago. It should have been you instead of Marina, and the wedding wouldn't have been called off, and I would have been here with you when Tina died, and—"

"Hush," she said, pressing her fingers over his lips. "We can't change what's past. We're together now. Maybe we . . . needed this time . . . to learn what we needed to learn."

"I believe that, actually. But I still feel like an idiot for not paying better attention." Looking into her eyes he felt compelled to share the thought that disturbed him most. "Do you remember when I came into the office and asked for a CBC for Rebecca? And you called me with the results?"

"Yes, I remember."

"I was dating Marina at the time, but feeling confused I think. Looking back, I'm not sure what I was feeling. When you called me, there was something I wanted to say so badly that it almost jumped out of my mouth, but I told myself it was ridiculous, and I didn't say it."

"It doesn't matter," she said. "We can't change it and—"

"Okay, so we can't change it, but it still ticks me off."

She smiled as she said, "The only thing that matters to me is to know that you were thinking of me, while I was thinking of you." She touched his face and asked, "What did you want to say?"

He thought for a moment. "It's like . . . the thought just came to me out of nowhere . . . that I wanted to tell you I thought you were an amazing woman . . . and that I hoped your husband was treating you the way you deserved."

Laura sucked in her breath, trying to imagine how that would have struck her at the time. "He was long gone by then," she said.

"I know that now, but I didn't then. If I'd brought him up you would have told me you were no longer married, and it might have made a big difference in the steps I took in my life after that."

"It doesn't matter," she said again, gently, soothingly. "You're here now," she whispered and kissed him. "And I'm grateful."

"Oh, so am I," he said and took her into his arms, kissing her again.

When he started to enjoy it way too much he was grateful to hear Laura say, "Why don't you read what else I wrote?"

"Okay," he said and cleared his throat loudly, putting some distance between them.

Laura opened the third journal to the first place she'd marked. He read a brief entry about her relief when he'd told her that he hadn't gotten married after all, but it was immediately followed with the statement, *It's all very silly anyway, because I know a man like that would never show any interest in a woman like me.*

Wade looked up at her and said, "Are you kidding? Are you *kidding?* Where does this come from?"

"What?" He pointed out the sentence and she read it. Without apology she said, "That's how I felt. I still have trouble believing it's real, that you're really here, saying such things to me, crying over my journals." She smiled and added, "Read the last one."

Wade found it and read,

> *Rebecca Morrison is two years old, and she's still my favorite patient. Her father is still available. I wish I could apply for the job of being Rebecca's mother. Maybe I should just come right out and ask if there's an opening and where I could get an application. Since that idea is completely ludicrous, I should probably just start getting serious about dating again. It's been a while. If nothing else, Rebecca's father has made me suddenly rather discontent with being alone, so I'm going to get my profile on the web again, and I'm setting a goal to get out more. A goal is good.*

"So you see," she said when he'd finished reading, "seeing you made me get my profile back on that website, which made you come and ask me out. How weird is that?"

"It's amazing," he said and kissed her quickly.

Again she touched his face. "You are an answer to my every prayer, Wade Morrison. And I love you."

"I love you too, Laura Dove."

The temptation to kiss her again—and again—motivated him to say, "I hate to admit it, but I've got to get some sleep tonight if I ever hope to become a doctor."

"Okay," she said, clearly disappointed. "I don't want to keep you from becoming a doctor."

They stood in the center of the front room and he took both her hands into his. "When will I see you again?" she asked.

"Well," he said, "tomorrow my shift at the clinic goes until late evening. The doctor I'm working with is on call. Friday?"

She sighed loudly. "I'm taking an elderly sister in the ward to the temple; I'm her visiting teacher."

"Okay then . . . I guess that brings us to our Saturday date. I'll pick you up at ten. Is it okay if I call you tomorrow when I get home?"

"Of course," she said. "I'll look forward to it."

He pressed a hand over the side of her face and into her hair before he took a step closer and bent to kiss her. "I love you, Laura," he muttered and kissed her again, only because they were standing up, and he was on his way out the door.

"I love you too, Wade," she said and pressed her lips on his once more.

He wrapped his arms around her, hugging her tightly as he'd done this morning. She returned his embrace, feeling immersed in his love.

"I'll talk to you tomorrow," Wade said and kissed her brow before he hurried out the door.

The next couple of days dragged for Wade while he fought to stay focused on what he was trying to learn by following doctors around and taking mental notes on everything they did. He kept Rebecca close to him while he did some self-inflicted studying, wanting to understand everything that was going on in the clinic where he was currently spending long, tedious hours. He read his daughter some stories and took her for a long walk in the stroller. But everything he did felt hollow and empty without Laura there. They talked on the phone a handful of times, but the timing was always difficult—either Rebecca needed his attention, or one or the other of them needed to be somewhere.

He woke up Saturday morning feeling as "happy as Christmas," he thought, recalling one of his favorite songs. After he'd showered, he bathed Rebecca and dressed her in her favorite outfit, an old-fashioned flowered sundress with daisy appliqués on the skirt. And little white sandals. He packed the diaper bag and loaded the stroller into the trunk before they had breakfast. Jane commented on Rebecca's pigtails and said, "You're getting pretty good at that."

"Practice," he said with pride.

When they arrived at Laura's house, he got Rebecca out of her seat and set her on the front porch. "Knock on the door," he said, and she did, but it was barely a little tap. He picked her up and pointed to the doorbell. "Push the button." She pushed it and giggled when she heard the chime. He set her down and stepped off the porch.

When the door came open, Laura laughed and squatted down in front of Rebecca, talking to her as if they were peers. Rebecca just held up two fingers and said, "I two."

"I know you are," Laura said, lifting the baby into her arms while she smiled at Wade. "Hi," she said. "I've missed you."

"I've missed you too," he said and moved close enough to give her a quick kiss.

"Ooh," she said, "now the neighbors will be talking."

"Is that a problem?"

"Not for me." She laughed. "Most of them will be saying . . ." she raised her voice, "'It's about time she got a man in her life, poor soul.'"

"Let them talk," he said and kissed her again. Wade pointed at Laura and said to Rebecca, "That's Laura. Can you say Laura?" She looked puzzled but said nothing. "Say Laura," Wade added. She only shook her little head. "Oh well," Wade added with a chuckle.

"Go hoosey," Rebecca said, and Laura laughed.

"She knows where we're going, and patience is not one of her strong traits." Wade took her from Laura and put her back into her seat while Laura locked the door of the house. Wade opened the passenger door to help her in. By the time he got in on the other side, Laura was buckled in, but she turned as far as she could to talk to Rebecca in the backseat. Before he got out of the driveway, Laura was singing the five little piggies song, playing with Rebecca's toes where they stuck out of her sandals, and making the child giggle.

When that apparently got old, Rebecca said, "Daddy, cup."

Wade pointed toward the bag and said to Laura, "She wants her drink. Would you mind? It's just in the side pocket there."

Laura gave Rebecca the cup with a sippy lid and smiled as if just watching her drink it was entertaining. "She's adorable," Laura said.

"Yes, she is."

"She must look like her mother, because I only see a very subtle resemblance to you."

"Yes, she does," Wade said.

Rebecca finished with the cup and threw it to the floor as usual, before she said, "Moozah, Daddy. Moozah."

Wade chuckled. "She wants music," he told Laura and turned on the stereo. "She likes *Collective Soul*." One of the songs they'd danced to the other day filled the car, and Rebecca immediately started bouncing in her seat and clapping her hands, which Laura thought was hysterical. Wade spoke loudly enough to be heard above the music. "I have this bad habit of listening to music very loudly when I'm aggravated or stressed. After Elena died, I did it more than usual. And again after the Marina thing blew up. Rebecca's rarely gotten into the car without loud music playing. So I trained her, I suppose. She only goes for two volumes. Loud or off."

Laura laughed again. "So, is this like emotional eating?"

"Yeah, I think it is."

"Doesn't bother me," she said. "I prefer it loud myself."

"How very compatible we are," Wade said, kissing her hand.

At the mall Wade got the stroller out of the trunk while Laura unbuckled Rebecca and got her out of the car. Wade put

Rebecca in the stroller and buckled her in, saying to Laura, "We call this the all-terrain vehicle. It's got a lot of miles on it." As they started across the parking lot, he pushed the stroller with one hand and put an arm around Laura, saying with a smirk, "One-hand steering for our convenience."

"How delightful," she said and put an arm around his waist.

As they came through the door directly in front of the carousel, Rebecca immediately became excited and tried to get out of the stroller. "Kitty, Daddy, kitty," she said.

He explained to Laura. "She likes to ride on the kitty, as opposed to the horses or whatever else they've got on there. But she does call the carousel the hoosey, which I assume is a horsey."

Wade took Rebecca on the carousel twice, and Laura sat where she could watch. Then they walked through the mall and had a delightful time perusing all the sights. They spent a ridiculous amount of time in the toy section of one of the department stores, where Laura bought Rebecca a baby doll when Wade wasn't looking.

"You don't need to buy my daughter presents," he said as they left the store.

"I can if I want to," she insisted. He could only laugh, and had to admit that Rebecca loved the doll. She was making quite a display out of talking to it as they continued their excursion. For lunch Wade and Laura had Chinese food, but Rebecca's tradition was a corn dog.

Laura felt thoroughly enchanted with her observance of Wade and Rebecca. She'd always enjoyed the few minutes here and there when they'd come into the office. But this was completely different. He clearly understood every word of her two-year-old language, when Laura often didn't know what she was saying. And Wade spoke to Rebecca directly, no baby talk, as if she were his equal. When she fussed he was patient and loving.

It became evident that lunch at the mall was a practiced ritual when Wade put Rebecca into a highchair. He cut Rebecca's corn dog lengthwise and then in bite-sized pieces, saying to the child, "It's hot. It needs to cool, and we don't want you to choke if it's too big." He put a puddle of ketchup on her plate and poured part of his lemonade into her cup with the lid.

"Hot, Daddy," she said, touching a piece of the corn dog. She held up her finger and he kissed it. He tested the temperature of her food and assured her it was okay now before she started dipping pieces into the ketchup and eating them, getting it all over her hands and face.

"How's the Chinese?" he asked Laura.

"Marvelous," she said.

"Emotional eating?" he asked with a smirk.

"Absolutely."

"And today's emotion would be . . ."

"Euphoria," she said, and he laughed.

"Amen," he said and gave her a quick kiss.

Laura made a production of opening her fortune cookie for Rebecca to see the paper appear in the middle. She let Rebecca take the paper out, then Laura read it to her in an animated voice. "It says here that you should be open to new opportunities that are just around the corner. I think that means we need to ride the carousel again." She broke off a tiny piece of the cookie and put it into Rebecca's mouth. "You want to ride the kitty again?"

"Kitty, kitty," she said.

Laura said to Wade, "It's my turn to ride the carousel . . . Daddy."

"Go for it," he said and started washing Rebecca's hands and face with a baby wipe from the bag. "But she needs a diaper change first. We're not up to potty training yet." He picked up Rebecca and the bag, saying, "We'll be back."

A few minutes later Wade was watching the carousel go around, with Laura standing next to Rebecca, who sat on the big kitty. He savored the moment, recalling the emotion of the day: euphoria. Yeah, that was it.

With the carousel ride completed, Laura declared that they needed to go look at shoes. Wade sat on the floor in the shoe store for more than forty minutes, watching the women in his life trying on shoes. *Euphoria.* When they'd agreed on a pair of pink hiking boots for Rebecca, Wade insisted that he was also going to buy the white shoes with the ankle straps for Laura.

"I have nothing whatsoever to match these shoes," she said.

"Well, I like them. Maybe we should go find you something in white."

"What for?" she asked, not wanting him to keep spending money on her. Then she realized he was staring at her, as if to imply some silent message.

She recalled what had just been said, and her heart quickened just before he took the shoes to the checkout counter, saying over his shoulder, "I'm not going to propose in a shoe store."

Laura took Rebecca into the mall corridor while Wade bought the shoes. Her heart beat so fast that it almost hurt as she considered what he'd just said and the implications attached. Surely it had to be a dream! Surely it was all too good to be true! But something in Wade's eyes let her know it was real—as real as anything in this world could be—more real than anything she'd ever encountered, because it was real right down to the deepest part of her spiritual and emotional self. She could never articulate the idea, but she knew beyond any doubt that her feelings for Wade were not coincidence or happenstance, and they were not to be taken lightly. He was the best thing that had ever happened to her, and if she had any say in the matter, she had no intention of ever letting him go.

She watched Wade walk toward her, shoe purchases in hand, and she felt as if her spirit had known his for all eternity. She loved him so much! He put the packages into the storage area at the bottom of the stroller, then took Rebecca and buckled her into the seat before he took Laura's hand, saying, "We have not yet begun to shop."

Rebecca soon fell asleep in the stroller, which prompted Wade and Laura to take a break in the furniture section of a department store and just talk for a while. At a lull in the conversation, Laura took a long look at Rebecca and said, "She's so precious. I just want to hug her all the time. She's like a cross between a Cabbage Patch doll and a teddy bear."

"That's very well put," he said. "I know exactly what you mean."

Following more time at the mall, they went to a park and had a marvelous time playing on the swings and the slide with Rebecca. By that time they were hungry again and went out for burgers and fries, because Rebecca loved to dip her french fries and suck the ketchup off until the fry was worn out. Once they were done eating, Wade asked, "So now what?"

"Truthfully," Laura sighed, "I hate to, but . . . I should go home. I have a lesson to prepare for tomorrow, and some laundry to do." She took Wade's hand across the table. "But . . . there is one more thing I'd like to do . . . unless you don't want to."

"Okay," he drawled, wondering why she sounded so nervous.

"Would you take me to Elena's grave?"

Wade swallowed carefully. He was so touched he could hardly speak.

"Is it very far?" she asked when he said nothing.

"No, it's nearby."

"If you're not comfortable with it then—"

"It's not that," he said. "I go there often. I would love to take you there. It just . . . means a lot to me that you would even think of such a thing."

Laura smiled and shrugged. "I think Elena and I would understand each other."

"Yes, I'm certain you're right," he said.

Laura wasn't sure why she felt like this was an important step, but she did. They made a quick stop to buy some flowers, then drove to the cemetery where Elena was buried. Once Rebecca was out of the car she ran straight to her mother's grave and touched the words carved there, the way she'd likely seen her father do countless times. Laura actually felt teary as she observed Wade guiding Rebecca through the process of putting the flowers above the headstone in a ritual that was obviously customary. Then he stood and put his arm around Laura, pressing a kiss into her hair. She heard him sniffle and asked, "Are you okay?"

"Oh, yeah," he said, his voice breaking. "If you must know, these are happy tears. It's the first time I've ever come here and felt real hope." He wrapped both arms tightly around her as if to silently express gratitude. She returned his embrace, and he added, "I should take you home."

"It's been the most wonderful day of my life," she said firmly.

Wade kissed her and said, "May there be many more just like it."

"Amen," she murmured, and he reluctantly took her home.

* * *

Wade did little that evening but care for Rebecca and try to catch up mentally with all that had happened since he'd found Laura's photograph on the Internet. He was glad to be alone in the house with his daughter, just needing some time to let it all settle in. And the bottom line made him smile. He loved Laura, and she loved him. The inevitable path before them was all he could ever hope for and more. And he felt deliriously happy.

He forced himself to prepare his own lesson for his class of teenagers and made certain all was in order for Sunday. Alex and his family came in from a movie, asking how his day had gone. He just told them, "It was great," and left it at that.

"You need to invite her over to dinner tomorrow," Jane insisted. "Do you think she'd come?"

"Unless she has plans," Wade said.

"I work from six to six tomorrow," Alex said. "So let's do it at six-thirty."

"I'll ask her," Wade said and went upstairs to get Rebecca ready for bed.

Wade was glad to have Laura call him soon after Rebecca had gone down for the night. Her lesson was prepared, and she was folding clean laundry. She eagerly accepted the dinner invitation, and Wade was pleased to have an excuse to see her tomorrow. They finally said good night at some time past eleven, and Wade had to call her first thing the next morning just to hear her voice before the day began. Their church schedules were opposite, which made it impossible for them to see each other before evening, since they both had lessons to teach.

At six o'clock Wade arrived at Laura's home. He was getting Rebecca out of the car when he heard Laura call, "I'm back here. Come this way." He saw her peeking through an open tall wooden gate at the other end of the driveway. He walked past where her car was parked and through the gate, greeting her with a kiss.

"Hi," she said, touching his face, "I missed you."

"I missed you too," he said and kissed her again as Rebecca took off across the yard. Wade turned to see her go, then said, "Wow," when he realized how beautiful it was. The backyard was completely fenced in, with a little shed in one corner, a little vegetable garden, a variety of flowerbeds, a couple of old trees, and a little wrought-iron bench beneath one of them. It was all well groomed without being so immaculate that it didn't feel real. He loved it! "It's so great," he said.

"Thank you," she replied, taking his hand. "This is my haven . . . even when it's cold out, I often just walk through the yard or sit on the bench for a while."

They found Rebecca bending over a little plastic gopher set in the center of a patch of flowers, looking as if he'd just poked his head up out of the ground. She was chattering to it as if it might respond. Laura laughed softly and said, "I'm not much for yard ornaments, but that one was just too cute to resist."

"Rebecca likes it," Wade said and watched Laura pick a flower and give it to Rebecca, showing her how to smell it. She eased closer to Laura, obviously wanting to be held. Rebecca held the flower up to Laura's nose for her to smell it. "That's Laura," Wade said. "Can you say Laura?"

Rebecca just smiled at him and smelled her flower. "Fower," she said and held it up for him to smell.

"Are we in a hurry?" Laura asked.

"We have a few minutes. Why?"

"I'd like to show Rebecca something, if that's okay."

"Of course," he said and followed her through the back door, into the kitchen. They went down the hall, past the bathroom and into what appeared to be a spare bedroom where dolls and stuffed animals were strategically arranged on the bed, the dresser, the cedar chest at the foot of the bed, and on the floor. Rebecca squealed with delight and squirmed to get down.

"There's nothing in this room that she can hurt, or that can hurt her," Laura said, then she laughed to see Rebecca trying to pick up as many dolls and animals as she could possibly hold. Wade put his arm around Laura and laughed with her. While

Laura watched Rebecca, her eyes sparkling, Wade became more focused on Laura, wondering how it was possible for one human being to actually feel so intensely for another. Impulsively he pushed her hair back from her face and kissed her cheek, then her temple, then just behind her ear. She laughed and shivered visibly, making him chuckle. He kissed her throat, then let her hair fall back into place as he said, "You are so beautiful."

She turned to look at him, her eyes glowing with admiration and warmth. "You are so sweet, so good to me."

He kissed her lips quickly and said, "I think we should go. I'm not sure how good Rebecca's chaperoning skills might be."

Laura laughed softly, and they turned to see that Rebecca had settled for a soft pink stuffed kitty with a big purple bow around its neck. "Her favorite colors," Wade said.

"Well, good," Laura said. "She can keep it."

"Come along," Wade said, picking her up, along with the kitty.

"You want to keep the kitty?" Laura asked her, and Rebecca nodded.

"Say, 'Thank you, Laura,'" Wade urged.

"Tan cue," Rebecca said, but she made no attempt to say Laura's name.

"You're welcome," Laura said, and they went out through the back door.

CHAPTER 18

Driving toward Alex's home, Laura asked, "So, we're going to your brother's house, where you're living, right?"

"That's right," Wade said.

"I've actually been there before . . . just for a minute."

"Yeah," he chuckled, "that's pretty weird to think of now."

"It's an amazing house," she commented. "I believe you told me it was a family home."

"Yeah, Alex's family, not mine."

"I think you told me that too; now I understand the difference. So . . . did he inherit it or . . ."

"Yes and no. His great-great-grandfather, on his mother's side, was Alexander Barrett. He came west with the original Saints and built the house. Alex is named after him."

"And Barrett, too."

"That's right." He smiled. "Anyway, Alex's cousin Susan—actually she's his mother's cousin—inherited the house many years ago. Apparently at the time it was a neglected wreck, so no one else really wanted it. They've put a lot into restoring and renovating it, spending at least as much as they would have on a typical home, I'm sure. Alex didn't meet Susan until he was already a doctor, but they quickly became close. Susan and her husband Donald kind of became surrogate grandparents to Alex's kids, and when Barrett was going through his leukemia, they let the family live here and helped with the kids. Susan didn't want the house to just be sold someday when she no longer needed it, and she knew her kids would do just that if they inherited it. So, she sold it to Alex and Jane for about half of what it's worth, I'd guess. Donald and Susan are on a mission right now. Actually, they kind of do one mission after another; I think this is their third. They stay here when they're around, which isn't much. But Alex and Jane technically own the house now, or at least they're paying the mortgage on it."

Wade pulled the car up in front of the house and looked up. "I love this house; it's amazing. There's a wonderful spirit here, but I'm sure that has a lot to do with the people who live here." He winked at Laura. "You're going to love them."

"I can't wait," she said and fought back a rush of anxiety.

"And they'll love you too," Wade said, noting the way she put a hand over her stomach.

"Hope so," she said with a nervous smile.

"No question about it," he said and got out to open her door before he helped Rebecca out of her seat.

Laura was overcome with nervous excitement as Wade led her through the front door of the Barrett home. It felt like stepping into heaven. He set Rebecca down and she ran into a room off the hall. Laura could see a beautiful, narrow, upward-winding staircase with a lovely polished wood banister. The atmosphere of the home was everything Wade had promised, both in its beauty and in the spirit of the people who lived here.

"Come on," he said, taking her hand. They followed Rebecca into a comfortable family room where she had joined a child near her same size with blonde hair—her little cousin Ruth, no doubt. *The twins,* Laura thought fondly and could certainly see why. In spite of no physical resemblance, they were nearly identical in size, and the way they played together made it evident they spent a great deal of time together. They were both digging in a box of dress-ups, while an older girl, obviously Katharine, was supervising the assignment of princess paraphernalia.

"Hey there," Wade said, and Katharine looked up, clearly annoyed by the interruption. Laura knew from what Wade had told her about his nieces and nephews that Katharine enjoyed mothering the younger children and actually took very good care of them.

"Hi," she said. "I'm glad Rebecca is here. She can be the Cinderella, since Ruthie wants to be Ariel."

"Okay then," Wade said. "This is my friend Laura."

"Hi," Katharine said again.

"That's Katharine," Wade said, pointing at her. "She's eight."

"Hello, Katharine," Laura said, but the girls were too busy to respond.

Wade led her down the hall and past the stairs to where the kitchen was. They entered to see a woman with blonde, curly hair, which was pulled up in a clip, wearing jeans and a white blouse, sitting at the table reading from the latest *Ensign*. Laura knew this was Jane.

"Hey, sis," Wade said, and she looked up.

"Oh hi," she said brightly. "It's all in the oven staying warm; we're just waiting for Alex to get home. He's on his way."

She stood up, and Wade said, "Jane, this is Laura Dove. Laura, my brother's wife, Jane."

"I've heard nothing but wonderful things about you," Jane said. Then to Wade, "You weren't lying; she is very beautiful."

"Indeed," Wade said, smiling at Laura.

"Oh stop that," Laura said. To Jane she added, "It's so nice to meet you. Wade has told me how good you are to him."

"We love having him around," Jane said, then surprised Laura by giving her a hug. "It's really nice to have you here. I hope you'll make yourself at home."

"Thank you," Laura said, and they heard a door come open nearby.

"There's the man of the hour," Jane said, and Alex walked into the kitchen, wearing standard hospital scrubs. Laura had heard Wade mention that his brother was a doctor, but seeing him in his scrubs helped her make the connection. He was obviously the brother who had stitched up Wade's wrist, and she recalled briefly seeing him with Wade at the hospital cafeteria.

"Hi," Jane said and greeted him with a kiss.

"Hi," he said to her. Then he turned and added, "This must be the famous Laura. It is so nice to finally meet you. Well, there was that minute at the hospital, but that hardly counted."

"Finally?" Wade asked as Alex took Laura's hand. "I only asked her on a date six days ago."

"Yes," Alex said, holding onto her hand, "but you admitted that you've known her for a couple of years." He looked directly at Laura. "I hope my kid brother is treating you like a queen."

"He is indeed," Laura said, winking at Wade. "It's great to see you again, Alex. I've heard nothing but good about you."

Alex gave Wade an exaggerated glare. "When did you take up lying?"

"I don't lie, and you know it," Wade said.

"Well, dinner is ready," Jane said, taking something out of the oven. Alex stuck his head into the hall and called the kids to dinner before he went to the sink to wash up. The girls came running in, and Wade put Rebecca into her highchair and got a bib on her while Laura didn't hesitate to do the same with Ruthie, since Alex and Jane were putting food on the table.

They were all ready to sit down when Alex said, "I guess the boys didn't hear. I'll just . . ."

"No, I'll get them," Wade said and took Laura's hand, leading her up the stairs. The house almost felt like a bed and breakfast to Laura, except that it wasn't so formally decorated. They went into a room that was obviously another family gathering place. It had comfortable places to sit, a TV that was turned off, and shelves filled with games, puzzles, and videos. Laura noticed a young boy on the floor, putting together a puzzle that was simple enough for his age. She knew this had to be Preston; he was five, just about to begin kindergarten. And the boy that she knew had to be Barrett was putting together a thousand-piece puzzle on a large coffee table.

"Hey there, guys," Wade said, but Barrett was concentrating. "It's time to eat." Preston jumped up and rushed out of the room without even acknowledging them. Wade chuckled and said, "I guess he's hungry."

"Okay, I'm coming," Barrett said without looking up.

"Remember how I told you about the gorgeous babe I had a date with?"

Barrett put a piece into place and said, "If she's so gorgeous, how come she went out with you?"

Wade smirked at Laura, then said, "I don't know. Why don't you ask her? I brought her to meet you."

Barrett looked up, and Laura was struck with how much he looked like his father. Recalling that he'd once had leukemia, and Wade had given bone marrow to save him, she felt an unexpected rise of emotion just looking at him.

"Hi," he said, his eyes intrigued.

"Hello, Barrett," Laura said. "Wade has told me that you're the coolest kid in the world."

Barrett chuckled. "He just says stuff like that because we have the same blood. I guess he thinks that makes me much cooler than I used to be."

"Well, yeah," Wade said as Barrett walked past them and into the hall. Wade said quietly to Laura, "He's ten going on seventeen." Barrett hurried down the stairs, and they followed more slowly. "Alex tells me he always acted older than his age, but it's even more obvious since he recovered from the cancer. It's like he has this spirit that's much older and wiser than any of the rest of us. Of course, when you go through what he's been through, there's got to be some level of superhuman something."

"I'd like to hear more about that," she said.

Laura enjoyed every moment of dinner with Alex and Jane's family. She felt marvelously comfortable and welcome; she felt as if she could just move in and be a part of them without even causing a hiccup. The idea sounded both glorious and ludicrous.

She loved watching Wade care so tenderly for Rebecca, even when she was making a horrible mess of her dinner, and her antics created many interruptions. She also loved the way he interacted so naturally with the other children. Preston was sitting next to him, and the child asked Wade more than once to help him with something, as if it were a common and natural occurrence. And when Ruthie dropped her cup, Wade was the first to get up and give it to her.

Laura also enjoyed observing Alex and Jane. She felt intrigued by the way they so naturally exhibited respect and admiration for each other. She'd seen a lot of bad marriages— some that were blatantly dysfunctional, and others that were an idealistic farce in public and a horrid nightmare in private. She knew playacting in a relationship when she saw it, and this wasn't it. They were genuinely comfortable with their relationship, and they clearly had a great deal of love and respect for Wade.

When the children were finished eating, they ran off to play. The little ones were washed up and set loose, with Katharine eagerly telling her mother she would watch out for them.

"Oh, she's such a blessing," Jane said as the girls ran out and the room became suddenly very quiet. The adults remained at the table, talking and laughing as they told Laura stories about the family and their unique connection. Alex told his slant on learning that Wade was his brother. At moments he made it sound very funny; at others it was touching.

"It's hard to believe you haven't known you were family forever."

"It feels that way," Wade said, "but I initially met most of the family at the hospital."

Laura looked confused, and Alex added, "Barrett was in isolation at the time; we practically lived there."

"I can't even imagine how difficult that must have been," Laura said.

"It was certainly an adventure." Alex sighed loudly. "One we're glad to have behind us."

"I can't help being somewhat . . . fascinated," Laura said. "Maybe it's because I work for a pediatrician."

"Jane has scrapbooks," Wade said.

"Really?" Laura said as if she she'd been told she'd won a lifetime supply of ice cream. "Could I see them?"

"Sure," Jane said and left the room. Wade and Alex both stood up to clear the table, and Laura helped. By the time Jane returned, the table was cleaned off, and she put two thick books in the center.

"Some people thought I was morbid," Jane said. "Others thought I was crazy—taking pictures to preserve memories that were so horrible. But I wanted a history of it, I suppose. And there were many times we didn't think he'd make it. I guess I decided to default on the possibility that I might want the pictures someday; and I could always throw them out if I ended up hating them."

"I'm glad she did it," Alex said. "They're still hard to look at—at least they are for me. But I think it's something that will have meaning for Barrett someday—to see what he survived."

"However," Jane said, "I must say you're one of the few people who has actually wanted to see them. Most people have a hard time looking at the ugly side of life. Thankfully we were blessed with people in our lives who weren't put off by it; they helped get us through."

"Then there are people like us who had no choice but to look at it," Alex said. "We had to live it. We're just grateful Barrett survived. It was all worth it because we still have him. If we didn't, I'd probably have to burn the pictures."

Laura felt touched by his words and the way these people were being so open with her. She opened the first book, and on the first page it read, "The Journey Through the Valley."

"The valley?" Laura asked.

"The valley of the shadow of death," Alex said.

Laura nodded, almost feeling near tears even before she started looking at pictures that documented the chronological order of Barrett's three-year battle with leukemia. There were photos of him at Primary Children's Medical Center during what his parents explained was the regular outpatient chemo regime they'd started out with. They had shots of Barrett with different people he had obviously gotten to know—doctors, nurses, staff, and other patients. He quickly lost his hair, and there were pictures of him doing what appeared to be many normal activities, wearing a variety of hats. A couple of pages were filled with pictures of him in exactly the same pose, wearing different hats.

"Everybody gave him a hat," Alex said. "He still has his hat collection and takes great pride in it."

Laura laughed softly but couldn't speak; she felt hard-pressed not to cry as the pictures told the story. Here was a family who had tried very hard to give their son some degree of a normal life, while nearly every photo showed a bald-headed child, looking tired and unhealthy. The age progression of

Katharine and Preston through Barrett's illness was also evident. And Jane and Alex showed an evolvement of weariness in their candid expressions.

The photos showed the documentation of the bone marrow transplants, where Barrett often looked so horrible that Laura finally reached a point where she couldn't hold the tears back any longer. Wade just handed her a tissue, and they answered her questions about what he'd gone through and why. While she understood a great deal about general medicine, she'd never encountered anything like this before. Alex told her that even as a physician he'd been ignorant of many aspects of Barrett's illness.

Tucked haphazardly between a couple of pages was a newspaper article. Laura unfolded it to see a picture of Alex in an exam room, wearing scrubs, and Barrett sitting cross-legged on the table, listening to his father's heart with a stethoscope. The headline read, *Doctor Gives Life to Dying Son.* The article's focus was on raising funds to pay for Barrett's transplant, but Laura caught her breath as she clearly remembered seeing this when it had come out. Before she could comment, Alex said, "I hate that headline, especially when my bone marrow didn't even work."

"The article did a great deal of good," Jane pointed out. "So much money was raised that it helped with other kids as well."

"I remember this," Laura said. "I'd just barely started working at the clinic, and somebody hung it on the bulletin board there; I guess it was of special interest in a pediatric clinic." She looked at Wade and felt something magically eerie as she said, "We all pitched in, and the clinic made a significant contribution."

Wade took a sharp breath. "Oh, that's weird," he said.

"It's amazing," Jane commented.

Wade looked at the date on the article and said to Alex, "I didn't even know you were my brother when this came out."

Alex just smiled and said, "Funny where life takes us, isn't it?" To Laura he said, "Thanks for the contribution. We owe you one."

"I don't think so," Laura said and tucked the article back into the book before she turned another page.

There were pictures of Barrett in the PICU with so many tubes and wires going in and out of him that it was downright shocking. And then he'd obviously recovered from that and was back in the isolation unit. As she looked through the photos, Barrett's parents explained their meaning or what had been taking place. Alex or Jane were often in the pictures, with evidence of long bedside vigils around them. Laura was especially taken by a photo of Alex sitting on Barrett's bed with the child in his arms, asleep but looking dead. The picture was perfectly candid and had captured a moment that actually made Laura's heart quicken. Alex's expression manifested despair; his eyes were closed as if in prayer, while he held his son close to him. It was the kind of photo that Laura might have expected to see in *Life Magazine* or *National Geographic*. While she couldn't stop staring at it, Jane said with reverence, "This was the day before we were told there was nothing more we could do. We really believed we were going to lose him."

Laura's tears escalated, and Wade handed her another tissue before he put his arm around her shoulders. "I'm so glad you didn't lose him," she said.

"We all are," Wade said.

"Yeah, a couple of days later," Alex said, "we were feeding Wade's bone marrow into him. It still took a while for him to come around, but it was the miracle we needed."

Laura turned the page and saw the point where Wade started showing up in the pictures. It was obvious that he too had become a part of the bedside vigils, and he was in many pictures that showed the slow but steady progression of Barrett's recovery. There were pictures from a trip to the zoo where Barrett was in Wade's arms, looking at the elephants. And Laura couldn't help noticing that Elena was in those pictures. She was also in the pictures that were taken the day that Barrett was baptized and celebrated his eighth birthday with his family. She was extremely pregnant, and so was Jane. Wade chuckled and pointed at Elena's belly, saying, "There's Rebecca. She's changed since then."

"So she has," Laura said comfortably. "But she looks like her mother; they're both very beautiful."

When Laura was finished looking through the pictures, she looked at the people surrounding her and felt deeply bonded with them. She felt compelled to say, "Thank you for sharing that with me. It's nice to have a glimpse into something so . . . profound."

"Thanks for actually being interested," Jane said. "It was a life-altering experience for us, to say the least."

Alex stood up to put the leftovers in the fridge, and Wade started rinsing dishes to go in the dishwasher. When Laura started washing a pan Jane protested, but Laura insisted. By the time she had a couple of pans washed, the kitchen was in order, then Jane got dessert out, which happened to be the makings for banana splits.

"Ooh, emotional eating," Wade said, winking at Laura, making her heart skip a beat. "And the emotion of the day would be . . ." He motioned toward her with his hand.

"Delight," she said, and he smiled as if he agreed whole-heartedly.

They decided against alerting the children to the fact that ice cream was available, so that the adults could eat dessert in peace and then fix it for the children afterward. Laura enjoyed the simple pleasure of eating banana splits with these wonderful people. She'd already accepted that she was completely and hopelessly in love with Wade, but she'd not expected to become so quickly and utterly taken by his family—at least those she'd met so far.

Laura was completely entertained by the children being given their dessert. All but the "twins" made their own banana splits with varying degrees of assistance. Rebecca and Ruth were put into their highchairs and given ice cream and banana pieces with which they made an incredible mess. Once the mess was cleaned up, Wade gave Laura a brief tour of the house, telling her some stories he knew of its history.

She was admiring a wide variety of framed photographs set out on a long hall table when she noticed one of Wade and Rebecca that wasn't very old. She picked it up and cooed over it, saying lightly, "Oh, can I steal this?"

"No," Wade said, "but you can have it if you really want it. Jane took the picture and put it in the frame. She gave it to me; I know she won't mind if I give it to you."

Laura smiled and hugged him quickly. "Thank you," she said. "I think it is now my most precious possession."

Wade made a comical scoffing noise and continued the tour. They also wandered around in the yard, holding hands and talking until it was time to put Rebecca to bed.

Laura watched Wade helping Rebecca get ready for bed, which included a ritual of tickling her feet, counting her fingers and toes, and what Wade called, "Blowing bubbles on the baby's belly." Rebecca wiggled and giggled and begged for more until Wade calmed her down by reading her a story. When she wanted *another* story, Laura eagerly volunteered.

Wade sat back and watched Laura reading his daughter a story, using an animated voice and pointing out little details in the pictures. Her tenderness and level of comfort with Rebecca

threatened to make his heart burst wide open. He felt so overcome with warmth in seeing them together that he wondered
what he'd been thinking with Marina. The comparison was . . .
well, there was no comparison. Everything about Laura didn't
just *feel* right; he knew it *was* right. He didn't even have to
question it. He realized now that what he had considered right
with Marina had merely been the absence of wrong. It may
have been okay had she possessed the integrity he'd considered
mandatory, but it never would have been like this.

Once Rebecca was asleep, Laura thanked Alex and Jane
profusely for their hospitality, and they each hugged her at the
door. Alex discreetly gave Wade a thumbs-up when Laura
wasn't looking. Through the drive to Laura's home, Wade felt
as if the Spirit were knocking him over the head. He felt as if
he couldn't live another day without taking the step that he
knew he needed to take.

He pulled the car into the driveway and turned it off before
he said, "Would you mind if I come in a for few minutes?
There's something I want to talk to you about."

"That would be great," she said.

Inside the front door she turned on the light, and he
noticed a dramatic change from the last time he'd been here.
The furniture had been rearranged to accommodate a beautiful
tall glass curio cabinet that now housed all of the little things
she'd had lying about on his previous visit. The room had been
completely baby-proofed. He almost felt like crying as the
implication of her efforts only strengthened his resolve.

"Nice cabinet," he said. "It wasn't here last time."

Laura shrugged. "I've always wanted one; got sick of
dusting all that stuff." She motioned toward the couch. "You
want to sit down or—"

"Actually, could we go out back? You have a beautiful
yard."

"Sure," she said and led the way to the back door. She flipped on a porch light, and Wade was glad to see that it shed a warm glow over the yard. Once they were seated on the little bench, he took her hand and said, "I've been thinking a great deal lately . . . trying to figure out this place I've come to in my life, and what to do about it." He looked at her and asked, "Is it okay if I talk about marriage . . . hypothetically? That won't scare you off, or anything, will it?"

"Go for it," she said with a smile.

"Okay, well . . . I was wondering what it might be like to live in a time or culture where marriages are arranged, or based simply on matters of practicality. I'm sure it would have many drawbacks, but then . . . people getting married because they fall in love certainly brings its own set of challenges."

"That's true."

"So . . . I was wondering what makes a marriage really work. And I'm not sure I have the answers, but . . ."

"Your marriage with Elena worked."

"Yes, it did. But who's to say that if she'd lived we might not have reached stages in our lives where changes might have occurred, challenges might have come up? I think marriage requires a level of commitment where two people are willing to work through the changes and challenges. But it takes two. Obviously, if one or the other of the people involved isn't willing to work it through, or their behavior isn't appropriate for a marriage, then it can't succeed. Love is obviously important, but I believe it's something that two people build more than fall into. Or maybe one kind of love brings two people together, and another kind keeps them together."

"I could agree with that."

"So the trick then, is to fall in love with someone who has the strength of character to work with you to build the kind of love and commitment that keeps a marriage strong, no matter what comes up. Would you agree with that too?"

"Yes."

"And it certainly helps to use your brains and your instincts enough to learn from the past and trust the present, and believe that the person you love will be as committed to the marriage as you are."

"Absolutely."

"Okay, so . . . after thinking all of that through, it occurred to me that the heart, the mind, and the spirit all have to agree. That's how I felt when I married Elena, and I didn't feel that way with Marina. My heart was in love with her, and my spirit felt compelled to move forward, but looking back, I believe that was the Lord's Spirit guiding me through some necessary lessons. And the lesson was that my brain kept seeing problems that I chose to ignore. It's like God was saying, 'Use your brain, Wade. If there are problems staring you in the face, you don't need me to tell you not to marry her.'"

Laura laughed softly, and he asked, "Was that funny?"

"Funny because I think that pretty well describes why I married Randall. He was a very good actor, and I think he put a lot of effort into deceiving me, even if it wasn't conscious. But I can look back and see that I ignored a great many warning signs because I was in love with him, and I naively believed that it was enough. Love isn't enough, you know. Not romantic love, anyway. It takes Christlike love, and commitment, and respect to make a marriage work. I didn't grow up seeing a good marriage, so I guess it took me some hard knocks to figure that out."

"Well, I grew up seeing a good marriage—then I learned that before I was born it hadn't been. And obviously the fact that it wasn't did a great deal of damage. The world we live in is tough, Laura, and it's going to get worse. We need to be strong in order to get through without letting it overtake our values or damage our children. If a marriage isn't based in integrity and fidelity—and unity with God—how can it ever have any hope?"

Laura looked into his eyes, feeling his every word penetrate her heart and her spirit. Did he have any idea what his convictions and beliefs meant to her? She could only hope that with time they might come to a place where he could know the deepest wish of her heart. She wanted nothing more than to be his wife, and she knew it was right—heart, mind, and spirit.

Wade returned Laura's gaze and couldn't hold back a smile. He wondered if she knew what was coming. And he prayed her response wouldn't disappoint him.

"I love you, Laura," he said, touching her face.

"I love you too, Wade," she answered, her eyes sparkling.

"If I told you that I would forever do everything in my power to make you happy and take good care of you, would you believe me?"

Laura took a sharp breath, and her heart quickened. What was he trying to say? Without hesitation she said, "Yes. Would you believe the same of me?"

"Yes," he said and immediately went down on one knee, keeping her hand in his.

"Wade?" she said breathlessly, her eyes widening.

"Shhh." He put his fingers over her lips. "Don't say anything—not yet."

Laura felt her breathing sharpen, and her hand tightened in his. Could this possibly be happening? She had longed for it, wanted more than anything to cross this bridge with him. But she hadn't dared hope that he would feel as strongly as she did, and so quickly. But what other explanation could there be for his getting down on his knee like that, considering the conversation they'd just had?

"I know it seems ludicrous, Laura. Anyone on the outside looking in would say I was crazy. A week ago I was just getting up the nerve to ask you out, and now I'm proposing. But I have absolutely no question that this is right. My mind, heart, and spirit are not only in complete agreement, they are all three keeping me awake at nights, demanding to know why I'm wasting my time and not doing something about it." He took a deep breath. "I cannot go another day—another hour—without asking you to be my wife." Wade blew the air out of his lungs, more nervous than he'd realized. She looked stunned, frozen, completely unreadable. If only to fill the sudden silence, he made his intentions unmistakably clear. "Will you marry me, Laura?"

Wade watched her expression closely while his heart beat painfully hard. She was clearly dumbfounded and stunned. But why exactly? He had every reason to believe that she felt the same way he did, but how could he know for certain until she told him? Was there some factor he wasn't aware of? Some issue that might cause her to hold back? He felt completely vulnerable and utterly helpless while the silence became intense.

"Laura," he said, unable to bear the tension. "If you need some time to think about it, or—"

She put her fingers over his lips to stop him. "I don't need to think about it, Wade," she said, a tremor in her voice. "I've never felt so right about anything in my entire life." He let out a burst of relieved laughter, and she added, "You're the best thing that's ever happened to me, Wade, and I love you with my whole heart. I would be a fool not to marry you."

Wade laughed again and wrapped his arms around her, drawing her embrace into himself. He eased back and took her shoulders into his hands. "Does that mean yes?"

"Yes," she laughed softly, "it means yes." He kissed her, and she added, "You can get up off the ground now, although it was very effective."

Wade sat beside her on the bench. "I wouldn't want our children to think I hadn't done it properly." She laughed again, and he took both her hands into his. "Laura," he said intently, "I've been thinking about all of this a great deal, and . . . if you don't agree with me, it's okay. We'll do this however you want, but . . ." Wade hesitated, realizing he didn't want to influence her approach to this. He knew how he wanted to go about it, but he was only half of the equation, and he wanted to honor her wishes. Rather than telling her his ideas, he simply said, "Tell me what you want, Laura. A long engagement, or a short one—or in between. A big wedding with all the works, or something quiet and simple. As long as it's in the temple, the rest doesn't matter to me. I'll do whatever will make it perfect for you."

She smiled and touched his face, as if she completely understood the awe he felt over this life-altering step they were taking. "You know what I really want?" she asked. "It might sound crazy, but . . . I don't want to wait, Wade. I want to get married as soon as it's humanly possible. I'm tired of being alone, and no amount of time is going to change the way I feel or my knowing that it's right. And truthfully, I would prefer quiet and simple. Unless you have any objections, I think we should just . . . get married and . . . send out announcements later just to let people know that we did."

He laughed and hugged her. "It's like you read my mind," he said. "We can just invite immediate family and close friends to the ceremony, and maybe have a luncheon afterward and call it good."

"That sounds perfect," she said.

They began talking about whom they would invite and how to go about it. Since Wade had a large family and most of them lived close, he suspected all of the adults would likely want to be there. But his best friend was Alex, and he couldn't think of anybody else at the moment. "What about you?" he asked.

Laura looked down and shook her head. "There's no one I care to invite," she said, and he was taken aback. "Truthfully, I would prefer to just let my family know after the fact. They're less likely to cause any drama that way. None of them would be temple-worthy anyway. I don't really have any close friends except Rochelle, and that's arguable. She lives out of state, and she's obviously not going to the temple."

"Okay, but . . . wouldn't you like to invite her to the luncheon? What about your parents? Your siblings?"

Laura sighed loudly and felt her insides tighten. She took courage and looked into Wade's eyes. "I mentioned that I came from a difficult home, and I told you a little, but . . . if I were to have any hesitation over this, it would be that I don't want to bring my family's influence into our lives." She sighed again. "For a long time I tried to maintain contact with them, and help them when I could, because I believed it was the right thing to do. But it created so much havoc and stress in my life that it was making me crazy. That's when I gained a better understanding of why the Nephites separated from the Lamanites. It was a matter of self-preservation. I've learned how to draw boundaries with them, and I can usually do it without too much trouble as long as we only keep in touch minimally." She chuckled tensely. "Truthfully, I can't deny that I have some fear related to . . ."

"What?" he pressed when she hesitated.

"I fear that . . . if you actually knew my family . . . you would renege on that proposal."

"Laura, look at me," Wade said earnestly. "It doesn't matter to me what kind of family you come from. What matters to me is the attitude you take in trying to rise above it, and I'm not the least bit worried about that. I'm not going to judge you by your family, Laura. And don't forget," he added lightly, "that you just agreed to marry an illegitimate Mormon boy raised under false pretenses."

Laura smiled with tears in her eyes. "I love you, Wade Morrison."

"Good," he said. "Let's get married. How about Saturday?"

She caught her breath. "Are you serious?"

"Dead serious," he said. "Of course we'll have to make sure it can be arranged and that the important people can be there, but we could try. I'm tired of being alone, too. What do you say?"

Laura could only throw her arms around him and cry. She'd never been so happy in her life.

They talked for more than an hour, discussing a tentative plan and negotiating the details, what was important and what could be disregarded. Wade kissed her once more before he left, then Laura just stood with her back against the door, pondering the miracle of how he had changed her life. Recalling the picture he'd given her, she rushed to find it, staring at the image of him and Rebecca until she almost fell asleep. She set it on the bedside table and got ready for bed, thanking her Heavenly Father for blessing her life so abundantly.

CHAPTER 19

Wade was pleased to find Alex home for breakfast; sometimes it was hard to keep track of his shifts. Alex and Jane both commented on how much they liked Laura, and how they had enjoyed her visit the previous evening.

"She enjoyed it too," Wade said. "I think she really likes you guys." He smirked, "I know I do." A minute later he casually asked Alex, "What's your schedule this weekend?"

"I'm off Friday, Saturday, and Sunday, and I start a four-day night shift on Monday. Why?"

"You got plans Saturday?"

Alex looked at Jane, who said, "Not that I know of, nothing important. Why?"

"Laura and I are planning to go to the temple on Saturday and we want you to be there; in fact, if you wouldn't be able to make it, we would have figured out a different time. We'd like to do lunch afterward."

"The temple sounds great," Alex said.

"What a marvelous double date," Jane added.

"It's a little more than that," Wade said, secretly delighted by the setup. "We're getting married while we're there, provided that it can be arranged."

"I knew it!" Jane said with excited laughter. "I took one look at her and knew she was the one."

Alex chuckled. "Obviously you don't have any reservations."

"Not in the slightest," Wade said and went on to briefly repeat their plans. When he mentioned that he would be moving out, the mood suddenly became very somber; Jane actually got tears in her eyes.

"Hey," Wade said lightly, taking her hand, "just think how much less complicated your life will be."

Her tears increased, and Alex said, "I don't think that helped."

"It's not like I'm going very far," Wade said. "Alex and I are practically joined at the hip, you know. I won't be able to stay away. And I'll still need help with Rebecca."

"I know," Jane sniffled, "but it's not the same. We just . . . love having you here; that's all."

"Well." Wade couldn't help smiling. "It's nice to feel loved, and not to have to feel like we've been a burden."

"Not even close," Alex said.

"I guess it's just . . . time to move on," Wade said.

"Yes, and that's a good thing," Alex added. "We're just going to miss you."

"Just consider this a gradual weaning," Wade said. "Eventually I'll have to start my internship, and I would probably have to leave the state for a while anyway."

"Good thing you're getting a wife to help take care of Rebecca before that happens," Alex said lightly, "otherwise, you'd have to lease her to us."

Wade chuckled. "Yeah, I probably would. And I'd lose my mind."

They all hurried to move on with their day, which ended up being extremely busy for both Wade and Laura. He had to buckle down and try to stay focused at the clinic and make certain he was at the point of progression where he needed to be. Even though he wasn't actually going to miss any education time to get married, he wanted to be able to spend as much time with Laura as he possibly could. The temple was closed on Monday, so he couldn't call to make arrangements, but he did call all of his parents and asked them to keep Saturday open. He didn't want to alert them to the fact that it was big news, so he just casually told them he was in a hurry and he'd give them details later.

Wade did manage to talk to Laura on the phone a couple of times, and he went to bed Monday night feeling happy and content. On Tuesday all of the arrangements were made with a little help from Jane. The temple could accommodate them, and a cancellation had occurred at the Joseph Smith Memorial Building so they would be able to do the luncheon. And appointments were made with both Wade's and Laura's bishops and stake presidents.

Wade called his mother Tuesday afternoon and told her he'd like to bring someone over to meet her.

"Is it a woman?" she asked, sounding more positive than she'd sounded in a long time.

"Yes, actually it is."

"You should come for dinner."

"That's not necessary, Mom. We can—"

"No, I insist. It will give me something to do. Your dad will help me."

"Okay, you talked me into it. Can we bring anything?"

"No, just come. Is six-thirty okay?"

"We'll be there."

Wade met an appointment with his bishop at six o'clock, and knew Laura was doing the same. They both had appointments with their stake presidents on Wednesday. As soon as he was finished he hurried to pick up Laura, knowing she was there because her car was in the driveway. Knocking at her door he felt a jittery excitement. He'd not seen her since Sunday evening, and he'd missed her terribly.

"Hi," she said, absolutely glowing when she opened the door.

"Hi," he said and stepped inside and closed the door before he took her in his arms and gave her a long, savoring kiss. "Okay, we can go now." He smiled. "I thought that might be a bit much for the neighbors to see."

Laura laughed softly, and he followed her out to the car. On the way to his parents' home, Wade explained more of the situation to Laura. He'd told her about his mother's cancer and that she was recovering from chemotherapy, but he'd said nothing about her recent struggle with depression and what had precipitated it. Even though she was doing better, she still wasn't quite herself.

"Maybe that gives us something in common," Laura said, and Wade took her hand.

"Maybe it does." He smiled. "I'm sure you would have better empathy for her struggles than I would. For me, it's just . . ."

"What?" she asked when he hesitated.

"I feel responsible . . . at least partly. People are aware of her past sins because *I* was so firm on not being afraid to admit publicly that I belong to two families. She's told me a dozen times she's okay with that; she's said she would do anything to compensate for the heartache her bad choices brought into my life. But . . . the reality is that she hasn't hardly stepped out of the house for months except for medical needs, and she only started going to church again recently."

"You can't take responsibility for that," she said. "It's good for you to care and acknowledge your involvement, but you can't fix depression for a person who is depressed. My guess is that . . . it's not so much public knowledge of her sins that makes her depressed; it's the way she's perceiving it."

"What do you mean?" he asked, intrigued.

"Well . . . perhaps if she hadn't been facing cancer when this issue came up, she would have had the inner strength to face it with more confidence and let it roll off. Perhaps the combination just hit her with too much all at once, and now she's in a spiral that she's having trouble breaking. She's obviously improving rather than getting worse, so that's good. But it probably all ties in to a lot of tough memories associated with her past. Even though it's technically in the past, sometimes it can come back to haunt you."

She said it so firmly that Wade wondered what might regularly come back to haunt *her.* From what she'd told him of her childhood, it wasn't too difficult to imagine. Yet her insight and strength were so evident—and inspiring. He felt his admiration for her growing as she went on. "From what you've told me, I think she means it when she says she doesn't care what people think of her, but this has just brought too many things together all at once. I think one day she'll get past it."

"That's what Dad says."

"Which dad?"

"Brad. Her husband."

"The father who raised you."

"That's right." He chuckled. "I know it can be confusing sometimes."

"If I ever wonder who you're talking about, I'll just ask."

"Okay," he said and kissed her hand.

When they arrived, Wade could tell Laura was a little nervous, but she was immediately put at ease when Wade introduced her to his parents. He noted that his mother's hair was growing back in, thick and curly, and she looked better than she'd looked in a long time. And he told her so, which made her smile.

Laura loved watching Wade interact with his parents. She'd always heard that the way a man treated his mother was a good indication of how he would treat his wife. Randall had put on a good act; however, looking back, she knew she had sensed the phoniness in it, but she'd chosen to overlook it. In contrast, there was no denying the genuine warmth between Wade and his mother—and the father who had raised him. She sensed a mutual respect between them that was made more meaningful, knowing that the circumstances of Wade's birth were so sensitive—probably to this man more than anyone involved. Yet his love and admiration for Wade were sincere and readily evident.

Brad and Marilyn asked Laura many questions about herself, and Wade told them of their many encounters through the years, making it sound like a romantic movie.

Marilyn said to Laura, "Well, you must really be something, because I haven't seen him this happy since before Elena died."

"You got that right," Wade said. "Which brings me to an important point." He smirked at Laura. "I mentioned that you should keep Saturday open." He used the same tactic that he'd used on Alex and Jane. "We're going to the temple and want you to join us."

"I suppose we could," Marilyn said, sounding hesitant. He wondered how long it had been since she'd attended the temple, given her frame of mind and health challenges.

"Well, you'd better," Wade said. "I'm getting married Saturday and I want my parents to be there."

Brad smiled. Marilyn gasped, then said with glee, "Really?"

"Really," Wade said and chuckled.

"Oh, that's wonderful!" Marilyn said, getting a little teary as she stood up to hug Wade, and then Laura. "Oh, my dear." She took Laura's face into her hands. "I couldn't be more pleased."

"Thank you," Laura said, and they all sat back down.

"So, you'll be there, right?" Wade said.

"We wouldn't miss it," Brad said, taking Marilyn's hand.

"Mom?" Wade said, wanting to hear it from her.

"I'll be there," she said, and Wade smiled at her. Maybe the incentive to come to his wedding would help get her out of this bad cycle.

Wade insisted that he would load the dishwasher. He was rinsing dishes while Laura helped Brad clear the table, when his mother came up beside him and said softly, "She's wonderful, Wade."

"Yes, she is."

"This is different from Marina."

"Much different, yes. Is it obvious?"

Marilyn laughed softly. "Yes, it's *quite* obvious—just by that light in your eyes."

Wade glanced discreetly toward Laura, who was laughing at something his father had said. "Yeah, she has that effect on me."

When the dishes were done, Wade took Laura's hand and led her to the front room, entering a minute before his parents arrived. Hanging on the wall above the couch was a beautiful framed print of an artist's depiction of the woman taken in adultery. Laura noticed it immediately.

"It's beautiful," she said. "And dare I say it speaks volumes . . . especially with *your* family."

"I gave it to her," Wade said. "I told her if she didn't like it she could exchange it, but she hung it here; tells me regularly how she loves it. I still wonder if it was too . . . bold."

Laura had no opportunity to respond because his parents came into the room, and they all sat down to visit. Following several minutes of chitchat, Laura said, "There's something I would really like to say."

Wade noted the way she intently looked at his parents, and he wished he had any idea what was coming. She took hold of his hand as she continued. "Wade's told me that the two of you have always encouraged direct communication, and so I'm hoping that it's okay to just say what I want to say."

"Of course," Marilyn said.

Laura smiled at Wade before she looked again at his parents. "Wade's told me about his unique situation with both of his families, and he's told me that it's treated very openly, and I'm glad for that. It makes it easier for me to say how . . ." Her voice cracked and Wade squeezed her hand, wondering where this was headed. "How grateful I am for the way you raised Wade to be such a fine man. I want to thank you, Marilyn, for bringing him into the world, for giving him a mother's love, in spite of the difficulties associated with the situation. And I want to thank you, Brad, for being such a good father to him, for teaching him by example how to be a good father himself." She smiled again at Wade, and he wished he could tell her what her words meant to him, because he knew they meant a great deal to his parents. "And he is a very good father," she added.

"Yes, he is," Brad said, smiling toward Wade. Marilyn was crying.

"Are those happy tears, Mom?" Wade asked.

"Yes, of course," she said and wiped her eyes. "It's just . . . nice to hear . . . something like that . . . now."

"Well, it's from the heart," Laura said. "Wade's told me how wonderful you both are, and it's easy to see that he's right."

"You're very sweet, Laura," Brad said, putting his arm around Marilyn. "But as long as we're being forthright here, you must know that Wade has been a great blessing in our home. He's always been one of those kids that we never had to worry about."

"Now, that's not true," Wade said.

"Well, less than usual," Brad added with a smile. "He's always been a good kid. It was never a sacrifice to claim him as my own."

"See what I mean?" Wade said to Laura, motioning toward his parents. "They're amazing."

Laura smiled and impulsively said to him, "Do you think they'd adopt me?"

"I don't know." Wade turned to his parents and asked with mock severity, "Will you adopt Laura?"

"Absolutely," Brad said. "You make her a Morrison and we'll keep her forever."

"It's a deal," Wade said and laughed as he put his arm around Laura.

A few minutes later Wade insisted that they had to leave; there were other people who needed to be informed of the big news. Wade felt so happy watching Laura and his parents exchange tender words of kindness and appreciation, he almost feared his heart would burst.

"They're wonderful people," Laura said in the car. "Just like you told me they were."

"I've been very blessed," Wade said.

Laura couldn't help thinking about her own family, people that she would consider far more a curse than a blessing. She dreaded the day when Wade would meet them, but she had to admit, "So have I."

"How's that?"

"Well, my family's a little scary, but God blessed me with yours."

Wade smiled and kissed her hand, then she watched him pick up his cell phone and do a speed dial. He waited a few seconds, then he spoke with pauses in between. "Hi, Dad. What are you doing? Would it be a problem if I come over?

Okay, but be warned. I'm bringing someone to meet you." He laughed. "Yes, it's a woman. Don't sound so surprised. We'll be there soon. We just left Mom's place."

He ended the call, and she asked, "Your other dad?"

"That's right," he said.

"But you've only known him a few years."

"Give or take; it's hard to keep track. But it hasn't been long."

"That must be strange."

"It was at first. Now, it's like we've been close forever. When I first met him I was pretty angry with him, but he's forgiven me for that." He grinned at her. "You're going to love him, and he's going to love you."

Laura felt as comfortable with Neil and Roxanne as she had with Wade's *other* parents. She found the contrast fascinating. Brad and Marilyn's home had been clean and homey, but very practical and down to earth. Neil and Roxanne's home had more evidence of affluence, but not in a showy way. Both homes had a good spirit in them; both homes were comfortable and filled with the warmth of the people who lived in them, something that had been completely absent in the home where Laura had grown up.

Laura was intrigued with the interaction between Wade and his biological father. The resemblance was clearly evident, and Wade was every bit as comfortable with Neil as he'd been with Brad. The situation certainly was unique; it was much like having divorced parents, which some of her friends had dealt with, except that this was obviously a little more sensitive.

Neil and Roxanne were thrilled with the news and eagerly agreed to be at the wedding. Neil then said, "And I'll be paying for the wedding luncheon; if you haven't already got it arranged, we can help with that."

"Okay, I accept," Wade said so quickly that it was humorous. He shrugged and added to Laura, "I gave up trying to refuse his money a long time ago. I just try not to be too big of a burden and be grateful."

"Never a burden," Neil said firmly. "But certainly a joy."

"Amen," Roxanne said with a warm smile toward Wade, and Laura felt like she could have reached out and taken hold of the love in the room. Wade had once told her that his parents were fine examples of overcoming the past and becoming the best of people. She could see what he meant, and she deeply admired such examples—especially considering her own upbringing with people who never put any effort into striving to become better or overcoming their dysfunctional behavior.

Wade took Laura home, and they shared a reluctant parting kiss at the door. He told her he needed to go home and call his siblings to invite them to the wedding. After he left, Laura seriously pondered calling her parents to at least invite them to the luncheon, but she just couldn't bring herself to do it. She'd call them *next* week and tell them the good news. She did call her friend Rochelle. Even though she was in a later time zone, Laura knew she was always up late—if she would even be home. There was no answer, so Laura just left a message on the machine.

"Hi, it's me. I've got some good news. I'm getting married this Saturday. It'll be in the Salt Lake Temple. I know it's terribly short notice, but I'd love to have you come to the luncheon we're having afterward. If you decide you want to come, let me know, and I'll give you the details. We'll catch up soon. Hope you're doing okay. Love ya. Bye."

Laura then stared at the picture of Wade and Rebecca for a while before she got ready for bed, happier than she'd ever dreamed possible. She'd not been in bed long when Wade called to tell her he'd talked briefly with each of his siblings, and they all planned to be there. "I told them it was short notice, and if they couldn't come I'd understand. But they all say they're coming; even Charlotte and Becca."

"Remind me," she said, still having trouble keeping all of his siblings straight.

"Alex's sisters," he said. "They both live out of state, but they insist they'll get here. They're great. You're going to love them."

"I can't wait to meet them—all of them," she said. "But more than that, I can't wait to marry you."

"Amen," he said, then added intently, "I love you, Laura— more every hour of every day."

"The feeling is mutual," she said. "I only hope you don't regret it."

"And why would I do that?" he asked, almost sounding upset. She hesitated, and he added firmly, "Laura? Why would you think that I could ever regret making you a part of my life?"

"You haven't met my family," she said, trying to sound light but he didn't go for it.

"And I've told you that's irrelevant."

More seriously she said, "And I've told you that I struggle with depression."

"Yes, and so does my mother."

"But she's your mother. You have a choice of whether or not you commit your life to me."

"And I'm choosing to commit my life to you. I will take on whatever that entails."

"Your commitment means a lot to me, Wade. Don't get me wrong. But I can't help worrying that . . ."

"What?"

"That saying such things is . . . perhaps naive. Maybe you don't really have any idea how bad it can get."

"Maybe I don't," he admitted. "But I know beyond any question that marrying you is the right thing to do, Laura. And

I mean it when I say that we will take on whatever life brings us—together. Are you hearing me?"

"Yes," she said tenderly. "You're really very good to me."

"It's not hard," he said, but Laura feared that one day it might become hard for him to be good to her. She prayed that whatever happened he would hold to his word. If she lost him she felt sure she could never survive it.

* * *

On Wednesday, following his time at the clinic, Wade went to pick Rebecca up at her grandparents' home, glad for an opportunity to talk with Elena's parents. After he'd greeted Rebecca, Melba gave him the usual hug. "How are you?" she asked.

"I'm doing great, actually."

"What's up?" Harry asked from the other side of the room where he was sitting in the recliner.

"Well," Wade said, "I'm getting married. And I'm happy to say that so far it's all going much better than the last time I tried this."

"That's good then," Melba said. "When do we get to meet her?"

"Soon," he said. "The wedding is Saturday, actually. It's just a family thing, but you *are* family. We'd love to have the two of you there, if you're not busy . . . if you're comfortable with it."

"Why wouldn't we be comfortable with it?" Melba asked. "We talked about this before. Elena would want you to move on. Rebecca needs a mother who can be with her now."

"I know all of that, and I appreciate your attitude, truly."

"It probably goes without saying," Melba said, "but I have to say it anyway. Promise us that we can always be close to Rebecca, and that you'll always be a part of our family."

"Of course," he said. "Not that it matters really, but . . . Laura—that's my fiancée—her family lives out of state and they're not much of a family. A kid needs good grandparents."

"I can agree with that," Harry said. "And maybe we'll get to have Rebecca's little brothers and sisters around too, huh?"

"I sure hope so," Wade said with a little laugh.

"When and where is this wedding?" Harry asked.

"Salt Lake Temple," Wade said, and they both smiled. He told them the time and the details of the luncheon afterward, and he was pleased to know they would be there. In a way the whole thing felt a little odd, but then he was pretty good at fitting into all kinds of families.

Wade took Rebecca home and left her with Jane and went to pick up Laura. She had taken the afternoon off to go buy a gown and see to some final details of the wedding. As soon as he saw her face he knew something wasn't right.

"Okay, talk to me," he said. She looked startled, then guilty. "What's wrong?"

"It's not important," she said as he held the car door for her.

He walked around the car and got in, but he didn't start it. "If it's upset you, it's important. What's wrong?"

Laura sighed loudly. "My mother called; she was drunk. It just has a way of . . . ruining a day."

Wade took her hand. "Did she say anything . . . particular that's upset you?"

"Just the same old things. I finally hung up on her. She just has a way of making me feel so . . . worthless and . . ."

"It's not true," Wade said and pressed a hand to her face before he gave her a tender kiss. "You're amazing, and I love you."

Laura felt compelled to say, "I'm really trying to believe you."

He smiled and kissed her again. "Give it time, Mrs. Morrison-almost. I will convince you of just how amazing you are, if it's the last thing I do."

She sighed and smiled, and he started the car. They went to a jewelry store and picked out wedding rings in record time. Neither of them were fussy about the rings, as long as they symbolized being husband and wife. Laura's fit perfectly, but Wade's needed to be sized and picked up the following day.

With that done, they had time for a quick supper before they met with both of their stake presidents, then Wade called Alex from his cell phone to tell him they were on their way.

"Where are we going?" she asked.

"It's a surprise," he said and kissed her hand, making her laugh softly.

When he pulled the car into an empty church parking lot, she looked confused, and he said, "This is a rehearsal."

"For what?"

"Well, it's a tradition." He chuckled. "Okay . . . it hasn't been a tradition, but it's going to be now. My brother did it at his wedding, and now I'm doing it at this one. That makes it a tradition."

"Okay," she drawled skeptically.

"We must share a wedding waltz, my love," he said. She looked surprised, then she smiled.

"What makes you think I even know how to waltz?" she asked with a sly smile.

"It was on your Internet profile."

"Oh, so it was. And you know how to waltz?"

"I do now," he said. "I learned it along with the swing, hoping to win you over. Did it work?"

She laughed softly. "It didn't hurt any. The swing was fun, I must admit. But . . . it's been a long time since I've actually waltzed. I had a guy friend in high school who was into that kind of thing and taught me. It's been years."

"Hence the rehearsal," he said. "But we have to wait for Alex and Jane."

"Why?" she asked.

"He has the key to the building, for one thing—but they're my dance teachers."

"Oh, I see," she said. "I think I saw some pictures of them at the house, dance competitions or something."

"That's them," he said. "They're spectacular. I only know how to do the pretty basic stuff, but it'll work."

Alex and Jane arrived and they all went inside, talking and laughing. Laura asked for a slow reminder of the steps before they tried it with the music, but she was clearly pleased and Wade couldn't help being glad for this opportunity. He thought of what Alex and Jane had taught him about the meaning of the dance. When the music began and he found himself sharing a simple waltz with Laura, he looked into her eyes and realized this was a dream come true. He'd imagined this moment, longed for it, and now it was here. He was astounded at how easily he was able to do the dance, and how fluidly she followed his lead. Seeing the same expression on Laura's face that he'd seen on Jane's when she'd danced with Alex, he decided that he couldn't be happier.

After they'd gone through the dance a few times, laughing and having a marvelous time, they watched Alex and Jane for a few minutes. Wade told her how they had started having a weekly dancing date since the time when Barrett had nearly died from leukemia and how they had nearly lost their marriage due to the trauma. He told Laura how they'd come together as partners on a dance team, and she commented on how great they looked together.

"Yeah," Wade said, "sometimes I just like to watch them." He turned to look at her. "But now that I have you, I think I prefer just watching you while *we* dance."

"I could go for that," she said.

After they'd left the church, Laura took Wade's hand and said, "Thank you."

"For what?"

"For learning the waltz, for creating this new . . . tradition. It really means a lot to me, that you would notice such a simple thing and go to so much trouble."

"Hey, Alex insisted once he read that part about your interest in dance. I think he's wanted an excuse to teach me for years. You'll have to thank him."

"I'll do that. But you *did* learn it. So . . . thank you."

"A pleasure, my love," he said and kissed her hand, counting the hours until she could be his wife.

* * *

That night as Laura lay in bed, the miraculous moments she'd shared with Wade meshed into the horrible conversation she'd had with her mother. With little sleep behind her she got up the next morning, her thoughts still churning. She hated herself for wondering if she was delusional to think that Wade could really love her as much as he claimed. She hated herself even more for wondering if he might just be deceiving her the way that Randall had.

Wade called her at work that afternoon to see how she was doing. She told him she was fine, then felt guilty for lying to him once she'd hung up. A few minutes after Laura got off the phone, she knew she couldn't keep holding it together enough to stay at work. She made sure all the bases were covered, then left the clinic. Not wanting to go home and be there alone, she went instead to see if Jane might be home. She was, and they sat and talked for quite a while, which made Laura feel a little better. While Laura felt hesitant to open up completely with Jane, it was evident that she firmly believed Wade was a good man. When Jane said she needed to do some errands before the three older children got home from school, Laura offered to watch Rebecca and Ruthie, but Jane insisted on taking them.

"I just have to drive through the bank and get a couple of things at the store, and they love it. I'm used to it. They'll be fine. Take a nap or something."

Laura wondered if her lack of sleep the previous night was that obvious. As soon as Jane left she made herself comfortable on the sofa in the study, just off the front hall. Again doubts crept into her mind, but she fought to force them away. She felt certain she wouldn't be able to sleep, but the next thing she was aware of was the doorbell ringing.

CHAPTER 20

Wade was able to get away from his rotation a little early, since he'd started at the crack of dawn, and he arrived at the house to see Jane's car gone and Laura's there. She'd obviously left work early, and he was pleased with the thought of seeing her. When he went in the back door and found no signs of anyone there, he figured Laura must have gone somewhere with Jane. Just thinking of the two of them spending time together added to the warmth inside of him.

When the doorbell rang he hurried to answer it, stunned to see Marina standing there. Her timing was unbelievable. He couldn't help sounding agitated as he asked, "What are you doing here?"

Marina stepped inside, even though he hadn't invited her to, and the next thing he knew she was crying and babbling about how she'd made a mistake by letting him go. He resisted the urge to look heavenward and ask if this was supposed to be a test, or if it was simply opposition. He listened patiently while Marina told him that he'd been right about so many things, that she was getting some counseling, that she wanted to change, *that she wanted him back.* They remained in the entry hall, mostly because Wade didn't want to invite her to sit down; he didn't want her getting too comfortable.

"Marina," he finally said, interrupting her stammering, "I'm glad you're getting some counseling; that's great. It's good to see you, but . . . you must know that it's too late for us. Way too late."

"Why is it too late?" she demanded. "We can try again. We could—"

"Marina," he said, looking at her hard, "I'm getting married."

"Married?" she echoed as if it were criminal. "When?"

"Saturday, actually."

"But . . . how could something change . . . so fast?"

"The last time we talked I told you I was hoping it would become serious. She's the one for me, Marina; I know it beyond any doubt. This is for the best."

Wade wondered what he'd done to deserve this when she started to tell him he was surely making a mistake, and then she started to cry again. She reminded him very much of her mother and the thought of how close he'd come to marrying her made him feel a little queasy.

"Marina." He interrupted her ongoing prattle. "You're wasting your energy here. It's too late for us, and your standing there making a drama out of it will not change that fact. It's better this way for both of us. I'm glad you're willing to work on whatever you feel your struggles may be, and I wish you every happiness. But our paths cross no longer, Marina. I have found a woman who is so perfect for me that I could never deny being led to her. I love her more than life, and I know she loves me. We're getting married."

She looked completely stunned, and he was amazed to see that the drama was immediately over. He had to believe that she wasn't really as upset as she'd been putting on.

Sounding mildly annoyed, she asked, "Am I invited to the wedding?"

"No," he said. "It's just for immediate family at the temple; that's it."

Marina then apologized for making a fool of herself, and she wished him all the best, but there was a subtle martyr-like attitude about it. When she finally left, he leaned his head against the closed door and groaned.

"Amazing," Laura said.

Wade turned and gasped. "What are you doing here?" he demanded, wishing it hadn't sounded so sharp. Attempting to explain, he added, "You scared me to death."

"I was taking a nap on the couch in the study, actually—at least until the doorbell rang. I didn't sleep well last night."

"You heard all that?" he asked.

"I'm afraid I did," she said, and he wondered how she might have perceived it. "Good thing you weren't trying to hide something from me."

Wade felt taken aback. "Did you think I would?"

"You've never given me any reason not to trust you. If there is any issue of mistrust, it's from inside me. But I have to admit that I've struggled a little with wondering . . . if we're moving too fast, if I'm setting myself up again for a fall. However, what I just heard made me feel . . ."

"What?"

She smiled. "I am absolutely certain that the man I'm marrying the day after tomorrow is a man of integrity, and marrying him is the best thing I could ever do with my life."

Wade let out a breathy sigh.

"However," she said, "I am a little concerned about your taste in women."

"Oh, my taste in women had a little glitch, but I only get to the altar with the most amazing women."

She smiled again. "I love you, Wade Morrison."

Wade couldn't resist kissing her, then he decided they needed something productive to do. They loaded up some of his and Rebecca's things into both of their vehicles, then he followed her to her house where they unloaded them, and Laura told him three times how happy it made her to see her house becoming filled with the evidence that she was about to become a wife and a mother. He had to agree.

When everything was taken care of for the moment, they sat together on the couch, holding hands, talking about the hours they had left to endure being single. Laura avoided bringing up the way her mother's words kept troubling her. Instead, she kissed Wade, then she kissed him again. He took her into his arms, and their kiss became lengthy and warm. She was startled when he moved away and stood up as if he'd been kicked.

"I need to go," he said. "I'll call you."

He didn't look back or even wait for a goodbye. Laura suspected the reason for his hasty departure and couldn't help feeling flattered by his evident attraction to her, and it was also reassuring to know that she wasn't the only one struggling with temptation. She also felt a deepening respect for him. She regularly saw proof of the convictions that he had boldly declared on their first date.

Only a minute later he called her from his cell phone. "Okay," he said, "we can talk now."

"I don't remember what we were talking about," she said with a little laugh.

"Me neither. Which is probably a good indication that we should avoid being alone together until after the wedding."

"Yes, I'm sure you're right."

"So, we'll both find something to keep occupied with this evening, and I'll see you tomorrow after work."

"Okay," she said, then her doorbell rang. "Someone's at the door; I need to go."

"I love you," they both said at the same time, then ended the call.

Laura pulled the door open to see her friend, Rochelle. But she hadn't been a redhead the last time she'd seen her—at Tina's funeral. The heavy makeup, designer clothes, and professional nails all made Rochelle feel like a stranger, but Laura tried to overlook all that. It took her a moment to believe Rochelle was actually here, then Laura laughed and hugged her tightly before she motioned her inside and closed the door.

"Oh, my gosh. I can't believe it!" Laura said. "It's so good to see you!"

She was wondering why Rochelle would have shown up two days before the wedding, until she said without preamble, "Are you out of your freaking mind?"

"What are you talking about?"

"Oh, Laura, you can't possibly be that naive after all we have been through together. How is it possible that you—*you,* of all people—could think that you can meet a guy and marry him in a couple of weeks? There was absolutely no one in your life the last time we talked, and now you're getting *married?*"

Laura tossed Rochelle a disgusted glare and said, "It's good to see you too. Have a seat. Let's chat."

Rochelle sat down. "Okay, I'm sitting. Why don't *you* sit down and tell me what kind of evil has possessed your brain."

Laura sat down as well. "I do not have to justify any of this to you. My reasons for marrying Wade are something you could never understand."

"What? You had a spiritual experience?" she countered snidely.

Laura willed herself to remain calm. "Rochelle," she said firmly, "my life's decisions are no one's but my own. You don't have to agree with them, but I ask you to support me in them."

"The way I supported Tina? The way I supported you when you married Randall?"

"So, what's the answer, Rochelle? To spend our lives alone and bitter? I don't want to be alone, Rochelle. I want children."

"Is that what this is about? Loneliness? Maternal instincts?"

"It's about that and so much more. Wade is a wonderful man and—"

Rochelle swore and shot out of her chair. Laura watched her pace the room, listening to her recount the horrors that had happened to all of them as a result of poor choices in men—as if Laura might have never heard them before. And then Rochelle went on with a verbal inventory of all the dysfunction in the homes they'd all come from, all hinging on poor marriage choices. Laura just waited for her to get it out of her system. When Rochelle finally became quiet, Laura asked, "Are you finished?"

"For the moment."

"Good, now sit down and listen to me for a minute. Wade and I have talked a great deal about the struggles and challenges of our pasts, and how to work through our problems. And even though we haven't been dating very long, I've known him for a couple of years. He's a good man, Rochelle, and I know it with all my heart."

"How can you *know* it? You prayed about it?"

"Yes, I did. And if you'll recall, when you were engaged and actually started praying to have discernment, that's when the problems came to the surface. God helped save you from that marriage once you really bothered to ask for His help, then paid attention to what was going on. And then you turned your back on everything you believe in. Don't sit there and tell me how I should believe, or how I should make my decisions. I'm marrying Wade on Saturday. I would love to see you at the luncheon, and I would love to spend some time with you tomorrow while you're in town. But I'm not going to talk about this any more."

"Your mind is made up then," she said as if Laura had admitted to becoming a Nazi.

"Absolutely."

Rochelle shook her head as if it were pitiful. Then she left, saying she would be spending time with another friend while she was in town, but she would see her some time tomorrow. Laura felt certain that other friend would be a *male* friend, and probably someone Rochelle had become connected with since she'd changed her lifestyle.

"Can't wait," Laura said to herself after she'd closed the door.

Wade called her that evening and immediately asked, "What's wrong?"

"Nothing. I'm just tired."

"I don't believe you. What's wrong?"

"Rochelle stopped by; she came into town early. It was just . . . hard. Being with her has a way of stirring things up."

"You want to talk about it?" he asked gently.

"Not really. I just need some sleep."

"I'll see you tomorrow evening, right?" She knew he meant dinner with Neil and Roxanne's side of the family so she could meet Wade's sisters who had come in this afternoon from out of state.

"Of course," she said. "I'm looking forward to it."

"Laura?"

"Yeah?"

"I love you. We're going to have a good life together."

"I know," she said and meant it. "I love you too. I'll see you tomorrow."

Laura got off the phone and went straight to bed. An hour later she took something to help her sleep when Rochelle's words wouldn't leave her mind. The sleeping pill wore off early in the morning, but she couldn't find the motivation to get out of bed.

Curled beneath the covers, Rochelle's words started to swirl in her head with memories that spat and hissed at her. Memories of an ugly childhood, of a marriage gone bad, of seeing her friends suffer from abuse and poor choices. Then the conversation with her mother a few days ago threw itself into the mix. And with her thoughts came doubt, and with the doubt came fear. A familiar helplessness overcame her, and she couldn't find the will to hardly even breathe, let alone face the day.

* * *

At the first opportunity, Wade called the pediatric clinic, just wanting to hear Laura's voice and to remind her that they only had twenty-five hours left to be single.

"Oh, she's not in," he was told. "She called in sick."

Wade felt concerned and confused the moment he hung up. She'd usually left messages on his cell phone if she'd changed her plans. He called the house three times but got no answer. He wondered if she had just called in sick in order to do errands before the wedding, or perhaps to spend some time with Rochelle. He called her cell phone but again got no answer. Feeling decidedly concerned, he pleaded a family emergency and left the clinic where he was putting in hours. He kept trying to call her right until he pulled into the driveway, where her car was parked. The back door was locked, but she'd told him where she kept a key, and he went inside after hiding it again. The house felt hot and stuffy, and he flipped on the swamp cooler.

"Laura?" he called and walked through the kitchen, peering into the front room, then continued on down the hall. "Laura? Are you here?" The bathroom was vacant, as was the spare bedroom, but through the open doorway of her bedroom he could see that she was on the bed, wearing pajamas as silly as most of her scrubs, her back to the door. With as hot as the house felt, he didn't have to wonder why she wasn't under the covers.

"Laura?" he said loudly enough to wake her. He hesitated in the doorway while her lack of responsiveness made his stomach tighten even before the memory consciously took hold. Logically it was ridiculous, and he knew it. What were the odds? But emotionally the possibility felt horrifically real.

"Laura!" he shouted, unable to move.

"What?" she said without moving, her voice clearly alert. She hadn't been asleep. She'd been ignoring him. And he felt angry.

"Well, at least I know you're not dead. I was honestly wondering there for a minute."

She turned to look at him. "Don't be ridiculous. Of course I'm not—"

"I've found a woman dead in her bed before, Laura." He tried to keep his voice even, but he knew his terseness was evident.

"I'm sorry," she said gently.

He took a deep breath. "I'm sorry too. I just . . . for a moment there it all came back. Do you want to tell me why you were ignoring me?" She said nothing and he pressed his case. "You don't go to work but don't leave me a message? You won't answer your phone or say anything when I talk to you? What's wrong?" She didn't answer. "Is it feminine?"

"No."

"Are you sick?"

Still nothing.

"Then what's wrong?"

"Nothing. I'm fine," she said, looking away.

"Now you're lying, and you promised at the very least to always be honest with me. You're depressed, aren't you." It wasn't a question. Still she said nothing. Wade wanted to shake some sense into her, or at least make her look at him, but he had no desire to have this conversation in her bedroom. He didn't bother to warn her before he scooped her into his arms.

"What are you doing?" she demanded.

"We need to talk, and I'm not doing it while you're in bed." He carried her down the hall and to the couch where he sat her at one end, then sat at the other. "Talk to me."

"What are you doing here anyway?" she demanded.

"You told me where the key was, remember? Beyond the fact that I will not be sleeping here tonight, I live here now. Talk to me." Still she said nothing. Wade reached over to take her arm into his hand. "Look at me," he insisted, and she did. But her eyes were grudging. "Where are you, Laura? Where's the woman who loves me and trusts me?"

"I don't know, Wade. Maybe this is the real Laura. Maybe the one you've gotten to know so far was just an act."

"I don't believe that even a little bit, and neither do you. Now talk to me."

"I don't want to talk, Wade. I want to be alone."

"And do what? Eat ice cream and ignore the phone? Let me make something impeccably clear, Laura. If an episode of depression requires you to have some down time, some alone time, so be it. Shut the world out once in a while. But I am not the world. I am as good as your husband, and I will not leave you to brood without knowing why. I deserve better than that from you. What happened? What's bothering you? Talk to me."

"Maybe it's nothing; maybe it's just me. Maybe it's chemical, or hormonal."

"Is it PMS week?"

"No."

"Then convince me that you've just had some horrid, bizarre chemical downfall that occurred overnight, and it just happens to have occurred right before you're getting married." She said nothing. "What happened, Laura?" Still silence. He sighed and reminded himself to be patient. "Get used to it, Laura. I may have to adjust to dealing with my wife's depression, but you're going to have to adjust to the fact that your husband will not leave you in peace until he gets a reasonable explanation. You want me to leave you in peace and let you wallow for a while, fine. But I need a good reason, and don't expect me to let you wallow too long." He waited; still nothing. "Do we need to play twenty questions? Will it take a hundred? I'm not leaving until you tell me whatever thoughts may be rolling around in that pretty little head of yours. Talk to me." Nothing. "Okay. Let me try some logic. Rochelle came to see you last night. What did she say?"

Laura turned guilty eyes abruptly toward him. "Oh," he said, "now we're getting somewhere. What did she say?" She didn't answer. "I could venture to guess. I bet it had something to do with your probable insanity over marrying a man you only started dating last week." Again her eyes told the truth. "Consider the source, Laura. Rochelle would think that any woman is crazy who intends to get married at all."

He heard her sigh, saw her squeeze her eyes closed. "I've opened the door, Laura. You've got to trust me enough to walk through it. Talk to me."

She hung her head and sighed again. "I don't know, Wade. Maybe . . . we *are* moving too fast . . . making a mistake."

"No!" he said so abruptly it startled even himself. Her wide eyes reminded him to stay calm and think this through. It didn't take much thought to realize the emotion he had tied into the possibility of calling off the wedding. But he couldn't let his past baggage interfere with what was happening now. He reminded himself to keep his wits and uttered a silent prayer. He believed the real Laura was in there; he just had to reach her.

"Now listen to me, Laura, if you feel like it's too fast, I can accept that. We can postpone it if you feel that's best, but I need a reason—a *good* reason. Just having a bad day and some general doubts do not constitute a good reason. If it's more than that, talk to me, and we'll postpone it. But we are not going to call it off, because this relationship is *not* a mistake. We have the ability to work this through—together."

"I'm not so sure," she said, hanging her head again, pushing a hand through her matted hair.

In Wade's mind he could clearly see the choices she was likely examining in her own. Or if she wasn't now, she would be. He took her shoulders into his hands and forced her to look at him. "Listen to me, Laura. I am going to marry you, and it's going to be forever, and I am going to stand by you no matter where the depths of depression may take you. Are you hearing me?"

"Why?" she squeaked. "How can you?"

"Because I will *not* leave you alone to go through door number two, *or* door number three."

She looked at him, puzzled and confused—then enlightened. "Oh, so you'll marry me because you're afraid I'll do something stupid otherwise? Because you feel sorry for me?"

"No, Laura, I will marry you because I love you, because I know that marrying you is the right thing to do, and because I will not let you become a casualty of this world. So marry me tomorrow, or next month, or next year. I'm here for the long haul. I'm not naive enough to think that it will always be easy. If depression will be an ongoing challenge for you, then we need to work together to handle it and get through it. That's what marriage is, Laura; it's helping each other get through. I'm not leaving you. But it would sure be a lot easier to help you get out of bed in the morning if I'm sleeping in the same bed, and I'm not doing that until you have my name."

He saw something softening in her eyes, and then his cell phone rang. He glanced at the caller ID to see that it was his mother. "I'll be right back," he said. "Don't go anywhere."

"Dressed like this?" she asked, but she sounded a little more like herself.

Wade walked into the spare bedroom to answer the phone. Laura watched him leave the room, then she stared at the wall and contemplated everything he'd just said, everything he'd said and done since she'd met him, placing it all on one side of a scale. And on the other side she put everything Rochelle had said, and all the horrible experiences of her life, and in the lives of those she loved. All the garbage on one side of the scale had nothing to do with Wade Morrison. He had done nothing to warrant any mistrust or fear. He loved her, and he was good to her. But how could she make the scales balance with the experiences of life that had become a part of her?

A knock at the door startled her. She pulled it open just a little, then seeing Rochelle, she opened it wider, wishing she'd just ignored it.

"You look terrible," Rochelle said, her eyes scanning Laura from head to toe.

"I thought a friend was supposed to accept you as you are," Laura said. "Have a seat."

"Thanks," Rochelle said, and they both sat down. Laura put her feet up beneath her and hugged a throw pillow.

"Say whatever you came to say and get it over with," Laura said. "I can see it in your eyes."

"Okay, I will," Rochelle said. "Listen, I know I was a little harsh yesterday, but I'm begging you to reconsider this. I can't bear to see you go through any more pain."

"Wade has brought me nothing but joy, and love, and acceptance."

"And how long do you really believe that will last? How did you feel about Randall before you married him?"

"It was nothing like this."

Rochelle gave a disgusted sigh. "You are behind rose-colored glasses, girl. How can you know a man so short a time and possibly have any idea if he means what he says?"

"I don't want to talk about this any more, Rochelle," she said. "Either change the subject or leave."

Rochelle's disgust became more evident. "You're just not going to listen, are you? Why do you think he wants to get married so quickly, Laura? Any guy who wants to be engaged for what . . . a week? He cannot possibly have your best interests at heart. He's probably hoping to get you to the altar before you find out what he's really like. If you—"

"Actually," Wade said, and they both turned toward him, startled, "she already knows I belong to a satanic cult, and I have three previous wives buried in my backyard."

Rochelle made that disgusted noise again. "I'm not amused," she said.

"What a pleasure to finally meet you, Rochelle. I've heard so much about you."

"Funny. I've heard absolutely nothing about you."

"That would explain why you're so convinced that I'm going to destroy her life?"

Rochelle seemed to prefer ignoring him. She turned to Laura and said, "I'm begging you to at least give this some time. Come back to Chicago with me; get some distance. Look at life from a new perspective, Laura. And if you still want to come back and marry this guy, fine."

"Door number two," Wade said, and Laura met his eyes.

"What's that supposed to mean?" Rochelle asked him.

"That's between me and Laura, just as our decision to get married." He looked at Laura and asked, "Are you up to going to that dinner?"

"Yes, I'm fine," she said. "I just need to change."

She hurried from the room, and Wade sat where she'd been sitting. He resisted the urge to say what he was thinking and instead tried a more diplomatic approach. "Rochelle," he said calmly, "I know your concern for Laura is valid. She's been hurt, and so have you—and Tina." She looked surprised, as if she wouldn't have expected him to know such things. "You don't know me well enough to believe that I'm what I appear to be, but you don't know me well enough to know otherwise either. Laura and I have no secrets from each other; more specifically, I have nothing to hide. Hire a private investigator, Rochelle. Do a credit check. You won't find a police record beyond one speeding ticket about five years ago. Talk to everyone who knows me, or anyone who ever has. Whatever you're looking for, you won't find it."

"Being perfect in the eyes of the world does not guarantee that you won't be a horrible husband."

"No, it doesn't. But being male does not automatically make me a walking disaster. Perhaps you would do well to consider that maybe Laura's learned something from the life she's lived; she's not only smart, she's wise. She has good instincts, a strong spirit, and a good heart. Give her some credit, Rochelle."

"I'm ready," Laura said to Wade from the doorway. Then to Rochelle, "We have a dinner appointment. Will we see you at the luncheon?"

"Laura, please," Rochelle said. "Give this some time. Please tell me that you're not fool enough to go through with this so quickly."

Wade watched Laura's face, the confusion in her eyes, and he was taken back in time so quickly that his heart began to thud. How could he ever forget that moment when it had become clear to him that Marina would choose her dysfunctional family's behavior over marrying him? Would it come to that again? In spite of all he had promised her, all he had entrusted to her, all he had pledged to do to carry her through any possible struggle, would Laura still choose to be swayed against him? He felt so utterly sick at the thought that it was a strain to keep a steady expression.

"Laura," Rochelle pleaded, "after what Randall did to you, I don't know how you can expect me to—"

"That's irrelevant," Laura snapped, and Wade saw shame in her eyes as she looked to gauge his reaction. He would have thought it had something to do with what she'd already told him, except for that expression on her face.

"*What* did Randall do to you?" he demanded.

"Oh, so there *are* secrets between you," Rochelle said, and Laura's expression turned guilty.

Wade couldn't resist saying, "We've got to save something to give us some adventure once the honeymoon is over." Inwardly he prayed there would be a honeymoon, a wedding, a life beyond this day. He wanted to scream at Laura and demand that she say something. But the last thing he needed right now was to exhibit some kind of behavior to give any hint of credibility to what Rochelle was saying. Instead he just looked at Laura and said in a quiet voice, "Let's go."

"Okay," she said, then to Rochelle, "I wish I could say it had been good to see you. I wish that you could have found even the tiniest degree of happiness on my behalf. And it would be nice if you could believe that maybe I'm not as big a fool as you think I am. I'd like to believe that what I'm hearing is out of concern, but I think it's more about your own anger. And I don't need it. Whatever I decide to do with my life is, quite frankly, none of your business. You're not the friend I knew and trusted anymore, Rochelle. You're just going to have to let go and let me make my own choices. Whether or not you stick around to see the consequences is up to you."

Rochelle moved toward the door, ranting something about Laura digging her own grave, and she had no desire to stand by and see it happen. When she was gone, the tension hovering in the air was so thick Wade felt as if he might suffocate. What Laura had said to Rochelle had been more of a relief to him than he could ever tell her. She had stood up to her and said all the right things to draw her boundaries clearly. But that didn't necessarily let him know where he stood. She'd declared her right to make her own decisions, but she'd said nothing about actually going through with the wedding.

Unable to bear the silence he asked, "Are you okay?"

"It's hard to say. I didn't know choosing door number one would . . ."

"Come between you and your friendship with Rochelle?" he guessed.

"I think I lost my friendship with Rochelle a long time ago," she said. "Of course, I could probably restore it very quickly if I took her offer." She chuckled with no sign of humor. "Door number two."

Laura looked long and hard at this man she was supposed to marry tomorrow. There were so many thoughts spinning in her head that she just wanted her brain to stop; she only wanted to be in his arms and let everything else melt away. But she felt frozen and crippled, and she *hated* it. She wanted to feel happy and thrilled and alive.

She was startled from her weighted thoughts when she found him standing directly in front of her. Without a word he put his arms around her, holding her tightly. *A hug.* What had he said? *No expectations or implications; just a simple expression of concern, support, and acceptance.* She felt so completely safe that she wanted to never let him go, but she had to wonder if letting him go would be better for him.

"Let's get out of here," he said and locked the front door before they went out the back way, then he locked that as well.

In the car Laura's thoughts wandered through disturbing caverns while the stereo played loudly. Then Wade turned it off and said, "Talk to me, Laura. Tell me what you're thinking; anything." He took her hand. "It doesn't have to make sense. Just tell me your thoughts."

Laura watched him driving, wondering how he could be so kind and accepting. It wasn't as difficult as it probably should have been to admit, "I keep wondering why you're still here."

"Here?"

"With me."

"And why would I not be?" he asked.

"After what just happened . . ."

"Rochelle has nothing to do with you and me, Laura—unless you let her. But I think you made it clear to her that she has no place in our relationship." He was surprised to hear his own voice tremble as he added, "You will never know what it meant to me to hear you say what you did."

Laura tightened her gaze on him, somewhat taken off guard by his emotion. "I'll know if you tell me," she said.

Wade glanced at her and saw distinct signs that the Laura he knew was back now—or at least she was closer. His emotion became irrepressible, and he pulled the car over to the curb, unable to drive. He unfastened his seatbelt and turned to take her into his arms. "Oh, Laura," he murmured. "I was scared out of my mind." She drew back, silently questioning him. "After what happened with Marina, I don't know if I could cope with realizing now that there were problems we couldn't solve. The way you stood up to Rochelle was astounding, Laura. You didn't let her come between us."

Laura felt a little stunned. "I was wondering why you're still here . . . now that you've seen how pathetic I can be when I get depressed." When he said nothing, she looked away. "Maybe you should reconsider."

"Reconsider what?"

"Marrying me."

"Over depression? Are you kidding?"

Laura turned back to face him, her eyes angry and bewildered. "You can't honestly tell me that you like this." She motioned toward herself. "How can you like it when I *hate* it?"

"You or the depression?"

"I don't know; maybe both."

"Okay, well first of all, let's keep the differentiation clear here. You are who you are no matter how you might feel, and I love you. I will always love you. And no, I don't like the depression. But I wouldn't like it if you had diabetes either, or MS, or cancer. But I would still love you. Depression is an illness, Laura, and we're going to treat it like one. We're going to work it through together. You say you've tried all the antidepressants and they haven't worked. So, let's do some research, talk to a good counselor, see what we can do that *will* work. I don't admit to knowing a lot about it, but I do know a little, and I'm willing to learn." He hesitated, then forced himself not to leave any of his feelings on the matter unsaid. "Laura, there's only one thing about this depression thing I can't live with."

"What?" she demanded, far more defensive than he felt the conversation warranted. "You can't handle a woman who curls up in bed and just wants the world to go away?"

"No, I can handle that," he said firmly. "But you need to understand that we are on the same side, Laura. However low this illness may take you, I'm going with you. I'm not the world; I'm the man who loves you, the man you are going to exchange eternal vows with tomorrow." He paused a moment to ponder his analogy and felt certain he was being inspired.

"Laura, if this were diabetes, what would you do if you felt the symptoms of insulin shock coming on?" She looked confused. "Come on. You're a nurse. You know this stuff."

"You'd need to . . . get something with sugar in it . . . in your system . . . quickly."

"Exactly. You'd need to understand the onset of symptoms, and know what to do about it. What did you do last night when I called you?" She said nothing, so he answered for her. "You were already sinking, and you told me nothing was wrong, you were just tired, you didn't want to talk about it. The only thing that gave me a clue was your admitting that Rochelle's visit had stirred things up. What things, Laura? I'm guessing it was more than just what she said about me. She probably brought it all back. Tina. Randall. Am I right?" She didn't speak, but he could see it in her eyes. "And what do you think might have happened if you had said to me, last night, 'I'm depressed, Wade. I need to talk?'"

"About what?" she snapped. "What is there to say?"

"It doesn't matter what you say. You just need to let those thoughts spill instead of letting them roll around in your head and eat you alive. But you're in the habit of holding it all in. Who have you had to talk to? Rochelle?" He made a disgusted noise. "Her answer to everything is Sodom and Gomorrah." He touched her face. "Laura, I've been praying very hard that whatever might come up between us, I would know how to handle it, because I need you to know that I truly mean it when I say that I am with you in this, no matter what. But you've got to trust me. I really don't think this is chemical, Laura, as much as it's the result of a long string of tough things in your life, with nothing to counteract them, no outlet, no perspective."

Laura looked into his eyes and felt a sense of déja-vu. The moment felt so much like another moment not so many days ago when he'd sat right where he was now, proclaiming his convictions, which had sounded to Laura like manna from heaven flowing through his lips. And just like it had then, emotion now burst out of her with no warning. She took hold of him and pressed her face to his shoulder, savoring the feel of his arms around her, in awe of the miracle he was in her life. She didn't even have to question Rochelle's concerns. She knew Wade; she knew him heart and soul. And he knew her. She could never explain how she knew, but she *knew*. In spite of all her shortcomings, her temptations, and less than admirable thoughts and feelings, God had been merciful to her. He loved her, and He had sent Wade Morrison into her life to prove it.

CHAPTER 21

"It's going to be okay, Laura," Wade murmured, stroking her hair as he pressed a kiss to the top of her head.

"I actually believe you," she said through her tears, holding him more tightly. "For the first time in years, I actually believe that it's going to be okay."

"Promise me you'll talk to me, Laura. That you won't shut me out, no matter what happens."

"I promise," she said. "Promise me you'll never prove Rochelle right. I can face anything as long as you never stop being the man you are right now."

"I promise," he muttered and tightened his embrace.

Laura became calm, and Wade helped dry her tears before he started driving again. She was examining how red her eyes looked in the mirror when he made a call on his cell phone.

"Hi," she heard him say. "We're on our way over. Do you think before everyone else gets there that you could help me with something? I think Laura could use a blessing. Okay, thanks. See you soon." He hung up and said, "I hope that's alright."

"Alex?" she asked.

"Yeah."

"Yes, it's fine. Thank you."

He took her hand and kissed it.

"I look terrible," Laura said as they pulled up in front of the house.

"No, you look like you've been crying. It's family, Laura. No one cares if you look like you've been crying."

"But . . . I'm meeting your sisters."

"Not until later. Right now it's just Alex and Jane."

In the house they found all of the children but Barrett gathered in the family room, making a delightful mess. "Hey there, lady," Wade said, and Rebecca came running into his arms. He laughed as he picked her up. Then he pointed to Laura and said, "That's Laura. Can you say Laura?"

Rebecca just looked at her father and said, "Daddy."

Ruthie came running as well, and Wade lifted her into his other arm, laughing again. "The twins," he said to Laura, "even though they look nothing alike."

"They're both adorable," Laura said and followed Wade to the kitchen. He bounced the girls as he walked, making them giggle.

"Hi," Jane said as they came in to find Alex standing on a stool, handing plates to her from a high cupboard.

"It must be a special occasion," Alex said. "She's breaking out the china."

"Don't use the word breaking in the same sentence with the china," Jane said, carefully taking the plates from him.

"Special occasion, eh?" Wade said, setting the girls down.

"I hear someone's getting married," Jane said.

"I heard that too," Wade said and gave Laura a quick kiss as Alex came down from the stool. He was both surprised and grateful with the way Alex stood directly in front of Laura and asked, "And how are you, little sister?"

"I've had better days," she said. "But thanks for asking."

"Satan got his bullies working on you? He wouldn't want you to actually marry the right man in the right place and enjoy it, now would he?"

Laura glanced at Wade, then back to Alex. "There's probably a lot of truth to that."

"Let's see if we can help that out a little, shall we?" Alex said and put an arm around her shoulders, escorting her into the hall. Wade got a wink and a smile from Jane before he followed after them.

In the study, Alex closed the door and guided Laura to the chair near the desk. Wade met Alex's eyes and said softly, "I want you to do it." For a long moment they just looked at each other, and Wade wondered if Alex was remembering, as he was, the time he'd asked Wade to speak the majority of the blessing for Jane during an especially difficult time. Alex hadn't wanted Jane to think that the words of the blessing had come from his own feelings or desires. Alex nodded to indicate that he understood, and Wade knew he did. Alex always understood.

In the blessing, Laura was told of her Heavenly Father's love, and that He was pleased with the place she had come to in her life by holding to her values in the face of many challenges. She was promised peace of mind and happiness, and told that the greatest antidote for her present struggles would be going often to the temple with her husband, to return to the place where their vows would be exchanged, and to be strengthened by the power found there. She was told that as she held fast to her beliefs, she would not only find great joy in her life, but she would be a great strength and example to others. And she was also told to rely on the love and support of those around her, who had been sent into her life to be her new family. They would be there to help her through whatever struggles might lie ahead.

After the Amen had been spoken, Wade wasn't surprised to find tears on Laura's face. She wiped them away as she stood, and Alex gave her a tight hug. "It's going to be okay," he said.

"That's what your brother keeps telling me," she said.

"You should believe him. He's a pretty smart kid."

Laura turned to Wade and hugged him as well. "Thank you," she said. "Both of you."

"It's no problem any time," Alex said and left the room, closing the door behind him.

"Do we have time to talk a few minutes before the rest of your family gets here?" Laura asked.

"We have lots of time," he said, sitting on the couch. "It's still early."

Laura glanced at the clock as she sat beside him. "Oh, it is early. You ditched the clinic, didn't you?"

"Yes, I did. I'll manage. Talk to me."

"Okay, well . . ." She looked down at her wringing hands and Wade realized she was nervous. "Some thoughts occurred to me during that blessing. First of all, I want you to know that I think you were right. In fact, you were so right that I truly believe you were inspired, which is just one more thing that lets me know I'm doing the right thing." He took her hand and squeezed it before she went on. "I do let horrid thoughts and memories swirl around in my head, and it's nice to know I have someone in my life now who will listen to them, and not judge me, or try to tell me the answers to my problems are immoral."

She took a deep breath, and he could see her nervousness increasing. He wondered what she wanted to tell him that would create such a reaction, when she'd always been so open with him prior to today.

"You were right. I should have been honest with you last night and confronted it then. I'll do my best not to let it get so out of hand from now on."

"That's my girl," he said, touching her face.

"There is one thing that keeps going around in my head now, Wade. I didn't say anything about it before because, well . . . it kind of just fell under the category of my knowing very quickly that I couldn't stay married to Randall."

"Is this what Rochelle was talking about?" he asked, and she nodded.

"I'm glad Rochelle showed up and said what she did, and now that I'm feeling better, I'm glad you found me the way you did today. At first I was mortified, but . . . now I don't have to wonder how you're going to respond when you find me depressed. I don't have to fear that . . ."

"What, Laura?" he asked with concern. Now she was shaking.

"You see," she let out a harsh, humorless chuckle, "Randall's answer to solving my depression was to slap some sense into me—quite literally."

Wade's heart pounded, and his stomach tightened. Tears fell down her face, and her expression became shamed, humiliated. She reached for a tissue from the little table near the couch. "Sick, psychotic, deranged; those were the words he used." She sobbed and pressed the tissue over her mouth for a long moment. "He blamed every problem in the marriage on my being depressed, while I knew in my heart that the greatest source of my depression was knowing I had married a madman."

She sobbed again, and Wade pulled her into his arms, holding her as if he could keep her from ever being hurt again, as if he could erase every hurt in her past. She returned his embrace with fervor, finally crying herself into a conspicuous silence.

"I'm so sorry you had to live through that," Wade said, tightening his embrace further still.

"Do you have any idea what it means to me, Wade . . . the things you said to me today, the way you responded to all of this? Whatever fear or doubt I may have had inside of me has been completely erased. I have never felt so firm and confident about a decision in my life. I'm just amazed that you can feel the same way."

"Are you kidding?" he asked with a little laugh. "I'm asking you to marry a once-suicidal, widowed man with a two-year-old daughter, and he's asking you to follow him around the country for years of residency before he can become a doctor who will be taking on one of the toughest jobs in the medical profession. We'll see who gets depressed when he can't cure every kid with cancer."

She laughed softly and hugged him tighter.

"However," he said, "I think if I take you with me on my hospital rounds and you wear your funny shoes and silly scrubs, we'll make a lot more headway."

"Or I could just get you going on your own collection of funny shoes and silly scrubs."

"Whatever it takes to make a sick kid smile," he said.

"You made Barrett smile when he was sick," she said. "I saw pictures to prove it."

"Once or twice," he muttered and pressed a kiss into her hair.

At the risk of dampening the mood again, Wade said quietly, "Tell me more about Randall, Laura. I need to know so I won't have my imagination filling in the pieces. How bad was it? You said you were only together about a month before the annulment. How many times did he hurt you?"

"There were only two episodes," she said with a steady voice. "The second one happened after I told him the marriage was over and he needed to leave my house. As far as domestic violence goes, it wasn't so bad. He only hit my face, and it didn't leave any bruises. It's more the things he said, and there's something about such words combined with a good, hard slap that somehow embeds them into your spirit. I guess that's the hard part. You see . . . that's how it used to be with my mother. Most of the time I managed to hide or stay out of her way when I knew she was drunk, but once in a while she got me cornered. Randall hit me the same way she did. He didn't say the same words, but what he said brought all of my mother's words back to me. She called me awful things, Wade. Told me I would never be good for anything, that I was ugly and useless. I've worked very hard to convince myself that she was wrong, that those messages were false. Logically, I know they are. But sometimes, emotionally, they come back to me, and they feel very real."

"It's not true, Laura. You're beautiful and amazing; you're the best thing that's ever happened to me."

"Hearing you say things like that, I actually believe I can finally prove my mother—and Randall—wrong."

"And with any luck I can prove Rochelle wrong," he said.

Laura lifted her head to look at him. "You already have."

He smiled at her, and she kissed him before she leaned back and said, "There's something else that came to me during that blessing . . . something I need to say. I'm just not quite sure how to explain it."

"Just talk," he said.

"Well, first of all . . . this part's easy. I just have to say how grateful I am that you thought of a blessing. I can't remember the last time I had a blessing. Randall offered to give me one once. I declined. I couldn't possibly believe that he had the right to do so when he had hit me the day before."

"I wouldn't think so," Wade said, feeling angry on her behalf. "But you need to remember that theory I once learned from general conference."

"What's that?"

"Just because you have a bad experience with a toaster, doesn't mean you shouldn't trust the power of electricity."

Laura smiled. "Which I guess summarizes my point. My depression often made me avoid my home teachers, or lie to them when they asked me how I was doing. Getting that blessing a while ago made me wonder what I'd been thinking all this time. I should have asked my home teachers for a blessing a long time ago. So . . . thank you . . . for thinking of it, for following through with it, for being worthy to do it."

"It's a privilege, Laura, I can assure you."

"Why did you have Alex speak it?" she asked.

"So you wouldn't wonder if it was coming from me. He did the same thing once, years ago. Jane was struggling. He asked me to give that part of the blessing."

"It's hard to imagine Jane struggling."

"When I met her they were at the worst of the situation with Barrett. It was pretty bad there for a while. Alex told me that it was like Jane completely lost herself. Their marriage became pretty strained. Of course, for weeks they hardly saw each other except for changing shifts with Barrett at the hospital. It was horrid. I pray we never have to face anything like that. When I lost Elena I was so grateful that it wasn't cancer, that she didn't have to suffer."

Laura smiled and touched his face. "Do you think Elena approves of me?"

"Approves?" he echoed.

"To raise her daughter, to spend my life with the man she loves?"

Wade touched her face in return. "I'm absolutely certain of it."

"How do you know?" she asked.

"I just know, Laura. I have felt her joy on my behalf. She knows we're in good hands."

She looked puzzled, perhaps startled, and he went on to clarify a point. "Laura, when you told me that you remember

Elena, and about your talking to her, well . . . I remember her talking about you, and how she'd enjoyed visiting with you. I remember telling her it was too bad we were moving, or she could have taken you out to lunch or something." Laura's eyes widened. "I think the two of you could have been very good friends."

Laura smiled at the analogy but couldn't speak. She was so touched that it couldn't help but strengthen her resolve in their being meant for each other.

"Anyway . . . back to the subject," he said, reminding her of the difficulties they'd faced this day. "I know there's something else you need to say. What is it?"

"How well you know me," she said. "I just . . . I also realized during the blessing that . . . I don't like being alone, Wade. Especially at night. When I get in that frame of mind, being alone at night in that house is . . . almost frightening. I love my house, but . . . that's where Randall yelled at me and hit me. That's where I got the news about Tina. That's where I had those long, horrid conversations with Rochelle. That's where I've wallowed in self-pity for endless hours. Last night was horrible—like all the memories just seemed to come out of the darkness to haunt me."

Wade thought about that for only a moment before he said, "Okay, we'll work on that. Tonight you're staying here. You can sleep in Rebecca's room." They both knew there was a twin bed in there along with the crib. "I'm sure you can borrow stuff from Jane, and they keep some things around for impulsive guests. Tomorrow you'll be married." He laughed softly when he said it. "Anything else?"

She smiled. "Nothing that getting married won't solve."

"Like what?" he asked.

"I just want to spend a couple of hours holding you close and kissing you until my lips wear out."

"Ooh," he said, coming to his feet with her hand in his. "Time to find a chaperone. Where's Rebecca when we need her?"

Laura smiled and went with him to the kitchen, where Alex and Jane were laughing while they worked together cutting up vegetables for a salad. "Can we help?" Wade asked.

"Are you kidding?" Alex said. "You're the guests of honor."

"It's all under control," Jane said. "Just relax. Tomorrow is a big day."

"Is it okay if Laura stays here tonight?" Wade asked. "She can sleep in Rebecca's room."

"Do you have to ask?" Alex said. "Of course she can stay."

"I'll let Jane take very good care of her," Wade said. "And I'll lock myself in my room."

"What?" Alex chuckled. "Is there a full moon tonight?"

"Something like that," Wade said. "How long before the mob arrives?"

"An hour or so, I believe," Jane said.

Laura asked, "Mind if I freshen up a little?"

"Make yourself at home," Jane said. "Let me know if you need anything."

Wade took Laura upstairs to his own bathroom, where he said, "Before you do whatever you have to do with whatever you've got in that purse of yours, there's something I need your help with."

"Okay," she said warily just before he handed her a razor.

"Do you want to do it, or do you want me to do it?" She looked confused, and he added, "It's time for the beard to come off. I'm starting a new life."

"Oh." She sounded startled and quickly gave the razor back. "I can't do it. What if I cut you?"

"I'd take the risk," he said and kissed her quickly.

Laura put both her hands on his face, caressing the beard with her fingers as if to say a fond farewell. "Are you sure?" she asked.

"Yeah, it's time. But you never know when I might gain a new aversion to shaving. I think, however, that you shouldn't marry a man unless you've seen his real face."

"Okay," she said, stepping back. "I'm ready. I'll just watch."

Laura watched Wade's shaving ritual with a certain awe. He laughed and made dramatic noises as the hair came off of his face, and she could only wonder why she had been so thoroughly blessed to have him in her life. He rinsed off his face, then dried it before he turned to look at her directly, and she felt her breath catch in her chest.

"Still handsome," she said, touching his face while he reached for the aftershave lotion. "Oh, this part I can do," she said. She poured some in one of her hands, rubbed them together then pressed her hands over every part of his face where he'd shaved, then she held his face between her hands and kissed him. "Ooh, feels different," she said and kissed him again. "Still nice, though."

He made a noise of agreement, then said, "I'm leaving now. I'll see you downstairs whenever you're up to facing company."

"I won't be long," she said. He smiled and closed the bathroom door, leaving her there.

* * *

Laura wasn't surprised at how much she liked Wade's sisters, Charlotte and Becca. And as always, the other members of his family that she'd already begun to get to know were a joy to be around. Holding Wade's hand in hers, absorbing the obvious acceptance and warmth of these people, she felt a hope and peace unlike anything she'd ever experienced. It was as if all these years of struggling to live the gospel against a lifetime of challenges had suddenly become worth it. She was truly blessed!

After everyone had left for the night, Wade gave Laura a quick kiss at the foot of the stairs and put her into Jane's care to see that she had everything she needed. Wearing pajamas borrowed from Jane, Laura spent several minutes just watching Rebecca sleeping, pondering the privilege she was being given to raise this child as her own. She finally turned out the light and went to bed, feeling surrounded by a warm spirit. She didn't know if it was the house, her little roommate, or the fact that she was getting married tomorrow. Probably a combination. Whatever it was, she felt happy. And considering her state of mind earlier today, that was nothing less than a miracle.

* * *

After Wade said goodnight to Laura, he knew there was something he'd overlooked. It had occurred to him just a while ago that there was someone he'd forgotten to invite to the wedding. It was barely ten o'clock when he dialed Kirk's number, hoping it wasn't too late. His friend had checked on him regularly since Elena's death, but he'd stopped inviting Wade to dinner when he'd admitted that it was just too hard. Kirk had simply said that when Wade's circumstances changed, they would make up for it. Still, Kirk had called regularly, showing a genuine concern for him in a way that no other friend had. He'd been thrilled when Wade had become engaged to Marina, and disappointed when Wade had ended up hurt and alone. It was a pleasure to call Kirk now with the good news.

"Hey," Wade said when Kirk answered. "I hope it's not too late."

"Are you kidding? The night is young. How are you, buddy?"

"I'm great, actually," Wade said. "Listen, I know this is short notice, but . . . it was pulled together pretty quickly, and it's been crazy. Anyway, I'm getting married tomorrow, and—"

"Are you *serious?*" Kirk laughed. "Tomorrow?"

"That's right." Wade couldn't hold back a little chuckle. "Anyway, I don't know if you can make it or not, but—"

"I'll be there. Tell me when and where."

"The Salt Lake Temple," he said and let him know the time.

"This is great," Kirk said. "Tell me everything."

Wade spent nearly half an hour telling Kirk the story of his knowing Laura for two years, and how he'd finally come to ask her out, and then how quickly everything had fallen so perfectly into place. Repeating it all aloud only reaffirmed Wade's conviction that he was doing the right thing. He was the happiest man alive.

Wade had only been off the phone a few minutes when Barrett came timidly through the open door of Wade's bedroom.

"Hey, buddy," Wade said. "What are you doing up so late?"

"Dad said I could stay up and talk to you, and it *is* Saturday tomorrow."

"Yes, it is," Wade said, and they sat side-by-side on the edge of the bed.

"I like Laura," Barrett said.

"Well, I'm glad you approve."

"And I'm glad you're getting married," Barrett said. "I know you've been lonely since Elena died."

"Yes, I have," Wade said. "There's only one thing about this that's hard for me. It's that I won't be living in the same house with you."

Big tears welled up in Barrett's eyes, proving that he shared Wade's emotion over that point. Wade held him close while he added, "I know this is hardest of all for you, and I'm sorry about that."

"It's okay," Barrett said. "I mean . . . we'll still see each other a lot, right?"

"Of course. You are my favorite nephew. And you are coming to the wedding luncheon tomorrow, right?"

"You said I was invited," Barrett said, getting control of his tears.

"You'll be the only kid there except for Rebecca. How could I celebrate something so big in my life without you there?"

Barrett smiled and hugged Wade tightly. "I love you, Uncle Wade."

"I love you too, Barrett," he said, and returned the hug. "Don't ever forget, no matter how life changes or what happens, we share the same blood, and nothing can ever change that."

Barrett actually laughed, then he hugged Wade again.

* * *

The following morning everything was so busy and went so quickly that Laura didn't have a moment to feel nervous. Jane took such good care of her that she had to wonder if this was how it might be to have a sister who truly cared, a sister who shared your deepest beliefs. As they stood together in front of the mirror in the temple bride's room, Laura saw tears in Jane's eyes that coaxed her own joy to the surface. They shared a careful embrace, and a short while later she was in the celestial room with Wade, unable to even speak, but knowing that he fully understood her joy. She could see it clearly reflected in his eyes. As they walked together into the sealing room, she felt freshly overcome with the love and acceptance of his family members—from both families. His two fathers were serving as witnesses to the marriage, something that in itself spoke of the power of forgiveness and compassion. The very reality of seeing this uniquely blended family here together within temple walls, with no feelings of malice or contempt, gave her hope that her own challenges and issues could be overcome—especially with the love and support of so many good people.

Kneeling across the altar from Wade, the moment felt so unbelievably fantastic that she almost expected him to stop at any moment and declare that he'd changed his mind. But he spoke his vow with fervor and tenderness, holding her eyes with his through the entire ceremony, as if he too had trouble believing it was real. She'd never felt so beautiful, so loved and adored, so completely safe and secure. After rings and a kiss had been exchanged, she could hardly contain her joy. She was Mrs. Wade Morrison. Life could be no better than that.

After the ceremony, she and Wade were greeted by everyone present, and she accepted their warm embraces and congratulations as if she were living in a fairy tale. She met Wade's friend Kirk, and his wife, and she felt touched by Kirk's genuine happiness on Wade's behalf.

Back in the bride's room, Jane helped Laura unfasten the bustle at the back of her dress so that it fell into an elegant train. They met the men in the lobby before going outside to take pictures. Wade had changed from his white clothing into a classic black tux with tails, something that Alex had encouraged due to the tradition of the wedding waltz. Laura thought he looked absolutely adorable, especially when he kissed her and said, "I love you, Mrs. Morrison."

On the temple grounds they were met by everyone who had attended the ceremony, as well as Barrett and little Rebecca, since Wade's sisters had gone home to get them. Rebecca was wearing a white dress that Jane had picked out for the occasion, and she looked absolutely angelic. She went straight to her father when she saw him, and Wade laughed as he picked her up. He pointed at Laura and said, "That's Mommy. Can you say Mommy?"

Rebecca looked at Laura inquisitively while Laura recalled the many times Wade had tried to get the baby to say her name, and she'd never even attempted it. But now Rebecca clearly said, "Mommy," and she reached for Laura. Wade laughed softly as his eyes connected with Laura's, expressing his own joy in Rebecca's innocent acceptance.

Rebecca was included in many of the wedding pictures, and they did some group shots with everyone involved. The photographer asked for just a couple more of Wade and Laura on the temple steps while their guests mostly dispersed. Brad and Marilyn took Rebecca with them. Laura's heart quickened when she looked past the photographer and saw Rochelle hovering some distance away.

"Rochelle's here," she whispered to Wade.

"Is that good or bad?"

"I don't know. Just . . . stay with me."

"Like I would let you out of my sight," he said lightly.

When it became evident the picture-taking was completed, Laura moved toward Rochelle, holding Wade's hand in hers. "I'm glad you came," Laura said and gave her a hug.

"You look beautiful," Rochelle said, returning the embrace with strength. Stepping back she added, "I truly hope that you are deliriously happy, Laura. You deserve it."

"Thank you," Laura said, her voice cracking.

Rochelle then turned to Wade and said, "She's one in a million, you know."

"I know."

"If you hurt her," she added, her voice light while her eyes were severe, "I may be forced to do something criminal."

"I'll take very good care of her," he said. "I promise."

"I'm going to hold you to it," Rochelle said before other family members approached.

"I know everyone else here," Neil said warmly to Rochelle, "but I don't know you, young lady."

"This is Rochelle," Laura said. "We've been friends forever."

"A pleasure to meet you, Rochelle," Neil said with a warm smile. "This is my wife, Roxanne, and I'm Wade's father, Neil. Well," he chuckled and tossed a comical glance toward Wade, "I'm *one* of his fathers. I'm the biological one."

"I see," Rochelle said, seeming intrigued. "Well, it's a pleasure to meet you. Laura tells me that your son is a pretty amazing man."

"I would concur with that," Neil said. "In spite of me, he's still amazing."

"Or because of you," Wade said, then he added, "Don't listen to him, Rochelle. He's biased and partial, and he'll make me out to be superhuman. On the other hand, it's not hard to get him talking freely about all the skeletons in the family closet. It could be very entertaining."

Rochelle made an interested noise and Roxanne said to her, "Why don't you just come to the luncheon with us, my dear, and we'll take good care of you."

"Well," Rochelle said sheepishly, "I wasn't really planning on going. I just wanted to see Laura for a minute and—"

"Oh, you must come," Neil said and gently took her arm into his hand. He said to Wade over his shoulder, "We'll see you there."

Laura watched them walk away, certain Rochelle was in good hands, but not really caring what her perception of all this might be. She looked up to see Wade watching her and couldn't hold back a smile.

"So, Laura Morrison," he said, making her laugh to hear her married name spoken aloud, "what now?"

"Well, lunch is waiting," she said.

"And after that?

"We'll live happily ever after, of course," she said, and they walked to the Joseph Smith Memorial Building next door, where the luncheon was to be held. Just inside the door of the room on the top floor where everyone was gathered, Laura overheard Alex telling Wade, "We took all of your things from the temple to the car; you're ready to leave from here."

"Thank you," Wade said, "for everything."

"A pleasure, little brother," Alex said firmly, but with a smile.

The luncheon proved to be a delight. The food was wonderful, but Laura felt ecstatic just being Wade Morrison's wife. Rochelle appeared to be having a good time, and Laura noticed several family members approaching her. She was the only unfamiliar face in a group of people that had all shared many family functions with Wade previously. And this was obviously a family that didn't want anyone to feel excluded. Laura wondered how Rochelle could not be impressed with the genuine goodness of these people.

As the meal was winding down, Neil stood and offered some semblance of a toast to the married couple. With a cracking voice he expressed his love for his son, and for the privilege of being a part of such moments in his life. He then wished them eternal bliss before he invited everyone in the room to each take a moment and offer the bride and groom some words of advice or just well wishes. He sat down and motioned toward Rochelle, as if her sitting beside him made her the obvious choice to go next. She basically repeated what she'd said earlier on the temple grounds, but she smiled when she said it, and Laura couldn't help being pleased. Considering Rochelle's feelings, she couldn't hope for anything better than that.

Barrett stood next from where he'd been sitting next to Wade, and he declared as if he were ten years older, "Since Wade told me I was the best man, I just want you all to know he's the greatest uncle in the world, but he's gotten a lot more cool since he met me."

Everyone applauded, and Barrett sat down. Wade leaned over to him and said, "It's the other way around, buddy. Hello? I gave *you* some of *me,* remember?"

"Yeah, but I can draw Batman better than you."

"That's true," Wade said, and they turned their attention to Kirk as he stood next and offered sincere happiness on Wade's behalf.

What followed was both touching and humorous as every adult member of both of Wade's families shared their love and congratulations. Elena's parents were also there, and each genuinely expressed their joy for Wade and Rebecca to have such a fine woman to fill the emptiness in their lives. Laura couldn't hold back tears as Elena's mother said firmly that she absolutely knew Elena was pleased with this union, and her love would always be a support to them from the other side of the veil. Jane handed Laura a tissue, then she handed one to Wade too, and Laura realized he was crying as well.

Laura felt completely overcome with joy to be part of such a family, and she said so after everyone else had spoken. When it came time to share the *traditional* waltz, Laura wondered if she could possibly hold any more happiness—such a stark contrast to the depression that had assailed her on the previous day. She vowed to try to keep that perspective in mind when difficult moments arose in the future. Looking into Wade's eyes as he gracefully waltzed her around the minimal space available, she felt certain that no earthly experience could ever be so close to heaven as these hours she had spent with him, first in the temple, and now here, surrounded by family, filled with his love, and waltzing with this wonderful man who was now her husband. She wouldn't have been surprised to hear angels singing.

Dancing with Laura, Wade mentally glimpsed in the breadth of a moment all that he'd been through since Elena had died that had led up to this moment. His remembered the feeling he'd once had of dancing in the dark, groping through the mists of confusion and loneliness, longing to love and be loved once again. The contrast now was startling. All he could feel now was brilliant light, filling him, surrounding him, leading him forward with this incredible woman that God had sent into his life.

Following the waltz, more music was played, and Alex and Jane set an example for others to dance by doing exactly that. Before the song was over, more than half the guests were dancing, and following the next song, Wade took Laura's hand and spoke loudly enough for everyone to hear.

"Thank you. We love you. We're leaving." They all laughed and waved. Wade took a moment to hug Barrett, and then Rebecca, before he passed her to Laura to do the same. "Say goodbye to Mommy," he said.

"Bye-bye, Mommy," Rebecca said, and Laura laughed.

"Bye-bye, princess," Laura replied and hugged her tightly before turning her over to Jane.

Wade then hurried Laura from the room so quickly that she felt like the train of her dress was practically flying behind her. They stepped onto the elevator alone, and once the doors closed Wade pulled her completely into his arms, kissing her like he never had before. Her full skirts rustled as she eased completely into his arms, realizing now just how much he'd been holding back through these days between their first kiss and their marriage. Her bliss deepened with the evidence of his profound affection, and her respect for his convictions and his high regard for her knew no bounds.

"Oh, how I love you," he murmured against her lips and kissed her again.

The elevator bell rang to indicate that they had arrived, and Wade immediately stepped away from her, but he gave her a mischievous smile and kept her hand tightly in his. The doors opened, and they found themselves facing an elderly couple and three teenaged girls. They all smiled to see the bride and groom.

"Congratulations," the gentleman said with a smile.

"Thank you," Wade replied, and they eased past each other.

Laura was well aware that they made quite a spectacle, hurrying through the main floor of the building, decked out in classic wedding attire. She caught people turning their heads and smiling, while she had to keep telling herself this wasn't a dream.

In the parking garage they found the car with "Just Married" written across the back window.

"Why am I not surprised?" Wade laughed.

"That's what you get for letting your brother put our bags in the car," she said.

Wade just laughed again and kissed her before he opened her door and helped her in. Laura felt like she was sitting on a cloud of satin and lace and layers of netting as he carefully closed the door, and she struggled to fasten her seatbelt. Wade got in and put the key in the ignition, but before he started the car he turned to kiss her, and kiss her, and kiss her—until they both started to laugh. She had no idea where they were going, but he only drove about ten minutes before he pulled into the parking area next to an old Victorian home that had been converted to a bed and breakfast.

"When you only have twenty-four hours for a honeymoon," he said, "there's no point wasting any time driving."

"Hear, hear," she said.

With both of their overnight bags over his shoulder, Wade took her hand and led her inside. The manager smiled when she saw them, saying, "How sweet."

"We get that a lot," Wade said, and five minutes later they were on their way up two flights of stairs to the top floor.

"This really is happening, right?" Laura asked, breathless from both the climb and the butterflies in her stomach.

"It really is," he said, pausing at the door to their room. He looked into her eyes and said with fervor, "You are my wife, Laura Morrison, and I am your husband, and we are never going to be alone again." He opened the door and set the bags in the room before he scooped her into his arms to carry her over the threshold. "At least not for about fifty years or so," he added and kicked the door closed.

* * *

Wade was only vaguely aware of the early evening sun diffused dimly through the closed drapes, covering the room in a soft light that only enhanced Laura's perfect beauty. He'd lost track of the minutes they had spent just gazing into each other's eyes, their faces only inches apart, their heads sharing the same pillow. No words were needed to express the awe and measureless love they shared. Words would only taint the absolute perfection of the moment, while memories of the passion they had come to share hovered comfortably around them. *He loved her so much!* And he could see the truth in her eyes. *She loved him too!* He'd never imagined such happiness, such peace, such all-consuming gratitude. He was truly blessed.

The following afternoon Wade and Laura slipped into sacrament meeting as the opening song was in progress. They slid onto the bench beside Alex and Jane and the children. Alex smirked at him and whispered, "What are you doing here?"

"Going to church, hello?"

"Honeymoon over?" Alex asked, still smirking.

"Oh no. The honeymoon will go on for quite some time, I think. It's just going to have some work and real life interspersed."

"Whatever works," Alex said.

Rebecca saw her father and scrambled away from Barrett to move down the bench to get to him. He barely had a chance to hug her before she moved from his lap to Laura's, saying easily, "Mommy."

Laura's eyes grew misty as she took Rebecca and held her close for as long as a two-year-old would hold still. Laura met Wade's eyes while she held the baby, then Rebecca squirmed away to go back down the bench. Wade put an arm around Laura and murmured, "I love you, Mommy."

"And I love you," she said, then looked toward Rebecca. "Both of you."

ABOUT THE AUTHOR

Anita Stansfield, the LDS market's number-one best-selling romance novelist, is a prolific and imaginative writer. Her novels have captivated and moved hundreds of thousands of readers, and she is a popular speaker for women's groups and in literary circles. She and her husband Vince are the parents of five children and reside in Alpine, Utah.

If this story has touched you, and you would like to donate to the treatment of childhood leukemia, donations may be sent to Primary Children's Medical Center Foundation, P.O. Box 58249, Salt Lake City, Utah 84158-0249.